P9-DHS-799

Zombie Lover

TOR BOOKS BY PIERS ANTHONY

Alien Plot
Anthonology
But What of Earth?
Demons Don't Dream
Faun & Games
Geis of the Gargoyle
Ghost
Harpy Thyme
Hasan
Hope of Earth
Isle of Woman
Letters to Jenny
Prostho Plus
Race Against Time
Roc and a Hard Place
Shade of the Tree
Shame of Man
Steppe
Triple Detente
Yon Ill Wind
Zombie Lover

WITH ROBERT E. MARGROFF:

Dragon's Gold
Serpent's Silver
Chimaera's Copper
Mouvar's Magic
Orc's Opal
The E.S.P. Worm
The Ring

WITH FRANCES HALL:

Pretender

WITH RICHARD GILLIAM:

Tales from the Great Turtle (Anthology)

WITH ALFRED TELLA:

The Willing Spirit

WITH CLIFFORD A. PICKOVER:

Spider Legs

WITH JAMES RICHEY AND ALAN RIGGS:

Quest for the Fallen Star

Piers Anthony

Zombie Lover

A Tom Doherty Associates Book

New York

This is a work of fiction. All the characters and events portrayed in this novel are either fictitious or are used fictitiously.

ZOMBIE LOVER

This book is printed on acid-free paper.

Map by Jael

A Tor Book
Published by Tom Doherty Associates, Inc.
175 Fifth Avenue
New York, NY 10010

Tor Books on the World Wide Web:
http://www.tor.com

Library of Congress Cataloging-in-Publication Data

Anthony, Piers.
Zombie lover / Piers Anthony.—1st ed.
p. cm.
"A Tom Doherty Associates book."
ISBN 0-312-86690-9 (acid-free paper)
I. Title.
PS3551.N73Z43 1998 98-23526
813'.54—dc21 CIP

First Edition: October 1998

Printed in the United States of America

0 9 8 7 6 5 4 3 2 1

Isthmus Village
Black Village
Tall Hassle
Troll Bridge
Censor Ship
Ogres
Ogre-fen-Ogre fen
Void
Birds
Water
Griffins
Fire
Goblins
Elves
Earth
Air
Dragons
North Village
Fish River
Flies
Gap Village
Peace
Gap Chasm
Isle of Illusion
Books
Computer
Lake Kiss-Mee
Maze
Lake Wails
Isle of View
Good Magicians Castle
Castle Roogna
South Village
Kiss-Mee River
Castle Zombie
Magic Dust Village
Region of Madness
Lake Ogre-Chobee
Vortex
Mount Rushmost
Gateway Castle
Gold Coast
Mount Parnassus
Fauns & Nymphs
Ivory Tower
Ever Glades
Centaur Isle
XANTH

Contents

Prolog

She approached the Good Magician's Castle on foot: an obscure woman of indeterminate age in a flowing robe, steadying herself with a staff. She looked neither lovely nor regal, without being deficient in either quality. She carried a large book in the crook of her left elbow.

The castle was obviously not expecting visitors. The drawbridge was up, laundry was hanging from a window, and the moat monster was snoozing.

The woman was unperturbed. She touched the surface of the water with the tip of her staff, then stepped onto the moat. She walked across, her slippers denting but not penetrating the surface. Small ripples traveled out across the moat.

The moat monster woke with a start as a ripple gently lifted his nose. He blinked, then coiled into action. He raised his head high, opened his jaws, and oriented on the figure. He inhaled, ready to breathe fierce water vapor on the trespasser.

"Relax, Soufflé," she said.

The monster blinked, then sank back down into his snooze without even a snort.

The woman reached the inner bank and then the front door. It was locked closed. She touched it with her staff, and it opened. She walked into the castle. There was no clamor of discovery; whoever else was in the castle remained unaware of the intrusion.

She made her way through the dusky recesses, mounted the

crooked stairs, and walked into the dingy office. There was Good Magician Humfrey, poring over his huge archaic tome.

"Isn't it about time?" she inquired.

The gnomelike man's near ear twitched. He raised his head and focused a bleary eye on her. One or two synapses connected. "Oh, hello, Clio," he said.

"And a similar greeting to you, Humfrey," the Muse of History responded. "Now I'm sure you have the matters well in hand, but thought I should verify the details, purely as a courtesy. I do have an interest in the cases."

The Good Magician pondered, evidently sorting through his voluminous but dusty memory, until several more synapses fell into line. "I shall attend to it."

"Of course." Clio was too polite to suggest that he might have forgotten the matter. "I'm sure it will be a fine occasion. Are the invitations in order?"

Humfrey looked blank.

Clio gave the shadowy ceiling a you-men-are-all-alike glance. "Invitations," she repeated. "How else do you suppose the participants will know about the main event?"

"Invitations," he agreed, finally getting it. But his aspect seemed to be a trifle deficient in competence.

"Assign Jenny Elf to do them."

A rheumy eyeball widened in dull surprise. "But—"

"Who else?" she inquired rhetorically. "She's surely competent. Now do you have any proper notion of the other assignments?"

Humfrey started to turn the pages of the vasty old tome before him.

"Forget the Book of Answers," Clio snapped. "This needs to be more flexible than that. Ask your Designated Wife to make them. She will have proper taste and finesse."

"Wife," he agreed, relieved.

The Muse of History turned, about to leave, then paused. "I trust I will see you there."

Humfrey looked as if he had swallowed a stink horn. He hated to go out in public. But now he had no choice. "Yes."

Clio completed her turn and stepped out of the dismal study. Only then did she allow a small smile to hover in the vicinity of her lips. A person who did not know better might have supposed that she enjoyed discomfiting the notorious Good Magician.

1
Black Dream

Breanna felt fortunate. It was partly her appearance, which was filling out nicely: she had lustrous black hair to her waist, and glowing green eyes. Her dark skin fairly shone. That was because she was a bright healthy girl of the Black Wave, and proud of her heritage. She should really be something, she thought, when she finally turned sixteen.

She turned away from the mirror pond and looked for a blackberry pie to eat before dawn. And that was the main thing: alone among the teens of her village, she had a magic talent. Normally only a baby delivered in Xanth had magic, but she was special. She blessed the day she had discovered it, for it had changed her life. She had come to the Land of Xanth with her Wave six years ago when she was nine, and thought she would never have magic. How wonderfully wrong that had turned out to be!

Her talent was to see in blackness. That was why she now went about by night, and slept during the day. It was just so much more interesting at night, when other human folk were sleeping, and the weird creatures of darkness were abroad.

Oh, yes, there was danger. But she had obtained a safety spell that warned her of any direct threat to her tender flesh, and that was enough. She hoped. She hadn't renewed it recently, so the spell might be fading. She was able to move quickly and silently and lose herself in the night, foiling most monsters. She also had a sharp dagger, which she hoped she would never have to use as other than a threat.

Meanwhile the lure of the mysteries of darkness drew her to ever farther explorations.

There were no pie trees close by, but she did spy a tart bush. Tarts were a bit sharp on the tongue, but would do. She picked a black raspberry tart and bit into it, and it was fine. She found a coffee tree with a cup of black coffee, and that was fine too. At home she wasn't allowed to drink coffee yet, but that was yet another adventure of going out on her own: no one told her what not to do. Her folks were so dull that they could see only mundane things, despite living in a magic realm now. They would need special magic glasses to see most of the magic of Xanth.

Breanna really didn't miss Mundania. Xanth was so much more interesting. Oh, there were dangers, but they were mostly magical, instead of dreary things like robbers and drunk drivers. She might have liked to have some chewing gum, but here it was as apt to chew the person as to be chewed.

She saw what looked like a barrister bloom. Maybe if she wore its flower, it would enable her to argue her case better at home. It had a nice daisy-like flower. But as she touched it, something awkward happened. She jumped back. Oh, now she saw that it was a different plant, a bare aster. She wouldn't want to wear one of those flowers.

She came to a river that seemed a bit too wide and deep to wade across. Fortunately there were big banana plants, or plantains, growing by its banks, with the biggest fruits she had seen. Magic could be very good for plants. So she grabbed onto an old plantain and managed to haul it down. She wedged it open and scooped out the remnant of its pulp. Now she had a banana boat. She used an old stem as a paddle, and moved across the water.

Another craft came floating down the stream. It was small, and had two hulls, and several cats were on it. Oh—a catamaran. It figured. It had a sail, but one cat was busily shredding it with its claws. Then the cat spied Breanna, and dived down out of sight, terrified. That one would be called Fray D. Cat, she was sure.

She landed, and saw a big dog house with a small pup tent beside it. That too figured: big dog, little dog. Things tended to be literal, in Xanth.

She saw a bright rift forming in the east, and realized that it was the first crack of dawn. Night was over, and soon light would spill through the crack and inundate the region, flooding it with day. So it was time for her to sleep. She loved her talent, but it did have the small disadvantage of making daylight uncomfortably bright for her. She acclimatized when she had to, but preferred not to bother. Also, she got tired, after being active all night. So now she simply slept in the daytime, when away from home.

Unfortunately she wasn't sleepy yet. Oh—because of that coffee. She should have remembered that it had a mild wake-up spell. That was why her folks didn't let her drink it: they said she was enough of a handful by day, and they didn't need to have her active by night too. How little did they know! But though she hated to admit it, their rule would have helped her in this case. How could she get her rest?

She looked around. She saw a large dried fish mounted on a pole. Birds were coming in to sit on it. That was a perch; it was a favorite resting place for birds. But she was no bird.

There was a commotion, and several small metallic objects ran by. They looked like keys for doors, still new and shiny. Oh—those would be latchkey kids, running home. As she herself should be doing, if she weren't too ornery to give up her adventure. She saw them charge up to a big block marked WRITER. What were they doing around a writer's block? They climbed up on top of it, where there was a board. They settled down comfortably on that board, each little key evidently having its own spot. When every key was in place, the block put down wooden pegs and walked away.

"Oh, I get it," Breanna said. "The key board unlocks the writer's block." But her problem wasn't being blocked, but needing to get some sleep.

She saw a spreading tree whose branches might offer a decent place to be. But then she recognized it as a sycamore, and the last thing she wanted was to get more and more sick.

Then she remembered something she had seen nearby: dark glasses. They were supposed to have a spell to put folk to sleep. So she walked back to the spectacle bush she had passed recently and checked it over. Sure enough, one of its offerings was a handsome dark pair. And, conveniently close, was an open shelter with what looked like a comfortable bed under a pleasant canopy. Nobody was using it, so she would borrow it for a few hours.

She lay down on the bed, put on the dark glasses, and closed her eyes. Immediately she felt the magic taking hold, and sank into a lovely dark slumber.

Suddenly Breanna couldn't breathe; something was covering her mouth and squishing her nose. She struggled, reaching wildly with her arms—and discovered that a head was resting on her face. It was a man. In fact, he was kissing her!

She grabbed him by the ears and heaved him off her innocent lips. She tried to scream, but first had to inhale, and in the time it took to do that she was sitting up so violently that her dark glasses fell off. Blinding day assaulted her eyes, and she had to squeeze them tightly closed. When she shut her eyes, her mouth shut too, stifling her scream. She had never thought to practice screaming with her eyes closed.

By then she realized that maybe a scream was not in order. Who was this man who had taken such advantage of her? It might be better to find out before she took further action. After all, men did have their points, and it behooved a girl not to throw them away carelessly.

She squinted, letting only a little light in. The man was standing there, a somewhat hazy outline. He didn't look dangerous at the moment. "Who are you?" she demanded. "Why did you molest me?"

"I am King Xeth," he replied in a somewhat scratchy voice. "I kissed you awake."

"I know that! What made you think I didn't want to sleep in peace?" She was irritable, because of her rude awakening from slumber. Her systems were not yet back on track.

"You are in the Pavilion of Love." His speech was slightly slurred, but she could make it out. Her vision was improving as her eyes acclimatized to the daylight.

"The what?"

He pointed to a sign beside the bed. It said PAVILION OF LOVE.

Breanna drew a blank. "What's that?"

"When a woman wants to marry, she sleeps in the Pavilion of Love," he explained. "Only a man of good appearance, character, and breeding can enter. If he chooses her, he kisses her awake. I was so glad to find a sleeping beauty instead of a sleeping bag."

Things were beginning to come together, but not in a way that reassured her. "But I'm not ready to marry anyone!" she protested. "I'm only fifteen."

''I am thirty,'' he responded. ''I love your lustrous black hair and glowing green eyes. I am sure you will make a good wife.''

Breanna realized that she had blundered into real mischief. ''It was a mistake. I didn't see the sign. I was just resting. I can't marry you.'' She got off the bed and began sidling away.

''I will marry you and make you queen of the zombies,'' he said. ''You are young and healthy and fully alive, so it will be a long time before you rot.''

Breanna wanted nothing so much as to get well away from here, but this made her pause involuntarily. ''Queen of what?''

''The zombies. We felt it was time to have our own kingdom, so we held an election, and the healthiest zombie won. Me. But it is a condition of kingship that I marry, so as to summon a suitable heir and continue the line. That's why I came here, to find a wife.''

''You—you're a *zombie?*'' she asked, newly appalled. Her hand came up to wipe frantically at her mouth. Her lips didn't feel zombied, but she wanted to wash them ten times as thoroughly as possible. Was it contagious?

''Yes, of course. How else could I be king of the zombies?''

''This is absolutely impossible!''

''By no means. My mother is Zora Zombie, who married the living man Xavier forty years ago. It took them a while to summon the stork, because not all of her necessary innards were healthy, but—''

''I don't want to hear it!'' Breanna shrieked. Actually she had not meant that she doubted him to be a zombie; she could now see that there were some sagging places on him, incipient flesh rot, and the reason for his slurring was apparent: a mushy tongue. She had meant that it was impossible for her to marry him. She wasn't ready to marry anyone, least of all a zombie.

''There is no need for you to hear it, if it bores you,'' Xeth said equably. ''Come with me now to Castle Zombie, where the wedding will be organized. You will want to meet your new subjects.''

''No I won't!'' she cried. ''I won't marry you! I'm just a girl. A *living* girl. I'm getting out of here!'' Now at last she suited action to word, and charged out of the pavilion.

''But it has been decided,'' he protested. ''You slept here. I kissed you. All the zombie women will be jealous of your lustrous long hair and firm flesh.''

''Let them be jealous of something else!'' she flung back. ''Find another girl! I'm sure one will come to sleep in the pavilion soon. I'm gone!'' She dodged behind a beerbarrel tree and kept going.

''No, you are the one,'' Xeth called after her. ''I loved you the moment I entered the pavilion, as its magic decrees. I love your burned black color. I love your high emotion.''

She was running, but not out of range of his voice. ''What do you know of my emotion?''

''That is my talent: mind reading. I may fudge the details somewhat, but the power of your emotion comes through delightfully. I can tell that you have very strong feelings for me.''

''That's because I loathe the very notion of being close to you!'' she shot back.

''Yes, you love the notion of being close to me,'' he agreed. ''It will be a perfect marriage.''

She suspected that there was a bit of rot in his ear, too, but she didn't stay to argue the case. She tried to sneak behind a small tangle tree, but he still pursued her. ''Why don't you marry a nice zombie girl?'' she demanded over her shoulder.

''Because they are all too rotten,'' he said with considerable accuracy. ''While that is no fault ordinarily, it is a fact that the storks don't like to deliver babies to zombie women. That's why it took ten years to persuade the stork to deliver me to my mother. So I need a living woman, just as my mother needed a living man. You are just perfect.''

He had given her much too good an answer. She could not refute it logically. So she tried to do it emotionally. ''I'm *not* perfect! I'm too young and immature and unready to settle down. I don't love you.''

''You will surely grow older and more mature, and learn to settle down. You will be a fine inspiration for our corps d'esprit, our undead army. And I know where there is a fine love spring. The one where my mother learned to love my father.''

He was still out-arguing her. If there was one thing she detested worse than a zombie, it was a smart zombie. So she let fly with the truth. ''I don't want to marry a zombie!'' Then she ran as fast as her healthy living legs could propel her, and soon left him out of sight and hearing.

Soon she got smart. She knew he would follow, so she couldn't rest until she was so far away he would never find her. After that, she would figure out what else to do.

She slowed, so as to let some of her breath catch up with her, and picked her way carefully, so as to leave no obvious trail. When she came to a stream, she waded through it, pausing only to wash her fouled mouth out several times. She followed it upstream, then followed a dragon trail for several paces, before doubling back and wading farther upstream. If the zombie thought she had gone that way, he would encounter the dragon. She wasn't sure how dragons felt about zombies, but at least it would be a distraction.

At last she spied a branch hanging over the water. She reached up to catch it, and hauled herself up and into the tree. She made her way to a branch on the opposite side, and dropped off into a gully that led away from the stream. It should be just about impossible to track her this far.

But just to be sure, she climbed another tree, and hid herself carefully amidst its thick foliage. She would wait here until the end of the day, very quietly.

She was tired, after all that fleeing. She took a good grip on the branches, and relaxed, physically. She was too excited and horrified to relax mentally. She let her ears be her eyes, listening for any untoward sound.

All too soon it came: the clumsy crashing noise of a zombie in a hurry. She peered out between the leaves, just to be sure. Yes, it was a zombie, not Xeth, but another one, somewhat farther gone. He was headed in her direction.

How could he know? He wasn't even following her trail! What gave her location away?

Breanna decided to find out. She knew that the average zombie wasn't phenomenally smart, because its brain was rotten. "How did you know where I am?" she called.

"Wee cah feeel yooor maghic," it answered. It was not able to speak as well as Xeth, being farther gone. "Wee are aall loooking."

"You can feel my magic? What magic?"

"Your maghic tzalent."

Breanna waited no more; the thing was getting too close. She lurched out of her tree, dropped to the ground, and set off running again. Now she knew two things: they could feel her magic, and there were many zombies out looking for her. Maybe that wasn't surprising, since Xeth was a zombie king. Maybe they cast about aimlessly—that wasn't hard for a zombie to do—until one of them happened to come within sensing range of her. Then he oriented on her magic.

She saw another zombie ahead of her. She dodged to the side, but found the way blocked by a five-sided object. She recognized it: a penta-gone. Anything that touched it would be gone, nobody knew where, and she didn't want to risk it. So she slowed, and stepped very carefully around it.

The zombie behind her was less careful. It blundered right into the penta-gone—and suddenly was gone. That was a relief!

But now Breanna had blundered herself, into a bog. She was in danger of getting her black shoes all gooky. So she had to pick her way through it, going from hummock to hummock.

There was a huge fat monster. Breanna squished to a stop, concerned about just how dangerous it might be. So she asked it: "What are you?"

The monster oped its ponderous and mottled mouth and spewed forth an answer: "I am a hippo-crit."

"Are you dangerous?"

"No. I am a harmless friendly lovable cuddly creature."

But Breanna had an intuition that all was not quite right. Then she made the connection: hypocrite. One who said one thing but did another. She couldn't trust it.

But maybe she could use it. "Well, there's a really tasty morsel of a man following me," she said, sidling around the creature. "Too bad you're so friendly and harmless, because he would have made a nice meal for you." She found firmer footing beyond a hummock, and was satisfied that she could make a good run for it if she had to.

"Too bad," the hippo agreed, and shifted its bulk to block the passage of the next person passing this way.

She moved quietly on. She was getting tired, and hungry, but all she saw was some shortening, and she knew better than to eat any of that. She didn't want to be any shorter than she was. She would avoid largening too; neither food appealed to her. Then she spied a variety of pie tree bearing mun danish; those were tasteless, boring pastries, but she was used to them from her own term in Mundania, so could handle it. She picked several and chewed on them as she went.

Where could she go where the zombies could not? Her mind was blank. So Breanna just kept running, fearing that wherever she stopped, a zombie would close in on her. What an awful mess she had gotten herself into! All because of that inviting bed in the pavilion.

She was getting hot as well as tired. The sun was glaring. "I *know* I was stupid!" she yelled at it. Mollifed by her admission, the sun eased its glare.

She came across a small village marked Norfolk. Maybe someone here would help her. "Hey, can you block off zombies?" she called to the nearest man, who was digging in a garden.

He paid no attention. Irritated, Breanna ran on to where a woman was washing clothing in a stream. "Can you help me?" she asked. But the woman didn't even glance at her.

She came to the far edge of the village. The sign there said YOU ARE NOW LEAVING IGNOREFOLK. GOOD RIDDANCE TO YOU.

Oh, that was why they had ignored her! She must have misread the first sign.

A side stitch caught up with her. The only way to get rid of one of those was to slow down until it zoomed on ahead, for they were speedy things. When she slowed, Breanna's mind began to work a bit better. She got an idea: maybe the zombies couldn't go into the Region of Madness. She could maybe hide there; it wasn't far away. That was fortunate, because she was getting too tired to continue much longer.

There was a small patch of it north of the Gap Chasm, though its main mass was south. That little patch should be plenty. But what was the fastest way to it? She wasn't sure, and didn't have much time. But she saw a fully living man walking along, so she approached him. "Hi! I'm Breanna of the Black Wave."

He shook her hand. "I am Ayitym. I absorb one property of anything I touch." His skin turned dark, like hers.

She wasn't certain whether he would be pleased or annoyed, so she didn't mention it. "I'm looking for the Region of Madness. I know it's close by, but—"

"I don't want to go anywhere near that!" he exclaimed. "It would make me mad." He hurried away.

That wasn't much help. But she saw another man, so approached him similarly. "Hi. I'm Breanna. My talent is to see in blackness."

"I am Tyler. I have a different talent each day."

She was impressed. "That must be some fun."

"No it isn't, because I can't choose them, and they are small. Today I have the talent of growing warts on little toes. Do you want a wart?"

Breanna's toes cringed. "No thanks! I want to find the Region of Madness. Do you—"

"Right that way," he said, pointing.

She changed course, and walked swiftly toward the nearest loop of madness. She knew its nature, because her girlish curiosity had led her to explore some of its fringes. It was really weird there, and she didn't care to get far into it. But maybe it would be worse for the zombies than for her. She hoped.

She spied a man walking the opposite way. He looked rather dazed. Beside him was an old small white dog who seemed less confused. The dog paused as they came together, looking up at her, showing a black left ear, and a curled furry tail.

"You look Mundane," Breanna said. "Hi. I'm Breanna."

The man became aware of her. "I'm William Henry Taylor, and this is my daughter's dog 'Puppy.' I don't know what I'm doing here. I was just so sick, for so long—and suddenly everything changed."

"I know how it is," Breanna said. "But I guess if Puppy found your way out of the madness, he knows where you're going. So maybe you should keep going that way."

"I suppose so," he agreed. "I hope my daughter is all right." They went on.

Breanna felt a bit guilty for not trying to help him more, but she was afraid the zombies would catch up with her at any time, while they wouldn't bother Mr. Taylor.

She saw a ragged doll. But then it moved, startling her. "You're alive!"

"Not exactly. I'm Ricky. I'm a golem."

"Oh, a doll who has been animated."

"More or less." He moved on before she could ask him to verify that she was going the right way to intercept the madness. But she was pretty sure she was close; the scenery was beginning to think about looking weird, and she had been meeting weird people.

She came to the fringe and plunged in. The weirdness closed in, and for once she welcomed it. Let the zombies try to orient on her magic, when it was overridden by the magic ambiance of this section.

Then, halfway satisfied that she just might maybe be safe, she dropped to the ground and rested. She was so tired that she fell almost immediately into a daze.

''Why child, whatever is the matter?''

Breanna looked up. There was Day Mare Imbri, her friend. Imbri had once been a night mare, but had gotten half a soul and turned too nice to handle the ugly job. Now she had become a tree nymph, and kept nice company with a tree faun. She was pure black; that was what had first attracted Breanna. What could be finer than a black mare?

''Oh, Imbri! I'm in trouble.''

Imbri formed a dreamlet image of a pretty black young woman in a lovely black gown. She always knew how to relate. *''I can tell that, dear. I felt your emotion from afar. What trouble?''*

''I did something ever so stupid,'' Breanna wailed. ''I slept in the Pavilion of Love, and a zombie king kissed me. Now he wants to marry me.''

''But didn't you see the sign?''

''I came to the bed just before dawn, from the other direction. I wasn't looking for any sign. I had been exploring all night, using my talent—and now the zombies are orienting on it to find me.'' That gave her an idea. ''Say, maybe if I got rid of the talent, Xeth wouldn't be able to find me!''

''But you can't do that,'' Imbri protested.

Still, Breanna had hold of a desperate notion. ''I love my talent, but I hate being chased by zombies. If that's the price of my freedom, well maybe it's a necessary sacrifice. Can you take my talent and put it back where you found it?'' For that was how she had come by it. Breanna had been born (not delivered) Mundane, and come to the land of Xanth with her Wave. No Mundane had magic. But the day mare had befriended her, and given her the talent she had found, and they had been friends ever since, all six months. So she was the only original Black Waver to have magic. The children who had been delivered (not born) since then did have black magic talents, but none of them were over six years old.

Imbri shook her head. *''No, I can't do that. You had better go to the Good Magician for an Answer.''*

"But he charges a year's service for an Answer—and often it's so cryptic that it doesn't do much good anyway. I'm too young to suffer through that."

"Nevertheless, I think it is your best chance."

"He'll probably just tell me to accept my fate."

"If he does, it will surely be the correct course."

"But I'm desperate! If that zombie catches me, he'll marry me and make me queen of the zombies—and I'm only fifteen! It's a fate worse than death." That was literal, for zombies were made from dead people. Death was bad enough, but to be forced to drag about after death was surely worse. And to have to summon the stork with a zombie—absolute ugh! She'd rather be chewed by a werewolf or sucked by a vampire any day.

"I know this is awful," Imbri said. *"But I can't take your talent back."*

"Why not? I'm originally Mundane. The magic can't stick to me very closely."

"I am not free to explain."

"But the zombies are after me!"

Imbri sighed. *"I know, dear, and it is indeed awful. I am not saying that I don't want to help you. I am saying that I can't—and I can't tell you why."*

Breanna began to cry. She was ashamed of herself for doing it, but just got overwhelmed.

Imbri was just as sensitive to that as a man would have been, to the girl's surprise. *"Maybe I can compromise."*

Breanna brightened. "You can?"

"I will tell you what I can't tell you, in a dream—but then I must take back the dream. So you will not remember it."

"But how can that help me?"

"I can explain everything, in the dream, so you understand. When you do, and agree that you need to ask the Good Magician, you will wake from the dream and remember only that when you knew the whole story, you agreed. Then you will be willing to do it, and know that I can't help you, though I want to."

This was almost as weird as the madness. But what did she have to lose? "What if I don't agree?" she demanded.

"That would be dangerous."

Weirder yet. Breanna knew Imbri was her friend, and trusted her. So there had to be something. But whatever could it be? "Okay. Give me the dream."

"First I will rehearse the sequence as you experienced it. Then I will fill in the parts you did not see."

"Okay." Breanna was really curious now.

The forest faded, to be replaced by a scene from Breanna's memory. There she was, walking out from the Black Village, perturbed about the unreasonable restrictions her Mundanish parents still put on her. Here she was, just fifteen, and still not allowed to date a boy and close the door. Or to wander out into the distant forest alone. They still treated her like a child.

She wished she could go far away, and have some fabulous adventure, free from parental restriction. Maybe even visit the shore, and see the sea. She had heard of a city there called Attle, where rude creatures retorted "Attle be the day!" to any expression of ambition. She'd love to tell off those creatures of Sea Attle. She'd like to eat a sea-mint, and see whether it really stuck the mouth tight shut.

She started to get angry. Why couldn't she go and do these things? What right did anybody have to tell her no? It made her so blankety mad!

She realized she was on a special path, with another path crossing it. Oh—she had blundered onto a cross walk. No wonder she had gotten so suddenly cross. She stepped off it, and her temper subsided. Still, she felt that some of her ire was justified. It was high time that the Black Village started spreading out and interacting more with the rest of this magic land, which really had so much to offer.

Then she saw the beautiful black horse. "Oh, you lovely creature!" she breathed.

Mare Imbri's head turned. *"You can see me?"* she asked in a dreamlet.

"Of course I can see you! You're pure black. You're the prettiest horse I ever saw. May I pat you?"

"I suppose, if you want to." Imbri was plainly taken aback.

Breanna approached. She patted the mare on the shoulder. "I didn't even know there were horses in Xanth," she said. "Or are you a unicorn, with your horn hidden?"

"I'm a— well, it is complicated."

"Oh, tell me!" Breanna pleaded.

"I was a night mare for two hundred years, then a day mare, and now I'm a tree nymph, but I can assume my old form when I want, and be solid, and make some dreams. My tree gives me that power. I forgot I was solid; that's why I thought you couldn't see me."

Breanna was intrigued. "Did you have a night foal?"

"Not yet. But maybe now that I'm solid, it will happen. I would settle for whatever I could get."

They talked, and soon Breanna told Imbri all about herself too. Then they parted, but agreed to meet again, for they liked each other. It seemed that girls and horses were attracted to each other just as strongly in Xanth as in Mundania.

A week later Mare Imbri asked Breanna if she would like a magic talent. "Oh, yes, I'd love it!" Breanna exclaimed, liking this mental game.

"If you could have any talent you wanted, what would it be?"

Breanna thought for a long time—at least a minute. "Not a big one, not a small one. One that's me. Only I don't know me well enough yet."

"What about the ability to conjure any kind of seed?"

"I suppose that's okay, but I'm no gardener. I'd rather change the world."

"Or perhaps the ability to choose the breed of your future children."

"Future children! I'm only fifteen. I don't want to even think of having children until I'm an ancient old woman of twenty five."

"What about transformation of the inanimate?"

"I already have enough trouble with living things. Why should I want to mess with dead things?"

"Then maybe the power to create a small void?"

That was tempting. "Like the big Void, only under my control?" But in half a moment she reconsidered. "No, it would be too dangerous. I might forget and sit in it, and be half-reared."

Mare Imbri considered. *"How about the ability to project a spot on a wall?"*

"A black spot? Maybe, but spot-on-the-wall talents are a dime a dozen."

"This is a special spot. It's actually a picture. It improves with time, getting larger and more detailed, until it is a very nice image."

"Maybe so, but its not me."

"Hearing from a distance?"

"That's not me either."

"Then perhaps the ability to conjure a geyser at any spot?"

That was intriguing. But a moment's thought dampened it. "Still not me. What would I do with all that spouting water?"

Imbri swished her tail. One might almost suspect she was becoming a smidgen impatient. *"What would you consider to be you?"*

Breanna had worked out her answer. "To see in blackness. That would be ideal."

"I think I have found a talent like that. I want you to have it."

Breanna laughed. "But talents don't just lie around waiting for folk to take them! You have to be born—I mean, delivered with them."

"There are many kinds of magic in Xanth. Come with me, but don't tell anyone what you see."

"I promise," Breanna agreed, intrigued. Of course she couldn't get any magic talent, but just imagining it was fun.

"You will have to ride me," Imbri said. *"It's some distance."*

Breanna was delighted by the prospect. "Okay. But though I love horses—especially black ones—I'm not an experienced rider."

"There will be no problem."

So Breanna climbed onto Mare Imbri's back, and the horse took off. She galloped somewhat faster than the wind, seeming to pass right through trees, and the girl was entirely at ease, not even close to falling off. That was part of the magic of it. Sometimes they even seemed to be flying through the air.

Still, she had a doubt to work through. "*Do* some talents lie around, waiting for folk?"

"In a manner. For example, there's the C Tree. Its seeds do marvelous things. If you need a lot of water, you can invoke a C big enough to sail a ship on. Or you could put a C on your eye and C much farther than before. Or if you are afraid of failure, you can put a C seed in your mouth and suck-seed."

"I C," Breanna said. "I mean, I sea—er, *see.* But that's not the same as a talent, because you are using something else."

"The right C might give you the talent of C-ing better than ever."

Breanna shrugged. "I suppose so. Though if I tried to hide one in my bosom, it might C too much. I'd rather have an innate talent."

Then, suddenly, Mare Imbri stopped. They were in a towering castle. As Breanna slid to the ground, amazed, the loveliest woman she had ever seen appeared. Her hair was long and pleasantly greenish, and the rest of her would make a professional model jealous. "Hello, Breanna," she said. "I am Chlorine. This is my friend Nimby." She gestured behind Breanna, and when Breanna turned, there was a huge dragon with a silly donkey head. Breanna started to giggle, but managed to stifle it down into half a peep.

"Nimby would like to share your dreams," Chlorine said. "Is that all right with you?"

"You mean, this dragon will appear in my dreams?"

"Not exactly. He will merely watch."

"Well, whatever, it's okay with me. My dreams aren't much."

"Thank you," Chlorine said.

Then Breanna was riding on Imbri again, back the way they had come. She wasn't quite sure how that had happened, but dreams did tend to be discontinuous, so she wasn't concerned.

What did concern her was the lateness of the hour. She realized that the day had passed without her noticing, and darkness was closing. "I'll be late getting home," she said. "I'll catch heaven." There were times she needed to swear, but that could get her into trouble, so she substituted words.

"There will be no trouble," Imbri's dreamlet image said. *"Look around you."*

Breanna looked—and realized that she could see everything. She could see in blackness!

That was the beginning of her wonderful private life. She never told anyone else about her visit to the mysterious castle with the beautiful woman and ugly dragon, or about her brand new talent. The castle scene was probably just a daydream, but the talent was delightfully real.

"That's the way it was," she agreed as the memory dream ended. "You, or maybe your friends, found the talent for me. But why can't I give it back?"

A new dream formed. This was of Imbri, grazing by a clog tree. Near it was a sandalwood tree, where a faun danced and played panpipes. Then Imbri changed to nymph form and went to tousle the faun's hair, and he patted her pert bare bottom. Obviously the two got along well.

A dragon appeared—the one with the silly donkey head. On its back was the fair Chlorine. They stopped before the faun and nymph. "Nimby wants to dream," Chlorine said.

"Dragons can dream," Imbri replied.

"But demons don't."

"Demons?" the faun asked.

"Yes, Forrest. Will you keep a secret?"

Forrest and Imbri glanced at each other. *"I think we had better,"* Imbri said.

"Nimby is really the Demon $X(A/N)^{th}$."

Both faun and nymph laughed, thinking this a joke. Then the dragon transformed into a huge glowing demon figure, and the scene turned inside out. After a moment the scene returned to normal, with the dragon back. There was no further laughter.

"You are the expert on dreams, Imbri," Chlorine said. "Can you teach Nimby to dream? By himself, without having to view it as done by mortals?"

Imbri was plainly awed. *"I don't know. No demon has ever dreamed. They don't have the mortal coils for it. They don't know what living emotions are. So there's nothing for dreams to fix on."*

"Living emotions," Chlorine said thoughtfully. "Like love?"

"Yes, that especially. Demons think love is silly. Of course Nimby—" She framed the word with a peculiar emphasis, now that she knew what it signified. *"Nimby is not just any demon. So possibly—"*

"Nimby loves. He learned it from Mundanes, among others."

"Oh. Then maybe he should start to learn dreaming from Mundanes too. They are less complicated than magical creatures. If he could follow the dreams of one, perhaps a young one, he might be able to pick up the essence. I can't deliver a dream to one who doesn't know how to do it. It's like love: you can't accomplish it until you learn how." Imbri glanced at Forrest Faun, and a little heart flew across to bop him on the nose. He smiled.

"The Mundane family we know returned to Mundania," Chlorine said. "Fresh Mundanes are hard to come by."

"I know one," Imbri said. *"She has been in Xanth almost half her life, but she remembers Mundania."*

"Bring her here."

"But is it wise to let a Mundane know Nimby's true nature?"

"It isn't wise to let *anyone* know Nimby's true nature," Chlorine said firmly. "We have told you only because we need your informed help."

"Make her a deal," Forrest Faun suggested. "Give her what she most wants, if she will share her dreams with you."

"What would she want?" Chlorine asked.

"What would any Mundane want?" the faun asked rhetorically. "A magic talent, of course. Don't tell her who Nimby is, just make the deal."

Chlorine looked at Nimby, who wiggled a long ear. She returned to Imbri. "Bring her to the Nameless Castle."

Imbri resumed mare form and galloped swiftly away. Chlorine mounted Nimby, and both vanished. Forrest waved at the space where they had been, and retired to his sandalwood tree.

The scene faded. Breanna was back in her regular daydream, facing Mare Imbri. *"Now you know how you came by your talent. The Demon gave it to you, in exchange for sharing your dreams."*

"But I haven't seen that dragon in any dream," Breanna protested.

"He merely watches without interfering. If he disturbed your dreams, they would no longer be innocent. It has been effective; he is slowly learning how to dream on his own. But it would be impolitic to renounce the deal now."

"Well, he can keep sharing, if that's what he wants," Breanna said, though she felt more than a smidgen queasy about having such a creature there. Some of her dreams were rather personal. "Just take back the talent."

"Demons don't work that way. He would not feel free, if he voided the talent. In any event, it's not smart to jostle any demon, and especially not this one. He has more power than all of Xanth put together. In fact the whole of the magic of Xanth is merely the incidental leakage from his body, in much the way heat leaks from mortal bodies. It is best to stay entirely out of his notice, if at all possible, like a flea on a dragon. Chlorine interprets for him, so that the mere power of his attention does not obliterate much of the surrounding landscape. So it is best by far to let things be as they are—for all of us."

"But he is already noticing me, if he is sharing my dreams,"

Breanna said. "And now that I know his nature, how can I avoid noticing him?"

"Precisely. That is why you must not know. Your dreams must continue as they have been. He observes them with only a fraction of his attention, and that won't change if you don't change."

Now Breanna understood. "I guess you're right. I can't give my talent back. So I'd better just go see the Good Magician."

"Yes. He always does deliver, and the deals folk make with him are always worth it, even if they don't think so at the time."

Breanna sighed. "Okay. I agree. Take back the dream."

She came out of her reverie. She knew that she had just had a phenomenal dream, and learned something that shook the very foundation of Xanth, but she couldn't remember what it was. Only that now she knew that it made sense to keep her talent and go to see the Good Magician Humfrey for some other solution to her problem with the zombie king. She had agreed to relinquish the dream; she remembered that much.

"Sleep here," Mare Imbri's dreamlet image said. *"I will keep watch for the zombies, and advise you if they come."*

"But don't you have to go home to Forrest Faun? I'll bet you had to censor that dream with him in it to avoid violating the Adult Conspiracy."

"Of course. But I can remain with you for a while. Forrest understands, and so does my tree. When night comes, you can go to the Good Magician's castle. You will be able to avoid the zombies, because you can see better in blackness than they can. I would carry you there myself, but it's too far from my tree. I have substance only within a certain range of my tree, for it is what provides that for me. But I will help guide you and warn you, in my soul-mare form, and you will get there safely."

"Thank you," Breanna said. She felt better about the prospect, though she didn't know why. Then she lay down and slept.

2
We Three Kings

"Oh, you're going to get it!" the floor said. "Queen Irene is looking for you."

"Then maybe she had better find me," King Dor replied, unperturbed. He was used to being addressed impertinently by various things, because that was his magic talent: to talk to the inanimate, and have it answer. Such things tended not to be very smart, but they were observant. "Where is she?"

"Do I look like the Book of Answers?" the nearest wall demanded flatly. "How should I know?"

Dor rephrased the question. "When did you last see her?"

"Ten minutes ago." The inanimate did have to give a straight answer if it had it, when he asked directly.

"What direction was she going?"

"Toward the library."

He went to the castle library. Queen Irene was just watering the flame vine she had growing there, to make light for reading. It was curled in a rising spiral, with hot little leaves, and the flower on the end was a ball of rose-like petals of red flame. Unfortunately it hated water, so tried to burn anyone who watered it. Irene was the only one who could do it, and it wasn't always easy. The plant wasn't smart enough to realize that its roots needed water if it was to survive.

"Need any help, dear?" Dor inquired. His wife's talent was growing plants, and she could make anything grow to any size in a hurry. But that did not necessarily make the plants tractable.

Irene turned to glance at him. She had been a luscious young woman, but now she was safely middle aged and rather beyond lusciousness. It would not be politic to mention that, however. ''Yes. Can you distract it a moment?''

Dor focused on the clock sitting on the far side of the vine. ''Is that a time fly flying toward you?'' he asked it.

''A time fly!'' it cried, alarmed. It was an alarm clock, that got alarmed by the silliest things. ''Don't let it near me! It will foul up my mechanism.''

''I think the fish tank just got it,'' the shelf said. The fish tank in the neighboring aquarium swung its turret around, searching for the fly. It rolled forward on its treads, but no fly was to be found. It fired off a watery shell, annoyed.

''Maybe it's a sapphire fly,'' the aquarium said.

The flame vine's flower whipped around, because those bright little flies were its kind. They set fire to the sap of plants, which made them unpopular with most other types.

During the flame vine's distraction, Irene whipped the spout of her watering can in and delivered a good dollop to its soil. Then she drew her hand away before the flame could return to burn her. ''Thanks,'' she said.

''Oh, she got you good, flamebrain,'' the pot said. ''Don't you ever learn?''

The flame vine took aim and scorched it, but the pot only laughed. ''I was fired long ago, tender-root. That's why I sought work here. You can't hurt me.''

''Oh, stop all this quarreling,'' Irene snapped.

''Who says?'' the pot demanded metallically.

''I say. Or I'll use the hair spray on you.''

''You wouldn't dare!''

Irene brought out a bottle and pressed the top. A jet of hair shot out and formed a cloud around the pot. Soon it got worse: the hair formed into choking tangles. ''Oh, ugh!'' it exclaimed, coughing. ''What a hairy mess!''

Dor smiled. It was never wise to call his wife's bluff. She did not like back talk.

Irene brought out a hare comb. ''After this perhaps you will behave,'' she said as the hare tackled the worst of the tangles, clearing the pot's surface.

''Yes,'' the pot agreed, chastened.

Irene moved on to the miniature hackberry tree. It bore small axe-shaped berries that waved about, trying to hack things. Her watering can had many little dents from prior times.

Dor looked in the aquarium. It was a fish bowl, and inside it pin and needle fish stood on their tails, waiting to be bowled over.

The floor tile Irene stood on spoke up. "Oh, guess what I'm seeing!" it chortled. "Feet, ankles, calves—"

Irene lifted a foot and stomped on it warningly, and it shut up. She knew how to handle the inanimate.

"I understand you are looking for me," Dor said. "Was it for a kiss?"

"That, too," she agreed, kissing him.

"Ooooo!" the ceiling exclaimed. "Look what she did—and at her age too."

Irene shot half a glance at the ceiling, and it went silent. She didn't like discussion of age. "We have news that the zombies are all stirred up. Mr. E brought it to our attention." Mr. E was a man who loved enigmas. In fact he could sniff them out from afar. He never solved them; he merely called them to the attention of others who were likely to be willing to undertake that chore.

"Zombies?" he asked, intrigued.

"People are getting annoyed. Do you think we should check into it?"

Dor considered. This was her way of saying that the matter needed immediate attention. He was bored with the dull palace routine anyway. "I will see to it immediately. You can keep an eye on the kingdom for an hour."

"Or a year. Zombies aren't necessarily nice creatures," she said. "Except for Zora. I wonder how she's doing?"

"She's rotting," the nearest table suggested.

Dor ignored it. "I think she had a son some time ago. But you're right: most zombies are a bit ugly. Maybe I should take Dolph along, for quick transportation." Their son Dolph's talent was changing into any other living creature; when he became a roc bird he could carry others swiftly and far.

"Maybe your father, too," she suggested. "He and Chameleon just got youthened, and I think he's still getting used to it."

Dor remembered. His mother Chameleon varied with the phases of the moon, becoming beautiful and stupid, or smart and ugly. She had been rejuvenated too, but was currently in her ugly phase, and not much company for anyone. "Yes; it will do him good to get out for an afternoon."

Irene waited, as if he had said something stupid. Usually when she did that, she had reason. So he pondered.

The nearest book helped him. "You must be missing something really obvious," it said. "Maybe you should read a good book."

Suddenly it came to him. "They've been what?"

"Youthened," she said with half a smile, or slightly more. "Instead of being eighty one, now he's twenty one. Physically. And Chameleon is a child of sixteen."

He was stunned. "Why? I thought they were getting ready to fade out."

"Nobody knows. There were two doses of youth elixir in the package the Good Magician sent to Jenny Elf this morning, and they were marked for them. So now they are both young again. Younger than their grandchildren."

"The Good Magician always has a reason," Dor said. "But he never gives away anything free. Do they have some arduous service to perform for him?"

"Surely so. But no one has been told. Jenny Elf has a huge chore to do, with instructions. Maybe you should ask her." Which was her way of saying that she wanted very much to know, but didn't deign to inquire directly.

"I will," he agreed. "Right after I locate Bink and Dolph. We'll check with Jenny, and then go out and check with the zombies."

Irene nodded, and continued watering her plants.

Dor went out looking for his son Prince Dolph first. Dolph remained slightly awkward at age twenty four, despite having been married to Princess Electra for nine years and having two bright daughters delivered. His magic was first rate, however, and he was of amiable disposition. Still, it seemed better that his more savvy older sister Ivy become the next King of Xanth, when the time came. Dor hadn't said anything about that, yet, but eventually he would have to.

The inanimate things and surfaces around him directed him to the kitchen, where Dolph and Electra were showing their daughters Dawn and Eve how to make punwheel cookies. The children were six, going rapidly on seven, and already seemed to have the hang of handling the required puns and wheels. Electra was 874 or twenty seven, depending on whether reckoned by date of delivery or amount of active living; she had taken a long nap in the middle of her life. The twins were cute in proportion to their mischief, which was considerable.

Electra was clean in blue jeans, but Dolph and the girls were covered with punwheel dough. It was clear where the competence lay in that family.

"The zombies are roaming Xanth," Dor said to Dolph. "I thought you and I and your grandpa Bink could go out and find out what's agitating them."

Dolph looked at Electra. "Go ahead," she said. "I think we girls can handle the rest of this by ourselves." She glanced sidelong at him. "But perhaps you should wash and change. You wouldn't want to make a bad impression on the zombies."

Both girls giggled. They were similar in a family sense, but differed in detail. Dawn was red-haired, green-eyed, wore bright clothing, was normally bright, and her talent was to tell anything about anything living. Eve was black-haired and -eyed, wore dark clothing, was more somber, and could tell anything about anything inanimate. Dor wasn't sure which of them would relate better to a zombie, because it wasn't quite clear which category zombies fit into.

"I'll do that," Dolph agreed. He left the kitchen.

"We'll meet you at Jenny Elf's room," Dor called after him. Then, to Electra: "I'm glad he married you."

Electra blushed, and the girls giggled again, well understanding her natural modesty. Electra had never aspired to be a princess, but had loved Dolph from their first magical meeting. Her innocent ways still clung to her on occasion.

Dor went in search of his father. Bink was an oddity in Xanth, because everyone knew he had Magician-caliber magic, but few knew what it was. When there was something especially tricky or dangerous to accomplish, Bink was usually the one to tackle it, and often accomplished it by a series of weird coincidences. Apart from that, he was as amiable as his grandson, which made him easy to get along with.

Bink and Chameleon were in a guest room, having evidently come to Castle Roogna for the youth potions. Maybe they knew why they had been selected. Dor knocked on the door.

"It's King Dor," the door called to the folk inside.

"Come in, Dor," Bink's voice called.

Dor opened the door and stepped in. And stood amazed.

Before him stood a lad of twenty one, and a girl of sixteen. The lad was handsome and muscular. The girl was ugly. Both were in ill-fitting clothing; indeed, the girl was in the process of pinning the boy's trousers so they would fit better.

"I think this is the wrong room," Dor said, embarrassed.

"No it isn't, son," the woman said in Chameleon's voice. "Don't stand there with your mouth agape; close the door behind you."

It really was true. These were his parents, youthened by—

"Sixty years," Chameleon said. "We each took the same dosage. We have no idea why the Good Magician sent the elixir, but concluded that he must have good reason. He has not made any requirement of us, as yet."

"But he surely will, in due course," Bink added. "I must say that apart from the awkwardness of ill-fitting clothing, it feels rather good to be young again. There's a certain vigor I had forgotten."

"Why did you come, Dor?" Chameleon asked. She tended to be abrupt in her smart/ugly phase, having little patience with the slower intellects of others. She was more popular when in her lovely/stupid phase.

"I came to ask Bink if he would like to go out with me and Dolph to question the zombies, who are stirred up. I thought a three generation excursion might be fun."

"Good idea," Chameleon said. "Go ahead, Bink; you're not much help around here. I'll fix your other clothes and mine in the interim." She paused. "Including a showy dress for my other phase."

Bink nodded appreciatively. Chameleon had been generally acknowledged to be the loveliest woman in Xanth, when young and in phase, and even in age she was elegant. Now she was young again. Dor found it awkward thinking of his parents having romantic interests, but realized it was possible. His mother's combination of traits at the far end—extreme beauty and extreme stupidity—made her a very fine romantic prospect. The extremes would be much sharper, now that she was a teenager. Well, soon they would return to the North Village, and he could put that awkward aspect out of his mind.

Chameleon worked swiftly with needle and thread, and Bink's trousers assumed a better fit. "Let's go," he said, with the seeming abandon of his youth. He tended to grow more interested in traveling away from the home, when Chameleon was in her smart phase, but of course it would not be kind to speculate why.

"First we must check with Jenny Elf," Dor said as they walked down the hall. "Maybe she has the answers to several questions."

"Good idea," the youth agreed. It was just about impossible to think of him as an aging father.

Dolph appeared, in newer and cleaner clothing. "I'm ready, Dad," he said. "Who's your friend?"

"Your granddad," Bink said.

"My what?"

"This is Bink," Dor explained, understanding his son's confusion. "He has been youthened to twenty one."

"But that's younger than I am!" Dolph protested.

"Physically," Bink said, smiling.

"You do sound like him. But why?"

"We hope that Jenny will know," Bink said. "She was the one who got the package with the potions. Maybe the other papers in it will say."

Jenny Elf was in an office chamber on the main floor, laboring at a desk. On her left was a huge pile of envelopes, and on her right a small pile of addressed envelopes. Before her, on the desk, was her cat, Sammy. She looked up wearily as they approached. She was a small girl, with pointed ears, freckles, big spectacles, and four-fingered hands. She had come to Xanth by accident, at the age of twelve, when some kind of hole had appeared in the fabric of whatever, and been stuck here since. It had been nine years, because it happened just before Dolph and Electra married.

"That's a big pile of papers," Dolph said sympathetically. "Can I help you with any of them?"

That was one thing about his son, Dor realized: his sympathetic nature. If anyone had a problem, Dolph always wanted to help out. He and Jenny had been friends since they met.

"I wish you could, Dolph," Jenny said. "But the instructions say that all of the invitations must be written in the same hand, and that's mine. They all have to be done in two days too, so I must keep at it." She shook her right hand, and little sprigs of tiredness flew out from it.

''Invitations?'' Bink asked.

Jenny glanced at him, startled. ''Why, you're Bink!'' she said. ''I didn't recognize you.''

''Chameleon and I took the potions as soon as we got to our room,'' Bink said. ''They worked.''

''So I see.'' She concentrated, and recovered the question. ''Yes, these are wedding invitations.''

''Wedding?'' Dor asked, surprised again. ''Who is the groom?''

''The note says he is no one we know. But he is a prince or king, who will marry a common girl and make her a princess or queen. It is scheduled to happen here at Castle Roogna in just one week, so everything must be ready by then, and the invitations have to go out in time to bring all the participants.''

''Who is invited?'' Bink asked.

''Everyone, I think. Of course I haven't looked at all the names on the list yet.'' She indicated a long scroll. ''Some of them have assignments too.''

''Assignments?'' Dor asked.

''Matron of Honor—things like that. That's Electra.''

''Are any of us on that list?'' Dolph asked.

''I don't know.''

Then Sammy Cat moved his paw. It landed on one section of the list. ''Oh, thank you Sammy,'' Jenny said. Her cat's talent was to find anything—except home. That was part of the reason Jenny was stuck here in Xanth. Sammy had led her here, but couldn't lead her back.

Jenny checked the list where the paw was. ''Yes, here it is: King Dor is to be in loco Father of the Bride.''

''But my daughter Ivy's already married!'' he protested.

''In loco,'' Bink reminded him. ''That means instead of. Maybe her real father can't do it, so you will fill in.''

''Oh.'' It was obvious in retrospect.

Jenny read farther. ''Bink is to be Best Man.''

''But I don't even know the groom!'' Bink said.

''And Dolph is an Usher. Head Usher.''

''Okay,'' Dolph agreed. ''I guess I can handle that.''

''What about you, Jenny?'' Dor asked. ''Since you're doing all this work.''

The girl's eyes widened in surprise. "I didn't think to look. Sammy?"

The cat lifted a paw—and set it down again, off the list.

"But you can find anything," Jenny reminded him.

Dor caught on, unpleasantly. "Not if it's not there. I fear you aren't invited, Jenny."

"Not invited!" Dolph said angrily. "She has to do this mountain of work, wearing out her poor little hand—and she's not even invited?"

"It's all right," Jenny said quickly. "My birthday is on the same day. Sammy and I will have a chance to celebrate by ourselves."

A glance bounced back and forth between the three men. "It's not fair," Dolph said. "She's not a slave. She should at least be invited."

"Maybe there's a mistake," Dor said. "We can ask the Good Magician."

"No, please don't bother him," Jenny said. "Really, I don't mind helping. I'm sure it will be a very nice wedding."

Another glance bounced around between them. Then the desk spoke. "It had better be."

Dolph still wasn't satisfied. "Jenny, I don't need to be an usher for somebody I don't even know. I'll join you for your birthday instead. We've been friends for a long time." He stroked Sammy, which was proof of what he said, because the cat did not accept the touch of just anybody.

The girl was plainly touched. She blinked back a tear. "That's very nice of you, Dolph. It's true that you and Electra have been very kind to me. But it's not right to go against something the Good Magician has set up. There is surely excellent reason for you to be Head Usher. Sammy and I will be just fine."

"She's right, son," Dor said. "And you don't have to choose one or the other. The wedding won't take all day."

"It's at three in the afternoon," Jenny said.

"Then let's have your birthday in the morning," Dolph said. "I know Electra will want to be there too. And Che Centaur, of course, and Gwenny Goblin." They were Jenny's closest friends, though Gwendolyn was now Queen of Goblin Mountain, making the goblins behave. Che was tutor for Sim, the Simurgh's chick, who would some millennium inherit the position of Wisest Bird in the Universe.

If Che came, so might Sim, and that would go far toward making the occasion significant. Every winged monster in Xanth was pledged to protect Che, and every living thing was pledged to help Sim and his guardian nanny Roxanne Roc. Che Centaur was destined to change the history of Xanth, by influencing Sim, and no one could be sure what events they attended might thus become truly significant.

"So will Irene and I," Dor said, sharing his son's disquiet about the way the girl was being snubbed. He didn't care who else attended; he would be there regardless.

"And Chameleon and I," Bink said.

Jenny had to blink back several more tears. She removed her glasses and dabbed at her eyes with a hankie. "Thank you. That would be nice. But I had better get back to work on these invitations, so as to finish them in time."

They needed to leave before Jenny's tears overflowed and fell on the invitations. "Next week," Dor said firmly, guiding his son and young father to the door.

"It still bothers me," Dolph muttered as they walked down the hall. "How complicated would it have been to add her name to the list? The Good Magician couldn't have forgotten her, because he's making her do the handwriting chore."

"He's a century old," Bink reminded them. "And not known for manners. Maybe he figured that doing the invitations was enough of a privilege for her."

Dolph snorted.

Dor remembered something. "Didn't Jenny get a gene-tic to fix her eyes so she wouldn't need those spectacles?"

Dolph smiled. "Yes. But she has worn those spectacles so long that she forgets to take them off."

They walked on out of the front gate. There in the moat was Soufflé Serpent. Dor glanced at him in surprise. "I thought you were on duty at the Good Magician's castle," he remarked.

The moat monster hissed. The surface of the water translated: "Who do you think brought the old gnome's package to Jenny Elf?"

"Well, when you return," Dolph said hotly, "tell him we don't like the way he snubbed Jenny Elf, after—"

"Don't do that," Dor said quickly. "I'm sure it was just an oversight."

Soufflé hissed again. ''His Designated Wife made the guest list and assignments. MareAnn. Except for Jenny to do the invitations. That was Clio, the Muse of History, who decided that.''

''MareAnn was Humfrey's first love, who couldn't marry him until last, let she lose the ability to summon unicorns,'' Bink said. ''She knows how it feels to be left out. She shouldn't have left Jenny out.''

''Omissions happen,'' Dor said. ''We will do what we can for Jenny. Now let's focus on our mission: the zombies.''

''We need a name for our group,'' Dolph said.

Dor hadn't seen the necessity, but humored him. ''We three kings.''

''But I'm not a king,'' Bink protested.

''You're the father of a king, and Dolph is the son of a king,'' Dor said. ''That's close enough.''

Bink shrugged. ''It will be nice to be a king for a few hours, even if in name only.''

''I'll change into a roc bird and carry you up high so we can spy the zombies,'' Dolph said.

''Don't drop us,'' Dor said, smiling. He knew his son would be careful.

Dolph walked out beyond the moat, so as to have room, and suddenly he was a monstrous bird. ''Squawk!'' he called.

''He says to get your sorry donkeys over there,'' a nearby rock translated helpfully. ''And don't soil his feet.''

''We suspected it was something like that,'' Bink murmured. The inanimate sometimes overstated the case, not having much judgment.

Each of them took hold of one of Dolph's huge legs and sat on his feet. Dolph took two steps, pumped his enormous wings, and launched into the air. Soon they were spiraling into the sky, making Castle Roogna look small.

Dor had seldom flown, so was intrigued by the patchwork of Xanth that spread out below them. He recognized the good Magician's Castle to the east, and the Gap Chasm to the north, and the Isle of View to the west. Much of the rest was forest and mountain and lake, as it should be.

''There's one,'' Bink called, pointing slightly south. Dor realized that he was doing what he was supposed to, watching for zombies, instead of getting distracted by the scenery.

The roc headed down, and soon landed in a glade near the slogging creature. The two of them dismounted from the feet, and then Dolph reappeared.

But by the time they landed, the zombie had disappeared. However, there was a female centaur practicing her archery, so they approached her.

"Hello," Dor said. "We three kings are looking for a zombie."

She glanced at them. "Hello. I am Cindy Centaur. A zombie passed this way two moments and an instant ago, bearing north."

"Thank you."

"You are welcome." She loosed her arrow, and it neatly severed the stem of high root beer mug. The roots cushioned its fall so that it did not break or spill, and she was able to pick it up and drink from it.

"No one can shoot an arrow as well as a centaur," Bink remarked as they walked north.

The zombie was typical of its breed, which was to say loathsome. It had evidently once been a human man, but it must have rested in a grave with some ambitious worms for some time, because now half its face had rotted away and its clothing was in a similar mess. It shambled along, leaving decaying chunks of itself behind. Most zombies did that; it wasn't clear why they didn't soon degenerate into nothing. Probably their substance was magically regenerated at the same rate it sloughed off, so they were in a steady state.

Dor tackled the ugly business. "Excuse me, zombie," he said, stepping as close to the thing as he cared to.

"Zzure," the zombie agreed.

"Why are you and your kind walking around Xanth?"

The thing considered. It took zombies time to think, because their brains were rotten. "Xxeth," it said after a decomposing pause.

"Can you elaborate?" Bink asked.

"Nnooo." It shambled on, as if searching for something.

Dor shrugged. "I think we need to find a fresher one."

Dolph changed form, and they got aboard his feet. They flew across Xanth until they spied another likely figure. Three figures, in fact, suitable tattered. They came down for a landing on the beach on the southern shore of Xanth. They walked toward the place where the figures stood.

But what they had taken to be tatters of clothing and odd bits of flesh turned out to be three women with veils and ruffles. The first woman spied them. ''Ah, you are the men who have come to marry us!'' she exclaimed.

''We are?'' Dolph asked, perplexed.

''Aren't you?'' she asked, coming up to embrace him. ''I am Miss Conception. Do you wish to kiss me before or after the wedding?''

''But I'm already married!'' Dolph protested.

The second woman approached Bink. ''Yes, he is eager to be married,'' she said. ''And I hope you are too, even if you do seem a bit young for me. I am Miss Interpret.''

''I'm eighty one,'' Bink said.

''Now I know I misheard that! You can't be over twenty one.''

''Something is not right about this,'' the third woman said, approaching Dor. ''Is there something wrong with you too? I am Miss Givings.''

''I'm afraid there is,'' Dor said. ''We are looking for zombies.''

''Your taste in women is weird!''

''I mean that we wish to question zombies. We thought you were—that is, that you looked like—'' He realized that they might not take kindly to the comparison.

''Like girls ready to marry,'' Miss Conception said. ''Of course. And you are right. Let's do it right now, and summon lots of storks.''

''Wow!'' her veil said. ''That should be fun.''

''We are all married!'' Dolph said desperately.

''Yes, you all want to get married,'' Miss Interpret agreed, staring blissfully into Bink's young eyes. ''It's so nice that we are in agreement. I'm sure you will mature in due course.''

''In a pork's eye,'' a tassel said.

''But you do look a bit old,'' Miss Givings said to Dor.

''He certainly does,'' the ground said. ''Any day now he'll start to totter and dodder.''

''This is all a misunderstanding,'' Dor said firmly. ''We three kings are merely trying to find out why the zombies are stirred up.''

''You are kings?'' Miss Interpret asked, delighted. ''What a great marriage this will be!''

''We can visit Castle Zombie on our honeymoon,'' Miss Conception said. ''The Zombie Master should know.''

''The Zombie Master!'' Bink exclaimed. ''Why didn't we think of that?''

''Because your hearts were set on marriage,'' Miss Interpret said reasonably. ''But as soon as the ceremony is done, we can set out for there. We want you to be happy.''

''I don't think so,'' Miss Givings said regretfully. ''I fear we are confusing things. These men mistook us for zombies.''

''Mistook us for zombies!'' Miss Conception exclaimed. ''Does a zombie have this?'' She lifted her tasseled blouse and showed her bare but healthy upper torso.

''Wow!'' a nearby stone said. ''She must have nymphly ancestry. I haven't seen boobies like that since that flock of dodos waddled by.''

''That's boobs, you boob!'' another stone said. ''You got rocks in your head?''

''Whatever,'' the first said stonily.

Meanwhile, Dolph stared. He was still young enough to really appreciate such a sight. ''Maybe not as full or firm, for a zombie,'' he said. His eyeballs were beginning to glaze.

''I should hope not. How about this?'' She tugged at her skirt.

Dor knew he should do something, but his own eyeballs were locked, and he knew that Bink's were too. It wasn't possible for a man to look away from such a sight voluntarily. The effect was similar to that of the hypnogourd. And if she showed her panties—

''This is really getting interesting,'' a piece of deadwood said. ''What does she have under there?''

Then a bug happened to fly by just at eyeball height, interrupting Dor's view. He clamped his eyes closed and turned his head away, so as not to get caught again.

''That's fine,'' Dor said quickly, before she could freak anyone out and have her will of him. He stepped between Bink and the sight, freeing him. Then he did the same for Dolph, and took the young man by the shoulders, turning him around. ''No zombie can match any of you, I'm sure,'' he said over his own shoulder. ''We are sorry we can't marry you, but we must be on our way. We have pressing business elsewhere.''

''I knew there was a catch,'' Miss Givings said. ''There always is.''

''Yes, they are surely a great catch,'' Miss Interpret agreed.

''But you haven't seen what else,'' Miss Conception cried. ''You can't conceive what—''

''We're looking, we're looking!'' several stones said.

Dor bustled Dolph away. ''Don't look back,'' he warned. ''You have no business being amazed by anything not offered by your wife.''

''Oh, yes,'' Dolph agreed, remembering.

''Now take us to Castle Zombie.''

Dolph changed to roc form, and in a moment they were up, up, and away, winging toward the Zombie Master's edifice.

''Squawk,'' Dolph remarked sadly, glancing down at the three forlorn figures below.

''Yes, I know,'' Dor agreed. ''But we were really not eligible. I'm sure they will find three other men, in due course, and make them very comfortable, after their glazed eyeballs heal.''

''I wonder if their dialogue is entirely innocent?'' Bink asked. ''It is almost as if Miss Conception acted only when their words were not enough.''

''She may indeed have had a concept,'' Dor agreed. ''As it was, only an unlikely coincidence enabled us to escape.'' As he spoke, he realized that it had been exactly the kind of coincidence that happened around his father. Could there be a connection? He wasn't sure. In fact the frustrating thing about his father was that he had never been able to be sure.

Now Castle Zombie hove into view. It was rather battered and worn looking, as if chunks of corroded blocks were falling off. The moat was a puddle of slime. This could not be from inattention, because a zombie gardener was working there. He was carefully raking more dirt into the water, to be sure it was properly foul.

They landed just beyond the decrepit drawbridge. Dor hesitated to cross it, lest the worm-eaten planks give way and dump him into the muck below.

Bink considered. ''I suspect that magic makes this look worse than it is,'' he remarked.

''No doubt,'' Dor agreed. ''Maybe some illusion, or some debilitating spells. Either way, I wouldn't care to chance it without testing it.''

"I'll test it." Bink, with the carelessness of his new youth, went right ahead and crossed without trouble. So Dor and Dolph followed, now assured that the planks would hold. But Dor made a mental note: he would have to watch to make sure his father didn't do something more foolish than risking a mere dunking in slime. Youth had its liabilities.

They came to the inner portcullis, which was badly rusted. A zombie guard challenged them with a corroded spear. "Halsh!"

"Hey, who you talking to, wormface?" a paving stone demanded.

"We three kings have come to speak with the Zombie Master," Dor said.

"Heesh nough inn."

Dor was getting the hang of zombie speech. "He's not in? Then may we talk with Millie the Ghost?" Actually she hadn't been a ghost for fifty five years—the same as Dor's age, coincidentally—but for about 807 years she had been a ghost, so her friends still thought of her that way.

"Ghoo onn inn."

"Thank you." They walked on into the castle proper.

The interior was a good deal nicer than the exterior, because this was Millie's domain, and she was no zombie. The floors were clean, and there were curtains on the portals. Even the air was fresher. Castle Zombie showed the fallacy of judging a thing by its exterior; it was actually a nice residence.

"Get a load of this," a stone lintel remarked appreciatively. A woman was approaching them.

"Oh, hello!" Millie exclaimed. "How nice to see you again, King Dor and Prince Dolph and—" She paused.

"Bink," Bink said.

"Oh, you've been youthened!" she exclaimed, delighted. "Chameleon too?"

"Chameleon too," Bink agreed. "She will be lovely, in about two weeks."

"Come in and have some tee and crumples," Millie said, ever the gracious hostess. She was now in her early seventies, in terms of active living time, and in her eight hundreds chronologically. Like Electra, she had taken a number of centuries out, remaining her then-age of seventeen. She was still a lovely woman. Her talent was sex appeal, and age had masked but not abolished it. Dor remembered how she had been his baby-sitter when he was twelve, and how her beauty and talent had affected him then. He was still a little bit in love with her, but he had it well under control. Her present physical age helped.

Her tee and crumples were delicious, of course. The tee was in cups shaped like the letter T, and the crumples were twisted and crunched bits of pastry that looked like failed efforts but weren't. They were appropriate for a place in which zombies thronged. "And to what do I owe the honor of this visit?" she inquired.

"Actually, we came to see your husband," Dor said. "But perhaps you can help us."

"Jonathan is away right now. What is your need?"

"We wish to know why the zombies are stirred up and walking all over Xanth."

"Oh, are they? I didn't realize. I haven't been out recently, because we don't like to leave the castle unattended. What are they doing?"

"Just walking everywhere. They don't seem to be doing any harm, but ordinary folk are bothered, you understand."

She smiled, and Dor felt the lure of her again. What a creature she had been, in her physical twenties, when he was in his impressionable childhood! "I understand. I do love Jonathan, but somehow I never quite became accustomed to his business of making zombies. Of course it's not the zombies' fault that they are rotten; some of my best friend are zombies. But they do lack social grace."

That was a substantial understatement. "Yes. We would like to ascertain what is rousing them, so as perhaps to put it to rest."

"Quickly," Dolph said.

"Of course," Millie agreed. "But I really can't think what the matter might be. The zombies have been doing well recently. They even elected a king from their own number, so as to form their own kingdom. He is Xeth—Zora and Xavier's son."

"Xeth!" Dolph exclaimed. "That's what that zombie was trying to say."

"He is a fine figure of a man now; you would hardly know he is part zombie. But he's a responsible person; he would not try to stir things up in the living world. Not without considerable reason."

"A zombie king," Dor said thoughtfully. "He could stir them up, if he did have reason. Perhaps we should talk with him."

"I don't know where he is. Jonathan knows where all the zombies are; that's part of his talent. But he is away, in a manner of speaking, and I don't know how soon he will be back."

"We have an important wedding to attend to in a week," Dor said. "We really need to get this straightened out soon."

"Oh, I see." Women related well to weddings. "But it would be very difficult to find Jonathan right now."

"Exactly where is he?" Bink asked.

"That's complicated to explain."

"We will try our best to understand," Dor said firmly.

"I will try, then. Of course you know about Princess Ida's moon."

"Ptero," Dor said.

"Last year we learned that it is more sophisticated than we supposed. It is actually the manifestation of her talent of the Idea. All the folk who ever lived on Xanth, or ever will live, or ever might exist, are there, in their soul forms."

Dor was startled. "All the folk? But what about those of us who are here, now?"

"You are there too, only with the current year of your lives absent there. And time is different there; time is geography. But that's only part of it. There is an aspect of Ida herself there, and she has her own moon. And on that moon is another Ida, with—"

"Please," Dor said. "My comprehension is being strained. What has this to do with your husband?"

"Each little moon is different," she explained. "With different magic. Jonathan thought there might even be a zombie world. If so—"

"I see. That would be the perfect place for the zombies to be. Especially if they had a kingdom. Their own world!"

"Exactly. So Jonathan is exploring to see if he can find such a world. He does what he can for his flock."

"Maybe the zombies are looking for it too, in regular Xanth," Bink suggested.

"No, I don't think so. They were supposed to wait."

"How long will it be before the Zombie Master returns?" Dor asked.

"I don't know. He said to wake him up if he is gone more than three days, and it's only been one day."

All three of them did a quick reassessment. "He is sleepwalking?" Bink asked.

"No, just sleeping. In our bedroom. I check on him often, just in case."

"But then how can he be exploring worlds?"

"He made an arrangement with Princess Ida and the Night Stallion to explore them in the dream realm," she explained. "It's more convenient that way, and safer, because he can't truly be lost or hurt, and he can search more efficiently."

Dor was having trouble with comprehension again. "But if he's only dreaming, it isn't real. So whatever he finds won't actually be there."

"Oh, no, it's real. *He's* not real, while there, but the worlds are exactly as they are. I think. It is a controlled dream, relating to reality. He just won't be able to take anything from there, except information."

"He's like a ghost," Dolph said. "You must have thought of that."

"Why yes, I did," she agreed. "I have had experience. He seems real while there, and can talk with the people, but can't stay. If he gets chomped by a dragon, he'll be gone, though, and will wake on his own, and maybe unable to return. So I'm sure he's being very careful. I understand that there are remarkable sights there."

"There are some here in Xanth too," Dolph murmured, rubbing a bit of glaze off an eyelash.

"I don't think we can wait two days," Dor said. "We need to get the zombies settled well before the big wedding. Could you wake him early?"

"Oh, I wouldn't do that!" Millie said, horrified. "He said not to disturb him for anything short of an emergency, because he might not be able to find his way back to a choice site if he doesn't have time to mark the way."

"Mark the way?" Bink asked. "How can a dream be marked?"

"It's part of the magic the Night Stallion lent him. He can draw a glowing chalk line around something, that will stay in place after he leaves. So he can return later and make sure it's what the zombies want. But he can mark only one place at a time, so he has to be careful."

"Could we go after him?" Dolph asked. "So we can find him, and ask him, without interrupting his search?"

"Why, I hadn't thought of that," Millie said. "I suppose if you sniffed the sleep spell, you could."

This, weird as it was, seemed to be a way. "Is there enough of that spell for all three of us?"

"Oh, yes, we have plenty of it."

"But how would we find him, in that dream realm?" Dor asked.

"Oh, that wouldn't be hard. He leaves glowing footprints. That's so I can find him, if I need to."

"Then why couldn't he follow his own footprints, on another visit?" Dolph asked.

"They won't stay after he goes. So he has to remember the way, and mark his place."

"Then perhaps that is our best course," Dor said. "We can find him, ask him, and return in time to get the zombies settled."

Millie had no problem with that. "You can use a guest chamber," she said. "I will bake more crumples for your return."

That seemed like an excellent arrangement.

3

Solitaire for Two

Breanna woke at dusk, refreshed. It was time to go see the Good Magician, since she was now satisfied, for no reason she knew, that this was her only feasible escape from the zombies. So she quickly ate some hasty pudding she found, and set her face toward the darkest east.

''There is an enchanted path leading to Magician Humfrey's castle,'' Mare Imbri said. *''But the zombies seem to be able to walk those paths, so that's not safe for you. However, I know of another path that is privately enchanted, that should do about as well.''*

''What's a private enchantment?''

''One that's not officially sanctioned by King Dor. This one was set up by Com Passion, and—''

''Is this a dragon or tangle tree?''

''Oh, no, nothing like that. Com Passion won't hurt you. In fact Forrest Faun and I are her friends; we visit her sometimes to play dreams vs. realities. But you won't have to enter her cave; just keep on going toward the castle. You should be there by dawn.''

''Okay.'' Breanna started walking.

Imbri trotted along beside her. *''It's right this way, beyond the Jackpot there.''*

Breanna saw a man sitting on a big glowing pot. She paused. ''I know the centaurs are open about natural functions, and maybe some other folk are too, but I'd prefer to wait until he gets off the pot.''

Imbri made a laughing neigh. *''He's not having a function! He's giving away money. Everyone who passes him has to take some, to get on the path.''*

Sure enough, as they approached Jack reached down under himself, into the depth of the pot, and pulled out a handful of grubby coins. Imbri took one in her mouth, and Breanna took another in her hand.

''But what's the point?'' she asked as they stepped onto the path.

''Jackpots just like to give away lots of money.'' Imbri still held the coin; she wasn't speaking with her mouth, but with a dreamlet.

''I can see that. I mean, what's the money for? No one buys anything in Xanth, does she?''

Imbri considered. *''Well, you might encounter a slot machine some time. They eat coins.''*

Breanna nodded, and put the soiled coin in her purse. She didn't like dirty money, but perhaps it would be useful sometime.

Imbri's ears perked up. *''Oops, I'm being summoned. I have to go see about a daydream; I still do a few of them for my friends.''*

''You did some good ones for me, I think,'' Breanna agreed. ''Thanks for everything.'' She waved as the mare faded out.

The path was clear enough, and Breanna walked swiftly along it. Soon she came to a sign marking an offshoot: COM PASSION. That was the maker of the path, who evidently lived in a cave. But it wasn't necessary to go into the cave, so she walked on by.

But then she saw a ragged shape ahead. It was a zombie! They had found her again.

Breanna hardly took time to think. She turned about and ran back along the path. But soon she saw another zombie coming from the other direction. She was trapped between them.

She turned at the sign and ran into the cave. At least it wasn't supposed to be dangerous, and maybe it would provide a place to hide from the zombies. It was dark, but of course that was no problem for her. She saw several jars of currant jelly, and realized that there must be something electrical nearby.

She saw a box of some sort on a pedestal of some sort. A screen on the box lighted. Words appeared: *Well, now.*

What was this? There didn't seem to be any danger, but she didn't feel exactly at ease either. This cave was spooky. But with the zombies outside, she would have to bear with it. That meant dealing with this Com Passion character. ''I'm looking for—''

Of course, dear, the screen printed. *Did you bring me a little gift?*

Breanna suffered a flash of realization that illuminated the cave for half a split second. This was Com Passion herself! A screen machine. And she expected a little gift. It would be best to oblige her. But what did she have? Only one thing she could spare.

''It's very small, and somewhat dirty,'' she said apologetically. She fished out the coin.

Why thank you, Blackwave girl. I love it. There followed a row of little hearts. ♥♥♥♥♥♥

Breanna looked for a place to set the coin. *Give it to my mouse,* Com Passion printed.

Breanna looked around nervously. There was a mouse in this cave?

Then the cave shimmered, and became a regular room. A door opened, and a young brown woman walked in. ''I am Mouse Terian,'' she said. ''I normally sleep in my mouse pad.''

Oh. Breanna handed her the coin. Terian took it and set it on a shelf. Then she turned again. ''What is it that you wish of my mistress?''

''I—I don't understand.''

Terian frowned. ''What word do you not understand?''

''It's not that. I mean, I didn't come here to ask for anything. I just—well, it gets complicated to explain.''

''You do not understand our natures?''

''Yes. I think that's what I don't understand.''

''This is the cave of Com Passion, a machine who can change reality in her demesnes.''

''Oh, I hope she's not mean!'' Breanna blurted. Then she tried to take it back. ''I mean—''

The screen appeared. *Not mean or demean. Demesnes. My territory.*

Breanna felt even more stupid than before. ''I apologize.''

''I am her mouse,'' Terian continued. ''Com Passion loves people, but can't move her body, so I do what needs to be done. In real life I am like this.'' She shimmered, and became a real brown mouse. It squeaked.

''Eeeek!'' Breanna screamed, stepping back.

The woman reappeared. ''Precisely. So Com Passion enhances me to resemble your form. Normally folk come here to ask some favor of my mistress, for which they must pay an equitable price. Therefore we inquire what favor you desire, and what you are prepared to do in return.''

''I—I—'' Breanna hauled herself somewhat together and tried again. ''I'm on my way to see the Good Magician, who can maybe tell me how to stop the zombies from chasing me. When they were about to catch me, I ducked in here. Unless you have some way to get rid of them, I don't think I have a favor to ask of you.''

''My mistress can give you a charm to make you invisible to zombies. But it lasts only a few hours, so is a temporary expedient. Probably it would suffice to get you to the Good Magician's castle.''

''That's great!'' Breanna exclaimed. ''Yes, I would like that!'' Then she remembered the other part of it. ''But I don't know how I can pay for it.''

Terian considered. ''A love spring flows through my mistress' cave. Therefore she is very affectionate, and craves company. I have become overly familiar to her, and my intellect is not great, so she wishes for more. She is lonely and bored. Have you any relief for that?''

''But I can't stay forever and talk to a screen!'' Breanna protested.

''In my mistress' experience, most human beings have areas of expertise or knowledge that can be diverting. Is there anything you might teach Com Passion that would make her less bored or lonely?''

''Not unless she likes playing cards,'' Breanna said, laughing ruefully.

''Cards?''

A notion coalesced. Cards could be really useful for boredom. So maybe that wasn't such a far out idea. ''Suppose I taught her some card games? Ones she could play by herself, like solitaire?''

''Can you demonstrate such a game?''

''Sure.'' Then she reconsidered. ''Except I don't have a deck of cards. They don't play cards in Xanth. It's a Mundane game.''

''Describe them.''

''Well, there are fifty two of them in a pack, in four suits: Spades, Hearts, Diamonds, and Clubs. Each suit has thirteen cards, going from Ace—that's one—to King. On the backs there is some design or picture.''

As she spoke, the image of the cards appeared. Breanna tried to take one, but her hand passed through it: it was illusion. So she asked

Terian to lay them down on a table which obligingly appeared. Terian was able to handle the cards as if they were real, because Terian herself was mostly illusion in this form. Probably Com Passion could make her solid, but illusion was more energy efficient. Soon they had a pack of cards on the table, with a picture of Com Passion on the back, and the suit designs on the front: shovels, little beating hearts, scintillating diamond gems, and cudgels. Mare Imbri evidently served as the model for the queens, and a faun Breanna didn't recognize stood for the kings, while the jacks had black faces and looked like Breanna. They were ready to play.

"I know only three solitaire games," Breanna said. "But they're pretty good. First there's Klondike. Deal out seven cards in a row, with only the first one face up." Terian did so. "Then six more, starting with the second row, only the first face up. And so on, until there are seven face-up cards. Now you try to find aces and set them above, and build on them by suit right up to the king. You can build down from any card in the tableau, like putting that red four on that black five." Breanna continued her instructions, and found that Com Passion was a very quick study; nothing needed to be repeated.

"Now you just keep playing, until it stalls out," Breanna concluded. "Which it usually does, after a while. It's hard to win unless you cheat."

"Cheat?"

"Break the rules."

"But how can it be a game with no rules?"

Breanna realized that the machine was wired to be honest, and didn't understand dishonesty. "It can't be," she said. "So go ahead and play."

There was a pause. "My mistress is not an original thinker," Terian said after a moment. It seemed that she had direct communication with the machine. "And I lack the intellect on my own. You will have to direct the play."

"But it's easy to play," Breanna said. "Just not easy to win."

"Perhaps if you direct a game through to victory, my mistress will then have a sufficient sense of the whole so as to be able to play variations herself."

"Well, I'll try, but it will probably take several games."

"Shall we say that when you have played a game through to completion, your service is completed?'' Terian inquired. ''Then I will give you the spell, and you may proceed on your way.''

''Okay.'' It seemed a fair bargain.

So they played several games, with Breanna directing them. But every one blocked up before victory. She wished she had chosen an easier game to win.

Finally she broached the matter. ''Suppose I teach you another card game, one that's more winnable? Would that be all right?''

''That would be satisfactory,'' Terian agreed.

''Okay. Here's one I learned off my computer in Mundania.'' She paused, realizing that Com Passion *was* a computer. So this should be good. ''It's called Free Cell. It's a little like Klondike, and a little different. Deal out eight rows of cards, face up, and keep dealing more, overlapping them until they are all there. You want to build up on the four aces, same as in Klondike, and you can build down with alternating colors too. You have four free cells where you can park cards.'' She continued, and Terian laid out the cards and played according to directions. ''Every game is supposed to be winnable, if you play right, but it's usually too complicated for me. But maybe you, with your logical mind—''

''We must see a game played through to victory first,'' Terian reminded her.

So Breanna tried, but game after game blocked up. She knew she was making misplays, but couldn't help it. In fact, as time wore on, she was getting worse. She wanted to quit—except for the zombies outside.

''Suppose I teach you another game?'' she suggested desperately. The night was passing, and she was getting nowhere swiftly.

''That would be satisfactory,'' Terian agreed, exactly as she had before. Breanna could see that it really was true that this computer and mouse set lacked originality.

So she proceeded to her third and last game. ''This one's called Accordion. It's pretty simple to play, but almost impossible to win.'' She quailed inwardly as she said it. But since she was messing up on the theoretically winnable game, maybe she would luck out and win this one. It wasn't much of a hope, but what else was there? ''It's called that because it tends to expand and contract, like an accordion.'' She paused. ''Do you know what an accordion is?''

"No," Terian said.

"It's a musical instrument that you pump like a bellows. Do you know what a bellows is?"

"Yes."

Breanna was learning caution. "What is your definition?"

"A person who shouts loudly."

Just so. "There is another type of bellows: a device that pumps air by flexing in and out. It's used in Mundania."

Terian nodded. "Secondary definition noted."

"And the accordion has a keyboard on one side, and harmony notes on the other side, and—well, it doesn't matter. Deal out the cards face up, a row of about six, face up."

"About six?" Terian asked. "Surely it must be exactly six."

"Not according to fuzzy logic. Uh, do you know—"

"There is a colony of warm fuzzies nearby. They are not known for their logical abilities."

Breanna decided to avoid further analogies. "Never mind. What I mean is that you can deal out four five, six, seven, eight, or any number; it doesn't have to be six. That's just for convenience."

"A span of four to eight cards when inconvenient," Terian said, getting it straight.

Breanna let that pass. "Now you play by matching up the cards by suit or number, the first or third from the right." Terian looked blank, so she moved right on into a demonstration. "Deal the cards; I'll show you."

Terian dealt six cards: The Queen of Hearts, Two of Diamonds, Nine of Clubs, Six of Clubs, Ten of Spades, and Ace of Spades.

Q♥ 2♦ 9♣ 6♣ 10♠ A♠

"Now see, you can put the six of clubs on the nine of clubs, because the suits match and the nine is right next on the left," Breanna said. She paused. When nothing happened she said, "Put the six on the nine." She kept forgetting how literally these folk took things. "And put the Ace on the ten. Now you have four piles and four suits; you can't do any more. So now deal out another card on the right."

The next card was the Two of Hearts.

Q♥ 2♦ 6♣ A♠ 2♥

"Now this is nice, because you can close it up some more. Put the Two of Hearts on the Two of Diamonds, because the numbers match and the diamond is the third card to the left; remember, you can match either the first or third.''

''I remember,'' Terian said. She moved the card.

''Now you can match the two hearts, because they are next to each other. Do it. Move the whole pile; the buried cards no longer count.''

Terian did it.

2♥ 6♣ A♠

''So you see, we have boiled seven piles of cards down to three. Now deal out some more cards.''

''How many cards?''

Breanna tried not to roll her eyes. ''Three more.''

Terian dealt out the Four of Diamonds, Jack of Spades, and Eight of Diamonds.

''See, now the accordion is expanding again. We don't do anything. Deal a couple more.''

Terian dealt the Three of Hearts and Seven of Diamonds.

2♥ 6♣ A♠ 4♦ J♠ 8♦ 3♥ 7♦

''See, still nothing. I hate it when they alternate like that. Sometimes I wind up with half the deck spread out. Anyway, the object is to finish with all the cards in a single pile. Two piles is a very good score, three or four piles is still credible, and beyond that is pretty much of a washout.'' She grimaced. ''I wash out a lot.''

They played the game on through, and sure enough, finished with nine piles of cards. They played again, and finished with five piles. A third game was fifteen piles.

Breanna was about ready to tear her hair, but refrained, because it was really nice hair. ''Look, I can't seem to win a game for love nor money, and I need to get on my way. Is there any other way I can get that zombie-no-see spell?''

''You are offering love or money?'' Terian inquired.

Oops. ''Not literally. It's zombie love I'm trying to escape, and money isn't much use in Xanth. I mean, is there any other deal I can make with you, since this one isn't working out?''

There was the barest pause. ''We are intrigued by these games. Find another person to play them in your stead, one who can play one through to victory. At that point we will give you the spell.''

''But how can I find anyone else, when I can't even go out of this cave for fear of the zombies?''

''We will lend you the spell for that purpose.''

That was so logical that Breanna knew she would never have thought of it. ''Okay. But how can you be sure I won't just bug out?''

''Do what to what?''

Oops again. It did sound as if she meant to pull an insect from its hole. ''How do you know I won't run off to the Good Magician's castle the moment I have that spell, instead of finding you another player?''

''You will do what you agreed to do.''

She realized that a machine had little concept of dishonesty. ''Okay. I'll go find somebody. Seems fair to me.''

Terian lifted her hand, and in it appeared a marble-sized globe. She gave it to Breanna. But as Breanna took it, it faded out. Had she somehow broken it?

''The spell is now part of you, and will carry through the night,'' Terian explained. ''If you are unable to find a suitable player by dawn, return here and we will provide another spell for the next night.''

Breanna hoped she could do it much faster than that. ''Okay. I'll see you soon, one way or another.''

She walked out of the cave. Almost immediately she saw the zombies milling about. Maybe they knew she was in the cave, and were waiting to nab her when she emerged.

She nerved herself and walked down the path toward the zombies. If they gave even the slightest, teeniest, weeniest sign of seeing her, she would bolt back into the cave as fast as her fine black legs would carry her.

But the zombies gave no sign of being aware of her. They seemed to be patrolling, shuffling back and forth, dropping putrid bits of themselves behind. Yuck!

She timed her route to pass between the two of them while they were both walking away from the intersection of paths. She got through, and was on her way beyond without their noticing.

Then she reconsidered. How did she know the spell was working? She might have slipped through on her own merit. She had better make sure.

She nerved herself again, and turned back. Now the two zombies were approaching each other on their route. She could see the route, because it was marked by blobs of decayed flesh. They were definitely on guard duty.

She walked toward them. ''Hey, you rotters!'' she called.

There was no response. The zombies shuffled past each other and walked on out toward the ends of their routes. So she went to the center and stood there, waiting for their return. She was terrified, but she made herself stand there. She had to know.

They turned and shuffled back. Their faces were blank masks of disgusting decomposition. It was a marvel they could see anything, with those putrefied orbs.

"Hey, foulface!" she called to one. "Can you see me?"

The zombie ignored her. He continued to shuffle toward her. She realized that they would collide if she didn't get out of the way. So she moved clear, just in time, and the zombies passed behind her.

"Have you sheen anyshing, Seymour Bones?" one inquired of the other.

"Noshing, Rick R. Mortis," the other replied.

Satisfied, Breanna proceeded on her way. Now whom could she find who liked to play cards? There might be a small problem, because no one in Xanth knew about cards. But surely many folk were bored, and this was a good treatment for boredom.

Another problem was the fact that it was night, which was her prime time but was sleep time for others. But there should be a few folk active.

Sure enough, soon she spied the light of a lamp, and by the lamp a young man was putting handfuls of dirt into a bag. "Hello," she said by way of introduction.

"That is a pointless interjection," he replied, not looking up.

"What is?" she asked, vaguely nettled by his attitude.

"Your stupid salutation."

Breanna had never been a person to accept rudeness unchallenged. "Who says it's stupid?"

"I do. I am Smart Alec. I always know a detail others don't think of." He paused reflectively. "I can't think why I'm unpopular."

"Gee, it sure beats me," she retorted sourly. "What are you doing?"

"I'm collecting magic dust, as any idiot can plainly see."

"That looks just like ordinary dirt to me. Did you get some in your mouth, to make you talk dirty?"

"I'm not talking dirty, I am merely making statements about the incapacities of others who evidently don't realize how dull they are."

Breanna had had just about enough of this. She was ready to blast him with some real information on dullness, but remembered her mission. Maybe he would like to play cards. So she stifled her justified retort and tried to soften him up for the kill, as it were. "Thank you for explaining about the magic dust. But how is it you know that this particular dirt is magic, and what do you want it for?"

"All dirt in Xanth is magic," he said in superior fashion. "It is what carries the magic. It emanates from the center of Xanth, and slowly spreads out, and the magic diminishes as the dust thins. This is near the center of Xanth, so should be pretty strong. I'm going to take it to Mundania, where it should enable magic to be operative."

"That's a great idea!" she said, putting more enthusiasm into it than she felt. She had lived years in Mundania, and doubted that anything could budge its dreariness. "How would you like to play a great new game?"

Now at last Alec glanced at her, appraisingly. She wasn't entirely easy with the places his gaze landed. "Very well. Take off your clothes."

What a jerk! "Not that kind of a game. I'm only fifteen."

"Oh. Then you wouldn't know about that sort of thing."

Actually she did know, but preferred not to tell him that. "This is a card game. It—"

"Forget it. I'm not interested." He focused on his dust.

Irritated anew, Breanna walked on. If this was the kind of reaction she was likely to encounter, her quest was more difficult than she had believed.

Then she thought of a way to get something useful from this jerk. She turned back. "I'll bet you don't know who would want to play a card game."

"Com Pewter," he said, and ignored her.

Com Pewter. She had heard of him. He was a machine like Com Passion, who resided in a cave and could change his local reality. What better partner could she possibly find? Smart Alec *had* known the answer, and had done her a huge if inadvertent favor.

But Pewter lived far away, south across the Gap Chasm, not actually all that far from her home in the Black Village. How could she get there quickly?

Well, maybe the same way she had gotten here. But first she had to prepare. Could Pewter's activities possibly be construed as censorship? In Mundania that was the suppression of certain political, ribald, or otherwise objectionable speaking or writing, and it happened a lot. No matter how innocent or well meaning the expression, there was bound to be somebody who found it offensive and wanted to abolish it, dictating that only that particular person's beliefs and expressions were truly free. In Xanth it was brought by the Censor Ship, a dread craft whose docking meant awful mischief for those in the vicinity. She recalled when the Black Wave had suffered some of its effect. They had managed to escape it, fortunately, but all of them remembered. That was why they had made it a point to get on good terms with the De Censor Ship. Wherever that went, it abolished the evil suppression of the other ship, and even nulled the dread Adult Conspiracy of silence. So the DC Ship wasn't welcome in most quarters, because the Adult Conspiracy was almost universal in Xanth; even dragons and ogres honored it. But because the Black Wave had emigrated from Mundania six years ago, its elder children mostly knew the secrets, and weren't affected. Breanna herself understood perfectly how to summon the stork. She just didn't much care to do it yet, and not ever until she found someone really worthwhile. Meanwhile it was convenient to pretend that she was as innocent as a regular Xanth juvenile. The words "I'm only fifteen" scared off just about any pushy male. Except, unfortunately, one whose brain was rotten, like a zombie king. So she had no fear of the De Censor Ship, and in fact it could be useful on occasion. It was just a matter of proper management.

She concluded that Pewter's habit of revising reality could indeed be called censorship, because he didn't allow opposing folk to have their say. Therefore his activity should be of interest to the Ship. And that was all she needed.

She cupped her hands around her mouth. "Fee Fo Fi Fip—I smell Censorship!" she called.

Immediately the lights of a ship hove into view. It was magic, and could sail through land rather than water. That was because it was the opposite of the Censor Ship, which sailed on water.

"Hello there, Breanna," a girl in a sailor hat called.

"Hello, Tsunami," Breanna replied. Tsunami's magic talent was liquidation, which was why she was a vital crew member. She could turn any solid to water, and back again. Without that, the ship would become landbound in a hurry.

"What have you found?" Tsunami asked as the ship sloshed to a stop beside Breanna. She felt the land making little waves; it was weird.

''I just realized that Com Pewter is guilty of censorship,'' Breanna said. ''I want to go there and remonstrate with him.''

''Then get aboard,'' Tsunami said, rolling down the gangplank.

Breanna went aboard. The ship turned and picked up speed. It did this by using Nots: if it was Not here, it must be There, and so it moved there. But if the skipper said Not again, it had to move on to another there. It was said that a speed of thirty Nots could get it just about anywhere in a hurry.

Indeed, it was soon Not in northern Xanth, and was crossing the Gap Chasm. This was interesting, because it couldn't cruse in air, so had to sail down the chasm wall, across the bottom, and up the far wall. ''Not here, Not here,'' Tsunami kept saying, and the ship kept gaining velocity in its hurry to obey.

Breanna spied a line extending across the chasm. ''Why not use that as a guide to cross more quickly?'' she asked.

Tsunami looked. ''Oh, no, that's a time line. Follow that, and it takes you back in time.''

Breanna nodded. ''I guess we don't need that right now.''

Tsunami looked ahead. ''Ah, there's Clappy. His reports are always useful.''

Breanna saw a nondescript man standing near the ship. ''Reports?''

''Yes.'' Tsunami called out to the man. ''Hey, make us a report!''

The man clapped his hands together. Instead of a clapping sound, they made a report: ''The weather is fair on this day.'' He clapped them again and made another report: ''The Gap Dragon is foraging at the far end of the chasm at this hour.'' He clapped a third time: ''Three kings are traveling to Castle Zombie to inquire what is stirring up the zombies.''

''I could tell them that!'' Breanna exclaimed.

''Thank you!'' Tsunami called, throwing Clappy a kiss. He caught it and bowed.

They sailed on up the far side of the chasm, then resumed normal travel across the land. ''Oh, there's a lady bug,'' Tsunami said, pleased.

In a moment the lady flew low and landed on the deck. She folded her bug wings and her glossy shawl covered them. It was brightly colored, with spots. ''May I ride with you a while?'' she inquired.

''Certainly,'' Tsunami said. ''I love lady bugs. You are all so pretty.''

''Thank you. I have never sailed on a ship before. This is fun.'' She looked around. ''I am Lady Chelle.'' But soon she tired of the novelty, lifted her shawl clear, spread her insect wings, and flew away.

''They never stay long,'' Tsunami said, a trifle sadly. ''Sometimes whole flocks of bird-winged humans pass by, but they don't have much interest in sailing when they can fly. They can change into birds when they want to.''

Soon they were approaching Com Pewter's cave. ''Not beyond the cave,'' Tsunami said, and the De Censor Ship sloshed to a sudden stop, making the land ahead of it form into a wave.

Breanna stepped off. ''Thank you. I don't suppose you'd care to wait while I deal with this?'' She was concerned about getting back to Com Passion.

''I'm afraid we can't,'' Tsunami said with regret. ''We just got another call, and must tend to it immediately. Nothing is more important than opposing the Censor Ship.''

''I understand.'' She would just have to figure out another way, when the time came.

The ship turned and sailed back north, leaving a wake that caused the land on which Breanna stood to rise and fall gently. As the ship disappeared, the effect subsided, until the land was as solid and steady as it had ever been.

Then the ground shook in another fashion. Trees crashed in the distance, and monstrous footprints appeared, coming this way. Breanna remembered that there was an invisible giant who herded visitors into Com Pewter's cave.

''It's okay,'' she called. ''I'm going in to see Com Pewter anyway.''

The shaking stopped. ''Oooga,'' the invisible giant called, sounding like a fog horn. Indeed, a bit of fog drifted down.

''Right,'' she said.

A hugely toothed creature loomed up before her. It wore a vest on which the word MEGA was printed. It roared and opened its mouth, ready to take a big bite from her tender flesh. Several similar creatures were beyond it, guarding the cave entrance. How could she get inside?

Then she caught on. "You're mega bites!" she exclaimed. "For Com Pewter!"

Abashed at being fathomed, the creatures retreated. Breanna walked quickly by them, and entered the cave. She knew it might be hard to leave again, but if her mission were successful, Pewter would be glad to let her go. She hoped.

The cave was quite dark, and she liked that. She proceeded confidently until she came to the motley collection of junk that was the body of the machine. "Hello!" she called.

The screen lighted. PRETTY BLACK GIRL FAILS TO SCREAM AND FLEE, it printed.

"You don't need to change my reality," Breanna told it. "I'm here on business."

This surprised Pewter. She could tell, because his screen blinked and went fuzzy for three quarters of an instant. BUSINESS?

"I think you are guilty of censorship, and I want you to stop it."

The machine seemed to be set back. I HAVE NEVER BEEN ON A SHIP.

"I mean that you change reality, so that others don't get their fair say. That's what they try to do in Mundania. I want you to stop it at once."

GIRL CHANGES SUBJECT.

That was exactly what she meant, but now she couldn't say it. However, she wasn't annoyed, because that was only her pretext for getting a ride on the De Censor Ship. She had made an honest attempt, and now could get on with her main business. "I have come to teach you a great new game."

The screen formed an eye. The eye ran over her form in much the way Smart Alec's eye had. I AM UNABLE TO PLAY SUCH GAMES, TO MY REGRET.

"Why do you males have only one thought in your head?" she demanded rhetorically. She had mixed feelings about such looks. On the one hand she resented being sexually appraised, as if her body was the only reason for her existence. On the other hand, she was pleased to be noticed. So her protest was a matter of form as much as substance. "I'm going to teach you a card game. It's from Mundania, so you haven't encountered it before. Do you have a mouse?"

A mouse appeared by her feet. "Eeeek!" Breanna screamed, stepping back. She couldn't help it; surprise appearances of mice always set her off. She knew it was ridiculous, and that the mouse wouldn't hurt her. In fact she had once had a pet mouse that contentedly walked and pooped on her hand. But her reaction was hard-wired. "Change form!"

The mouse was replaced by a troll. "That's worse!" she cried, now more sensibly alarmed. "Trolls eat girls. Or worse."

"Please, you misunderstand," the troll said. "I am Tristan Troll, doing service as Pewter's mouse. I never ate girls. In fact I got into trouble with my village for letting a girl go."

His voice was very cultured and reassuring. Breanna decided to trust him, for now. It wasn't as if she had much choice, if she wanted to accomplish her mission. "I'll need you to deal the cards." She glanced at Pewter's screen. "Make the semblance of a table, and fifty two cards with symbols on them." She described the deck, and soon Tristan was holding it.

In due course she had demonstrated the three types of solitaire, but of course succeeded in losing all the games badly. "I wish I could win one for you, so you know how it's done," she said. "But for now you'll have to take my word that it can be done."

"Of course it can be done," Tristan said. "I didn't realize that that is what you were trying to do."

"You can play one through to victory yourself?" Breanna asked, amazed. "I thought your lack of originality prevented you."

"It might prevent Pewter, but I have an intellect capable of original thought." The troll smiled, and the expression no longer seemed as horrible as it might have. "In fact it used to get me into serious trouble."

"I know how that is," Breanna said ruefully. "I get in trouble all the time."

Tristan dealt out the cards for Free Cell on his own, and played quickly and accurately, making it look easy, and soon had won the game.

"You really are smart!" Breanna said. "I could never do that."

"I am not that smart," Tristan said. "But my creativity, buttressed by Pewter's logic, makes this feasible. This is a straightforward exercise of alignment."

This was a great break. "Okay. Now I am here at the behest of

Com Passion, who needs a partner to play these games through to victory.''

WHO? the screen asked.

''She's a computer, like you, only female,'' Breanna explained. ''And she's bored and lonely.''

''I know how that feels,'' Tristan said.

She was actually developing some sympathy for the ugly male creature. ''Nothing wrong with you that a girlfriend couldn't cure.''

''No female of my kind will associate with me. That is one reason I accepted this position.''

I CAN MAKE THIS FEMALE ASSOCIATE WITH YOU, Com Pewter offered.

''No!'' Breanna cried, suddenly really truly awfully alarmed. ''I'm only fifteen! I'm only fifteen!''

I CAN STORE HER IN THE BACK OF THE CAVE FOR THREE YEARS UNTIL SHE COMES OF AGE. THERE IS PLENTY OF GRUEL AND WATER TO FEED HER.

''No!'' Breanna screamed. ''You can't—''

FEMALE IS SILENT.

She was unable to speak. What an awful turn this had taken! She was escaping the zombie only to be caught by a troll.

''Let her go,'' Tristan said. ''If I believed in abusing children, I would never have gotten in trouble with my kind. She has come on legitimate business, and should be allowed to complete it.''

The screen made a flicker of resignation. FEMALE RESUMES DIALOG.

Breanna was free to talk again. She wanted to protest that she was no child, but thought the better of it. She really appreciated the troll's decency. ''So Com Passion needs a partner to play cards with. I thought you might like to do that.'' She hoped.

''This is interesting,'' Tristan said. ''We did not know of this entity. Perhaps we can set up a data link.''

''I guess. I'm not exactly sure how you do that.''

''By changing reality,'' the troll said. ''I can work it out in theory, and Pewter can implement it.''

GET THE GUI, Pewter's screen printed.

Tristan went to the back of the cave, and came back with a double handful of goo. He lifted it high, letting it stretch down in a gooey sheet along the wall. ''This is a graphical user interface,'' he explained. ''It helps show what you are dealing with.''

"Uh, sure," Breanna agreed faintly as the goo covered the entire stone surface, making it glisten.

Tristan stepped back, wiping his hands. "The GUI is in place," he reported.

Suddenly the wall of the cave became a huge window. There were Com Passion and Mouse Terian, glancing across in surprise.

"I have found you a solitaire partner who can play to victory," Breanna said, not letting the moment escape. "This is Com Pewter, and his troll-mouse Tristan."

Why how nice, Passion's screen printed.

"Tristan, if you would demonstrate a Free Cell win for Com Passion . . ."

The cards appeared, and the troll swiftly dealt and played and won.

Terian assumed girl form and clapped her hands. "How thrilling!" she exclaimed. "Now we can do it too."

Tristan gazed at her, his eyes traveling down in an hourglass pattern. It was true: Passion's mouse did have that type of figure, in her nymphly aspect. The germ of a notion wiggled into Breanna's mind.

Soon Terian was dealing and playing, buttressed by Passion, and won.

"That's very nice," Tristan said, still gazing at Terian.

Terian smiled at him. "Thank you."

Breanna realized two things: one was that there might be a future in the interaction of the two mice, because though they were of different origin species, they had similar positions and would surely understand each other. If the one was lonely, surely the other was lonely too. The other realization was that the two computers would have no further reason to associate, once both knew how to win all the types of card games. So they would separate, that being the logical unimaginative course, and Com Passion would be lonely again. Her nice mouse would be lonely too. Breanna decided that she ought to do something about that. She had a romantic nature. After all, Tristan was smart and decent, and Terian was lovely in her human image; what more was required?

"Solitaire can be interactive," Breanna said, remembering. "For example, Klondike: deal two decks opposite each other, and either player can play on the other's ace piles. Whoever finishes first wins, and you can't be sure who that will be."

The two tables merged at the interface, with Tristan at one, and

Terian at the other, facing each other. Terian's decolletage seemed to be lower than before, especially when she leaned forward, and Tristan seemed to be standing taller. They dealt out their hands of Klondike and played rapidly. Soon they were playing on each other's aces. The cards had no trouble crossing the barrier of the screen, as they were mere images themselves.

Both games blocked up. That was the thing about Klondike: much of it was the luck of the draw, so that no amount of skill or strategy could prevail. But Breanna seemed to remember that Double Klondike was more winnable than Single Klondike.

They played again, and this time it was evident that there was going to be a victory. Tristan was leading.

Breanna thought of something. She squatted down by Pewter's screen. "It might be more interesting if you arrange to lose," she murmured.

A question mark appeared on the screen.

"Trust me," she said.

Tristan had surged ahead, and was about to place his final card on a pile. But he hesitated, and Terian was able to place her last card first.

"Oh, you let me win," Terian said, blushing. "How romantic!" She threw a kiss at him. The kiss passed right through the interface and landed on his mouth.

Tristan stepped back, looking stunned. Pewter's screen became a series of exploding spirals intermixed with hearts, spades, diamonds, and clubs.

"Of course you know that was really Com Passion kissing you," Breanna murmured to the machine. "In her fashion. She's very romantic. If you want more of that sort of thing, you have a notion how to behave."

The screen slowly coalesced into a single large heart. Pewter was definitely interested. Meanwhile the two mice were staring at each other in wild surmise. His mouth was open in awe, and her bosom was gently heaving. They might have wildly different origins, but they were indeed well matched in the context. If the machines wanted to find out what love was like, they had only to give their helpers leeway.

Breanna looked across to Com Passion. "I think I'll go now. I think I have fulfilled my commitment."

More than fulfilled it, dear girl, Passion's screen scripted. *If you ever need a favor, come to me.*

"Thank you," Breanna said, gratified. She caught Terian's glance and winked, and was pleased to see the lady mouse blush. Yes, this was definitely working out.

She walked out of the cave. She didn't care if there were zombies in the vicinity, because she knew she was now much closer to the Good Magician's castle than she had been, and could reach it before dawn, and the zombies wouldn't even know she was there.

Yes, taken as a whole, this night was well worthwhile. Breanna set her face east and began to walk.

4

Dream Chase

The three kings followed Millie up the winding stairway. This gave them an excellent view of her posterior, reminding Bink forcibly of her talent of sex appeal. In this rejuvenated state he noticed such things, and it tended to catch him off guard. He wasn't eighty one anymore, physically. So, to avoid the embarrassment of an untoward thought, he focused his attention elsewhere.

He heard a faint moan. He would not have been aware of it, had he not been trying to avoid what was in front of his nose. He had not heard a moan quite like that before, and it bothered him.

"What is that?" he asked.

"If you don't know, you're a lot less man than you look," the stair right under Millie's rump said.

"I heard something," Bink said quickly. "Like a moan, to the side."

Millie paused. "Oh, that's the blob. The zombies brought it in, and Jonathan tried to rescue it, but all it does is suffer."

"It suffers? Maybe we could give it some healing elixir."

"We tried that, but that doesn't seem to be the problem. We don't know what to do."

"Maybe I should look at it." Bink's interest was only partial, but he had to finish what he had started.

"By all means." Millie led the way down a side passage, to an end chamber.

There it was, as described: a blob. It might have had the size o
man if shaped that way, but it just hunkered down into a quivering
mass. There were splotchy colors on its surface. Overall it wasn't very appealing.

"Hello," Bink said. "Are you sentient?"

The thing merely groaned again. Bink wasn't sure how it groaned, as it seemed to have no mouth. But of course the inanimate had no trouble speaking in Dor's presence, not needing any mouth either. All things were possible, with sufficient magic.

"It does seem to be alive," Dor said. "But without eyes or ears or whatever."

"I'd be miserable too, in that state," Dolph said.

The matter continued to bother Bink. "If it's not injured or unhealthy, this must be its natural state. But it obviously isn't happy. Could it be something that's gone wrong? That was meant to be a regular creature, but didn't get there? Maybe if we could figure out what it is meant to be, we could help it."

"That would be nice," Millie agreed. "We hate to see it suffer, but we don't feel free to throw it out."

There was nothing to be done here, so they moved on. Bink tried to put the matter out of his thoughts, but it kept bobbing back into them. If there was no other way, he would go to Good Magician Humfrey himself and ask what to do about the blob. But right now he had to solve the zombie problem.

They reached the spare room. It was nicely set up, with three beds. "Here is a jar of the sleep spell," Millie said. "Just sniff it and sleep. It works immediately. I will close the jar. Remember: follow the footprints."

They lay down, each on a bed. Millie brought the jar to Dolph. He sniffed, and his head dropped on the pillow, snoring. She brought it to Dor, and in a moment he too was asleep. Then she came to Bink. "Maybe if you let the blob sniff it, the moaning would stop," he suggested.

She brightened. "I'll try that!" She held forth the jar.

He sniffed.

Xanth was without form and void. He was zooming through that void at a horrendous rate, seeing clouds of surplus dreamstuff all around him. Then he slowed, and found himself standing in what he recognized as the Castle Roogna Tapestry Chamber. There was the splendid Tapestry, whose animated pictures showed any aspect of the history of Xanth the viewer cared to watch.

There was also a ghost hovering beside it. The ghost saw him and spooked, fading out of sight with a soundless exclamation.

"That's a new one," Dor remarked. "People spooking ghosts."

Bink looked around. Dor and Dolph stood beside him. So they were all present, in the dream.

In a moment Princess Ida, who was Princess Ivy's twin sister, entered the room. She paused near the door. The ghost hovered near her. "I am told that someone is visiting here in a dream," she announced. "So I will sleep, and join you in a moment."

"The ghost brought her!" Dolph said.

"The Castle Roogna ghosts are shy, but friendly," Dor said. "As a child I used to know them better."

Ida sat in a chair facing the Tapestry, and leaned back, closing her eyes. In a moment her even breathing showed that she was falling asleep. Then a second version of her appeared, standing before the sleeping figure, only this one was awake. "Oh, hello, brother," she said, spying Dolph.

"I didn't know you could dream!" Dolph blurted. "I mean—"

Ida smiled. "We did not have the advantage of growing up together, Dolph," she said. "Maybe that was just as well; I don't think you would have survived two elder sisters." She glanced around at the others. "Hello, Father Dor. Hello, Grandfather Bink."

"Hello," Bink answered awkwardly. He had never quite gotten used to the notion of having twin granddaughters. That was because there had been just Ivy as a child; only when she was an adult had the twin sister the stork had misplaced finally found her way to claim her heritage, at age twenty two. Ida was a nice person, with the extremely powerful but devious talent of the Idea: whatever idea she had that originated with someone who did not know her talent, was true. Now it turned out that her cute little moon, Ptero, was a function of that talent. So Bink knew that Ida was legitimate, but still he tended to think of her as unrelated.

"I gather you have come to visit the worlds of maybe," Ida continued, glancing up at the little globe that circled her head, even in the dream state. It was obviously a dream moon, because the real one was visible hovering by the sleeping Ida's head. "I must advise you that we now know of four moons, and there may be many others. They are Ptero, Pyramid, Torus, and Cone. The rules of magic differ for each one, and most of their inhabitants never existed in Xanth. You will be able to leave any of them simply by waking up, as can the Zombie Master, who passed this way before you."

"We are looking for him," Bink said.

"Ah, that explains it. You will be in no danger, but if you suffer what would be death in real life, you will lose the dream and wake up immediately, and be unable to return without going through the whole process again. So it is best to be careful. I will guide you to Ptero; after that I will wake up and go about my business, but the dream world will exist independently, because you are dreaming it. Once all three of you leave it, it will fade. If you need to go to the other worlds, you must find the Ida who resides on each. You will not need to have her sleep, because the entire derivative structure already exists in the present dream; just go on as you need to. I hope your mission is successful."

"Thanks, Sis," Dolph said, kissing her on the cheek. "Have a nice day when you wake up."

"When this is done, I hope one of you will come to tell me what you found," Ida said. "I can't go to those worlds, even in my dreams, unfortunately, so I am dependent on others to learn about them. I am most curious."

"We'll do that," Bink promised.

"Thank you. Now you must focus on Ptero, and think small. Very small. Make sure you stay together, because it is easy to get lost there. Time is geography; east is From and west is To. But you will not be affected by the time, because you are not really there. In fact you will have to form your bodies from filler material, as the natives do, in order to interact. Nothing you do there will be permanent, because this is only your dream."

"We understand," Dor said. "We just need to talk with the Zombie Master."

"Good fortune." Dream Ida stepped back toward her body. "Orient on Ptero." The tiny moon swung around before her head.

"Let's hold hands," Dor suggested. "So we don't get separated."

They linked up, and focused on the moon. Bink tried to think small, and suddenly the moon was growing. It seemed to swell to the size of an apple, then to a bowling ball. Then they seemed to be floating toward it.

He looked down. The Castle Roogna chamber was gone; they were in empty sky, dropping toward the distant planet. Their velocity increased. Suddenly the world was looming scarily close. Too close. It was no longer a ball, but a broad landscape, with mountains and fields and lakes.

"Oops," Dolph said.

Then they plunged into the ground. Darkness closed around them. Their impetus had carried them down into the rock.

"Maybe we can rise a bit," Dor suggested.

Bink concentrated on rising, as did the others. In a moment they burst out of the ground and sailed up into the sky.

"We're ghosts," Bink said, remembering. "We need to get some substance. Some filler."

They were hovering in a cloud. Dolph reached out and grabbed some cloud-stuff, pressing it into his body. That seemed to work, so Bink and Dor tried the same. The more stuff they pressed in to themselves, the more solid they became, and they began to fall. But they were able to control it, so that they finally made a soft landing in a forest.

Bink dusted himself off, and patted firm the last of the filler. He felt much like himself. Dor and Dolph seemed similar.

"Now we need to find the Zombie Master's footprints," Dor said.

They looked around, but there was no sign of glowing footprints. They had probably gone astray in the course of their inexpert landing. Even in dreams, things needed to be done approximately right.

"I'll change form and fly up and see if I can spy them," Dolph said. "If my talent works here."

"It should," Dor said. "We should be at least as talented in our dreams as in our reality. But don't lose track of us."

Dolph became a hawk moth and flew up, combining the flight powers of the one and the sensitive antenna of the other.

"So this is a dream," the ground said.

Dor glanced at Bink. "It seems my talent too is present."

"Sure it is," the ground agreed. "I can tell you where those footprints are: straight north."

"Which way is north?"

"Toward the blue."

Bink looked around. The air seemed to be bluer in one direction, and redder in the other. Cold north and warm south. All right.

They walked north. In a moment the hawk moth descended. It landed, and Dolph reappeared. "You're going the right way," he said. "I saw a trail of footprints there."

"We are on our way," Bink agreed.

"I also thought I saw something following us, but I couldn't make it out."

"How could anything be following us?" Dor asked a bit sharply. "We are in a dream, and on a unique world."

"Maybe a creature of this world," Dor said uncertainly. "But maybe I just imagined it."

"We'll keep alert," Dor said. "Just in case."

That made sense. But privately Bink wondered. Dolph had his juvenile confusions, but paranoia wasn't one of them. They didn't know what kinds of predators this world had. So he decided to hang back a bit, so that if anything came on them from behind, he would be the first one it encountered. It wouldn't be able to hurt him, and the effort might give warning for the others. They had been assured that they couldn't really be hurt while in this dream, but if they got sufficiently messed up, they would be forced to wake up and lose their place here.

Soon they found the trail: glowing footprints headed west. That meant toward the future, assuming that made sense.

"Say," Dolph said. "It's green that way." He looked back. "And yellow to the east."

They checked. Again Dolph's younger nature had picked up on something the elders had missed. So they couldn't get confused about whether they were traveling into the future or the past; the colors ahead would warn them. That struck Bink as a nice feature of this world.

They followed the prints, which seemed to know where they were going. They led past a small village. There was a gnome working outside his house. "Hello, hello, it's great to see you!" the gnome exclaimed in friendly fashion. "Haven't we met before?"

"I don't think so," Bink replied, as he happened to be closest. "I am Bink. Who are you?"

"Well."

"What?"

"No. Well. That's my name. Everyone knows me."

"Gnome Well," a nearby rock said helpfully.

Another gnome emerged from the house. "And this is my neighbor Metro," Well said. "Metro Gnome keeps track of ticks and tocks."

"That seems useful," Bink agreed. He knew that ticks could be real mischief if not supervised. A friend had once eaten an emi tick by accident, and gotten really sick. Another had been bitten by a psycho-tic, and gone crazy. A third had run afoul of a spasmo tic, and convulsed. "What ticks are you watching now?"

"A group of across ticks," Metro answered. "They are useful for word puzzles. Do you need any?"

"Not at the moment, thank you."

"So can I help you with anything?" Well inquired, in the manner of an old friend.

"We're just following these footprints."

The gnome looked. "What prints?"

So it was true: others could not see them. "Magical prints that only we can see," Bink explained.

"Well, I wouldn't recommend going that way," Gnome said. "There's a bad comic strip, and beyond it is only old age."

"We can handle it," Bink assured him.

"You must love punishment. I couldn't stand it."

"What's so bad about a comic strip?" Dolph asked.

Both gnomes rolled their eyes. "You're new here," Metro said.

"Maybe some things you just have to learn for yourselves," Well said.

They went on, and came to the edge of what seemed to be the comic strip. Beyond it things looked wild indeed. But the footprints went there, so they followed.

When they stepped across, they found themselves on a path labeled PSYCHO. They followed the prints along it. It wound crazily around, seeming to go nowhere in particular. It passed a huge feline creature who seemed to have no eyes, so they thought it safe to tiptoe by. Then it yawned, and there were eyes in its mouth: eye teeth. They hurried on, before the eyes could focus on them.

There was a sign saying BOWLING. That seemed safe. Then a bowl flew by Bink's head. Someone was throwing bowls at them!

They ran on, escaping the bowls. There was a cat staring at them.

It scanned Bink, then Dolph, then Dor, as if it could see their innards; the process was disquieting.

"It's a cat scan, dummy," a little figure with a big mouth said, and ran on.

Next were several little dogs running in circles. "Lap dogs," the figure said. "Doing their laps."

Beyond them were other dogs that just lay in the way. There were too many to step over, so Dolph bent down to lift one out of the way. "Ouch!" he exclaimed. "It's burning hot!"

"Hot dogs," the running figure explained.

There was a cacophony of barking as mud puppies formed from nearby mud, and suds puppies formed from soap bubbles. Then it stopped as a hush puppy commanded silence.

"What gives with all these animals?" Dor demanded.

"It was just raining cats and dogs," the big mouth answered.

"I think I'm beginning to appreciate why we were warned against the comic strip," Dor muttered.

They managed to get beyond the animals, but were not clear of the strip. Dolph saw a purse lying in the path, so he bent to pick it up—and it exploded, spattering him with dirt. "That's a disperse, dummy," the mouthy figure said, chucking. "So now are you going to try to play the lute?"

Sure enough, there was a stringed musical instrument there. "Let me try it," Bink said, and picked it up.

The strings of the lute snapped free of their moorings and tried to wrap themselves around him. But he happened to be standing beside a wall of colored blocks, and the strings got tangled around the blocks instead. Suddenly the blocks moved, manifesting as a big snake composed of blocky segments. It looped away, dragging the lute.

"Sidewinder captures disso-lute," the figure said gleefully.

"We've got to get out of here!" Dolph cried. "Let's follow that snake."

They charged after the sidewinder, but it swerved back into the center of the strip. They were in danger of losing the footprints, so they stopped and looked for them.

The prints led to the side, but that trail was blocked by a big picture of a collection of pins, labeled TING. "We'll have to move that out of the way," Dor said.

"Uh-uh-uh!" the running figure said. "This is a pain-ting."

"Just what are you?" Bink demanded of the little creature.

"I thought you'd never ask! I'm a running commentary. If you think I'm bad, you should meet my cousin the running gag. You can get rid of him only by telling lame jokes, so his legs stop working."

"So can you tell us how to get out of this comic strip?" Dolph demanded. But the commentary had already run away.

"There's an open space," Dor said, peering to the side.

They made for it. It turned out to be a square section paved with linoleum. It looked harmless.

Then a wild-eyed woman appeared with wild roses in her hair. Her body was luscious, but there was something dangerous about her. "Hi! I'm Meriel Maenad. Do any of you want to indulge in floor-play with me?"

"No!" Bink said quickly. He knew about the maenads; they were bloodthirsty wild women who loved to tear men apart, literally.

"Just as well," the running commentary remarked, reappearing. "Those who indulge on that floor get trampled by the families of their partners, who don't much like them."

"How do we get out of here?" Dolph demanded, but again the commentary had run off.

Then a large serpentine head loomed over them. "That looks like a hydra," Dor said nervously. Sure enough, in a moment several more heads appeared.

The first head's mouth opened. Fire shot out, just missing them. "That's a fire hydrant!" Bink cried. "Run!"

They ran so fast their surroundings became a blur. Their feet stepped on egregious puns, getting all pungent. Bink was disgusted.

Suddenly the surroundings cleared. They were out of the comic strip.

They eased to a halt. "Now I know what Gnome Well meant," Dolph said. "I don't want to go through that again."

"At least the regular landscape is relatively clear," Dor agreed. "But have we lost the trail?"

They looked around. Soon Bink saw the footprints emerging from the strip and proceeding west.

Bink, lagging back a bit, heard a faint stirring in the comic strip. Then there came the voice of the running commentary. "And another foolish traveler braves the ticklish zone.'' There was the sound of stifled laughter, as if someone was being unwillingly tickled.

Was that coincidence, or was there really someone or something following them? Bink decided not to say anything until he had more definite evidence.

''This is slow,'' Dolph said. ''Why don't I assume roc form and carry us swiftly along it?''

''And fly over any other comic strips,'' Dor agreed.

That would get them well ahead of any pursuit, Bink thought with satisfaction. If there was any.

Dor became a roc, and they got onto his huge feet and caught hold. Then he spread his wings and took off, flying low. Bink saw the footprints becoming a streak, because of the speed. They were traversing a great plain. This supposedly tiny world was huge, from this close.

There was a bank of clouds sheltering a storm. They veered around it, and passed a rainbow. Dor pointed: ''Look—rainbow trout!''

Sure enough, there were pretty fish swimming in the rainbow.

They passed over another comic strip, and Bink realized that these were the boundaries between regions of Ptero. They were surely effective; no one would cross such strips carelessly.

The footsteps passed through the strip and emerged on the other side, unchanged. The Zombie Master must have had a cast-iron sense of humor.

They crossed a forest, catching glimpses of the prints under the trees. Then something familiar loomed ahead. ''Castle Roogna!'' Dor exclaimed. ''How can it be here?''

''All the creatures who ever were, will be, or might be are here,'' Bink reminded him. ''So I suppose that all their houses and architecture can be here too.''

Dolph came to land before the castle. He missed by a little, and almost wound up in the zombie graveyard. ''Hey!'' a man cried.

''Sorry about that,'' Bink called.

Dolph managed to clear the graveyard and land safely. They got off his feet, and he resumed manform. ''So is this really Castle Roogna?'' Dor asked.

''Sure it is,'' the man answered. ''What did you think it was, an outhouse?''

"We were merely surprised, for we know of a similar castle far away."

The man approached. Then he did a doubletake. "Why you're Consort Dor! I didn't know you were out today."

"Consort Dor?" Dor asked blankly.

"Have you lost your memory? King Irene's husband."

"I suppose I have," Dor said, evidently taken aback. "Irene is here?"

"Of course. If you've lost your memory, I'd better introduce myself. I'm Zafar the zombie lover; I tend their graveyard while they rest."

"That's good," Dor agreed.

"I've got some forget-me-not extract," Zafar said. "It nullifies the effect of a forget spell. Maybe that will help you."

Dor shook his head. "I don't think so. But thanks."

Zafar returned to the graveyard. The three kings exchanged most of a glance. They shrugged.

The footprints led on in. They followed.

A huge head rose out of the moat. It was Soufflé Serpent, the moat monster. He looked at the three with surprise, as if also not aware that they had gone out, then nodded and sank back under the surface.

"Why do I think this is about to be strange?" Dor inquired rhetorically.

"Because it is," Bink said. "Even for a dream."

A woman came to meet them at the front gate. She was about twenty seven, and was so lovely that the halls brightened as she passed.

Bink stared. *It was Chameleon.*

She recognized him at the same time. "Oh, Bink, you look eleven years younger! How did you do it?" Then she stepped into him, embraced him, and kissed him.

Bink's head orbited another realm, as it did when she did that. But he knew this couldn't really be her. Because she had not entered the dream and gone to Ptero. And she was the wrong age: not her real seventy six or her youthened sixteen. And she was in the wrong phase, at the height of her beauty, instead of ugly or just this side of ordinary. So how could this be?

Dor and Dolph stood motionless and silent, as confused as he was. Chameleon was, after all, their mother and grandmother.

She drew back half a notch. "Oh, Bink, I've missed you so! I didn't expect you back until tomorrow. Let's go up to the bedroom right now."

And she was in her stupid phase, so didn't have the wit to be discreet. How could he explain, if he figured it out himself?

He glanced at Dor, desperate for guidance. Dor was their son. He should know. But he looked blank.

Meanwhile, Chameleon was tugging him toward a stairway. He tried to hang back, but couldn't. "Oh, go on up," a stair told him. "You're only young twice."

"We'll meet you—after," Dolph called helpfully.

After a few confused moments, Bink found himself in their chamber. Chameleon closed the door, pushed him onto the bed, so that he had to sit, then sat on his lap. Her bottom was marvelously soft. She wrapped her arms around his head and pulled him in for a welcoming hug. Her divinely firm bosom pressed against his face. She smelled of heaven. His senses melted into one great blissful mass of joy.

But she couldn't be his wife! The real Chameleon was back in Xanth, in Castle Roogna, maybe in this very chamber. But it wasn't the same castle; it couldn't be.

She got up and began removing her clothing. "I can't get over how young you look," she breathed. "Almost the way you were when we were first youthened. You look wonderful." Her dress came off. She was one of those women who looked better with every glance.

If he didn't do something soon, he would lose all control. His twenty one-year-old body was eager to summon a battalion of storks in a quarter of an instant. He loved Chameleon, and desired her, especially when she was like this. But how could it be?

She stood before him in bra and panties, not only unbearably lovely, but excruciatingly sexy. He was in danger of freaking out. Only his real mental age of eighty one enabled him to tide through the sight.

Bit by bit, he worked it out. All the people and creatures who ever existed or might exist were here on Ptero. That included all of the Xanth folk. So Chameleon was here too. She really was his wife.

She took off the underwear. His eyeballs were heating; he had to blink repeatedly to prevent them from frying.

But she was older. No less desirable, but older. Time was supposed to be geography here, or vice versa; people could be any age. So she was twenty seven, here in Castle Roogna.

And this wasn't even the real Ptero, but a dream image of it. So this was a dream Chameleon, not the real one of either Ptero or Xanth.

She started to undress him. Her touch was wonderfully gentle yet compelling.

It still felt like adultery.

"Chameleon," he said. "There's—there's something I must say."

"Can't it wait?" she asked, drawing off his shirt.

"Chameleon, I'm from Xanth."

"We're all on Xanth, in our off year," she said. She started work on his trousers.

"I mean I'm not from Ptero. I'm visiting from Xanth. I'm not—not the Bink who's due back tomorrow."

"I don't understand," she said. "Can you stand up, so I can get these off?"

"Chameleon, please! We can't do this."

She paused. "We can't? But it's so much more fun when we're young."

"Chameleon, I love you, but I'm not the Bink who lives here. It would be wrong to—"

She began to get the message of rejection. Her eyes turned moist, making him feel unbearably guilty. "You don't want to?"

How could he explain? The smart Chameleon would have understood the moment she saw their age differences, but this was the stupid one. Alternate worlds within worlds were beyond her limited comprehension.

He tried another tack. "Chameleon, suppose I was someone else who just looked like Bink but wasn't him. Would you still want to do this?"

She struggled with the concept, but it was too much. So she kissed him instead.

Bink gave himself up for lost. He still felt it was wrong, but he loved and desired her so much that he couldn't fight it any longer. He knew she was completely innocent of bad intent; she loved him and wanted him, and that was the whole of her present understanding. Would her opposite phase be angry, when she came into play? Or intrigued?

Chameleon got back to work on his trousers. Bink offered no further resistance.

Then the door opened and a man entered. ''Hello.''

''Hello, Bink,'' Chameleon said without looking, recognizing the voice.

Then, slowly, the realization sank in. She paused. Then her head turned.

There was Bink, thirty two years old, her true husband. ''I had some lucky breaks, and managed to get back a day early,'' he said.

''Yes, I know,'' she agreed. ''We're—'' She paused again, her head slowly turning back to the Bink on the bed.

''Yes, there are two of us,'' Bink-21 said.

''So I see,'' Bink-32 agreed.

Chameleon's head turned back and forth between them. ''I don't understand.''

Now Bink-21 could explain again, knowing that there was someone present who would understand. ''I am the Bink from Xanth. I am visiting Ptero in a dream. I'm not really here. Except in spirit. So I think I should turn the bed over to the real Bink at this point.''

But now Bink-32 protested. ''I'm the dream?''

''I'm sure you're real,'' Bink-21 said. ''But my image of you is in a dream. Just as I'm real, but not really here. Since Chameleon is a dream too, she's yours.''

''She is a dream,'' Bink-32 agreed.

''A perfect dream. And I love her. But I have my real Chameleon back on Xanth.''

''There's another woman?'' Chameleon asked plaintively.

The two Binks exchanged a glance. ''No,'' Bink-32 said. ''There is only you, Chameleon. And two of me. So one of us will go, and the other will be with you.''

She smiled. ''That's nice.''

Bink-21 got up and hastily donned his shirt. ''I think my talent is operating. It will not allow me to be harmed by magic. Since at least one of us is me, the other can't do anything harmful to the one. So it enabled you to get home in time.''

''Yes,'' Bink-32 agreed. He took off his shirt.

''We must talk, when we can,'' Bink-21 said.

''Yes. Soon.'' Bink-32 lay on the bed.

As Bink-21 went out the door, Chameleon was resuming where she had left off. Her confusion had been abated. That would not have been the case with a smarter woman. Both Binks understood that. Neither could stand to cause her the slightest pain. He closed the door behind him and headed for the stairs.

He had done the right thing. Yet there was that in him that almost wished that his other self had been too late.

He turned a corner and saw something just vanishing into a chamber, as if hiding. He remembered the suspicion that something might be following them. Could it be doing so even here in Castle Roogna? No, surely it was just a castle servant getting out of the way, or maybe a shy ghost.

Downstairs he found two Dors and one Irene in animated dialogue. For a moment he couldn't tell them apart. Then one Dor spied him and smiled. "How was it, father?"

"I didn't—I mean—"

Suddenly that Dor and Irene burst out laughing. "Fooled you," he said. "We're the natives."

Bink looked at the other Dor, who nodded. Then he saw that the natives, like Bink-32 and Chameleon-27, were older. He was sixty six instead of fifty five, and she was sixty five. He shouldn't have been fooled. "You aged well," he admitted.

Then two Dolphs came down the wall, with one matronly Electra and two stunning young women. The women spied Bink and charged him together. One was a redhead with green eyes and bright clothes, the other a dark-haired, dark-eyed creature in black clothing. They embraced him from either side. Who were they?

"What a handsome young man you are," the redhead said, kissing his right cheek.

"Yes, just right for us," the jet-blackhead said, nibbling on his left ear.

Finally he put it together. Dolph—Electra—eleven years hence—twin seven-year-old daughters who would now be eighteen. Each. "Dawn and Eve!" he exclaimed. "My great-grandchildren."

They laughed together. "Aw, he caught on," Dawn said. "Now we can't show him this." She leaned forward just enough to provide a glimpse of her fine cleavage inside a bright halter. She had evidently inherited an aspect of Chameleon.

"Or this," Eve agreed, lifting her short skirt just enough to show the edge of a dark panty on a firm bottom. There was another aspect.

"Girls!" Electra cried, appalled. "Behave yourselves!"

They laughed again, hardly chastised. "What brings you here, Great Grandpa?" Dawn asked innocently.

"If it's not to sneak peeks at your demure descendants," Eve added mischievously.

"It's to talk with the Zombie Master," Bink said. "The traveling one." Then he paused with another realization. "But you already know this, because you have just touched my flesh and my clothing, and your talents are to know anything about anything animate or inanimate."

"Shux," Dawn said, pouting cutely. "He's getting harder to tease."

"But maybe worth the challenge," Eve said.

"You girls were sheer mischief when you were seven," Bink said. "I think you're worse now."

"Thank you," they said together, blushing with pleasure.

"But we shall have to let our visitors go on," Irene said. "Before their trail gets cold. The Zombie Master didn't pause here long, and he's still a day ahead of them."

"Where did he go?" Bink asked.

"To Pyramid," Dawn said.

"We've been there," Eve said.

"With a nice faun," Dawn agred.

"With whom we really had fun," Eve concluded.

Electra looked about ready to explode. "Teasing," Dawn said quickly. "Nothing more."

"Unfortunately," Eve said.

"But we helped him save us all from dread marginalization."

"And clued him in on his true love: Mare Imbri."

"So would you like a pair of guides?" Dawn asked, inhaling, showing a pair.

"Really friendly guides who can show you—" Eve spied a deadly glance coming her way from her mother, and changed course before it reached her skirt. "The lay of the land?"

"What would your boyfriends think of that?" Irene inquired musingly.

The girls instantly sobered. ''We'll just tell you what to expect,'' Dawn said.

''Each triangular face of Pyramid is a different color,'' Eve said. ''When you cross from one to another, your orientation is still fixed by the first, so you can no longer stand up.''

''You can get help to change,'' Dawn said. ''But whoever helps you gets bigger, and you get smaller.''

''This is weird,'' Dolph said.

''But I'm sure we'll manage,'' Bink said.

''And if you happen to go on to Torus, that's where doing a favor makes you love the one you do it for,'' Dawn said.

''So you have to exchange favors within the hour, to avoid love trouble,'' Eve said. ''If you want to.''

''But what about time and geography?'' Bink asked.

''The rules are different for each world,'' Dawn explained.

''So is the terrain, and the people,'' Eve said.

Dor shook his head. ''This may become more of an experience than we anticipated.''

''We can provide you with a place to sleep, where your bodies will be safe,'' Dor-66 said.

''Will we need them, since we're already dreaming?'' Dor-55 asked.

''Oh, I suppose not. But first we should check with King Ivy.''

''How did Ivy come to be king, and not Grey or Dolph?'' Bink asked.

''The others were lost during the marginalization, so it fell to her,'' Dor-66 said. ''After that, it seemed easier just to leave it that way.''

''Here she comes now,'' Electra said.

Indeed, a forty-year-old woman wearing a crown was approaching. She did look like an older version of Bink's granddaughter.

''King Ivy,'' Dor-66 said. ''These are three visitors from Xanth, who are here in a dream. Grandfather Bink, who has been severely youthened, Father Dor, eleven years younger than I am, and Son Dolph, similarly younger than our Dolph.''

''I am pleased to meet you,'' Ivy said gravely. ''You all seem oddly familiar.''

''So do you,'' Dolph-24 said.

''This will get in my way,'' Ivy said, removing her crown and handing it to her father, Dor-66. Then she stepped into Dolph-24 and hugged him closely. "I love you, little brother." After that she hugged Dor-55 similarly, and finally Bink. "You seem even younger, Grandpa," she murmured in his ear.

"I was just rejuvenated," he said. "It still seems strange."

Ivy stepped back, took back her crown, donned it, and became suitably sober again. "You will want to go on to my sister Ida," she said. "Please come this way." She evidently had been briefed on their business.

They followed her to the Tapestry chamber. There was Princess Ida, with her moon—and sure enough, it was the shape of a little pyramid, with four triangular faces.

"These are the Xanth originals," Ivy said. "They need to locate the Zombie Master."

"I will be glad to help," Ida said. "The Zombie Master's experience clarified the way. You will not need to sleep, as you are already asleep in your own realm. Simply think small, and you will fade from here. If you need to find my next derivative, she lives on the blue face."

"Thank you," Dor said. He glanced around. "You have all been most kind." He hesitated. "Would it be permissible to visit again, when we are not on pressing business?"

"Certainly," King Ivy said. "We would be glad to talk with you, as we have no knowledge of events in your year of animation."

"You can't just go back in time to when you were that age?" Dolph asked.

"We can travel there, but must skip over the year during which you live," she said. "We become younger as we go toward From, but for me the year when I am twenty nine does not currently exist; I go from thirty to twenty eight. My memory takes a similar skip, so that I can't recall what I did that year. Next year the following year will be missing from my experience. Similar is true for all of us."

"Weird," Dolph said.

"I'm sure that we would find it as odd in Xanth," King Ivy said.

Bink wondered whether it could possibly be stranger yet on Pyramid. They would soon be finding out.

Then the three kings held hands, faced Pyramid, and thought small.

5

GOOD MAGICIAN

At dawn Breanna reached the vicinity of the Good Magician's Castle. She could tell, because there was a sign saying VICINITY OF GOOD MAGICIAN'S CASTLE. But then the path petered out, leaving only interspersed forest and field.

She stopped at the end of the path, perplexed. How could this be the place, if there was nothing here?

She ticked off possible reasons on her fingers. One: this was a fake sign, and this was not the right vicinity. But everything else suggested that it *was* right, because she had seen other signs saying things like GMC NEXT LEFT, GMC obviously being the abbreviation for Good Magician's Castle. GMC HALF HOUR'S WALK. This was an enchanted path, so the signs should be accurate.

Two: maybe the castle had moved. But then there should be a forwarding address or detour sign. There wasn't.

Three: this was a challenge. But in that case—

She paused, her refutation foundering before getting established. She knew that challenges could be anything, and were generally tailored to the folk who sought to bother the Good Magician with their stupid Questions. She was a person who liked to be forthright, to go straight to the person she wanted, to tackle a problem directly. What could be a bigger challenge for her, than not to be able to *find* the one she sought?

''Very well, Good Magician,'' she muttered. ''You want to play

Hide & Seek. I'll play your stupid game. But I'll bleeping well expect value for my effort.'' She had learned not to try to swear; she could do it, being originally Mundane, but nasty effects tended to occur as the surrounding atmosphere of the Adult Conspiracy tried to suppress it. The De Censor Ship couldn't be everywhere at once, unfortunately, so until someone—maybe Breanna herself, in due course—mounted a successful campaign to suppress the Adult Conspiracy, it remained in force. Native Xanthians were inducted into the Conspiracy as they came of age, and thereafter made 180-degree turns and supported what they had opposed as children. It was ludicrous hypocrisy. But Breanna wasn't native, and there was nothing for her to learn that was going to blow her mind. It had been blown before she was six years old, when she got into her cousin's porno collection. So she would not change sides when she passed eighteen. Then, armed with the awful power of adult initiative, she would see what she wanted to do.

All of which was halfway irrelevant at the moment. Right now she had to find the castle. So how should she go about it?

First, she had to figure out just where the castle was. Had it been buried underground? She didn't see any sign of heavy construction. Of course with magic there might not be any telltale marks. Still, that seemed like an awful lot of trouble just to make one minor questioner pause. So probably the castle hadn't been buried or moved, just hidden.

So how was it hidden? That was easy: with illusion. Illusion was cheap and versatile and effective, sort of the basic currency of Xanth. So the castle must be right there, somewhere in front of her, but made to look like part of the forest. The path probably went right to it, but illusion covered the path, making it look like untouched forest floor. She could probably walk right along the path, feeling it with her feet.

She tried it. Sure enough, there was a path where it looked as if it ended. Her feet became invisible at the ankles, so it looked as if she were ankle deep in forest loam. Illusion covered reality.

She continued—and suddenly stepped off the hidden path and lost her balance, almost falling. The path had curved, while she hadn't. So she backed off, looked around, and found a stick she could use as a cane. Then she walked into the illusion again, tapping ahead of her in the manner of a blind person, making sure the path was there before she stepped on it.

Then it ended, again. She tapped all around, but there was no continuing path. Yet she was sure it was there, because she had been right about the illusion; why have illusion cover a few feet of a path that ended soon anyway? So what was going on?

A moment's thought brought an answer: it must be more illusion. Illusion wasn't limited to sight; it could be sound or touch too. So now the illusion had been expanded to touch; she could no longer feel the path.

So what could she do? Walk through the area in a criss-cross pattern, hoping to bump into the castle? She'd probably just fall into the moat and get gobbled by the moat monster. So that wasn't the best idea. She needed a way to penetrate the illusion, to know exactly where the castle was, even if she couldn't see or feel it.

This was a real problem. Her experience seeing in the dark had gotten her used to never being blind. Now, suddenly, she was really sightless. The good magician had targeted her pretty well, finding her weakness, that she hadn't realized until now.

She would have to do some heavier pondering. She sat down in the illusion, seeing her bottom disappear, and leaned back against a tree. And fell flat on her back. The tree was illusion!

She scrambled back to her feet, dusted herself off, and walked back beyond the fringe of illusion. Then she sat down again and leaned against a real tree. She closed her eyes, trying to make her brain work better. But she seemed to have run out of creative notions.

"Hello."

Breanna looked up without opening her eyes. There stood a black horse. "Oh, hello, Imbri. Did you bring me a daydream?"

Mare Imbri assumed woman form so she could talk more readily. *"I'm actually on business for that other party I had to attend, and saw you here. Are you all right?"*

"Mixed. I'm in the middle of a challenge, and it's getting the better of me."

"Oh, this is your challenge? I thought it was mine. Or Justin's. The invisible castle."

"Well, I thought it was mine. Who's Justin?"

"Justin Tree. He was a man who opposed the Evil Magician, the year Chameleon was delivered, seventy six years ago, and was transformed into a tree. He's been there by the North Village ever since."

"The Evil Magician?" Breanna asked blankly.

"That's what he was called. Later he assumed power, and became known as King Trent, now retired."

"King Trent! Him I have heard of. The transformer. But why didn't he transform Justin back into a man?"

"Justin didn't want it. He was satisfied as a tree. For one thing, he would be pretty old now, as a man, but remains in his prime as a tree. But still, he misses the adventure of being a man, of traveling, fighting, loving, and so on. So he would like to have that. But he wants to remain a tree."

Breanna shook her head. "How can a tree have an adventure?"

"That's what he wants to ask the Good Magician. So I agreed to carry his dream to Humfrey. But I can't find the castle."

Breanna laughed. "Now wouldn't that be an irony. If I struggled to conquer a challenge that wasn't even meant for me. Or you did. Or Justin Tree did. So how do we know who it's for?"

Imbri looked thoughtful. *"It might be for all three. A general purpose challenge, and the one who gets past it and the others gets his Question Answered."*

"I don't want to compete with anyone. I don't want to freeze your friend out by taking it myself, or to get frozen out. Does it have to be one or the other?"

"I'm not sure. Sometimes two or more folk come as a group, and the challenge applies to all of them."

"Then maybe we should cooperate. Combine our resources. Can Justin do that, if he's not really here?"

"Yes, because I am carrying his dream. His body isn't here, but his mind is. In fact, if he has to handle challenges, he'll need help, because he can't actually do *anything here."*

"Then why don't I be the body, and he can be the mind? Because I'm sure stymied on this invisible castle. If he can help me here, maybe I can help him on the next challenge. And when we get in, we can both demand Answers."

Imbri flickered, and Breanna knew she was checking with the tree. *"Yes, he agrees. I told him of your situation with Xeth Zombie, and your desire to escape. He understands. So I will put you in touch with each other, via my dreams."*

Then Breanna saw a tree. It was growing in a glade near a village, and it was a handsome specimen of its kind, whatever kind that was. This was Justin. "Hello. I am Breanna of the Black Wave."

A face formed in the foliage, making the whole tree seem to be a head on a trunk of a neck. This was Imbri's design. *"Hello. I am Justin Tree."* His voice in the dream seemed vaguely archaic and vegetative.

"So you want to tackle this challenge together? I'm stumped. Uh, excuse the expression."

The face smiled. *"No problem. May I use your eyes?"*

"That depends. I need them myself."

"I merely wish to look through them, to see what you see, so I can assess the problem. I merely need you to look in directions I request, on occasion."

"Oh. Okay. As long as it doesn't hurt."

"It would be a shame to hurt such a pretty young woman."

There was something about this tree she liked. He seemed not to be aware of her color or her age, and he didn't mind associating with her gender. "So where do you want me to look?"

"Perhaps I should explain. I have had some time viewing a forest scene, and have learned something about it. There is the phenomenon of parallax, in which distant objects seem to change their positions as the viewer moves."

"Oh, sure, that happens all the time," Breanna agreed. "So what?"

"It may be possible to use it to penetrate the illusion. Because illusions are normally two dimensional, while reality is three dimensional."

"Well, I guess so. But if you look through my eyes right now, you'll see that it's bleeping convincing illusion." She opened her eyes. "I don't care whether it's one dimensional or ten dimensional, it's covering up what I need to see."

"Yes, I do see. But if we can define exactly where the illusion is, we should know where the castle is."

"I don't get it. But if you have a way, go to it."

"If you will walk back and forth while looking in the direction you think the castle is, I can test my theory."

So Breanna got up and walked back and forth, staring in the direction the path went before it faded. It seemed pointless, but she had nothing better to offer.

"Yes," Justin said. *"I see it."*

"See what?"

"The lack of parallax."

"I guess I'm not seeing what you're seeing."

"Let me help you. Walk again, and attune to my vision."

She tried, though mystified. And suddenly she saw what he meant. The distant trees were shifting their positions in most of the forest, but in one area they weren't. They looked just the same from one angle as from another. Like a picture, whose perspective didn't change. "That's the illusion!" she exclaimed. "That unmoving picture!"

"Yes, by elimination. So now we can define it by continuing parallax, reducing the area of search."

"You're pretty smart," she said admiringly.

"No, just old, with time to think."

She walked back and forth, and soon narrowed the "picture" down to an area just about the size of a castle and moat. Then she used her cane to probe ahead, and walked to the edge of that region. When she got there, her cane came up against something solid. It was a low wall. She poked beyond it, found footing, and stepped over.

The illusion vanished. The Good Magician's Castle stood there in all its glory. They had conquered the illusion.

Curious, she stepped back over the low wall, which was evidently there to prevent anyone from blundering into the moat. The castle disappeared, and the picture of forest returned. She stepped back inside, and the castle returned. That was the inner limit of the illusion. All she had had to do was find her way through it; it didn't work from the inside. Just as a person couldn't look at a painting from the back of it.

"Well, that wasn't so bad after all," Breanna murmured. "Thanks to your insight, Justin."

"And your sight," he replied, seeming as pleased as she was.

"Where's Mare Imbri?"

The mare appeared in a day-dreamlet. *"I am here, maintaining the contact between you."*

"Oh, okay. You just faded out."

"It's my nature, except when I'm with my tree and faun. Daydreams seldom last long."

That made sense, maybe. Breanna walked toward the drawbridge, which was down. But as she did, the ground became sticky. At first it was just a nuisance, but with each step it got worse, until she could hardly drag her feet up. She was stuck to the ground.

"I think we have encountered the second challenge," she murmured. "I'm in a sticky situation."

"Can you back out and circle around the bad patch?" Justin asked.

She tried, but now she was completely stuck. "No. Like a fool, I barged right in until it was too late."

"Like anyone encountering the unexpected," he corrected her.

There was just something about this tree that appealed. Her folks were quick to rebuke her when she messed up; Justin made her action seem reasonable. "So what now? Do I take off my shoes and jump?"

"And get your pretty feet dirty? No, there must be a better way, if this is a challenge. Let me ponder."

Meanwhile, something happened beside the drawbridge. The lid of a large container slowly lifted. There was a picture of a skull and crossbones on the box. "This is not a good sign," Breanna muttered, feeling a chill. Was a monster going to come from that crate to gobble her, since she couldn't get away?

A skull appeared, followed by a skeleton. It looked around with its eye sockets, spied her, and rattled forward. It stopped just beyond the sticky section. "Apop Tosis at your service," it said.

Breanna was terrified, so she bluffed. "Not at *my* service. Whatever you're selling, I don't want it."

"Skeletons aren't generally dangerous," Justin said. *"They lack desires of the flesh."*

That helped. "What do you want?" she demanded, still not exactly settled.

"I see you are in a sticky situation, so I have come to help you."

"I don't think I want—" she started.

But Justin was more cautious. *"This must be part of the challenge. It is better to hear him out."*

"To be impolite," Breanna improvised. "How do you want to help me?"

"Let me make myself more comfortable," Apop said. He brought out a bottle labeled Boot Rear and lifted it to his jawbone. There didn't seem to be any fluid in it, but suddenly he sailed into the air, flying apart. The bones fell to the ground in a pattern, forming a rocking chair with the skull on the seat. "I always carry some boot rear with me," he explained. "So I don't have to depend on someone else to boot me in the rear so that I can change configuration."

"Good policy," Breanna agreed guardedly. "I'm not exactly in a position to boot anybody's rear right now." Skeletons were not her favorite companions, though they weren't as bad as zombies. At least they weren't rotting.

"Now I will ask you three questions," Apop said. "If you answer them well, you will get out of your sticky situation. But if you don't, you will find it embarrassing."

"Yeah, sure," she muttered.

"First question: Are you a bigot?"

"What the bleep kind of a question is that?" she demanded, outraged. "Of course I'm not! How could you even suggest it?" But as she spoke, something awkward happened. Her clothing was shrinking. Her blouse felt tight, and her skirt was riding up on her hips.

"What is happening?" Justin inquired.

"Can I talk to you silently?" she subvocalized.

"Yes, we are dream connected, so I can hear whatever you direct to me, as well as what you hear from outside. I heard the skeleton's question. But then you started wriggling, and I don't know why. I am unable to fathom your actual thoughts, so that you retain your natural modesty."

He couldn't read her mind. That was a relief. She also liked the way he phrased her desire for mental privacy. She had never been to a court, but suspected Justin was courtly. "Because my clothing suddenly shrank," she said silently. "Maybe it got wet."

"Maybe," he agreed. *"Meanwhile, I'm not sure you gave a satisfactory answer to the question."*

"It was a lousy question!"

"Perhaps it is intended to make you react negatively."

"Well, it succeeded! It's outrageous to suggest that I could be a bigot. I'm black!"

"I hadn't realized. But does your color relate?"

"Sure it does. I'm a victim, not an oppressor."

"I fear I am being slow in comprehension. What is the definition of bigot?"

''It's a person who is utterly intolerant of any differing belief or opinion. We were up against it in Mundania. That's one huge reason we left.''

"Then your answer must be no. The penalty must be because you objected to the question rather than answering it."

He had to be right. She had let the question blow her equilibrium, like an idiot. ''For sure.'' She faced the skeleton. ''No, I can't be a bigot.''

Apop didn't answer. But her clothing shrank another notch. Her blouse was constricting her breathing, and in danger of tearing, and her skirt was becoming a mini.

''My clothing's still shrinking,'' she told Justin, alarmed.

"There must be a connection to your answer to the question," the tree concluded. *"Perhaps it is a penalty for what is considered an unsatisfactory answer."*

''I don't give half a bleep what a stupid skeleton thinks is unsatisfactory,'' she retorted. ''He has no business asking such a question.''

"Now I don't wish to be offensive," Justin said carefully. *"But it strikes me that if the skeleton desires a certain answer, and can make you uncomfortable when you don't give it, some consideration may be required."*

''Meaning I'm stuck here, literally, and getting my undies in a knot, so I'd better watch my mouth.''

"I'm sure they are very nice undies."

''You didn't tell me anything useful.''

"Perhaps some finesse is in order. More than one answer may be acceptable, or perhaps more than one phrasing."

''Okay, I'll try.'' She took a breath and spoke aloud again. ''Maybe it depends on your definition of bigotry.'' Her clothing didn't tighten, but neither did it loosen. ''Maybe every person is a bit bigoted in some respects, and not in others. Maybe I am too. But I don't want to be.''

Now her clothing loosened. ''By bleep, Justin, you were right again! I gave a more reasoned answer, and my clothing relaxed. This is weird, but who's to argue with what works?''

"Most situations merely respond to the proper key, if it can be found," the tree said.

The skeleton spoke again. ''Second question: What is your fondest wish?''

''That's easy: to be a queen, with all the privileges thereof.''

Her clothing writhed warningly.

"Isn't that zombie you encountered a king?" Justin asked. *"So that if you married him, you would be a queen?"*

Breanna felt an awful sinking sensation. She hadn't thought things through. ''Yes. Scratch that answer. I don't want to be a zombie queen.'' She addressed the skeleton. ''I want to get away from that zombie who's chasing me. That's why I'm here.'' But her clothing tightened again.

''Hey, wait a minute!'' she cried. ''Who the bleep would want to marry a zombie? I've got a right to get away.'' But her clothing tightened worse than before.

"Perhaps a zombie might see that as bigotry," Justin said.

''Well, who cares what a bleeping bag of rot cares! It isn't as if he's a person.''

Then she paused. ''Hoo, boy, I just heard myself talking. That's the way the bad whites talked about us, in Mundania. The bigots.''

"But you aren't a bigot."

''I'm not quite so sure, anymore. I mean, how do I know that zombie king isn't a decent person, apart from his physical condition? All I could see was his rot, and I freaked out.''

"Well, zombies are not fun to be around."

''Nevertheless, in retrospect I'm not exactly proud of my reaction. I still don't want to marry Xeth, but I think I could have been more polite about it.''

"Fortunately you are already past the first question. There should be a better answer for the second one, though."

''There sure should be.'' She faced the skeleton again. ''I think that wasn't my fondest wish. I think I need more tolerance. To maybe grow a bit in attitude. So maybe at some point I'll talk with the zombie, and explain myself better. I guess what my fondest wish really is, is to be all that I can be, in every way I can be, including understanding and open-mindedness.''

Her clothing loosened entirely.

''You sure put me on the right track,'' she told Justin. ''The funny thing is, I believe it. I wasn't reacting well before.''

''Third question,'' Apop said. ''Is the Adult Conspiracy worthwhile?''

"Brother," she muttered. "Am I ever going to flunk this one!" Then she faced the skeleton. "No, it's worthless. It's stupid, pointless, inconsistent nonsense. It exists only to browbeat children."

Her clothing tightened so much that her blouse pulled out of her waistband and threatened to uncover her bra, and her skirt was trying to expose her panties. It was really trying to embarrass her.

She laughed, almost hysterically. "I just caught on! These are embarrassing questions. Em-bare-ass-ing. I should have known there'd be a dirty pun in this."

"You may have to stop opposing the Adult Conspiracy," Justin said. *"It can be vicious."*

"Damn it!" she cried aloud. "This is too much! I'm *not* going to lie and say the Adult Conspiracy is good. It's a cheat and a shame, and it should be abolished. And that's the way I truly feel. And I don't care if my knickers twist right off my little black mule. I mean *ass.* So there!"

Now her blouse shrank to the size of a handkerchief, and her skirt almost disappeared. The magic was calling her bluff. She stood there in awful squeezed exposure.

"I don't care! I don't care! What you want me to say is wrong, and I am not going to say it. And now that I think of it, why the hell should I even be embarrassed by a bare ass? What is wrong with the human body the way God made it? Only a bigot would think it's obscene." She ripped off the rest of her clothing, which was painfully tight, and stood naked. "I have been catering to that stupid Conspiracy, and it's time to stop. I renounce it. If that means I flunk this stupid test, well that's tough, because I think I'm on the side of the angels. So there."

"Well spoken!" Justin said. *"I never had the courage to say that."*

"Well, someone had to. Even if—" She stopped. "My feet! They're unstuck!"

"And the skeleton is departing. You did not fail the test, you passed it. By asserting your true belief, instead of allowing the bigotry of others to govern you."

"Gee, I guess I did," she agreed, bemused. "So I guess we got through the second challenge. Just when I thought it was lost."

Not wasting the moment, Breanna marched on to the drawbridge, half expecting it to rise just before she got there. But it didn't, so she set a cautious foot on it, and when it didn't turn out to be illusion or worse, she walked on across the moat.

There was a space between the moat and the castle wall, and in this space were several large hoops with what looked liked two puffs of cotton tied to them on either side near the top, and three strings with three colored beads and three brightly colored feathers on each. Nine beaded straps reached inward to support a leather disk that filled most of the interior. The whole was hung by another beaded strap.

"What are those things?" Justin asked.

"I don't know. They look somehow familiar, but I can't quite place them. It's almost as if I've seen something like them in Mundania, but I can't think where. I suppose they could be a modern art exhibit."

"I doubt that they are mere decorations. Could they be a challenge?"

Breanna considered. "In a vague way, they remind me of spider webs. But there are no spiders on them, so I don't think they are traps. Just to be sure, I won't touch them; I'll walk around them." She proceeded to do that.

Inside the ring of hoops, she turned. "So that was no sweat. What next?"

"I don't know," Justin said. *"There doesn't seem to be much point to this excursion. I doubt it's worth the effort."*

"You're right," she agreed, surprised. "Why am I going to all this effort to see the Good Magician anyway? It isn't as if I have anything to make of my life."

"Oh, I thought you wanted to be all that you could be, and abolish the Adult Conspiracy."

"Why?"

"Because it's stupid, pointless, inconsistent nonsense?"

"Well, sure, but someone else can tackle it. I have no ambition."

"I don't care much about having an adventure, either. Maybe we should just leave off and forget about foolish dreams."

"Yeah." She walked back to the drawbridge and started to cross.

"Wait," Justin said. *"Not that I care, but I wonder if there isn't something wrong here. How is it that we both had such high ambitions a moment ago, and now don't?"*

"We just came to our senses, is all."

"Maybe, but I'm not satisfied with that. I distrust sudden changes, maybe because they can be bad for foliage. We ought at least to understand the change. What led us to our sudden revelations of pointlessness?"

"Dreams are foolish," she said. "They just lead to mischief. So sensible folk ignore them and get on with life. Not that there's much point to that, either."

"I agree. Still, I notice a change in you. You were full of fire and verve, and now you seem, if you will pardon the expression, mundane."

"Well, I'm an immigrant from Mundania."

"Breanna, I am still not satisfied. You were a pleasure to associate with, and now it doesn't seem to matter."

"Well, so were you, and now you're just a vegetable."

"We were two interesting folk, and now we're dull."

"So?"

"Doesn't that bother you?"

"Why should it?"

"I don't know, but somehow I feel it should."

"Well, let's go home and forget it." She reached the far end of the drawbridge.

Still, he seemed to lag. *"Where's Mare Imbri?"*

"She must be here, because we're still connected."

"No, she finally connected us directly, so that she wouldn't have to mediate every exchange. She was trotting along in case we needed other assistance. She didn't say she had to leave."

"That's right." Breanna looked around. "Imbri! Where are you?"

There was no answer.

"This bothers me increasingly," Justin said. *"Do you suppose something untoward happened to her?"*

"I don't care if its toward or away, this makes me nervous." Breanna turned and walked back across the drawbridge. "Maybe she got lost."

"That's impossible. She knows all of Xanth."

She spied the circle of disks again. Something clicked. "Uh-oh."

"What is it?"

"Now I remember where I have seen such things before. They're dream catchers."

"Dream catchers?"

''Native Americans made them to catch bad dreams, so folk could sleep in peace.''

"Imbri used to be a night mare!"

''That's my thought. If she went near one of those things—''

"We must find her."

''Yes.'' Breanna went from one disk to another, looking closely at each. Soon she found her: caught in the middle of the hoop, four feet, head, and tail bound to the rim. ''Imbri!''

But the mare was silent. She struggled to turn her head, but even this was difficult. She was fairly bound, physically and mentally.

"When she was caught, we lost our dreams," Justin said, working it out. *"We must free her."*

''For sure.'' Breanna reached out to untie a knot. But her hands passed right through it. In fact the whole dream catcher was illusion, for her. But not for Mare Imbrium.

"I think we have discovered the third challenge," Justin said gravely. *"It is to recover our dreams."*

''Right on. But I can't touch either the dream catcher or Imbri. What do we do?''

"The prior challenge was mostly yours," Justin said thoughtfully. *"I suspect this one is mine, because I am the immaterial person here. I must find a way."*

''Well, do it quickly, because Imbri looks uncomfortable.'' Indeed it made Breanna hurt to see the discomfort of the mare. She had never liked to see animals mistreated, particularly horses, and Imbri was the best horse of all. It was also weird to realize that Breanna's own ambition had been driven by her dreams, and that when Imbri had been caught, Breanna's life, and Justin's too, had lost their point. So they had personal reason to rescue the mare, apart from basic decency. It seemed that all dreams had been caught, hers and Justin's, and if they freed Imbri they would know how to free all the dreams. But regardless, Imbri had to be saved.

"I think I need to know more about dream catchers," Justin said. *"You say they are made by mundane natives?"*

''Native Americans; that's not quite the same. I don't think they're really mundane.''

"This is a type of magic I haven't seen before. Could one of those folk have come from Mundania?"

''Sure, why not? I did.''

"And if he found himself in a strange land, he might seek the advice of the Good Magician, and be required to undertake a year's service. Which could take the form of making big dream catchers to protect the castle from night mares."

"It works for me."

"Do those things need any kind of maintenance?"

Breanna pondered. "I don't know, but I don't think so. I think they are made once, then hung up and they just keep on working. But I really don't know much about them. I always thought they were superstition."

"Could it be that they didn't work well in Mundania, because they grew old and were not restored to optimum power?"

"Could be."

"So that perhaps these must be serviced every day or so, to be at full strength."

"Sure, why not. But what's your point?"

"Maybe we could rescue Imbri when the maker comes to refurbish the dream catchers. Each one must be deactivated for a time so he can work on it."

"Maybe," Breanna agreed doubtfully. "But I'm not sure how we can—"

"I wonder whether dreams are impossible for us, at present?"

"I can still dream," Breanna said sharply. "I just don't want to."

"Here is what may do it. If we can craft a dream of our own, we may be able to use it to free Imbri."

"How can we do that?"

"If we can dream that a day or more has passed, the one who services the dream catchers may think that it is time to go over them already. When he works on this one, we can rescue Imbri. You must hide, of course, so he doesn't see you and realize what we are doing."

Breanna was doubtful, but had no better idea herself, so went along with it. They found a nook or a cranny in the wall, and she scrunched down pretty much out of sight. She concentrated, and with Justin's help imagined that the day was passing, and night falling, and day coming again. She got into it, and soon it seemed that time really was passing swiftly. She tried to imagine that it was happening to the whole castle.

"He's coming," Justin said.

Sure enough, there was a man with reddish skin, wearing a feather tucked in a band around his head. He approached the dream catcher.

"What have we were?" he asked rhetorically. "A night mare? Well, just let me you lead you to a safe stall." He reached out and touched the dream catcher, and Imbri suddenly dropped to the ground.

He was going to take her away, captive! "No you don't!" Breanna cried, jumping from her hiding place. "That's *my* mare!"

The man looked at her. His mouth dropped open. Then she remembered that she had lost her clothing. No wonder he was staring. But it was too late to do anything about that. "Come, Imbri," she said, and led the mare to the castle wall. Her hand passed right through the horse, but Imbri came along with her.

Suddenly Breanna's dreams were back. She wanted to destroy the Adult Conspiracy. She wanted to be free and successful and beautiful and all the rest. She had ambitions. She had dreams.

"You did it!" Justin said.

She had, she realized, freed Imbri. They had broken the dream-catcher spell, freeing all their dreams. They were now beyond the dream catchers. The day mare might not be able to pass them without getting caught, but she had no need to go near them again.

"Yes, I think we got past the third challenge," Breanna agreed, satisfied.

"Thanks to your state of exposure, which I had forgotten."

"So had I," she confessed, trying to force a blush by her dark complexion. "You know, I do object to the Adult Conspiracy, but I still am not comfortable going around naked. People might stare, as the red man did. Would it be hypocritical for me to put something on, now that we're through the challenges?"

"By no means. The full name is 'The Adult Conspiracy to Keep Interesting Things from Children.' By asserting your freedom from it, you merely establish your right to say or do what you wish. You may go clothed or unclothed as you choose. Considering the weather, which I think is a trifle cool, it makes sense for you to wear something for the time being."

Once again, she found she liked his attitude. The region wasn't cold, but it remained a dandy pretext.

As it happened, there was a small lady slipper plant growing by the castle wall, with a pair of delicate slippers that just fit her. Near it was a cowslip plant with a ripe slip, so she harvested that and donned it. It fit a bit snugly, but covered the essentials.

She found a shiny facet of the wall and peered at her refection. It showed her that the fit was more than snug; the slip clung to her upper and nether sections in a way that made them bulge and seem twice as prominent as they really were. ''I look like a cow!'' she exclaimed.

"That does seem to be the penalty for wearing a cowslip," Justin said. *"But if you will accept the view of one whose days of being a human man are rather long gone, the reflected view is not an unattractive aspect."*

She reconsidered. If he thought it was all right, maybe it was, even if it did make her look way older than fifteen. ''I guess it will do.''

She went to the entrance. A woman was just approaching it from inside. The woman listened, then turned her head toward Breanna, her eyes seeming not quite to focus. ''Hello, Breanna and Justin,'' she said. ''And Mare Imbri. I am Wira, the Good Magician's daughter-in-law. I will show you to his study.''

''Thank you,'' Breanna said, surprised. ''How do you know our names?''

''The Good Magician saw you coming, and told me. He assumes you know the price of an Answer.'' Wira glanced at her, but again her gaze missed by a vague amount.

As usual, Breanna spoke before she thought. ''Are you blind?''

''Yes. But I know this castle well, and will get you safely where you need to be.''

''Oh, I didn't mean that you couldn't—'' But it was already impossibly awkward, so she cut her losses and shut up.

''She's not upset,'' Imbri murmured, assuming girlform in these closer quarters. *''She's Hugo's wife, and is one of the few folk for whom Humfrey is genuinely fond, though he doesn't speak of it. She knows, though.''* Then, after a pause: *''I need to go now. I think the Good Magician will take care of you.''*

''Sure, thanks,'' Breanna said. ''You've done more than enough for me.''

Mare Imbri faded out.

Breanna followed Wira through the labyrinth of the castle, up a tightly winding staircase, and to a dingy cubby where a century-old gnome pored over a huge archaic tome. ''Good Magician, here are Breanna of the Black Wave, and Justin Tree of the North Village, here to ask you Questions.''

The gnome looked up. ''State your Questions.''

''Justin Tree wishes to have a nice adventure, without changing from being a tree,'' Breanna said. She paused, in case Justin had a correction to make. He didn't. ''I want to find out how to escape the zombies.''

The Good Magician's gaze was disconcertingly like Wira's, and Breanna realized that he was looking through her to Justin. ''You could have an adventure as a tree if a dragon were to toast your foliage.''

''Not that kind!'' Justin protested. *''A human type adventure.''*

Breanna started to translate, but the Good Magician raised his hand. ''Rhetorical. I know the kind he wants. His best Answer requires the service of another person.'' Now his old eyes focused on Breanna. ''That person is you.''

''Me!''

''He must vicariously share the adventure of a person in human form, with that person's consent. The best person, considering availability, compatibility, and interest of adventure, is you. But there are two constraints. You are beneath the age of consent, which means indoctrination into the Adult Con—''

''No I'm not!'' she protested. ''I reject the Adult Conspiracy.''

''Therefore that is not an issue,'' he continued, unsurprised. ''The other is that you are female, and may not wish to share your feelings with a male mind. It is my policy not to require unkind service for an Answer. Therefore if you wish to decline, and to perform some other service for your Answer—''

''No, that's okay,'' Breanna said. ''I was just caught off guard. Justin's okay; I like him. He can share my adventure if he wants to.'' She found the decision surprisingly easy to make. It was almost as if she had thought something like this out before, and agreed. It wasn't as if she planned to do anything she might be ashamed of. She realized that Justin had been not only helpful on the challenges, but nice company. He didn't act superior, the way too many older folk were too likely to do, and he didn't come across as prejudiced against the Black Wave. She liked him. It was weird, because she hadn't been looking for any friends among whites, males, or trees, but there it was. There was just something about him. Maybe it was his archaic courtesy.

"Then that will be your service, which will terminate in a year or by mutual agreement." His eyes refocused on Justin. "Your service will be to be on call indefinitely as a consultant for selections, challenges, and solutions."

"You need help on such things?" Justin asked, surprised. Breanna repeated it aloud.

"It takes time to research and decide which querents are worthy, and to devise and institute challenges that will discourage those who are not serious without eliminating the worthy," Humfrey said. "The services of those who assisted before are concluding. Things have become awkward, and we stand in need of intellectual assistance. It will not be necessary for you to leave your tree site or to interrupt your personal adventure; the work is intellectual."

"I will be glad to do it," Justin said. *"It will make me feel useful again."*

Breanna realized that the Good Magician respected Justin's intellect in much the way she did. The tree-man was smart and balanced. Maybe his time as a tree had filled out his intellect.

Humfrey focused again on Breanna. "You can escape the pursuit of the zombies by going to the Isle of Women. This isle is not easy to locate, so you will be guided by one who knows the way. Wira will introduce you, and give you what you need."

"Gee, thanks," she said. But the Good Magician had already tuned her out, and was back in his tome.

"This way," Wira said, and led the way back down the stairs. Breanna suspected that there was plenty yet to discover. But that was okay, because not only was she about to escape the zombies, she had gained a good companion.

"Thank you," Justin said.

6
WORLDS BEYOND KEN

Dolph still found it strange, becoming small enough to enter a world he knew was the size of a large cherry. In fact, since they were already on a world that size, this one was that much smaller. It made his imagination begin to shrivel, so he tuned that out and just focused on where they were going.

The four-sided triangle that was Pyramid expanded. It was rotating, and he saw the triangles change from blue to red to green. He didn't see the fourth side, until he realized that it was at the bottom, and was somber gray, maybe because it didn't see much light.

The pyramid expanded, and some of the detail on the sides came clearer. There were mountains and valleys and plains and lakes, just as on Ptero. But everything on the blue side was a shade of blue, including the trees and houses. Everything on the red side was similarly a shade of red, including the lakes and clouds. It was rather pretty, in its monochromatic way.

Then the nearest face became too big to see around, and it was like dropping onto a map. It was the green side, which would have seemed natural if its sky wasn't green too.

This world's Ida was supposed to be on the blue side, but the green side was where they were landing. Actually they didn't know that the Zombie Master had gone on to that Ida, so they needed to find his footprints and follow them, as before.

This time they made a better landing, and dented the ground only a little. They let go each others' hands, dusted themselves off, and looked around.

They stood in a green glade surrounded by a green jungle. A green lake was to one side. Between them and the lake was a patch of green sand. There was no sign of glowing footprints.

"Maybe that sand will know," Dor said. He walked across toward it.

"Don't step on me," the sand said. "I'm a sand trap."

Bink picked up a green stone and tossed it into the sand. A sand bar jumped up and snapped across, pinning the rock. "Oh, you tricked me!" the sand said.

"Have you seen a stranger pass by here?" Dor asked.

"No." Then the sand reconsidered. "But would you like me to help you look?"

"Yes."

"Done." The sand patch became a size larger, and Dor became a size smaller.

"Oops, we forgot," Dolph said. "Things that do favors grow, and the receivers shrink."

"I'll survive," Dor said. "It's only filler material."

"Still," Bink said, "we had best be careful."

The sand humped up and formed into a green man shape. "Sandy Sandman, at your service," it said.

Dor, though slightly diminished in size, had not lost his common sense. "Since you have agreed to help us search, and been rewarded, part of that service should be some advice on how to get along here, so that our search doesn't get messed up."

Sandy considered for a moment and a half. "Yes, I suppose that's right. The first thing you should do is get your color right, because anyone can see you're not green."

It was true. They were the only un-green things in view. "How do we do that?" Dor asked.

"Wash yourselves with some green water, of course."

So the three of them stepped around the sand trap and knelt by the lake. They scooped out handfuls of green water and spread it on themselves. When that wasn't very effective, they simply waded into the lake, and came out green.

Green bubbles formed and rose to the surface around them. As each got there, it popped. "Who are you?" one asked. "Why are you here?" another asked. "Where are you going?" a third one asked.

"Ignore them," Sandy said. "They are just pop quizzes."

Bink emerged from the water and spied a green mint plant. He was about to pick a mint to eat when Sandy spoke again. "Don't. That's a govern mint. If you eat of its fruit, you will have so swear allegiance to it."

"This is a dangerous place," Bink remarked as the other two came out of the water.

"Now we can ask the ants," Sandy said. "They get around a lot." He peered down with his somewhat fuzzy eyes. "There are some, but we don't want to ask them."

"Why not?" Dolph asked impatiently. "You can translate what they say."

"It won't work," Sandy said.

But Dolph got down so he could spy the ants. "Hey, you!" he said to the nearest. "Have you seen a foreigner pass?"

The ant waved its antennae. "He says far pastures are always greenest," Sandy translated.

"But that's not relevant."

"Exactly. It's an irrelev ant."

Oh. So Dolph focused on the next ant. "Foreigner?" The ant waved its feelers.

"Native," Sandy translated.

"Native?"

"Foreigner," Sandy said. "That's an ant-onym. It always says the opposite of what it hears."

Dolph was getting impatient again. He spied a third ant. He opened his mouth.

"I wouldn't," Sandy warned.

Dolph paused. "Why not?"

"That's an ench ant. It will enchant you if you let it."

Another ant glowed brightly. "What about this one?" he asked.

"That's a brilli ant. It is very bright, but won't speak to those it deems dull, which is everyone else."

"Then what kind of ant will do?" Dolph asked, beginning to think about becoming annoyed.

"A reli ant. Maybe several reli ants. You can depend on them. But I don't see any of those here."

Dolph decided to give up on this approach. "I'm going to change form and look around myself," he said.

''Take us with you,'' Bink suggested.

So Dolph became a green roc, and they got on his feet.

''That's impressive magic,'' Sandy remarked.

''Squawk.''

''Thank you,'' Dor translated. ''And thank you for your help. We are going now.''

Sandy nodded and waved. As Dolph took off, he saw the sand man settling back into his comfortable sand trap. He had indeed been helpful, and had earned his extra size.

He also saw a stir of motion, as if something were nearby, perhaps following them. But he kept his beak shut, because probably it was just his imagination. In any event, they would soon leave it far behind.

Dolph rose high enough to get a good view of the surrounding landscape—and in a moment he saw a glow. He circled down. Sure enough, there was a trail of footprints. They led up to the edge of the green land and crossed over the sharp bend.

But when he tried to fly across that boundary, he suddenly went out of control. He found himself tilting at an awkward angle.

''Get back over the green!'' Dor cried.

Dolph, gyrating wildly, managed to cross back, more by chance than design. Then he straightened out and was flying level again. ''Squawk?'' he demanded.

''I'm not sure what happened,'' Dor said. ''Maybe we had better land, and I can ask something inanimate.''

So Dolph located a landing field similar to the first, complete with a lake and sand pit. The lake went right up to the boundary, where it made a sharp angled turn and became level blue water on the other side.

''I don't want to lose any more mass than I have to,'' Dor said. ''I'll see if I can make a deal, fair exchange.''

''What would sand want?'' Bink asked, bemused. ''Apart from more mass?''

Dolph changed back into manform. He saw that the sand was laid out in two colors, with bands of very light green on the edges, and a band of dark green in the center

Dor approached the sand. ''Hello,'' he said, not stepping in it.

''Hello,'' it responded. ''What do you want?''

"I need some information. Do you need anything?"

The sand heaved and humped and formed into a person-like figure. A female one, with a light clothing and dark body. She wore a conical hat and high-heeled shoes. "How about a man?" she asked, and cackled.

She was a sand witch!

"I know where a nice sandman is," Dor said. "His name is Sandy. I don't know whether he has romance in mind."

She cackled again. "He won't have a choice. Just tell me where."

"In exchange for some information we need," Dor said. "So nobody changes size."

"Done."

"He is by a small lake in that direction," Dor said, pointing carefully. "We flew the distance in an instant, but it might take an hour by foot."

"I'll find it. What do you want to know?"

"How to cross over to the blue side without losing our balancc."

"You want to orient for Blue?"

"Yes, I think that's what we want to do."

"The lings can help you," the sand witch said. "They can do change magic. They make the impossible possible. But it will cost you some size."

The three men exchanged glances. Then Dor nodded. "We'll have to pay it. Where can we find these lings?"

"I will summon them." She faced toward the edge, put two fingers to her mouth and made a sandy whistle. "Hey, Bluelings!"

In a moment there was a scurrying and chirping, and a swarm of squirrel-like creatures that ran on two legs. They lined up and peered over the edge.

"Make your deal," the witch said, and set off in the direction Dor had indicated. She had an interesting stride, with sand shifting forward to form a new leg while the trailing leg diminished.

"We want to turn blue and stand straight on the blue side," Dor said. "Can you do that for us?"

The lings seemed to understand. They chirruped excitedly.

"Deal," Dor said. He walked up to the edge and stepped over. As he did so, he turned blue and tilted at right angles to the new plane. He also grew another size smaller.

Bink crossed over, and changed similarly. This time Dolph saw that the lings nearest him became slightly larger.

Then Dolph crossed. As he did so, he felt that same imbalance. His body was almost horizontal to the blue landscape, and he couldn't seem to right it. Then he saw his hands turn blue before him, and he straightened out and became vertical. He also felt himself shrink a size. The lings had done it, for the usual payment.

But Dolph was curious, so he tried to step back to the green side. Now his body oriented almost horizontal again, making it impossible for him to walk. It was clear that a blue side person could not make it on the green side, and vice versa. So they probably didn't mix much. Such were the rules of the magic of Pyramid.

He crawled back to the blue side in time to see the lings running away. They had done their job and had their payment. It was a fair deal. This was a fair world, just awfully different.

He changed back into roc form, and the others sat on his feet. He ascended, this time having no difficulty, and circled to pick up the trail of footprints. He was careful not to try to cross the boundary between faces. This side was all in shades of blue, of course. Soon he spied the prints, and followed them.

They led past blue hill and dale, through blue forest and field, by blue mountain and lake, until they led to a blue isle with a bluestone ridge, up to a blue house.

The blue door opened, and Princess Ida came out to meet them. She looked to be forty, the same age as the one on Ptero. But the moon that circled her head was a different shape. This one looked like a little doughnut.

"You must also be visitors to this realm," she said.

"We are," Dor said. "I am King Dor, from Xanth. This is my father Bink, and my son Dolph."

"Are you sure they aren't both sons?"

Bink smiled. "I was recently youthened from age eighty one to twenty one."

"Oh, then perhaps you know Jonathan, who passed by here a few hours ago."

"Yes, we call him the Zombie Master," Dor said. "We are looking for him. We have been following his trail."

"I can help you find him. But there is a complication."

''Who cares?'' the blue pavement asked.

''That's my talent,'' Dor said quickly. ''To converse with the inanimate. Sometimes it speaks without being asked.''

''Oh. That's certainly interesting magic.'' She did not seem entirely thrilled.

''Dawn and Eve told us that the magic on each world is different. On this one the person who does a favor gains size.''

''Yes. I thought you should understand that, before you accepted any favor.''

''So let's exchange favors,'' Dolph said. ''What can we do for you?''

''What I want most is information about the other worlds. I now have freedom of this world, or at least the blue face, since the nice faun and mare abolished the evil Blue Wizard, but in the process I have learned that there is an enormous amount I don't know.''

''We can tell you all about Xanth,'' Dolph said.

''But we need to travel on, to catch up with the Zombie Master,'' Dor said.

''Perhaps if you can tell me how those delightful twin girls are doing.''

''They're both eighteen, and very pretty,'' Dolph said.

''Well, yes. I believe they will be that age as long as they remain in the place they are. Did they manage to solve the faun's problem?''

''Faun?'' Dolph asked, perplexed. She had mentioned a faun before.

''Last year Forrest Faun passed by here, with Mare Imbrium and the twin girls. I think they were taking rather a shine to him.''

Dolph looked at the others, who were similarly blank. ''I guess we don't know that faun. But we know that Mare Imbri became a tree nymph and is happy. And Dawn and Eve seem to have boyfriends now.''

Ida smiled. ''I think you have answered my question. Now I will tell you what I learned about Torus. On that world, the giving of favors does not change a person's size, but incurs a burden of emotion. The giver comes to like or even love the recipient. So you will want to be very careful.''

''That is a good caution,'' Dor said. ''We shall be careful, even if this is a dream.''

"I think you would not care to be bound into love with a dream figure you hardly knew."

"Agreed," Dor said. "Especially since we are all married."

"I understand that my analog on Torus lives on an island in a lake, much as I do."

"He probably went to her," Dolph said. "Because he's looking for a zombie world."

"Yes. I hope he finds it."

Then they linked hands and focused on Torus. Soon they were flying toward it, seeing its geography. It was weird, because its mountains and lakes and forests and fields wrapped all around it, even on the side facing inward. It seemed to Dolph that it must be really odd living there, and being able to look up beyond the sky and see the rest of that world.

Dor turned to Dolph. "Maybe we can simplify things, if you become a roc now, and fly across instead of landing."

"Great idea! Grab onto my feet." Dolph changed, and they clung to his feet. He leveled out as he approached the surface, peering down to search for the glowing footprints.

Soon he saw them, and followed them immediately to a lake, and an island. Just like that, they had found the place.

But he also saw another faint stirring, as if something watching them while trying to remain hidden. Yet how could anything be following them from world to world? Dolph pumped his wings and flew faster, to make sure to leave it well behind.

He landed before a nice little house with a pleasant garden. The others got off his feet, and he changed back to human form.

The footprints led up to the house.

Ida came out. Her moon was a little cone. "What, more visitors?" she inquired.

"We are looking for Jonathan, the Zombie Master," Dor said. "We are from his world, and need to talk to him. We believe he has gone on to Cone."

"He has," she agreed. "He promised to tell me about it, when he returns."

"May we have your permission to go there too?"

"Oh, I don't own Cone! I am merely its location. Why don't you just go there, without exchanging any favors with me?"

"That may be best," Dor agreed.

The linked hands again, and focused on Cone. In half a moment they were on their way, becoming small, falling toward it. They were getting better at this.

Dolph assumed the roc bird form, and carried the others on his feet while he searched for the trail. Soon enough he spied it.

But he couldn't follow it from the air, because it disappeared beneath a dense forest. So he came down for a landing at the edge of that forest. Soon the three of them were afoot again.

The trees were huge. They stared up, awed. The trunks gnarled upward, intersecting each other, sometimes spiraling around each other, forming dense knots of wood halfway between the ground and the distant crowns. And on these knots were houses. It seemed that the natives were tree dwellers.

A creature spied them and flew down. It looked like a dragon, but it had feathery wings like those of a harpy, and the head of a goblin. It landed nearby and stared at them. "Who the ΔΔΔΔ are you?" it demanded.

Dolph bristled. He assumed the form of a sphinx, because it was larger than the challenger and could also speak with a human voice. "Who wants to know?"

This evidently impressed the creature, for its tone moderated. "I am Drarplin, a dragon-harpy-goblin crossbreed."

"You must be very unusual."

"No, I'm ordinary. We are all crossbreeds here. So pay up."

"Pay what?"

"The thumb tax, of course. One blurse for each thumb."

"Blurse?"

"Don't you know anything? A blessing-curse. Blurse. Something useful that still sticks you with its point. If you want to enter this forest, all of you must pay."

Dolph looked at Dor and Bink. "We have six thumbs between us. How many blurses do we have?"

"Burn his wings off so he can grow clean new ones," a rock said.

"That's one," Drarplin agreed.

"It is? I mean, for sure." Dolph knew that his strength was in form changing, not brains, but he was finally catching on. Blessings and curses combined. Wishes that did good and ill together.

"That's an interesting unit of currency," Dor remarked.

"Who asked you, royal blockhead?" another rock asked.

"That's another," Drarplin agreed. "Royalty and stupidity combined."

This was getting easier, thanks to Dor's talent. "Go stifle in a bed of sweet roses," Dolph said. "Go soak your head until it swells into real beauty. Find a really pretty girl who hates you. And collect so many thumb taxes that you can't sit down for a week."

"Three, four, five, six," Drarplin said, counting on his toes. "Very well, you may enter Evil Prime Forest." He spread his wings and flew away.

They followed the prints into the forest. The forest Evil Prime closed over and around them. It got so thick that they couldn't see the way through, despite the footprints.

"We can't pass," Dor complained, wedging ahead.

"Can," a voice came.

"Can't can't," a half buried stone retorted.

A long vine dangled down before them. It sprouted many legs instead of leaves, and the legs began to dance. "Can can," it sang. And the way opened up somewhat.

"A chorus vine," Bink said, recognizing the species. "Thank you, vine; you have nice legs."

The vine turned from green to red. It appreciated being appreciated.

But soon the way became impassable. The glowing footprints disappeared; they had lost the way.

Dolph looked up. "There seems to be space higher up," he said. "Maybe I can fly us through."

"There's no room for a roc bird here," Dor pointed out.

Dolph considered. "Maybe there is room for a small one. I'll become a midget roc." He did so, and there did seem to be just enough room for his wings if he chose his route carefully. He was still a pretty big bird.

The others got on his feet, and he flew up. They seemed much heavier, but he realized that was because he was so much smaller. It was all he could do to stay airborne.

He made it through the labyrinth of the levels of the forest, and out the other side. And almost stalled out.

The world had ended.

Then he realized that it was merely the rim of Cone. The forest filled in right up to it, and halted at the end, where the world turned inside.

And inside was filled with a vast sea. It stretched all the way across the interior of Cone, filling it. The water took off at right angles to the rim, and as he flew over it, this became the level surface. There was no problem of orientation of the kind they had encountered on Pyramid; when they turned the rim of Cone, gravity turned too.

He rounded the corner and flew low over the water. All around the great circular rim he saw a flurry of activity. Apparently visiting the shore was great sport for the inhabitants.

Sport? Suddenly he realized that the activity consisted of couples summoning storks. Right in the open, splashing in the fringe of the water, in sight of all the other couples. There were children watching too. Apparently the process wasn't secret, on this world. Could there be a special license right by the shore?

He flew back the way he had come, peering closely. He could see the footprints emerging from the forest—who knew what route the Zombie Master had taken!—and going into the water. So flying over this tilted sea was pointless; they needed to get below the surface. Could they do that? How would they breathe?

He glided down and made a landing on the water. He gave the others time to get free, then changed into a sea serpent. He held out his flippers so as to support them, so the three of them could consult.

"Those prints go down the inside wall of the cone," Dor said. "That's where we'll have to go.

"Hisss," Dolph said.

"How will we breathe?" the surface of the water translated helpfully. Of course Dolph himself could breathe, because he had gills, but the others couldn't change form.

Dor considered. "Since this is a dream, we may be able to breathe under water. Evidently the Zombie Master did. Let's try it."

The two men put their faces in the water and breathed. Sure enough, they had no trouble. It would have been a different story, had they been real, but dreams had special privileges.

Dolph put his head under. Dor faced him. "You might as well carry us down, however; it will be faster than walking. We don't know how far the Zombie Master went."

So they clung to his fins while Dolph carefully dived below. He found the flowing prints, and followed them. He saw that there were creatures living along the cone wall, and they had houses and gardens and paths. For them, that was level ground, though it was actually at right angles to the upper surface of the sea and opposite to the outside surface they had first landed on. So Cone had its own rules of orientation, different from those of the other worlds.

The prints seemed to be heading down toward the very conic inside tip of Cone. Dolph increased his speed, making the trail a blur. In that manner he passed hills and vales and mountains, all populated by assorted creatures. This seemed to be a world of crossbreeds, so that the dragon-harpy-goblin was indeed typical. There was no counting the number of combinations there seemed to be; apparently any creature joined with any other, and the stork delivered constantly changing combinations.

That made him pause. Did Cone even have storks? It might have some other means of delivering babies. Maybe it had a different Adult Conspiracy to conceal the details. That was an interesting notion. He remembered when he had married Electra, and neither of them had known the secret of stork signaling. What a night they had had! By the time they figured it out, he had realized that he loved Electra, and no longer wanted to marry lovely Nada Naga. He had been satisfied ever since; Electra had turned out to be the perfect wife for him.

At last they neared the inner tip of Cone. And there where the conic surface of this world came together in a point, was a house. The prints led up to it.

They stopped outside it, and Dolph resumed manform. They were right: he had no trouble breathing without his gills.

The door opened, and Ida emerged. She looked forty; apparently their ages were fixed by that of the Ida on Ptero, whose age changed with her geography. Dor suspected that would be disquieting, not to have control of one's age.

But there was something wrong with her. After a moment Dolph figured it out: her body was human, but she had the head of a horse. She was a crossbreed, like all the natives of this world. But it had to be her, because there was a moon orbiting her head.

Dor stepped forward. "We are visitors from Xanth, several levels down. We are looking for the Zombie Master."

"Why yes, he did pass this way, two hours ago," she said. "He went on to Dumbbell." Her equine mouth seemed to have no trouble speaking. She had delicate gills in her neck.

"To stupid?" Dor asked somewhat blankly.

"My moon," she explained, angling her head to show it. It was a tiny object in the shape of a dumbbell.

"Would it be all right with you if we just went right on there? We need to talk to him and return to our own world."

"We are actually dreaming this," Bink explained.

"Of course. I can see that you are not crossbreeds, and that you breathe without gills. Straight species are very rare on Cone." She paused. "But I wonder whether I might ask a favor of you, before you go on."

"Oh, is this a world where favors carry burdens?" Dolph asked, intrigued.

"No, not at all. It's just that recently a misfit begged my help, and I thought it possible that you might be able to assist."

"What is it?" Dolph asked. He knew they needed to keep moving, but he was curious.

"On this world, folk live either on the outside, or the inside," Ida said. "This is the inside, under the water. Our magic is so construed that only couples that straddle the two environments can summon the storkfish."

Dolph nodded. That explained all that activity at the edge of the water. Land folk making trysts with sea folk.

"In each case, babies are delivered to the couples. If the baby has lungs, it goes with the land parent. If it has gills, it goes with the sea parent. But on rare occasion there is an error. That is the cause of my concern."

"But suppose the parents aren't together when the baby arrives?"

Ida looked blank. "Not together?"

"In nine months, they could lose track and be far apart."

"Nine months?"

"The time it takes the stork to deliver."

Ida shook her head. "There must be considerable bureaucratic delay in your realm. Here delivery is within two days, or there's an investigation. The couples remain together until the storkfish arrive with the bundles."

This world was more different than it looked! ''So one was mis-delivered?''

''No. One was—defective.''

''Defective?''

''Unsuitable for life on Cone.''

''But what kind of crossbreed wouldn't fit on a world like this?''

''Let me introduce you to Aurora.'' Ida turned her head. ''Dear, would you please come out?''

The door opened again, and a very shy girl swam out. Her eyes were downcast as if she was ashamed. It was hard to see why, as she was in her upper section a beautiful figure of a human female, and had a nice tail. She was a mermaid. She had red hair, brown eyes, and white wings.

Wings?

As usual, Dolph blurted out his question before he thought better. ''How do you fly in water?''

Aurora blushed. ''Not very well,'' she confessed.

Embarrassed, Dolph tried to make amends by assuming the form of a male of her persuasion. He became a winged merman with gills. He spread his wings, and found that they dragged heavily in the water. ''I see.''

''How did you do that?'' Aurora asked, amazed.

''It's my talent,'' Dolph said, balancing awkwardly on his tail. ''I can assume any living form I want.''

''Then why don't you assume the form of a handsome man?''

Then it was Dolph's turn to blush. He hadn't realized that he was unhandsome. Electra had never told him. ''I guess I didn't think of it.''

''Oh, I didn't mean—I mean—I'm sorry. I'm not socially clever. I haven't had much experience.''

''I know the feeling,'' Dolph said, smiling ruefully.

She smiled back, as ruefully. ''Yes.''

''How do you think we might help?'' Dor asked Ida.

''I gathered from Jonathan that your home world is oddly mixed,'' Ida said. ''That you have just one surface, on which land and water coexist.''

''True. But—''

''In such a realm, a winged mermaid might be able to flourish. She might live in a lake, and fly to other lakes, holding her breath.''

"She might even be able to breathe in the air," Dolph said. "By flying through thick clouds. They always have water hidden away."

"That sounds wonderful," Aurora said.

"It does seem feasible," Dor agreed. "But this is a dream. How could a dream native travel from here to our world?"

"I have pondered that," Ida said. "Between the time when I learned of your world from Jonathan, and your arrival. She can't travel there physically, but if there were some native creature who was willing to accept her spirit, it might work."

"I saw a winged mermaid once," Dolph said. "At Chex's wedding on Mount Rushmost. But she has lungs."

"Still, she might show me around," Aurora said. "If I could get there."

"I really don't think—" Dor began.

"What is needed is a creature who is unsatisfied with its form and mind," Ida said. "Who would be happy to let Aurora define those. And perhaps there is such a one."

"Even if there were," Dor said, "it would be back on Xanth, while Aurora is here. I don't see how they could get together."

"I'm thinking of the one who has been following you, by some wild coincidence."

The three kings hurled a glance around. "Something *has* been following us?" Dor asked.

"Yes. One of my friends told me that three foreign men were coming, followed by something else. We're not sure what that is, but it seems to be very unhappy."

"A monster?" Dolph asked, glancing back nervously.

"I don't know. But perhaps we can find out. Here it comes now."

The three of them looked back together. There was a stirring in the water, and a vague shape appeared.

"The blob!" Dolph exclaimed. "The one that was moaning in Castle Zombie."

"I told Millie to give it some sleep potion," Bink said. "That must have enabled it to join our dream."

"So it followed us, hoping for help," Dolph concluded. He had somehow suspected that Grandfather Bink would be involved, when Ida spoke of wild coincidence.

"Do you think it would like to become a winged mermaid?" Ida asked.

''Maybe I can ask it,'' Dor said. He assumed the form of a blob. Now he didn't have a mouth, so wasn't sure how to speak. He rolled across and touched the other blob with his surface. ''**?**'' he inquired.

''**!**'' the blob replied.

He returned to his normal form, unhandsome as that was. ''I think it says yes.''

''But still, we are in a dream, while the blob is in Castle Zombie,'' Dor said. ''I don't see how—''

''If you will return to your bodies when you wake,'' Ida said reasonably, ''wouldn't the blob do the same when it wakes? And if Aurora is with it, wouldn't she be carried there too? Then she could give it live definition in her nature.''

The three men exchanged another wondering glance. They shrugged.

Aurora approached the blob. She reached out one hand, tentatively. She touched it. ''Oh, I like it,'' she said. ''It's just miserable because when the storkfish—I mean the stork—delivered it, it had not been shaped into a creature. It was left as it started, raw material. So its mother dumped it in the forest, throwing it away, where the zombies found it.''

''You can tell all that, just from touching it?'' Dolph asked.

''Yes. Because our sprits are merging. It will be glad to have my template. And I will be glad to go to its world. I think I can manage to form lungs as well as gills, in that context.'' As she spoke, her hand was sinking into the blob.

''Then when you get there, tell Millie the Ghost what happened,'' Dolph said. ''She's not really a ghost, she's the Zombie Master's wife. She's nice. She'll help you find suitable water.''

''Thank you.'' Aurora's arm had disappeared to the elbow. Now she stepped the rest of the way in, and disappeared into the blob.

Ida walked over and clapped her hands over the blob. ''Wake!'' she said sharply.

The blob quivered as if surprised. Then it faded. But as it did, it assumed the form of the winged mermaid.

Ida looked at them. ''Thank you so much. I'm sure Aurora will be much happier in your world. Now please do go on to Dumbbell.''

They linked hands and focused on that little world. Soon it expanded, until it was a massive planet with two centers, connected by a bar. Dolph became a full-sized roc bird and sailed down, looking for the glowing footprints.

"I presume the inhabitants of this world are not very smart," Dor remarked.

"Zombies aren't smart either," Bink said. "Maybe this is the one."

Dolph flew down to one of the swollen ends of the world and circled it, descending ever closer, peering down. As with the other moons, there were varied features of the terrain, and signs of habitation. As before, he soon got used to the notion that this was a full-sized world with its own identity. It was mind-bogglingly tiny in one sense, but full-sized in another.

He spied a glow. He circled down, and sure enough, there were the prints. They started at the middle of the bulge, and went toward the connecting rod. He followed.

It was weird flying low overland as the rod came into view over the horizon. Now it looked like an impossibly massive and tall tower rising from the plain, with a ball balanced on its end. But as he followed the prints to its base, his orientation changed, and he was able to turn the corner in flight and follow them along the rod, which now seemed level rather than vertical. Only on Planet Pyramid, it seemed, was personal orientation fixed by its plane of origin; on the others the change was automatic. This was easier.

The tracks led to a neat house in the center of the bar. Dolph glided to a landing in a nearby field, and changed back to human form. "Good job, son," Dor said. "We are making better progress.

They approached the house. There was Ida, exercising in her garden. She was human rather than crossbreed, but was remarkable in another way: she was massively muscular. In fact she was lifting solid hand weights that were shaped exactly like the planet itself.

"Hello," Dor called.

She turned. "Oh, you would be the next group," she said.

"Yes. We are looking for the Zombie Master."

"You missed him by an hour. He went on to Pincushion." She angled her head, bringing her moon into view. Sure enough, it looked just like a pincushion.

"Why are you exercising?" Dolph asked.

"Oh that's right, you are from another world. I don't know how magic works there, but here it is directly related to physical strength. So we all are concerned about our development." She heaved the weights over her head, showing massive arm muscles.

The men exchanged yet another glance. They had thought the inhabitants would be stupid. Instead they were fitness freaks. Ida looked as if she could pick any of them up with one hand.

"If it's all right with you," Dor said cautiously, "could we—?"

"Oh, by all means, go ahead," Ida agreed.

They focused on the pincushion. It expanded, or they shrank, and soon they were flying toward it. This world was perhaps the oddest one yet, because it seemed to be a soft central blob from which hundreds of enormously long, thin pins projected.

Somewhere in here was the Zombie Master's trail. But where? The pins were like a forest, with many of them hidden by the ones in front, from any perspective.

"Maybe he landed on the cushion, and we can pick up his trail there," Bink suggested.

So Dolph found a halfway clear place and flew down to the base. The pins crowded in so thickly there that he had to fold his wings and drop the last part of it. But the surface was a soft cushion, so they weren't hurt.

They made their way through the forest. From here each pin was much larger in diameter than it had seemed from afar, as thick as a thin mountain. When they brushed too close to any, its orientation took over, causing them to rotate so as to stand on its surface. There were no people here; either they lived under the cushion, or up along the pins.

Then they found the prints, and followed them to a pin. They boarded that pin, and walked along its endless length. Now the pin seemed level, and the others near it seemed level too, pacing it like disconnected horizons to the sides and above.

"We need to find a faster way to travel," Dor said.

"I can't fly, because my roc wings would bang into the neighboring pins," Dolph said. Actually that was a slight exaggeration; the other pins weren't *that* close. But the area seemed so constricted it made him nervous; he preferred plenty of room as a roc.

"We didn't bring any travel spells along," Bink said.

"I'll ask around," Dor said. He faced down. "Hey, pin: what's the best and fastest way to travel along you?"

"Password?" the pin asked.

"What do you mean, password?"

"I am a protected PIN. I give access only via the right password."

Dor paused. Then he said, "Very well. PASSWORD."

"Thank you. The best and fastest way to travel along me is to get the flew."

Dolph realized again that the inanimate wasn't very smart. When it heard the word "password" it assumed that this must be the correct one.

"Tell me about the flew," Dor said.

"When you catch it, it makes you sneeze and fly for two minutes."

"Where can we find it?"

"Just stand in the breeze and suck in whatever's there, and soon a flew bug will fly by. Make sure you are facing backward."

So the three of them faced back toward the base of the pin, and breathed deeply. Soon Dolph saw a little bug flying along, so he sucked it in. Immediately he sneezed so violently that he shot backward along the pin. Before he slowed, he sneezed again, and again. By the time the paroxysm abated, he was far along, out of sight of the others. He gasped for breath and wiped his tearing eyes; that had been fast travel, but not the most comfortable.

He heard a distant explosion. It repeated several times. Then Dor came sailing backward along the pin, coming to rest just beyond Dolph. He too was gasping and tearing, but otherwise all right.

Finally Bink came along, propelled by similar jets of air.

None of them really liked this mode of travel, but it was effective. So after they had recovered their breaths, they intercepted more flew bugs and did another hitch of sneeze travel. Several bouts of this brought them to the end of the pin.

This was expanded and rounded, and on its knob was a nice little house. There was a tall, thin Ida. "Yes, I know," she said. "He passed this way half an hour ago. Just go on to Spiral."

They linked hands and oriented on the spiral-shaped moon spiraling around her head. It expanded until it became a scintillating pattern of sparkling lights. These spiraled inward toward a bulging center that glowed more brightly. There were also streamers of dust that obscured parts of the whole, but it was nevertheless lovely. They centered on one of the outer ends of a band, and searched for the glowing prints. When they weren't evident, Dolph flew to the next spiral, and there he spied them.

He flew on along the band, not caring to cut straight into the center lest he lose the trail; it was not obvious, because of the competing brightness of the spirals. Soon he came to the bulging center, and there was Ida's house. She seemed to be a central figure of whatever world she existed in. That seemed to make sense, as each world depended on her, in its fashion.

He landed by her house. She emerged immediately. "Why yes, your friend passed by here just fifteen minutes ago. Go on and find him on Tangle."

They oriented on her moon, which did indeed look like a tangled blob of string or spaghetti. It did not clarify as they swooped down on it; it seemed impossible to figure out all the intricacies of its convolutions. The prints could be hidden anywhere in this mass.

Dolph flew around and around the thing, but couldn't locate the prints. They could be in the inside of it, following a string that passed through the center.

"Let's try the center first," Dor suggested. "That's where Ida is likely to be, so is where he'll be going, as this obviously isn't a zombie world."

Dolph flew in to the center, where the worst tangle was. Sure enough, there was a nice little house, and the footprints led up to it.

He landed, and they approached. This Ida looked heavyset, as if she had eaten too much pasta. "You missed your friend by five minutes," she said. "Go on after him on Motes."

Her moon was a small cloud of dust. They oriented on it, and soon were approaching what turned out to be a cluster of little stones. Of medium stones. Of larger stones. Of great rocks. Of planetoids. In fact, the swarm was made of hundreds of rocky bits, each large enough to support a village.

How could they find footprints, when there was no land between rocks?

"Go to the center," Dor recommended. "Maybe we can catch him before he reaches Ida."

Dolph flew toward the center of the swarm. But before he reached it, he saw a glowing footprint. He veered toward it, but soon found that the trail abruptly ended.

"He must have jumped," Dor said.

Dolph saw that the last prints were opposite another planetoid, so he flew across to that one. Sure enough, the prints resumed. He followed them around the rock—and there, suddenly, was the Zombie Master. He was about to jump toward another rock.

"Wait!" Dor cried. "We need to talk to you!"

Surprised, the Zombie Master waited. Dolph landed nearby, discovering that his weight was very small here, and changed form. Then the three of them approached Jonathan. He looked extremely old, but that was because he was. Dolph suspected that the Good Magician gave him doses of youth elixir to prevent him from becoming too old. He was almost nine hundred years old chronologically, and somewhere around one hundred physically, because he had spent eight hundred years as a zombie.

"Hello Dor and Dolph," he said. "And—?"

"Bink," Bink filled in. "Chameleon and I were just youthened."

"How have you come to enter my dream?"

"We needed to talk with you, so Millie let us sniff the sleep potion," Dor said. "The zombies are all stirred up in Xanth, and we need to know why, so we can get them settled before the big wedding. Wedding guests don't much like zombies."

"Wedding? Who is getting married?"

"We don't know, but Jenny Elf is writing a huge pile of invitations, and many of us have important roles in it."

"That's interesting. Unfortunately I don't know why the zombies are stirred up. It is not by any design of mine. I had noticed the effect, and made inquiries, but had not received news by the time I started this excursion to locate a zombie world. When I do find the world, there should be no further problem."

"But how can the zombies reach it?" Dolph asked. "They can't go physically, can they?"

"They won't have to. They can dream their way to it, once I find the way."

"Zombies dream?"

"Of course. And they sleep quietly in their graves while dreaming. Unlike living folk, they can remain asleep indefinitely without deteriorating more than usual."

"That does seem like a good solution to the problem," Bink said. "Do you think you will find a zombie world soon?"

''I certainly hope to. There seems to be an endless chain of worlds, and since they embrace all the realms of maybe, one is bound to be suitable. I mean to locate it, mark it, and establish a direct route to it. Then most of the zombies can get to it within a couple of days.''

Dor nodded. ''That's not the information we were seeking, but it seems just as good. So we can go home and report that probably the problem will abate before the wedding.''

''That seems likely,'' the Zombie Master agreed.

''Then we had better let you be on your way, and we will return to Xanth and make our report.''

''Tell Millie I am making progress,'' the Zombie Master said.

Dor nodded. Then the three of them linked hands, and focused on waking up.

7
Road to the Isles

They came to a slightly larger chamber where a woman worked. She was tall, shapely, and veiled. She spied Breanna and Wira, and spun about to face them. ''So you dare enter my lair, my foul feathered fiend!'' she declaimed. ''This time you shall not escape my love!'' Her hair rose up on its own, and turned out to be composed of little snakes that hissed in time to the speech.

Breanna halted, taken aback. What had she done this time?

But Wira was unperturbed. ''Mother Gorgon, this is Breanna of the Black Wave, and Justin Tree.'' She turned to face Breanna. ''And this is the Gorgon, the Good Magician's Designated Wife for this month. She's an actress in the dream realm.''

''Rehearsing a role,'' the Gorgon agreed. ''In a really bad dream.''

Oh. ''But what's bad about love?'' Breanna asked.

''The sight of the Gorgon's face turns living folk to stone,'' Justin murmured.

''Love is wonderful,'' the Gorgon said. ''But in this case, I shall bare my face and kiss the miscreant. So will my snakes. He will wake screaming.''

''I hope he deserves it,'' Breanna said, slightly shaken.

''Oh, he does, he does,'' the Gorgon said with satisfaction.

''Mother Gorgon, Breanna needs protection,'' Wira said.

''Don't be silly, child; no one will hurt her here.''

Wira was clearly no child, but it was also clear that the Gorgon liked her. ''She must travel with Ralph.''

"Ralph!" the Gorgon exclaimed indignantly. "He's the one this dream is for! He is nasty, rude, scheming, selfish, stubborn, cruel, hateful, dirty, and generally reprehensible. Why would anyone travel with him?"

"Because he knows the way to the Isle of Women."

"Oh, that." The Gorgon sighed. "Then she had better have the protection racket." She reached into her ample bosom and pulled out a tiny toy tennis racket. "Keep this on you at all times, child, especially when you sleep," she said, offering it to Breanna. "It will protect you from all physical harm."

"Thank you," Breanna said, accepting it. She looked for a pocket, but her slip had none. She also realized, belatedly, that when she lost her clothing she had also lost her knife. That made her feel naked in another way.

"If you are going to travel, you had better dress the part," the Gorgon said. She studied Breanna from under her veil. "You are full fleshed, but I think one of Wira's dresses would fit you well enough."

"I will fetch one," Wira said immediately. She hurried out.

"Meanwhile you are surely hungry," the Gorgon continued. "I have some Gorgon-zola cheese." She lifted a plate from the table.

"Thank you," Breanna said, taking a chunk. She bit into it, and found it very good.

"I am serious about wearing that racket," the Gorgon said. "Ralph is the kind of jerk who doesn't pay much attention to the Adult Conspiracy."

"Don't protest," Justin advised. *"Ask her what she means."*

It seemed apt. "What do you mean, Gorgon?"

"You look to be about fifteen, so I can't be too specific. But some ilk aren't much concerned if a girl is underage. He might try to summon the stork with you."

That was specific enough. "I wouldn't like that," Breanna agreed. "But you say this little racket will protect me?"

"It will, dear. But only if it is on your body. Make sure not to lose it."

Good advice! "I will make sure," Breanna agreed.

Wira returned with a nice blue dress. Breanna put it on over her head, and it did fit well enough, though it bound here and there. It had zipper pockets, so she put the little racket into one.

"You may be in doubt about the protection," the Gorgon said. "Perhaps you should test it."

She was indeed in doubt. "Test it?"

"Try to hurt yourself."

So Breanna tried to bend one of her own fingers backward. It wouldn't bend. She tried punching the wall, not hard. It didn't hurt. She punched harder. Still no effect. So she put all her force into it. Her fist made a hole in the wall, but she felt no pain, and her hand was uninjured. "This is neat," she said appreciatively.

"If you have to," Wira said, "you can strike someone else. But you probably won't have to, because he will not be able to strike you. Not with any effect."

"Thank you," Breanna repeated. Now she truly appreciated the protection racket.

"However, you could be abused slowly, so do not depend on it overmuch," the Gorgon said. "It is an emergency measure."

"Abused slowly?" There was no answer.

"I think she means seduction," Justin said.

"Oh." Now she understood, and realized why the Gorgon would not say more. She did not know that Breanna was already party to aspects of the Adult Conspiracy.

"But you must be tired," the Gorgon said. "I understand you traveled all night."

"Well, that's what I do. My talent is to see in the dark, so I normally sleep by day."

"You may use my room," Wira said. "I don't need it by day."

Breanna was indeed tired. "Thank you," she said once more, as Wira led her to another chamber.

She lay down on Wira's nice bed and disappeared into sleep.

In the late afternoon Justin's voice woke her. *"You may want to clean up for dinner,"* he suggested diplomatically.

Not only that, she was fit to burst. She headed for the bathroom. Then she paused. "Do you have to be with me all the time?"

"I believe I can return my consciousness to my tree-self for a while, if you wish."

"Without Mare Imbri's help? And if you get there, could you return here?"

"I am not certain," he said uncertainly.

She reconsidered. "Don't risk it, Justin. If you don't know how girls do it by now, it's time you learned. Stick around." She resumed her trip to the bathroom. It wasn't as if he were physically present, after all.

Thereafter, she found a basin and pitcher with water, and a sponge, so she stripped and washed up. It was good to get clean, after her wearing night and morning.

"You still here?" she inquired as she found a towel and dried off.

"Yes," Justin said. *"But if you prefer me to depart—"*

"No, it's too risky, and by now you've seen it all." She was struck by another thought. "Did you have a girlfriend, when you were in manform?"

"I regret I did not. I was not—handsome."

"Handsome is as handsome does," she said, repeating an ancient outworn adage.

"I did not accomplish much, either. That's one reason I found I was satisfied to be a tree."

"I think that's sort of sad, no offense. You should have had some decent human experience, before you lost your chance." She found a mirror on the wall, and checked herself in it.

"It might have been nice, had a girl like you been interested," he said. *"As it was, I did not have much to regret leaving."*

She held her pose a moment longer, knowing that he could see her clearly in the mirror, because he saw through her eyes. "You would really have liked a girl like me?"

"Oh, indeed, were she but of age."

"I *am* of age, by my definition," she said hotly.

"I apologize. I forgot. Yes, I would have liked a girl like you very much."

She had been thinking of color and form rather than age, but concluded that he had answered those too. She was pleased. She wrapped the towel around herself and returned to the bedroom.

Another dress had been laid out for her, together with appropriate underclothing. The Good Magician's folk were good hosts. She got dressed, and found that this outfit fit her perfectly. Someone must have judged her measurements by the fit of the slip and other dress, and made alterations.

She touched up her hair, then went to the door. Wira was there. "If you care to join us for dinner, you are welcome."

"I'm famished." The cheese had been good, but hardly enough to sustain her.

There were the Good Magician, the Gorgon, Wira, and a nondescript man who turned out to be Hugo, the son of Humfrey and the Gorgon. His talent was summoning fruit, but it didn't work well, so that much of the fruit was spoiled. So their fruit was from elsewhere, fortunately.

Dinner was formal, with elegant plates, goblets, and dishes. Breanna suddenly realized that she wasn't up to this. She had never been at a formal dinner before. She didn't know the etiquette. She was sure to mess up.

"How do I get out of this?" she asked Justin desperately. "I'm hungry as all get out, but I'm a dunce at this sort of thing."

"As it happens, I am familiar with the protocol," Justin said. *"It was one of those useless things I learned. If you care for guidance—"*

"Yes!" There was a great answer.

And so he guided her through it, telling her which piece of tableware to use when and how, and to sip rather than gulp, and tear bread in half before buttering, and all the rest, and she behaved perfectly. She discovered a certain grace in the procedure, and by the end of the meal she was actually enjoying it. The food was very good too.

They had recovered her knapsack, and stocked it with extra food. Breanna was not used to such kindness, and didn't know what to say. But Justin stepped in with advice, and she was able to thank them all graciously.

At dusk Ralph arrived. He was a slovenly-looking man in rumpled clothing and a sneer. "So where's this nymph I have to guide?" he demanded.

Breanna opened her mouth, but Justin intercepted her retort before it got out. *"Don't get into a war of words with this dragon dung,"* he advised. *"You will only be dragged down to his level."*

So she stifled it, and merely said "Here I am."

He looked at her contemptuously. "A black brat."

Already she was getting to dislike him. But all she said was "Let's go."

They left the castle together. Breanna touched the pocket to feel the outline of the racket, making double sure it was there.

"So what's this nonsense about traveling in the night?" Ralph demanded with a sneer in his tone. "Afraid to be seen by day?"

She opened her mouth, but again Justin got to it first. *"Don't let him engage you in argument. He's just trying to make you react, so you will be in his power."*

He was right. "Trust a man to know the ways of a man," she said silently to Justin, but with a mental picture of a smile so he would know it wasn't serious.

"You are young, but you are pretty," he said seriously. *"They were wise to give you the racket. This is not the kind of adventure we want to experience."*

"For sure."

"You too stupid to answer?" Ralph demanded.

"I just happen to prefer night for traveling," she said aloud.

"So you can disappear in the darkness?"

He was trying to needle her about her dark skin. "Yes."

"You must be good at that."

"Yes." If she had had a cherry bomb, she would have stuffed it into his smirk.

They walked on for a while. Ralph had a magic lantern so he could see his way. Breanna of course did not need it, but she did not see fit to inform the man of that.

Unfortunately, he soon thought of it for himself. "So what's your talent?"

Now she had to tell him, or balk. That would get them into another verbal tussle. "How can I avoid telling him?" she asked Justin.

"It is best not to lie, because that puts you on his level. But if you refuse to tell him, he will simply keep badgering you until you do tell. Perhaps challenge is best: ask him his own talent."

"What's yours?" she asked Ralph.

"If I show you mine, will you show me yours?"

There was something about that phrasing she didn't much like, but it seemed a fair deal. It wasn't as if she were protecting life and death information. "Okay."

"Well, I can't."

"Huh?" she asked, and immediately wished Justin had intercepted that crude utterance.

"That's why I came to the Good Magician. To get my talent."

"But your talent's always with you," she protested.

"Not in this case. Do you want the whole story?"

"He's up to something," Justin warned. *"I can tell by the sneakiness in his manner. I think he wants to learn more about you, so he's telling you more about him. So as to get the two of you informationally closer. But he really doesn't care about your character."*

"I'm sure," she agreed sourly. "But he's got me curious. What's the harm in it?"

"There more he learns of you, the better he will be able to exploit your weaknesses, so as to have his way with you."

"Way? What way?"

"Stork summoning, for one thing."

"In his foul dreams!"

"To be sure."

"But if the racket protects me from harm—" She paused, suddenly alarmed, remembering the Gorgon's veiled warning. "That *is* considered harm?"

"Unwilling stork summoning? To be sure. Especially considering your age, no offense."

"Okay, so I should be safe if I resist it, and I will. I'm going to go for the information."

"As you wish. I admit to being curious myself."

"You seem to be a young woman of many dark silences," Ralph remarked.

There were some verbal digs again. Dark silences for a Black Wave girl. "I have a small brain. It takes time to process big questions."

He laughed, not nicely. "Few things are more appealing than a stupid girl. So have you decided, or do you need another hour?"

She wanted to let him have a dragonfire blast of invective, but stifled it with Justin's help. "Tell me your story."

"When I was young, I seemed to lack a magic talent. At first folk thought I was magically obnoxious, but various tests demonstrated that my personality was entirely natural. So obviously it was the others who did not appreciate my charm and intelligence. Maybe they resented my delightful nature."

"What a load of sphinx manure!"

"That must have been it," Breanna agreed aloud.

"In due course I tired of trying to discover my talent on my own," Ralph continued. "So I went to see Magician of Information. The challenges were horrific, but I demolished them by detonating cherries and pineapples, and managed to get inside. The stupid sluts of the household wouldn't speak to me, so I forged on up to the gnarled old gnome's cell and demanded my Answer."

"What cheek!"

"That must really have impressed him."

"Humfrey looked up with his fried-egg orbs and grumped, 'I know why you're here, and I'm not going to help, so you might as well go away now.'

"I was of course furious, with considerable justice. 'I can think of only two reasons why you won't help me,' I informed him forthrightly. 'You are either jealous of my talent, or incapable of discovering it. Both choices show that you are nothing but a pretender and a fool.' "

"The effrontery of this idiot is phenomenal!"

"You sure told him," Breanna agreed aloud. She discovered that she was after all enjoying this exchange. It was nice seeing Justin get worked up.

"But the over-the-hill Magician responded with faked patience. 'I know all about your talent, young man. It is currently residing safely in Mundania with a little boy named Lija. I suggest that you count your dubious blessings and go home.' "

"Beware, Breanna; he is walking too close to you."

"I noticed," she replied mentally. "I want to see if this racket works."

" 'What are you talking about, old man?' I demanded righteously. 'How can some horrid little brat in Mundania have my talent? No one in Mundania has any magic, as you would know if you weren't in your dotage. That's why we call it Mundania. Even the ogres know that.' "

"If I had a mouth, I would vomit."

Breanna kept silent. She had a mouth, but it was only a giggle she had to stifle. Ralph's self-described arrogance was a thing almost of beauty.

"Obviously he couldn't refute me, so he changed the subject. 'Not all magic is good magic,' he uttered.

" 'What are you talking about, imbecile?' I demanded reasonably."

"He is putting his arm around you."

"I know. He stinks. But I want to be quite sure I'm protected, in case he ever catches me off-guard."

" 'Some magic that is too dangerous or unpleasant for Xanth is sent to Mundania, where it can be safely disposed of,' he said. 'It is the best way to handle toxic waste. Somehow your particular talent was strong enough to survive in Mundania despite the extreme thinness of magic there. It took up residence with a small boy.'

" 'So my talent is strong enough to survive in Mundania!' I gloated. 'It must be Magician caliber! No wonder you're jealous, you decrepit has-been. I knew I was destined for greatness. I don't want some fool Mundane getting the benefit of my talent. How do I get it back?' "

"He is trying to squeeze your pert posterior."

"I can't feel a thing."

" 'You are not listening,' Humfrey said, seeming suddenly weary. 'Somehow I am not surprised. But trust me: you do not want your talent back. My best advice is to leave well enough alone.'

" 'Sure you would say that, you feeble freak. But I'm not going to let you get away with it. *Tell me how to get what's coming to me!*' "

"Now he is trying to squeeze the left portion of your bosom." There was a more specific word for the region, but Justin was too polite to use it.

"No force is coming through. It's as if my dress is armored."

" 'You would be better off going to Demon University, crashing Professor Grossclout's lecture on monster evolution, and mooning him. At least then your end would be roasted rapidly. Now go away.'

" 'Not until you get me my talent back, you stunted fraud. I DEMAND MY TALENT!'

"Finally I got through to the dimwitted midget. 'Very well, if that is the way it must be,' he said grudgingly. 'I will arrange to return your talent to you. But it will take time to accomplish. Meanwhile you must render me your Service.'

" 'I'll do that, you overcharging charlatan. What do I have to do?'

" 'Return in two days to guide a damsel to the Isle of Women.'

"And so you see me here, guiding you," Ralph concluded his narrative. "But before you tell me your story, how about a kiss?"

"Tell him no!"

"No."

"Girls have such quaint ways of saying yes." He put both arms around her, holding her securely, and brought his face down toward hers.

"I said no, you brazen creep! Let me go."

But he held her tightly. "One little kiss, to warm things up," he said, his mouth bearing down on hers.

"I'm only fifteen!" she cried, turning her face away.

"What delightful youth." He lifted her up so that her feet lost purchase with the ground, then dropped down to the ground with her. "Let's get that dress off you before it gets dirty." He reached across to get hold of it.

"If you are quite satisfied that he won't let you go voluntarily, it may be time to fight back," Justin remarked.

"How?"

"Remember, he can't actually touch you; he's just clasping the entire protected package. But you can touch him."

"Say, that's right!" Breanna's arms were pinned to her sides, and her legs were caught under his, but her head was loose. She remembered how she had punched a hole in the wall. Would it work the same way with her head?

"You want a kiss?" she said, forcing a smile as she turned her face back to his.

"Sure, before we get on to the main business."

"Then take this." She lifted her head, ramming her face into his, hard.

She felt nothing much, but his head rocked back, and a bit of blood appeared at his nose. She had banged it with her forehead. It was a dent rather than a smash, but surely painful.

He let go of her, grabbing his face. "Oooo!" Then he fished for a handkerchief.

Now her hands were free. She remembered a trick she had heard about, to stop the close approach of an unwanted face. She extended one finger and put it sidewise under his sore nose. She pushed up and inward, and his face moved back because of the discomfort. In that manner she shoved him off and got to her feet. "Oh, was that kiss too hard?" she asked with mock solicitation. "Want another?"

"Nooo!" he moaned, rolling away. It really wasn't that much of an injury, but maybe he wasn't used to getting pushed back.

"Maybe some other time."

"I suspect that suffices. You have made your point."

"Yeah," she said with satisfaction.

She waited while he got the handkerchief and tended to his nose. Then she pretended innocence. "Let's get on to the Isle of Women. Maybe you'll feel better by then."

He stared at her, but evidently decided to let things be for the moment. He didn't know about the protection racket; maybe he thought she had gotten in a lucky blow. So he might try again. But probably not right away. Meanwhile, she had truly verified the power of the racket. Now she felt safe. As long as she didn't cooperate, she could not be damaged.

They resumed their walk, and Ralph did not try to put his hands on her again. Soon it got dull.

"I didn't tell you about me," Breanna said, preferring any kind of dialog to silence. "I have this talent of seeing in the dark, so I mostly am up by night and sleep by day."

"That explains that."

"But I got kissed by a zombie prince who found me sleeping. Now he wants to marry me, so I'm fleeing. That's why I went to the Good Magician, and why I'm going to the Isle of Women. I should be safe there."

"I doubt it."

"You do? Why?"

"What will you do for me if I tell you?"

Justin cut in. *"Don't aggravate him needlessly. He might renege on his commitment to get you to the isle."*

Probably good advice. So she stifled her natural retort again, and tried to be polite. "I don't want to kiss you. I don't want to do anything with you except get where I'm going. So you can tell me what you want to, or let it be, as you prefer."

"There is something about that isle you really should know. But you ought to be a bit more friendly."

"Sorry. No touching."

"As you wish." His tone suggested that she was making a mistake, but she didn't trust his motive.

They continued moving. Breanna refused to let him know how he had piqued her curiosity. Was he faking it, or was there really something at the Isle of Women that would make her regret going there? She was annoyed that he was still trying to pressure her for something he knew wasn't allowed. At least he wasn't still trying to grab her.

They passed a hat rack with several nice hats just ripening. Intrigued, Breanna picked a nice black one with a white frill on the top resembling a cresting wave. "A black wave hat," she said, putting it on. It fit perfectly.

Ralph didn't comment, but Justin did. *"That does seem to match your nature. It is becoming."*

"Becoming what?" she asked, alarmed.

He laughed. *"Attractive. It makes you look cute."*

"Cute I can live with."

Then Mare Imbri appeared. *"I learned about Lija,"* she said.

"Who?"

"Elijah. The boy who got Ralph's talent. I can give you the whole story in a daydream."

"Great! Let's have it."

The surroundings mostly disappeared, though she continued walking on automatic pilot, and Breanna's awareness devolved on drear Mundania. There was a region shaped like a new jersey, and a town, and a house. Inside the house was a family with a daddy, a mommy, an eight-year-old boy named Lija, and his sister Rachel, who was there for him to quarrel with. By day he had a smile nearly as bright as the sun, and things were great. But everything changed at night.

The moment bedtime arrived, Lija's smile vanished. His head hurt. His neck, shoulders, back, or knees ached. His belly cramped, his chest felt heavy, and his breathing got wheezy. All the misery he had avoided during the day closed in victoriously at night. So of course he was unable to fall asleep without a heroic struggle by his parents.

When morning came, Lija would be perfectly fine and ready for a full and active day. But when bedtime returned, so did his problems. Lija called his condition the Bedtime Booboos. His parents had their own name for his condition, but they were very careful never to use it in Lija's presence.

Daddy and Mommy tried to be supportive and understanding, but they soon reached the limits of their patience. Sometimes they would not smile reassuringly when they placed a cool wet cloth on his head.

Sometimes they muttered under their breaths when they massaged his sore limbs and back. Once they even grumpily ordered him back upstairs to get his own cool cloth and then put himself back to bed and go to sleep.

Poor Lija! Not only was he feeling terrible every night, he was also in trouble with his folks. But there seemed to be nothing he could do about it. The Booboos never let him go.

One summer evening as Lija made his nightly announcement that he was once again suffering from Bedtime Booboos, Mommy, for no reason at all, got angry. "I'm really tired of these Booboos!" she yelled. "Every night, the same thing over and over again! Your head aches or your throat is sore or your stomach hurts or whatever you can think of to avoid going to sleep."

Now that was an unkind accusation. "I don't do it on purpose," Lija protested in a sad, small voice. "I really don't feel well. I can't help it if I can't go to sleep."

"I don't understand your condition, Lija!" Mommy continued. "It seems so convenient that the only thing it interferes with is bedtime. You are fine all day long, and then at bedtime you are suddenly sick." It was almost as if she were suspicious of something. "It's like a magic transformation, one minute well and the next minute sick, and I think you—"

Mommy paused abruptly in the middle of her tantrum. She sat down quietly on the bed next to him, looking very thoughtful. They sat in silence while they pondered the situation.

"Lija," Mommy whispered slowly. "I think you have a magic talent."

"I do?" he asked in wonder.

"Unfortunately, I think your magic talent is the Bedtime Booboos."

"But this is Mundania!" he reminded her, as if anyone could ever forget the dreary reality even for an instant. "There's no magic here." Which was of course the problem.

"There's a little bit of magic," she reminded him back. "Remember the beautiful rainbow, that stops you from ever catching up to it. So you must have gotten some of the ugly magic."

It did make sense, but Lija was definitely not pleased. "It's not fair!" he grumbled. "I'm the only kid outside of Xanth with a magic talent, and I get a stupid one! Now I'm stuck with Bedtime Booboos forever unless I can get rid of this talent.''

"I'm afraid so,'' Mommy agreed. "Believe me, I am as annoyed as you are.'' She seemed really sincere.

"What do people in Xanth do to free themselves of stupid talents?''

"They move to Mundania, and their magic disappears.''

"Oh, great! I already live in New Jersey! There *is* no place more mundane than here. So what do I do—move to Xanth?''

"No!'' Mommy cried in alarm. "If your talent is this much trouble in mundane New Jersey, imagine how much stronger it would be in magical Xanth!''

The family tried to figure out how Lija had acquired his unwanted talent. Lija supposed that it was the result of a mixed-up delivery by a really confused, overworked, and directionally impaired talent-distributing stork. His sister Rachel defended the stork by claiming that the talent was correctly delivered; it was just that Lija was actually in the wrong place. Daddy proposed that when the demons were disposing of unwanted talents, one of them escaped to Mundania where it hid in Lija. Mommy suggested that perhaps a large giant walking close to the Xanth/Mundania border was struck by a sudden sneezing fit. The poor man sneezed so hard that his talent flew out and went flying into Mundania, where it finally landed on Lija.

Unfortunately, not one of them thought of toxic waste disposal. Since no one could determine either how the talent had come, or how to make it go away, they resigned themselves to living with it as best they could. This was, after all, drear Mundania, where such things were commonplace.

The daydream ended. "But why is Ralph determined to get his talent back?'' Breanna asked Imbri.

"He doesn't know its nature. He thinks any talent is better than none. The Good Magician tried to warn him, but he wouldn't listen.''

"I know.'' Breanna smiled privately. "I think I won't tell him. I'll bet it's ten times as bad in Xanth, because the magic is so much stronger.''

"Yes. He will have to sleep in daytime, as you do, because he will not be able to settle down at all at night.''

"It couldn't happen to a more deserving lout.''

"The Good Magician has sent the Demoness Metria to see the Demon E(A/R)TH. Humfrey knows the Demon will give any help

needed to get rid of any stray magic, because he hates having his realm polluted by fantasy. He will arrange for the family to win flying tickets to Florida, so Lija can go to the very spot that corresponds with Ralph's house in the North Village. Then the Demon E(A/R)TH *will exorcise the talent, and it will be driven back to its natural home in Xanth. In Ralph. He will have his wish.''*

''Will he ever!'' Breanna said zestfully.

''And Lija will at last have peace.''

''Yeah. And Ralph will be really proud and happy. Right up until bedtime.''

''What's that?'' Ralph asked.

She must have forgotten herself, and spoken aloud. ''Dream Mare Imbri just visited me. She says the Good Magician is even now arranging for your talent to be returned to you, in all its awesome power.''

''It's about time,'' he said smugly. ''I thought that old fraud could come through if given sufficient motive.'' He glanced at her. ''Are you sufficiently bored yet? Are you getting motivated for something interesting?''

The jerk never gave up. ''I like being bored.'' She was speaking figuratively, of course.

They kept walking, following the enchanted path, making good time. Ralph did not try to grab her again, and she began to regret the way she had banged him. Maybe she could have just told him NO clearly, and it would have been all right.

"I don't think so," Justin said. *"He does not deserve the benefit of the doubt."*

''How can you be sure?''

"I don't wish to appear condescending, but I am a male, and have had time to think. I can appreciate your desirability as a woman, and the ruthless nature of some men. You are young, and have a certain naiveté about adult relations."

''I do not!''

"Please, I am trying to protect you from exploitation."

''You're trying to invoke the Adult Conspiracy!''

"Perhaps it will be possible to make a demonstration. You allowed me to be present when you performed certain natural functions. Would you wish to have him watch similarly?"

''No! What has that to do with the price of beans in Mundania?''

"Beans?"

"Just an expression. Ralph isn't going to watch me pee, okay? He's not a tree."

He nodded, mentally. *"Trees do collect urine. Here is what I propose: tell Ralph you need to take a comfort break, so need privacy for a time. Then spy on him. I think he does not appreciate the extent of your ability to see in the dark, so you will be able to hide from him."*

"This is pointless!"

"If I am correct, he will try to sneak a peek at you. Then you will know that you were not at fault when you struck him."

She considered. "Okay, I'll give it a try." Then she spoke aloud: "Ralph, I need a bit of privacy. Suppose I head off to behind that bush, and you wait here, okay?"

"Very well," he agreed, and found a rock to sit down on. He set his lantern on the ground beside it.

"See?" she said silently. "He's not going anywhere."

"Yet."

How could he be so sure? She walked to the bush, and around it. She set her black wave hat on the bush, marking her presence. She ducked down as if squatting, then ran quickly and silently behind the nearest tree. She peered past its trunk.

The first thing she saw was that Ralph was no longer sitting on the stone. He had left the light there as a seeming indication of his presence, but he was already circling around behind trees and bushes, hiding while closing in on her bush. As Justin had surmised, Ralph thought that the darkness covered him, not realizing that she could see as clearly as if it were daylight.

"He is finding a vantage where he can look behind your bush," Justin said. *"So he can see you with your dress up."*

"Sheesh, Justin, you were right! He's trying to sneak a peek at panties, and worse."

"Yes. Such sights fascinate men."

"Even you, Justin?"

"Even I, despite my age and loss of manform."

"Except that you didn't try to sneak. You offered to return to your tree."

"Yes. But I did not insist on departing, when you generously let me stay for the occasion."

"Well, I thought of you as a tree."

"I am a tree with the spirit of a man."

Ralph, discovering that the spot he spied on was empty, and that he had been had, quickly returned to his stone.

"Actually, I do need to do it," she said.

"I will depart to—"

"No, we've already been through that. Just don't comment. I'll pretend I'm alone." She found a place and squatted. "Anyway, you see through my eyes. If I don't look, you don't see, right?"

"That is correct. However, you did stand before the mirror, when—"

"I was showing off. That's different."

He was silent. She quickly did her business, then returned to recover the hat, and walked back to the stone where Ralph sat as if he had never moved.

She decided not to make an issue. "Thanks," she said dryly as they resumed walking. And to Justin: "You proved your point. I was naïve. This guy's a turd."

"So he is. Fortunately your racket and some common sense precautions will protect you."

"I must admit, I am coming to see some use in the Adult Conspiracy. It protects innocents like me from characters like him. At least it's supposed to."

"Few things are entirely good or entirely evil," he agreed diplomatically.

"Maybe it didn't protect me because I renounced it. I guess I couldn't blame it for that."

"You must do what you deem proper. Sometimes that incurs a penalty, but it remains your proper course."

"So maybe I'll go easy on abolishing it entirely, until I know what parts of it ought to be saved. Reform rather than abolition."

"That seems sensible."

"You're awful agreeable. How come you never tell me I'm being a foolish child?"

"I wouldn't think of saying that!"

"Come on, Justin. You have to have been tempted. What holds you back?"

"All my life, as a man and as a tree, I have been a sensible, principled individual. That has turned out to be supremely dull. You, in

contrast, proceed from one fascinating dilemma to another. As an adventure, it is marvelous."

"And you wanted adventure," she concluded, seeing it. "My crazy ideas and mistakes make my life interesting. Got it."

"Integrity requires me to make one additional confession."

"Why Justin, you must be blushing, because I feel the heat on my face. What are you talking about?"

"I am discovering that despite the extreme difference in our situations, and the likelihood that in due course we will separate and never again associate, I feel a certain appealing pleasure in that association, and I prefer not to jeopardize it."

"Why Justin—are you saying you like me?"

"I was trying to avoid saying that."

"And your tree bark was getting shrunk into knots," she said, remembering her session with the embarrassing challenge questions.

"Yes."

She laughed aloud, causing Ralph to glance warily at her. So she made sure her next statement was silent. "And I like you too, Justin. Even though you're nothing like any companion I would have chosen for myself."

"Sometimes odd associations occur."

"For sure." Pleased, she let it be.

By morning they were near the west coast of Xanth, because the enchanted path facilitated travel. Breanna had never seen the sea before, and was amazed. "So much water!"

"This is as far as I need to take you," Ralph said. "The Isle of Women is one of the occasional islands off the coast. It interfaces with Xanth one hour a day, so you must watch for it and cross over to it then."

"How do I get to it? I wouldn't care to try to swim out there."

He sneered. "True. The sea monsters would gobble your delicate dark flesh in a moment. You have to take the boat. It is there by the paradox."

"The what?"

"The paradox. I don't know why it's called that. When you see the isle, go down to that dock you see there and get in the boat. It will take you across."

"That's all there is to it?"

"That's all there is to getting there. That's not why it won't help you escape the zombie prince."

"And you're not going to tell me why."

"Not unless you care to purchase my favor with a little favor of your own."

"Meaning you want to get your hands on my black panties, and have me not fight."

"Precisely. Are you interested?"

"No."

"Then I am through with you." He turned and walked away.

"I'm glad to be rid of him," she confided to Justin. "But he did get to me on that business about why the isle won't help me. I was almost tempted to let him touch me, and hope that the protection racket stopped him from going too far. But I wasn't sure it would protect me, if I wasn't fighting—you know."

"I admit there could be doubt, if you were indicating that you liked his attention. I believe that was the warning the Gorgon was obliquely rendering. I think it was best not to risk it, because if the racket did prevent him from completing his vile design, he probably would renege on giving you the information."

"Yeah, you're right for sure. But it still bugs me."

"It bothers me also. But perhaps we shall ascertain the information via some other source."

"Well, let's go down and look at that dock. I want to know what's what before I do anything else foolish."

They walked to the dock. It seemed to be an ordinary wooden pier, with a small boat at its end. A pie tree grew beside it.

"There is something missing," Justin said. *"There is no paddle."*

"Say, that's right! How am I going to paddle it to the island?"

"Could that be what Ralph wasn't telling? The location of the paddle?"

"Dunno. He acted as if I would have no trouble making it to the island, but then wouldn't find it helped."

"True. Perhaps there is a paddle hidden under the dock."

She bent to peer under it, and saw a sheltered spot with several pillows. "Say! Someone slept here."

"It does look like a comfortable spot to take shelter from wet weather," Justin agreed.

"And it's dawn, and I'm tired. So why don't I eat one of those pies and turn in until the island shows? I'll paddle the boat with my hands if I have to, if it's not too far." Then she reconsidered. "Only I might sleep through, if it's only here for an hour."

"I can wake you each hour, so you can look to see if it is here."

"You can do that? When do you sleep?"

"I do not require sleep in the same way you do, in my vegetative state."

"Okay. Maybe make it every half hour, so I don't catch the isle at the end, and maybe it vanishes before I can get across to it."

"Agreed."

She harvested a chocolate pie, ate it, and found a nearby milkweed. She disliked eating anything as white as milk, but some sacrifices had to be made. Then she crawled in under the dock, set her hat aside, arranged the pillows, got herself comfortable, and closed her eyes.

"Breanna."

She came awake, startled. "Oh, is it time to look? It seems like only ten minutes."

"It is *ten minutes. Ralph is stalking you again."*

"He is? How can you tell?"

"I hear him with your ears. I have had decades to attune to normal environmental sounds, and can recognize a human footstep amidst background noise."

"Gee. What should I do?"

"Be ready to resist if he grabs you. So that your racket is quite clear that you need protection."

"Got it." Breanna feigned continued sleep, but was as tense as a spring. Now that Justin had alerted her, she did hear the faint scuffling of human feet. So that rat was still trying to nab her for underage sex! Well, this time maybe she would bash his nose right out the back of his skull. She had been a bit regretful for hurting him, before, but this was just too much. She was sorry she had lost her dagger.

He came to the dock. He must have been watching her throughout, so as to know exactly where she slept. He figured that if he grabbed her while she was still asleep, he could nail her before she worked up a sufficient protest. Well, he had a surprise coming.

He reached the dock, and paused. She realized that she probably should have scrambled out from under before he arrived, because here there was very little room to fight. But it was too late to do it now.

Suddenly he caught hold of her feet and pulled her out. No subtlety at all; he was just grabbing and hauling. As her legs came out, her skirt scraped up around her hips. He shifted his grip to her thighs and hauled again, getting her all the way clear. Then he bent over her and put his hands on her chest. He knew exactly where to grasp, damn him!

Breanna did it without even thinking. She brought up one foot and planted it in his belly, while clamping her hands on his hands so that he couldn't move them away. Never mind where his hands were; they would be gone soon enough. Then she shoved hard with that anchored foot. It was an adaptation of the stomach throw, that she had learned as a child in a Mundanian judo class. It was performed when Tori, the thrower, was on his back, and Uki, the throwee, was standing or leaning over. Just like this; it was a perfect defense for a girl on her back. She knew she was showing an awful lot of bare leg, but he wasn't in any position to gawk.

He went flying up over her head, his pinned hands becoming the fulcrum. He did a forced somersault and landed with a hard whomp on the dock. Only then did she release his hands. It had worked!

But as she scrambled to her feet, something weird happened. Ralph went sliding down the dock and landed with a thunk in the boat at the end. Then the boat took off, without paddles, as if it had a hidden motor. It cruised into the water, heading straight out to sea.

"Hey!" Ralph cried. But there was nothing he could do. The boat was taking him wherever it was going, and it wasn't stopping.

"Well, that answers the question of propulsion," Justin remarked. *"It's magic; it requires no paddle."*

"But where is it going?"

"Surely to the Isle of Women."

"But the isle's not there yet."

"So I see. Yet the craft is obviously going somewhere"

"Looks more like nowhere to me."

"Evidently the boat isn't smart enough to realize that its destination is absent. It assumes that anyone who enters it is ready to travel. There must be another dock on the isle to receive it, when the isle is there."

"Yes. And when the isle isn't there, the boat just goes right on, looking for it. So it really is going nowhere fast."

"That would seem to be a paradox: a boat going somewhere in a hurry, yet going nowhere."

"Paradox!" she cried, a light flashing over her head. She loved that incidental magic of Xanth. "That's it!"

"I beg your pardon?"

"That's the magic pun. Ralph said this dock is called Paradox. That's pair o' docks, with the boat going between them. That's all it knows to do—to shuttle back and forth. But when one dock is missing, it's got nowhere to go, so it goes nowhere. Somewhere becomes nowhere. Paradox."

Justin's astonishment washed through her. *"I believe you are correct, Breanna. There must be a pair o' docks, or there is paradox. And Ralph is caught in it."*

"Yeah." She watched as the boat sped out to sea, becoming smaller as it gained distance. A pair of arms was waving frantically over it. She didn't have much sympathy.

"Had you set foot on the dock, that might have been your fate," Justin said, shaken.

"Yeah. So I guess Ralph did us a favor, showing us exactly how it works." She stretched. "Meanwhile, I'm going back to sleep."

"To be sure."

"If I can relax enough, after that fracas. My heart's still pounding."

"I could sing you a lullaby."

She laughed, then paused. "Are you by any off-chance serious?"

"Yes. I used to be a fair singer, though that was not considered a masculine trait. I often imagined melodies of nature, as a tree, with associated images. I think I could do it in my mind, and you could hear it and see, if you wished."

"Gee. Sure. Give it a try."

He began to sing, and it was marvelous. It was as if the forest itself were serenading her, with the sound of wind through trees, the movement of birds' wings, the swishing of the tails of fish in a running stream, and even the gentle drifting of clouds against a deep blue welkin. Sound and image were one, and wonderfully soothing.

"That's really great, Justin! Can you do it until I fall asleep?"

"Yes, I can do it indefinitely. I am glad to have an appreciative audience."

"And thanks for alerting me about Ralph."

"You are more than welcome. I would not want anything untoward to happen to you."

"Me neither." Then she thought of something else. "Can you show me your tree again? I mean, the forest, and all, sure, but your own special tree specifically?"

"Certainly." A modified picture formed in her mind, with the tree centered.

"Thanks. Now I'm sure of it. You're cute too."

She felt her face heating, and knew he was blushing again. Satisfied, she sank back into sleep.

8
ISLES OF WO

Dor woke. He was on the bed in the chamber of Castle Zombie. On adjacent beds his father and son were stirring.

What a chain of worlds they had seen! He ticked them off on his mental fingers and toes: Ptero, Pyramid, Torus, Cone, Dumbbell, Pincushion, Spiral, Tangle, and Motes. That was nine in all, each seeming as big and competent as Xanth, despite being impossibly small. And perhaps an infinite number beyond them, that the Zombie Master was still touring.

Dor put his feet on the floor and stood up. Actually this was no worse than orienting on another dream world. This just happened to be the real one. Or was it? Could the Land of Xanth be on a globe or other shape orbiting the head of some giant Ida? The notion was mind boggling, so he set it aside.

The door opened, showing Millie. ''I thought I heard stirring,'' she said.

''Yes, we are back,'' Dor said. ''Jonathan says he is making progress, and hopes soon to find a suitable world for the zombies. He is on the ninth derivative at the moment, a cluster of floating rocks called Motes. So we shall return and report that the zombies should be out of the way by the date of the wedding.''

''That's good,'' Millie said. ''But there is another problem. The blob—''

''Has become a winged mermaid,'' Dor finished for her.

"How did you know?"

"Her name is Aurora. She couldn't make it on her own world, so has merged with the blob to give it identity and form. She should do well enough in Xanth."

"That's the problem: she has no idea where to go, and I don't know what to tell her. She is asking for the three kings."

Dor glanced at the others, then nodded. "I suppose it is our responsibility. We had better talk to her before we go home." He paused, seeing the jar of sleep potion. "You say you have plenty of that?"

"Oh, yes," Millie agreed. "Would you like to take that jar with you?"

"Yes, just in case. One can never tell when something like that might be useful."

Millie picked up the jar and brought it to him. Dor put it in his pocket. "Thank you."

"But remember," she warned him. "This is not for ordinary sleeping. It's for the dream worlds."

"Yes. I will use it only when warranted."

"You had better," the jar said from his pocket.

They went to the other chamber. There was Aurora, sitting on the edge of a wooden tub, soaking her tail in water. She was of course beautifully bare.

"Oh, you are here!" she cried, spying them. "See—I did manage to get lungs, so I can breathe your air." She inhaled, and her chest inflated, causing Dor's eyes to lock. She spread her wings and flew across to plant a kiss on Dor. "You must tell me where that other winged mermaid is!"

"Actually I saw her only once, at Chex Centaur's wedding," Dolph said. "Fifteen years ago. She would be of mature age by now."

"That's all right. She will surely know the scene." Aurora stood on her tail, keeping herself upright by flapping her wings at half speed. She was a most scenic female figure, with sightly attributes, in utter contrast to the former aspect of the blob. Dor was privately amazed that the same flesh could assume such different forms. This wasn't the kind of magic transformation Dolph did; it was a given mass reshaped. That made it special.

"We can ask some regular mermaids," Dolph suggested, trying

without success to wrest his gaze away from two attributes. "They should know where the winged ones are."

Dor nodded. "We will take you to the nearest merfolk colony and inquire."

"Oh, thank you!" she exclaimed, and kissed him again, in the process squishing an attribute against him.

"I am glad that is settled," Millie said, with a section of a reminiscent smile. "But first you must have more tee and crumples; I have them ready."

Dolph looked at Aurora. "I know you can fly, but I think I had better carry you, when we travel, because I'll be flying high and fast, and I am familiar with the terrain."

"I'm sure you know best," she said demurely.

In due course they exited the castle, and were ready to travel. But with three folk to carry, Dolph couldn't use the roc form. So he became a large six-winged dragon, and they straddled his serpentine mid section. Aurora had no legs, so couldn't straddle, so she sat sideways while Dor held her securely in place around the waist.

Dolph took off. He spiraled up into the sky, avoiding passing clouds. With each beat of those great wings, the dragon body lifted powerfully, and they felt extra weight, and Aurora's attributes pressed down against Dor's arm. Then on the return stroke the dragon seemed to be floating, and everything became light. Dor hoped that no one else was aware of his arm. He wouldn't care to try to explain his impressions to Irene.

"Do you have demons here?" Aurora asked, glancing around.

"Yes, many. In fact Dolph's ex-fiancee Nada Naga married Demon Prince Vore, and they have a two-year-old daughter named Demonica."

"What happened to them during the Time of No Magic?"

"How do you know about that?"

"Cone is part of Xanth too, indirectly. Our history and folklore say that all magic derives from the Demon X(A/N)th, and that when he departed for a day, so did most of the magic. We were protected, because our nested worlds were stored in a special cell in the nameless Castle that didn't let its magic escape. Of course that's just our legend; there may be no such place on your world."

"There is such a place," Dor reassured her. "So it could be true. I wondered where Ida's moon was, before it joined her."

"But I should think it was a difficult time for unprotected demons, who can't exist without magic."

"It was," Dor agreed. "I believe they became dust devils, as they do in Mundania. Then they recovered when the magic returned."

"That's nice. It wouldn't be the same without demons."

Dor hadn't thought of it that way, but found himself agreeing. Most regular demons were nuisances, but some were important, like Demon Professor Grossclout, and some were intriguing, like Demoness Metria in her several guises.

Soon they spied a river complete with merfolk sporting in a pool. Dolph spiraled down and made a good landing in an adjacent field. They dismounted, Dor set Aurora on her tail, and Dolph changed back to manform.

"I hope I didn't bruise your poor arm," Aurora said, concerned.

"No problem," Dor said gallantly.

They approached the river. The head of a lion popped from the water, spied them, and roared.

"Oh, go chomp yourself, mane brain," the river bank said.

The sea lion bared its teeth, but there wasn't much it could do about a section of ground. After a moment it bashed the water with its paws, then turned tail and disappeared with a flash of its flukes.

"The sea lions aren't dangerous if you don't invade their territory," Dor said to Aurora. "But you have to watch out for the ant lions. They can pursue you on land."

"We have uncle lions on Cone," Aurora replied. "They're really fierce."

They walked downstream to the pool. There were no merfolk showing. "It's all right," Dor called. "It wasn't a real dragon, just a transformed Magician. We are men, and one mer-person."

A blonde head popped out of the water. One eye was artfully covered by a trailing tress. "Men! Hello—I'm Ash." She lifted in the water just enough to show her own attributes.

"Three kings," Dor assured her. "We are looking for—"

A redhead appeared. "Kings! I'm Cedar. You are looking for brides?" She lifted a bit farther from the water.

This was getting dangerous to eyeballs. "No. We just want to—"

A dark gray-brown head appeared. "I'm Mahogany. We don't do one splash stands. Not even for kings." She lifted so high that her snug little waist was visible.

"We're not looking for splashes," Dor said. "We're looking for winged merfolk."

"Now there's nothing they can do, that we can't do just as well," Ash said, inhaling. "Except fly."

Dor indicated the mermaid balancing beside him. "This is Aurora. She is new to Xanth, and needs to find her own kind. Can you help us?"

They considered. "Well, there's Erica," Cedar said. "She hangs out around Mount Rushmost with the other winged monsters."

"That's where I saw her," Dolph agreed.

"She has a portable pool table for her tail," Mahogany said.

"That sounds ideal," Dor said. They turned away from the pool.

"Are you sure one of you wouldn't like a trial splash?" Ash called after them.

"Almost sure," Dor called back. "Thank you for the information."

A surly-looking man approached. "Hey, want something nice?" he inquired.

"Go away, BB!" Cedar cried. "They don't want what you give."

Dor paused. "What does he give?"

"He has the talent of bad breath," Cedar said. "If he breathes on you, your own breath gets stinky awful."

Dor quickly turned away from BB.

Then Dolph changed, and they boarded, and flew up.

"Well, no wonder!" Cedar exclaimed. "Look how he's holding her."

"But we can do that too," Mahogany said. "Just as bouncily too."

"We don't exactly have brass ears," Ash agreed.

Then the distance became too great, and their following words were lost. Dor was relieved. And glad that his father and son couldn't see how he had to hold Aurora. He couldn't risk letting her fall.

But what did brass ears have to do with anything? Dor couldn't figure it out.

"You look perplexed," Aurora murmured.

"I didn't quite hear what they said. It sounded like 'brass ears,' but—"

She laughed, which really bounced her attributes. "Not brass ears. Brassieres. Clothed girls use them, if they need to. At least they do on Cone."

''Oh.'' Dor felt himself trying to blush.

''Conic bosoms are popular in some circles,'' she continued. ''But we merfolk haven't felt the need.''

''There is no need,'' Dolph agreed fervently.

Aurora remained curious about Xanth. ''I see some boys dancing,'' she said. ''What is the dance, and why are they so ragged?''

Dor looked down. ''They are poor boys, so they are doing the Oliver Twist, the poor boys' dance.''

''Oh. Is there a version for poor girls? I might try that.'' She bobbed in place, banging his arm some more.

''Maybe Erica will know.'' It was all he could think of to say, lame as it seemed. Aurora was a most distracting armful.

They came to Mount Rushmost. This was a mountain with almost vertical sides and a broad plateau on top. Dor almost thought he could see huge faces in the rock, but concluded it was imagination or illusion.

There was a small gathering of winged monsters on the plateau. They were all female. Three were winged centaur fillies, another was a girl with reptilian wings, and another was—yes!—a winged mermaid. The group of them stood beside a living room that retreated as it saw the strange group descending. Living rooms were comfortable, but more nervous than inanimate rooms. The ladies were holding sun glasses, and those cups of light really brightened the premises.

The dragon landed at the edge, beside a patch of flowers. Dor recognized the larger ones as maxi mums, and the small ones as mini mums. They would make those who sniffed them correspondingly large or small. So, like most of Xanth's plants, they were best left alone unless a person really understood their nature.

Dor changed, and they approached the winged monsters. ''Hey, what are you men doing here?'' the centaur demanded. ''This meeting is limited to maidenly winged monsters.''

''Oh, you're in for it now,'' the ground said. ''You have trespassed on a private gathering.''

The centaur glanced down, startled. It seemed she wasn't used to hearing the inanimate speak.

''Our apologies,'' Dor said. ''We'll leave as soon as we can. That's my talent making the ground speak; ignore it. But we have a maidenly winged monster with us who needs help.'' He indicated Aurora.

The girls looked. "Oh," the centaur said. "Well, in that case we'll let you go with minor penalties."

"Penalties?"

"Now you're really going to get it!" the ground said zestfully.

"You're not supposed to be here, considering your maleness and lack of wings. Do you deny it?"

The three men found themselves unable to deny either their maleness or their lack of wings.

The centaur nodded, having won her point. "I'm Karla Centaur. I was transformed from a regular centaur. This is Serena." She indicated the girl with reptile wings. "She's of mixed parentage. Love spring, you know."

"Love spring?" Aurora asked.

"The water makes any male and female fall instantly into ferocious romantic love," Dor explained. "Except if one is a child; then the love is parental."

"Oh. Like the shoreline of Cone, the conic section, where the land folk meet the sea folk for love. That's nice."

Karla indicated another winged centaur. "This is Chea Centaur. She was rescued from a tangle tree by Che Centaur. Her folks were from the gourd realm, so she gave him a gourd-style apology for taking his time, and he turned bright red and flew away. It seemed he misconstrued her intentions." And one more winged centaur. "This is Sharon Centaur, transformed from human to help shore up the new species, but she's still learning the nuances of centaurism." And the winged mermaid. "This is Erica, one of the few of her kind. We are here visiting the virgini tree and discussing ways to avoid it in the future. We think maybe the lips plants will help."

"Lips plants?" Dor asked blankly.

"Loose lips sink slips," the ground said.

Karla indicated a patch of plants in pretty colors. "I'll show you." She picked a flower. It looked like a bright red pair of lips. She touched it to his face, and the lips kissed him. "This is a two-lips plant. The others are more potent: the three-lips, four-lips, or five-lips. We have to take good care of them, because when a lips plant dies, it becomes a zombie plant which sucks the soul from unwary travelers, called lip-o-suction."

"That sounds almost as bad as the banana cream pie tree, which creams anyone who picks its pies,'' Dolph remarked. ''Not all plants are friendly.''

''Now for your penalty for intruding here,'' Karla said. ''Each of you men must be kissed by one of us.''

''That doesn't sound so bad,'' Dolph said.

''Just wait,'' Karla said with an obscure smile as several of them applied red balm to their lips. Then Serena the winged girl flew up to kiss Dolph, and Sharon Centaur approached Bink, and Karla herself leaned down to kiss Dor.

Her lips touched his—and his head seemed to explode. As the dust cleared he found himself sitting on the ground, heart-shaped clouds dissipating around him, and ebbing waves of delight spreading across his face. He was unhurt; in fact it had been a remarkably pleasant experience. He looked around, and saw Bink and Dolph sitting similarly, and looking similarly dazed.

''Lip bomb,'' Karla explained. ''Do you think it will free us from maidenly bondage to the virgini tree?''

''Surely it will, in due course,'' Dor agreed, getting up.

Meanwhile Aurora and the other winged mermaid, Erica, were talking as they dipped their tails in a table whose surface appeared to be water. Then Aurora turned to Dor. ''Yes, she will help me get established here,'' she said. ''Thank you so much.''

''Then I think we can get on home now,'' Dor said. ''We trust that you ladies will treat Aurora with consideration. You will find the story of her origin to be quite interesting.''

''Oh, Cone is dull,'' Aurora protested. ''It's just land and sea. It's this odd Land of Xanth that is interesting.''

''That's what yoooou think,'' the ground said.

''All right,'' Karla said. ''If you are sure you wouldn't like another kiss. We do have more lip bomb.''

The three men backed away. ''Thank you, once was enough,'' Dor said politely. He tripped over a couch potato he hadn't seen, and landed flat on the couch. At least its pillows were better than the hard ground.

Dolph transformed to the dragon, and they quickly boarded. He flew off the brink and was immediately high in the air. But his flight seemed somewhat unsteady, and that made Dor nervous. That lip bomb hadn't worn all the way off yet; his mouth felt outsize. ''Maybe we should pause for a drink of water before flying home,'' Dor suggested.

Dolph flew down to the nearest little stream and landed with a jar. Yes, he was definitely unsteady. Dor kicked the jar aside and stood up. Dolph resumed manform. Then they went to the stream and drank. The water was deeply refreshing.

A cute little fire-breathing puppy came bounding along the bank. Every time it barked, another little puff of fire and smoke came out. Then a catfish lifted its head from the river and hissed. Dor nodded; he loved seeing natural creatures playing.

Dolph seemed to be steadier. The water had washed out the lingering effect of the bomb, so that he could focus on something other than a passionate kiss. There should be no further danger of crashing in flight.

Now they were ready to go home and report that the zombie problem would probably abate by the wedding day. But Dolph paused before changing form. ''Where are we going?'' he asked.

''Home,'' Dor said.

''Uh, yes. But where is home?''

Dor opened his mouth to answer, but then paused himself. ''Why, I seem to have forgotten. That bomb must have blown it away.'' He looked at Bink.

''I don't remember either,'' Bink said. ''It should be a harmless lapse, because—'' He broke off, shrugging.

Because he could not be harmed by magic, Dor suddenly realized. That was the explanation for all the weird coincidences. He could be harmed by nonmagical things, or embarrassed by magic, but not harmed *by* magic. That was why they didn't have to worry much about magical dangers. But something magical must have happened, because all three of them should not have suddenly forgotten where home was.

''I don't think it was the bomb,'' Dolph said. ''Because I remembered where home was, until just now.''

A dark suspicion enveloped Dor. Suspicions cruised around like invisible blobs, and when they caught a person, they were awful to get rid of. ''This stream—where does it flow from?'' For it occurred to him that the firedog and catfish might not have been playing. They might have been trying to warn folk away from the river, too late.

They traced it back, and discovered that it issued from a forgotten crevice in the mountain. "The River Lethe flows deep underground," Dor said. "This could be a tributary stream. The way that water works, whatever you speak of just before drinking it, you forget. They sometimes use it to cure children who have somehow learned forbidden words. And I spoke of going home."

"That's right!" Dolph agreed. "So we forgot where it was."

"An amusing yet harmless loss," Bink said ruefully. "But perhaps we can get around it by flying high and looking around. We should know home when we see it, and we can see all of Xanth from high enough."

"Good notion," Dor agreed. "If that fails, we might get some reverse wood, and use it with another drink of lethe. Then the water would serve as a memory enhancer."

"Or it might reverse the liquid properties of the water, and dry us out," Bink said. "Reverse wood can be treacherous stuff."

Dor nodded. "We had better stick to our search, so as not to complicate our situation more than it is."

Dolph looked around. "I wonder where this river goes? I don't remember any lethe water on the surface."

"It's not the kind of thing a person remembers," Bink pointed out.

"To the Forest of Forgetfulness," a nearby stone said. "Nobody who goes there remembers the experience, so word doesn't get around."

Dor was intrigued. "There could be really interesting things there."

"But we don't want to go there," Bink said. "We have already complicated our situation enough."

So Dolph transformed into the roc bird, and they got on his feet, and he flew up. He spiraled high in the sky, so that they all could look around. All of Xanth was laid out below them. But Dor still had no idea which part of it was his home.

"There's the Gap Chasm," Bink remarked. "I remember the first time I encountered that, just after I met Chameleon. I had to go down and cross on the bottom, where the Gap Dragon roamed. I met Donald the Shade, and kissed his wife and told her where the silver oak was."

"I'm glad you met Chameleon," Dor said. She was after all his mother. "But do you remember where home is?"

"Then it was the North Village, but I don't think that's where we were about to go." He peered farther. "There's Castle Roogna. Oh, didn't we have adventures there!"

"Yes, of course," Dor agreed, becoming impatient. "But right now we need to find home."

"Wherever it is," Bink agreed. He peered again. "There's the Isle of View, where Dolph was married."

"Squawk!" Dolph agreed.

"He says it was some wedding night," a metal button translated. "Neither he nor Electra knew how to summon the stork."

"Well, I suspect they finally figured it out," Dor said. "They have a fine set of daughters in Dawn & Eve." For a moment he pictured them as they were at eighteen, on Planet Ptero. Would Xanth be ready for them at that age?

They circled around Xanth, noting the familiar landmarks, but found no sign of home. That memory had been cleanly erased.

"Maybe we can ask someone," Bink suggested. "There should be some person in Xanth who knows where we live now."

"I agree."

So Dolph flew downward, and found a landing spot near the west coast. He settled beside a large envelope—which suddenly sprouted antlers and feet and bounded away.

"I guess it was really an antelope," Bink remarked. "There are some odd animals in the backwoods."

Dolph changed back to manform, and they looked around. Nearby was a man reading a book, so they approached him. "Hello," Dor said.

The man looked up. "Who are you?"

"I am King Dor. I wonder if—"

"Sure, and I'm a dragon ass," the man said sourly. "Go away and let me practice."

"Practice what?" Dolph asked.

"My talent, dummy. I can bring characters and items out of these scenes in books. See?" He reached into the page of the books he held, and brought out a scarlet pimpernel flower. "I'm trying to find something useful."

"Good luck," Dor said, and they moved on. He appreciated the man's frustration; useless talents abounded in Xanth.

They saw a young woman dancing. She seemed to repeat the same motions over and over. "Doesn't that get dull?" Dolph inquired.

She never paused. "It's supposed to repeat, idiot," she replied witheringly. "It's a re-done-dance."

They went on. They came to a man concentrating on a rock. "Hello," Dor said, somewhat warily. "I'm King Dor."

The man looked up. "Oh, really?"

"Yes, really, you jerk," the stone he held said.

That seemed to be persuasive. "And I am your lowly rebellious subject, Phil Istine," the man replied. "What do you want from me?"

"Some information, if you please. Can you tell me where I live?"

Phil stared at him. "You don't know?"

"It seems I drank some lethe water, and forgot where home is," Dor said, embarrassed. "But surely you know where it is."

"Surely I do," Phil agreed. "And I'll tell you, for a return favor."

Dor was wary of such things, but had to ask. "What favor?"

"Well, you see my talent is molding things into other things, like this." Phil moved his hands over the rock, and it became a loaf of bread. He bit a chunk from it and chewed, showing it was real.

"Hey, watch who you're chewing on!" the loaf protested.

Phil passed his hands over it again, and it became a model house. "But my girlfriend isn't impressed. So now I need a new girlfriend, and all the others around here are taken. Except the ones on the Isle of Women. So why don't you go and fetch me one of those, and I'll tell you where your home is."

Dor's mistrust of this continued. "Why don't you fetch her yourself?"

"Because only women and royal men can go to that island. I'm not royal. But you are, so you could go. There must be a woman there who would like my talent."

"It's a good talent," Dor agreed. "Where is this Isle of Women?"

"Just offshore. But there's a problem. It's one of several Isles of WO, and it's hard to tell them apart."

"Well, we can ask," Dolph said.

"And they only interface with Xanth an hour a day. So if you get the wrong one you have to leave it and try for another."

"I think we can do that," Bink said.

"Okay. Fetch me that woman, and I'll tell you where to go home."

It seemed a steep price, but at least it was sure. "Agreed," Dor said.

They walked to the shore—and suddenly an island appeared. So Dolph changed to roc form, and they flew across to it.

The trees seemed to be covered by vines. "Those look like bovines," Bink remarked. "And I see cow pies on the ground."

"Maybe those are bull pies," Dor said. "There's a bull sleeping nearby."

"A bull dozer," Bink agreed.

A flock of ungainly birds spooked as Dolph landed on the beach. They had the heads of cows. In a moment a swarm of flies with the heads of bulls took off after them.

"Cow birds and bull flies," Dolph remarked as he changed back to manform.

Frogs with the heads of bulls snapped up the flies as they passed. Bullfrogs, obviously.

The commotion woke the sleeping bull. It got to its feet, put down its head, and charged. Its horns dug into the ground, pushing up a mound of sand and dirt. It left a cleared path behind it.

Several men came running down that path. But they had the heads of cows. "And here come the cowboys," Dolph added. "With their bulldogs." Indeed, the dogs were bullheaded.

"This is udder nonsense," Dor said, disgusted.

One of the cowboys stepped into a bully pulpit and lifted a bullhorn to his mouth. "MOOOOO!" it cried. "We have a bulletin."

The three kings retreated. This clearly wasn't the Isle of Women. In fact it wasn't even one of the Isles of WO, because these were all bovines.

A bull whose head was a whip appeared. It snapped its head back and forth, and the whip cracked sharply.

Suddenly they were in a stampede. Water plants with the heads of bulls were charging past them, spooked by the bullwhip. "Bulrushes," Dolph said, identifying them. Then he changed to roc form, and they got quickly off the island.

Already another island was in view, so Dolph veered to intercept it. "Wait!" Dor cried. "How can we be sure it's an Isle of WO, instead of an Isle of BO?"

Dolph veered again, this time toward shore. He spied something and landed. There was a wooden sign beside a dock with a small boat:

BOARD FOR BO

"Well, it's a board," Bink said. "But I would have trouble figuring out what it means."

"What does it mean?" Dor asked the board.

"It's clear enough, knothead," the board said. "The boat takes the traveler to the Isles of BO. Get aboard when you're bored. What part of that don't you understand?"

"The Isle of Bovines," Dor agreed. "Suppose we want to find the Isle of Women?"

"Go to the sign for WO, mush-brain. Isn't it obvious?"

"In retrospect," Dor agreed without rancor. The inanimate tended to lack social graces, but by a similar token was unable to tell a lie: it was too stupid.

They walked along the beach. Soon they came to another sign: COME FOR CO. "That's not the one," Dolph remarked with two-fifths of a smile. "We've already seen the cows."

The next sign said DOWNLOAD FOR DO. Then ENTER FOR EO, FORGE FOR FO, and GO FOR GO.

"Let's skip some signs," Dolph suggested, and became a six-legged horse. They got on, and he galloped past fifteen signs. They stopped at the sixteenth. Sure enough: WORK FOR WO.

They looked over the sea. There was an island. Dolph quickly assumed winged form and carried them across to it.

This one was heavily wooded with everblue, everyellow, and evergreen trees. A thick forest extended from beach to beach, and there were wood thatched houses nestled under the trees. They landed on the beach, which appeared to be composed of sawdust rather than sand. They approached the nearest house, walking along a wooden boardwalk. Dor knocked on the wooden door.

It opened, and a wooden man stood there. His body was formed of polished planks, the limbs fastened by wooden pegs. Wooden eyelets peered at them. "What?" he inquired somewhat woodenly. His jaw had a wooden hinge.

"Is this the Isle of Women?" Dor inquired.

"Of course knot," the man said, and closed the door.

They exchanged three thirds of a glance. "It occurs to me that there might be more than one Isle of WO, as the man said," Bink remarked. "This may be the Isle of Wood."

"You bet it is, fleshface," the door responded.

"I never realized that there were so many isles off Xanth," Dor said as they walked back to the beach.

"That's probably because they aren't here all the time," Dolph said. "If each surfaces for only an hour a day, there could be—" He paused, counting on his fingers, but he ran out of them before coming to a conclusion.

"We assumed that the other isles were for the other letters," Bink said. "Apparently there are a number for each letter."

"Worse," Dor agreed. "Somewhere else there must be Isles of WA, WE, and WI. Xanth must be much bigger than we thought."

"As well as much smaller, considering Ida's moons," Bink said. "Perhaps it is just as well that we are making this journey of exploration. This is knowledge we might find useful."

"Yes," Dor agreed as Dolph became winged to take them into the air.

There was another island nearby, so Dolph flew directly for it. Its vegetation looked oddly woolly, as if a giant sweater had been pulled across it. When they landed, the beach was as soft as a woolen mattress.

Rather than waste time, Dor addressed the island immediately. "What isle is this?"

"The Isle of Wool, bone-skull," the mattress replied.

Without a word, Dolph changed back, and they took off. There was another close island, so he landed on that. This one seemed ordinary, except for a muted wailing sound associated with it.

There was a child gathering shells on the beach. "What isle is this?" Dor asked him.

"The Isle of Woe," the boy replied tearfully.

"Thank you." They departed.

The next island was overrun by small furry animals. Soon they ascertained that this was the Isle of Wombats. They moved on.

When they landed on the next, they saw a huge statue at its near end. The statue was a word. In fact it said WORD. As they approached, it spoke: "In the beginning was the Word."

On the next, everyone was too busy working to answer any questions, but they got the news from the inanimate: the Isle of Work.

The next turned out to be a huge worm, coiled into island shape. But the one after that was worse: the Isle of Worse. Then there was one whose beach was composed of precious stones of every type: the Isle of Worth. And one that was so marvelous that they stood and gazed at it in wonder: the Isle of Wonder.

At last they returned to the sign on the mainland. "There just seem to be more islands than we can fathom," Dor said, dispirited. "I'm sure that any of them are worth appreciating on their own terms, but how will we ever find the one we want? There may be hundreds, and the Isle of Women may appear and fade while we are checking some other Isle of WO."

"I hate to say it," Bink said, "but I think we may need to ask someone else where it is."

Dor shrugged. "Let's see who we can find."

They looked around, and saw the dock not far from the sign. It wasn't anything fancy, but seemed serviceable, and there was a boat at its end.

But before they could check the dock, three humanoid figures appeared. "There's someone to ask!" Dor said.

"I don't think so," Bink said. "Those are zombies."

"Well, we can try," Dor said. He walked to intercept the zombies, who were shambling toward the dock. "Hey, zombies!"

They paused. One turned its weathered head. "Yesh?"

"I am King Dor of the living humans. Do you know where I live?"

"I amm Dropsy. Wheere yooo livze?"

Dropsy. That sounded female, and now that he came close, he saw that it was indeed female. Portions of her showed that would have locked his eyeballs, had they not been decaying. "Do you know where I live?" he repeated carefully.

"Yooo livze. I livzing deadth." She gestured to her two companions. "Zeeze Dee."

"Dee?"

"Dee Composed andz Dee Ceased. Zhey deadth too."

Dor realized that he was not getting through, and probably would not be able to; the zombie's brain had rotted too far. However, he did not want the zombies going to the same dock that the three living folk were about to check out. "I talked with the Zombie Master."

"Zjonathzan!"

She understood that much. "Yes. He is looking for a world for you. A zombie world. You should go home, so you can go there when he finds it."

"Zzombiee worlz?"

"Zombie world. New home. Go there." Actually they would not be going there physically, but would lie in their graves and dream of it. But that was too complicated to explain.

Dropsy exchanged a wormy glance with her companions. "Ggo homze."

"Go home," Dor agreed. He knew the Zombie Master would be calling in all the zombies when he returned, so this would give these three a head start.

They turned and shuffled toward the east. He had succeeded in getting them to leave the beach.

They waited until the zombies were out of sight, then resumed their own trek toward the dock. From a distance it had seemed ordinary; from up close it seemed routine. But one never could tell, because even the dullest things could harbor magic.

Dolph peered under the pier. "Say, now," he murmured. "A sleeping beauty."

The others joined him. There was a pretty Black Wave girl of fifteen, sound asleep in a pillowed nook.

"Do you think she knows?" Dolph asked.

"She might," Bink said. "Because she is evidently waiting for something. Maybe she's a woman going to the Isle of Women."

"Then we should ask her," Dor said. "But she's asleep."

"Well, kiss her awake," the dock said. "That's what you do with sleeping beauties."

"Perhaps if I were young and single," Dor said. "But I am middle aged and married, so I don't feel free to disturb her."

Dolph sighed. "We're all married, so none of us can wake her," he said with regret. "We'll just have to wait. She is pretty, though."

"You're all hopeless," the dock said. "If I were a living man, I would know what to do with a pretty sleeping maiden."

"If you were alive," Bink said, "you would soon develop some notion of the constraints that life and ethics place on individuals."

"Aw, spoilsport!"

Dor studied the girl's face. "Yes, she reminds me of Irene when she was that age, with the appealing health and vigor of youth."

"And she reminds me of Chameleon when she is almost at perihelion," Bink said.

"I wish we could wrap up our mission and get on home," Dolph said. "Wherever that is. I miss Electra."

"Perhaps the maiden won't sleep long," Bink said. "We shall just have to see. Meanwhile, we can settle down for some rest ourselves; we have had a busy day."

They leaned against posts of the dock and relaxed. It was reasonably pleasant here, Dor reflected, and the mystery of the maiden was intriguing.

9

Serious Seduction

"Wake, Breanna, but feign sleep for the nonce."

''What's a nonce?'' she asked sleepily.

"For the time being."

''Being what?''

"There being three men approaching. It is too late to escape without being spied, so I think it best to remain still."

''Oh.'' She kept her eyes closed and her breathing even. She was under the dock, and possibly in danger. ''I don't think I could escape three men, even with the protection racket.''

"Precisely. Unless they believe you are sleeping, and then you move very suddenly. I should be able to judge when the moment is propitious."

''Okay, I'll fake it. But I hope it's a false alarm.''

"So do I, Breanna."

They waited while the men approached. ''Say, now, a sleeping beauty,'' one said.

Breanna tensed, but forced herself to seem relaxed and asleep. But as the dialogue of the three men proceeded, Justin suffered a revelation. *"I know these men!"* he exclaimed. *"I have heard their voices before, when they visited my tree. They are Magician Bink, his son King Dor, and grandson Prince Dolph."*

''Royalty!'' she exclaimed silently.

"Indeed. They are all Magicians, and good folk. We need have no fear of them."

"What they're saying is interesting. Who is Chameleon at Perihelion?"

"Chameleon is Bink's wife. She varies with the cycles of the moon, alternately extremely smart but physically ugly, and extremely lovely but very stupid. He is saying that you remind him of her of the latter stage."

"I'm not stupid!"

"No one implies that you are, Breanna. Just that you are beautiful."

She reconsidered. "I think I like this man."

"He is eighty one years old, and his wife is seventy six."

"Oh, ugh!"

"Still, I believe it is time for you to wake. We need to check for the island."

"Gotcha." Breanna stirred, sighed, stretched, and slowly flickered her eyes open. She hoped that she resembled a truly beauteous enchanted lovely maiden innocently awakening.

"She's waking!" one of the men exclaimed.

So far, so good. Breanna looked at the men as they came to look at her. One was a mature fifty five, but the other two looked to be twenty four and twenty one. That didn't compute. How could they be three generations?

"I recognize King Dor and Prince Dolph. But the third—why it's Bink, as he was when young! He must have been youthened."

"Euthanized?" she asked, alarmed.

"Youthened. Made young again. By about sixty years, it seems."

"Miss," the elder man said cautiously. "Do you know where the Isle of Women is?"

"He is King Dor."

Breanna sat up and worked her way out from under the dock. After all, it was less than enchanting to have mainly her feet visible. Her skirt slid up some, but a little of that was beneficial. "Why yes, King Dor," she said. "I am going there myself."

"Excellent. May we go with you?" Then the man did a doubletake. "You recognize me?"

She wasn't ready to tell them about Justin Tree. Just in case. So she evaded that. "I should hope so." She looked at the prince. "And you are Prince Dolph." And at the third man. "But maybe not you."

"I am Bink," he said. He didn't add more, which meant that he wasn't telling her everything either. Okay.

"I am Breanna of the Black Wave. I'm fleeing my zombie lover, and—"

All three men jumped. "The zombies!" Dolph exclaimed.

Breanna was surprised. "You know about them?"

"We are trying to find out about them," Dor said. "They have gotten all stirred up, and we need to get them settled."

"They're stirred up because the Zombie King Xeth kissed me awake and wants to marry me," Breanna said. "I told him I'm only fifteen, but that doesn't bother him. He likes my firm living flesh. So I'm fleeing, and the zombies are chasing me, and the Good Magician says I can escape them on the Isle of Women, so that's where I'm going."

"But if you escape them, they will continue to be stirred up," Dor said. "We need them to settle before the big wedding."

"What big wedding?"

"The one at Castle Roogna next week. We don't know who is getting married, but we all have important roles to play in it. We suspect it is a royal occasion, for it will be a prince or king marrying a common girl. We don't want zombies attending."

"For sure," she agreed.

"A horrible thought has occurred to me," Justin said. *"Could that be your marriage to Xeth?"*

"No!" Breanna cried.

Immediately the men crowded solicitously around her. "Are you all right?" Dolph inquired anxiously.

"I—I'm all right, I guess. I just had a horrible thought. Suppose—suppose the royal groom is King Xeth—the Zombie? After he catches me?"

All three had the grace to look appalled. "Oh, Breanna, we wouldn't want that," King Dor said. "We must help you escape."

"We saw some zombies a while ago," Prince Dolph said. "They must have been looking for you."

"For sure," Breanna agreed weakly. "I had a spell to make them not see me, but that must have worn off by now, so they're picking up my scent again. They can feel my magic talent of seeing in blackness. They home in on it. So I have to keep running. But I can't run from here, because I have to be here when the Isle of Women comes.''

''We've been looking for it all day,'' Prince Dolph said. ''We keep finding the wrong islands. How can you find it?''

''It's supposed to be the island we can see from this dock. I didn't realize there were several.''

King Dor nodded. ''We have been traveling north along the coast. Maybe we were simply in the wrong position to see the right island.''

''And I'm supposed to take the boat,'' Breanna continued. ''Were you using a boat?''

''No,'' Prince Dolph said with three-fifths of a smile.

''Maybe the isle won't show, unless someone's by the right boat,'' she suggested.

King Dor nodded. ''That seems possible. So we will wait here with you for it.''

But then four figures showed up. Breanna recognized them instantly. ''Zombies!''

''More zombies,'' King Dor agreed, looking. ''Others must be orienting on your talent. We might hold them back a while, but perhaps you had better get in the boat now, so as to be out of their reach.''

''I can't do that,'' she protested. ''The magic is wrong when the island's not there. Paradox—oh, never mind. I must wait.''

King Dor looked at Prince Dolph. ''Can you stop them without hurting them?''

''I can carry them away, two by two.''

King Dor nodded. ''Do that. Bink and I will try to stall the other two.''

Then the prince disappeared, and a roc bird appeared in his place. Breanna was so surprised her jaw dropped.

The roc bird spread its wings and launched into the air. It swooped toward the zombies. It caught two in its huge claws and carried them away. But the remaining two came straight on.

''Why—why don't you want to hurt them?'' Breanna asked.

''They mean no harm,'' the young-looking Bink said. ''The Zombie Master is our friend. His creations don't try to hurt living folk, and we don't try to hurt his folk. We just prefer to exist apart from them.''

How well she understood! But the zombies weren't letting her live apart from them.

The two men stepped out to intercept the two zombies. "What is your business here?" King Dor demanded of them.

"Bzeenna," one replied, spitting out part of its tongue.

There was no doubt of their mission: to fetch her back to Xeth.

"She does not wish to go with you," King Dor said. "You must leave her alone."

"Bzeenna," it repeated. It tried to push on past. King Dor spread his arms and blocked it.

Breanna shuddered. The thought of physical contact nauseated her. She was coming to understand that the zombies were entitled to their own lifestyle, if that was what it could be called, but she couldn't stand to be part of it.

Several more zombies were converging from other parts of the beach, and the roc bird wasn't back yet. Now she was surely done for!

"The island is appearing," Justin said.

"The Isle!" Breanna repeated. "Oh, thank you, Justin!"

Bink turned to glance at her. "Justin?"

In her excitement she had spoken the name aloud. There was no help for it now but to tell the rest of it. "He's a tree. He's with me, sort of. He gives me good advice."

"I know Justin," Bink said as he fended off his zombie. "We have been neighbors for a long time."

"True," Justin said.

"Well, the Isle of Women is appearing," Breanna said. "We'll have to get in the boat together. I think there's room."

The roc bird reappeared. King Dor signaled it, and pointed to the boat. The roc nodded and came down for a landing. Prince Dolph reappeared. "Zombies all over," he reported. "Dozens of them."

"Maybe we better link hands," Breanna said. "The dock—just link hands!"

King Dor and Bink shoved their zombies back, then turned and took the hands of Breanna and Prince Dolph. Together they stepped on the dock. The zombies followed, not yet quite there.

Suddenly all of them were sliding along the dock as if it were a slippery chute. They sailed off the end and landed together in the boat. The boat bounced, then started moving.

Two zombies stepped on the dock, and slid along it. They fell into the water behind the boat. They splashed helplessly. Breanna almost felt sorry for them.

"Water can't kill them," Justin said. *"They are already dead. They will wade back out."*

Breanna was relieved. She was getting more insights into zombie nature than she had ever cared to have, but slowly the recognition that they were after all people of a sort was gaining ground. She could almost wish them well—if only they would leave her alone. Dropsy—what kind of a woman had she been, in life? What kind of a woman was she *now,* apart from her awful undead status?

Meanwhile the boat picked up speed. It had no paddles and no engine, yet was propelling itself smoothly through the water. The dock was shrinking behind, and the Isle of Women was expanding before.

The young-seeming Bink looked over the side. "What propels this boat?"

"I don't know," Breanna said. "In fact, I'm not sure why this boat is here. When I went to sleep it was gone."

"It must have returned while you slept," King Dor said reasonably.

"That's for sure," the boat replied. "I dumped that mean man on the Isle of Blobs and came back to home base."

Breanna looked around, startled. "Who said that?"

King Dor smiled. "My talent is to talk to the inanimate, and have it respond. The boat responded."

She looked at the boat. "Oh. Yes. Can I ask it a question?"

"Go ahead, black beauty," the boat said.

"What makes you go?"

"My duck feet, dummy. What else?"

"The inanimate is too stupid to be polite," King Dor remarked.

"Yeah," the boat agreed with gusto. "So I can peek up under your skirt and blab the color of your—"

"Stamp on it," King Dor advised.

Breanna lifted one foot and stamped hard on the deck. The boat was silent. But she wrapped her skirt more closely about her legs, so that nothing was visible from below. The irony was that she was proud of the black underwear she wore, but she was not about to have a piece of wood think it was getting away with a sneak peek.

"I had forgotten what fun Dor's talent is," Justin remarked. *"Girls do have to watch their skirts."*

"What do you mean, 'fun'?" she demanded silently.

"No offense intended, Breanna, but seeing under skirts or into shirts is one of the great male pastimes. Your best strategy is to pretend to be unaware of it. That preserves your innocence even if something accidentally shows."

"Even underage skirts and shirts?" she asked sharply.

"You are very mature in outlook and poise. They obviously regard you as a young woman."

She pondered, and concluded that that was best. Justin had once again found a persuasive way to frame his insight. It wasn't as if she didn't already know that men were hopelessly juvenile in certain respects. "Okay. Anyway, it was the boat that tried to peek, not the men."

"They are all honorable. Still, it is probably best not to put them in an awkward situation. Their good wives would be upset."

"For sure." She kept her knees together.

"It is nevertheless a fault that can give women great power over men. The sight of an uncovered bosom—"

"You mean breasts?"

"To be sure. And the surprise glimpse of well-filled panties can freak out an army. Keep that in mind for emergencies."

"I'll do that," she agreed.

Meanwhile the boat was rushing toward the island. Breanna decided to risk another question to the boat. "Who set you and the dock up here?"

"The women of the Isle, dodo. So princes can cross."

What a contrast between Justin Tree and this dead wood! "Princes?"

"Only women and princes can cross to the Isle of Women, idiot. Because it is entirely populated by women who want to marry princes and spend the rest of their lives in comfortable leisure. Everyone knows that."

"Now that's interesting," Bink said. "Our group just happens to consist of a woman and three kings or princes."

"Darn right, stupid. Otherwise I'd have dumped you on some other isle. Those are my orders."

"So it wasn't just timing that messed up Ralph!" Justin said. *"He wasn't a prince or a woman."*

"For sure he was neither princely nor female," Breanna agreed sourly.

"Maybe the boat knows what Ralph wouldn't tell you."

"Say, yes! I'll ask." Aloud, she said: "Boat, do you know why the Isle of Woman may not help me escape the Zombie King?" But as she spoke, she got it: "King! He's a king! So he can follow me!"

"For sure, splinter-head," the boat agreed smugly.

King Dor shook his head. "If the Good Magician told you that the Isle would solve your problem, then it will. He always knows."

"But sometimes a person has to help herself somewhat, also," Bink added. "Perhaps Humfrey meant that you could find the solution to your problem on the Isle of Women. You assumed that the Zombie King could not follow you there, but that's not the rationale."

"That must be it," she agreed. "So my quest is not yet done. But how will I know what to do there, to save myself?"

King Dor considered. "You are helping us to reach the isle, so perhaps we can help you to fend off the Zombie King. Actually that may help put the zombies to rest before the wedding, so we may have a common mission after all."

"We do want to make sure that the wedding is not yours," Bink said.

"These are good men," Justin reminded her. "It would be expedient to accept the offer with thanks."

"Gotcha." Aloud, she said: "I thank you most kindly for the thought. Justin Tree appreciates it too."

"That's right," King Dor said. "Justin is with you. But if I may inquire, why is this?"

"He wants to have an adventure, but he's getting sort of old to return to human form. So it's a deal: I got my answer in exchange for giving Justin a ride in my head. He sees and hears what I do. It's a vi—vi—"

"Vicarious."

"Vicarious adventure for him. Too bad it's from the female perspective."

"By no means, Breanna. I am enjoying the experience."

"But he says he doesn't mind. And he does give good advice."

''Surely so,'' King Dor agreed. ''I am glad he has this opportunity to experience human life anew.''

The boat caught up to the island shoreline, but didn't slow. Suddenly it rose from the water. All five occupants (counting Justin) were astonished. ''How can a boat go on land?'' Prince Dolph asked.

''With duck feet!'' Breanna said, realizing. She leaned over the edge to peer under the boat. Sure enough, there were multiple pairs of orange webbed feet.

''But where is it going?''

''To the paired dock, blockhead,'' the boat replied. ''So the women can check you out.''

The boat ran on, carrying them inland. The island seemed ordinary, with trees, fields, and houses. There was a well-worn path with no obstructions for the duck feet. They pattered swiftly along.

"Well, now we know why there were no paddles," Justin said.

They came to a pond. By the pond was a dock like the first one. The boat ran into the water and paddled across, coming to a halt by that dock.

''It seems we have arrived,'' Bink said, standing and stepping onto the end of the dock. King Dor followed.

It was Breanna's turn. She stood, then hesitated. To get on the dock she would have to take a wide step, giving the boat a chance to peek and make an embarrassing remark.

''I believe the step is steep,'' King Dor said. ''Dolph, if you would lift the lady up—''

''Oh, sure,'' Dolph said. ''By your leave, miss.'' He put his arms under Breanna's shoulders and knees, and lifted her sedately up. He passed her up to King Dor, who set her onto the dock.

''Awwww,'' the boat said, before Prince Dolph stamped on its hull.

At the end of the dock a small group of women stood. Breanna hadn't noticed them before; they must have arrived in the past moment.

''Hello,'' a lovely young woman in furry halter and shorts said. ''I am Voracia. I will be your guide, until you marry appropriate women and depart the Isle. You are of course three princes.''

''Three kings,'' King Dor said. ''However, we have not come here to find wives, as we are already married.''

''What?'' she asked, horrified. She looked severely at the boat. ''Didn't you verify marital status?''

The boat sank somewhat in the water. ''I forgot.''

Voracia was grim. ''Well, you're here now. So you will simply have to provide three of us with princely husbands in lieu of you. Only when you have accomplished this will you be allowed to leave the Isle.''

King Dor evidently was not accustomed to being addressed in this manner. ''I think we shall leave when we choose to leave, when our mission here is done.''

''No you won't. The boat won't take you.''

He gazed at Voracia. ''We can fly from here.''

''No you can't.''

Prince Dolph assumed the form of a winged man. ''I think we can,'' he said. ''This is not the only form I can assume.''

Voracia frowned. ''I suggest that you try it.''

Prince Dolph spread his wings and flew up into the air. He spiraled high, looked around, then flew back down to the ground. ''Xanth is gone!'' he exclaimed.

''Gone?'' King Dor asked.

''We have erased the interface between Xanth and the Isle of Women,'' Voracia said. ''You will go nowhere, because you will have nowhere to go—until we restore the interface.''

''So there, numbskulls!'' the boat exclaimed from behind them. ''Ha, ha, ha!''

Breanna felt guilty for getting them into this mess. ''This isn't right,'' she said. ''They're just helping me.''

Voracia turned to her. ''And whom might you be?''

''Breanna of the Black Wave. I'm here to escape being married to a Zombie King.''

''Zyzzyva can handle that. I'll call her.''

''Who is Zyzzyva?''

''She's our zombie member. She—''

''No way!'' Breanna cried. ''I'm not going near any more zombies! I'm trying to get away from them.''

Voracia shrugged. ''Well, then, let's get you settled. Then we can see about the three princes here.''

''Three kings,'' King Dor said.

''Whatever. Maybe we can persuade you to dump your present wives and marry three of us. That would settle your accounts nicely.''

''I don't think so,'' King Dor said.

Voracia gazed at him. "Not even if I show you my talent?"

"Don't ask her talent," Justin warned.

"What's your talent?" Prince Dolph asked, once again seeming to speak before he thought. Breanna knew how that was.

"This." Suddenly she was standing before them in lacy white bra and panties.

"This is mischief."

"For sure." Because all three men froze where they stood, staring at the woman. Breanna had to admit that Voracia was impressive; both items of apparel were very well filled.

"You will have to rescue them."

"Right." But then she discovered something weird: her own eyes were fastened on Voracia. They were starting to lock in place. "Hey! What's going on here? *I'm* not fascinated by the sight of a woman's undies."

"You're not male."

"Oh, no! *You*, Justin?"

"Me," he confessed. *"I see though your eyes. When you focused them on—"*

"Oh, for screaming out loud! Look away, Justin."

"I can't. But you can. They're your eyes."

Oh. He was right about that. She wrenched her eyes away, and felt Justin's presence relax. He had been a tree for a long time, but recent experience must have attuned him back to the human state, making him vulnerable. Now it was up to her to rescue the others similarly.

Breanna stepped in front of King Dor, breaking his line of sight. She put her hands on his shoulders and turned him away from the compelling sight. He relaxed; then she stepped in front of Prince Dolph. When she had him free, she did the same for Bink.

"What's the matter?" Voracia asked, sounding concerned.

"As if you didn't know!" Breanna snapped, turning back to face her. "You stunned them with your unmentionables."

"But I was only showing my talent," the girl protested. "Which is to change my bra and panties to any style or substance." Her outfit turned into blue halter and shorts, then into striped tank top and slacks. "When I was a child, not so long ago, I thought I had no talent, because I didn't wear those particular items. Then one day—"

"You mean those are the same things?" Breanna asked, amazed.

"Yes. I can even turn them into armor." Now she wore woven metal uppers and lowers. "But that's sort of heavy, so mostly I keep it simple."

The kings were turning around again. "So your halter and shorts were actually—?" Prince Dolph asked, his eyes starting to sweat.

"Yes. It's all the same." Voracia appeared in a string bikini whose strings threatened to snap at any moment.

"Get a load of that!" the nearest stone exclaimed. "You can string me along any time, honey."

"Don't do that!" Breanna cried as Prince Dolph began to fall like a petrified tree. "You're freaking him out."

"Oh." Voracia changed to a jacket top and heavy culottes. "I didn't realize. I've been so long on the Isle of Women, seeing no men, I just forgot. When he asked my talent, I just—I'm sorry."

"I'm not," the stone said. "I wish I were a stone man."

"I'm happy the way I am," Voracia's halter said.

"What?" Voracia asked, looking around.

"It's my talent," King Dor said quickly. "I talk to the inanimate, and it talks back. Just ignore it."

"Oh, how delightful! But I apologize for showing you anything you would rather not have seen. I meant no harm."

She seemed genuinely penitent, though Breanna had about a forty percent share of doubt.

"I understand women try things on men, just to make sure they work," Justin said. *"So it may be half innocent."*

Breanna thought about the way she had sort of shown off to Justin, before the mirror in the Good Magician's castle. Just because she could get away with it, being physically alone. She had claimed to be informal because they were sharing awareness, but there had really been more to it than that. Part of her wanted to hide her assets; another part wanted to advertise them. "I guess," she agreed. Then, aloud: "Well, if you are to be their guide, keep it in bounds."

"It's almost like an aspect of the Adult Conspiracy. Bounds have to be set, to protect the innocent."

Good point. It wasn't always best to do what a person could do, just because she had the chance. The sensitivities of others had to be considered.

"Here is how it works," Voracia said. "Every woman on this

island intends to marry into royalty. Unfortunately there are many more of us than there are royal visitors, so we have set up a roster based on a complicated set of rules it would be tedious to elucidate. Those at the top of the list get the first choices, and as they get placed, others rise to take their places. So at present I am number one on the list. Thus I get to associate with the prospects, and to interview them, to see whether any are right for me.''

''Well, they aren't,'' Breanna said. ''So you can just forget about that aspect.'' She realized that she was starting to pick up words like ''aspect'' from Justin Tree. She liked his influence; it made her seem more adult.

''We shall see.'' Voracia's outfit turned momentarily translucent. Breanna's doubt about her innocence increased to sixty percent. However, it wasn't convenient to challenge it right now. ''But first, as I said, we should get you settled, Breanna.''

"Translation: she wants you out of her hair, so she can be free to vamp the kings without interference."

''For sure.'' Aloud, she said: ''Thank you.'' Voracia wasn't the only woman who could mask her private agenda.

''Let's see that string again,'' the stone said. ''I want to develop a String Theory.''

''You will have the house left by the last woman who trapped, I mean succeeded in finding her prince. It is a good residence. Right this way.'' She turned and walked away from the pond.

Most of the other women had faded back. But two remained. ''Ahem,'' one said assertively.

''Oh, how nice to see you, Claire,'' Voracia said with artificial sparkle. Her clothing turned smoky for an instant.

"Translation: Get lost, Claire. This hunt is mine."

Breanna giggled, then quickly stifled it. ''You're a good judge of women, Justin. That's exactly the way it is.''

''Since there are three prospects,'' Claire said firmly, ''three of us may see to their welfare. Since I am number two on the list, I qualify.''

''Do you ever!'' the stone agreed.

''And I am number three,'' the other woman said. ''So I also qualify.''

''Yes, of course,'' Voracia said. ''Thank you so much for reminding me.'' Her outfit flashed metallic with spikes. She turned back to the kings. ''Normally we see only one male visitor at a time, so it has been a while since the protocol has been invoked. Three of you are entitled to three guides. This declarative female is the Demoness Claire.''

''So very pleased to meet you,'' D. Claire declared. ''Especially if any of you have an inclination to be blissfully freaked out for days at a time. I can be extremely accommodating when I wish to be, and I would wish to be for a prince.'' Her body seemed to expand here and here, and contract there, becoming suggestive of an hourglass.

''We really have no wish to be—'' King Dor started. But Claire's whole form, body and clothing, turned smoky, and the smoke coalesced to form a tightening body stocking around a body no mortal woman could match. King Dor's eyes and jaw began to glaze.

''Stop that!'' Breanna said, stepping between them. ''This isn't the time.'' Not that there would ever be a time.

''My apology,'' Claire breathed. She was very good at breathing. Her garment thickened just enough to enable the men to resume their own breathing.

''I love the view from here,'' the stone said. It was on the ground near Claire's feet.

"These women are dangerous," Justin observed. *"They have no intention of letting three kings escape."*

''And this is Nefra Naga,'' Voracia said, indicating the other woman.

"Really dangerous. Prince Dolph almost married a naga princess."

''Hello,'' Nefra said. She had very dark brown hair framing a small heart-shaped face with large aqua eyes. She wore an aqua dress trimmed with dark brown, so as to accentuate her features. ''I was at your wedding, Prince Dolph.''

Prince Dolph looked startled. ''You were?''

''I thought you were going to marry my cousin Nada Naga, who didn't love you, but instead you married Electra, which I think was a good decision.''

''You *were* there,'' he said, still surprised. ''I didn't know she had a cousin.''

''I was young. Nada's Aunt Nera fell in love with a human type guy named Nathan, and I'm their daughter Nefra. Because I am part human, I have a magic talent, along with the normal naga abilities. I have the talent of switching.''

''Switching? You mean with a switch?''

She laughed. ''How clever! No, I can switch any two things, including talents.'' She looked around. ''Like this.'' She gestured, and suddenly the rock switched places with a small nearby tree.

''Hey!'' the rock cried out. ''I can't see the sights from here.''

''You have already seen more than enough of Voracia and Claire's legs,'' Nefra said. ''You don't need to see mine.''

''I didn't want to see your legs. I wanted to see your tail.''

''If I assumed snake form now, I wouldn't be able to return to human form without showing way more flesh than I ought.''

''Yeah,'' the stone agreed.

Nefra returned to Prince Dolph. ''So you see, I have no designs on you or your father or grandfather. But if I am not your guide, I will be replaced by someone who *does* have such designs. So I thought it best to keep my place.''

"Nefra is all right," Justin concluded.

''I guess so,'' Breanna agreed with less conviction.

''I think you're here under false pretenses,'' Claire muttered darkly.

''I was almost related to Prince Dolph by marriage,'' Nefra said. ''I'm not going to betray a family connection.''

''Exactly.''

''Now if we can resume travel,'' Voracia said with a slight edge. ''The house is this way.'' She walked along a path.

Soon they came to a pleasant little log cabin in a glade. ''Oh, that looks sweet,'' Breanna said, falling instantly in love with it.

''Go on in,'' Voracia said, ''See how you like it. In due course someone will come to explain the intricacies of our listing system to you, so that you can get in line for a prince to marry.''

''But I'm only fifteen,'' Breanna said. ''I don't want to—''

"Maybe best not to tell them that," Justin warned. *"Lest they evict you from the island."*

Good point. ''Don't want to be pushy,'' she concluded. She opened the door and entered the house.

It was small but beautiful inside. There was a table with two chairs, a pretty rug on the floor, a nice little kitchen alcove, a bathroom alcove with a basin and potty, and a bedroom with a queen-sized bed. ''Why so big, for one person?'' she asked Justin.

"One established way for a woman to prevail on a man to marry her is to share her bed with him. Therefore it needs to be large enough for two."

"Oh," she said, blushing. "I knew that."

Stairs led up to a storage attic where there was a chest with extra blankets. There was a window opening onto the back, with the island shore in sight.

All in all, it was very nice. She would like it here. But first she needed to figure out how to prevent Xeth Zombie from coming to share that bed with her. The zombies had traced her to this area, and surely Xeth was on the way now. The boat would bring him here, because he was royal. So she might not have much time. Maybe just one day, until the isle interfaced again with Xanth.

But the three kings had agreed to help her solve this problem. Maybe they could share the house with her, until the crisis passed. She would go out and invite them in. She would be glad to give them the bedroom, and she could take the attic.

She opened the door and stepped out. And looked around, dismayed. The three kings were gone. Everyone was gone.

"But they wouldn't just have deserted me like that, would they?"

"Of course not," Justin said. *"But I think I can fathom what happened. The women of the Isle preferred to be free of you, because you interfered with their designs. So when you were out of sight, one of them showed her panties, freaked out the men, and carted them off to another section."*

"But what of Nefra Naga? She had no designs on them."

"So she said. She might have simply been trying to reassure you and the kings, the better to close the trap. Such subterfuge is not beyond the capacity of the gender."

"Translation: women can be bitches," she said bitterly.

"Perhaps I am being unduly suspicious."

"No, I don't think so. I just got myself suckered." She looked around. "But they can't have gone far. I'll get out there and find them."

Then she glimpsed something walking through the forest. A shiver of sheer horror ran through her. "Justin! Is that what I'm afraid it is?"

He looked through her eyes. "I very much fear it is. A zombie."

"He's here already!" she yelped. "They must have sent the duck boat back for him immediately.'' She dived back into the house and slammed the door. There was a set of braces and a bar on the inside. She slammed the bar into place, locking the door.

Then she ran for the back door, and barred it too. But by that time she heard something at a window. She ran up and slammed shut its inside storm shutter, and barred it. Then she hurried to do the same for the other windows.

Breathless, she surveyed the situation. The house seemed to be secure for the moment. But she was trapped inside it. ''How am I ever going to get out of here?'' she asked. ''To get something to eat? To dump the potty? I don't want to be a prisoner here forever!''

"I am not sure. Perhaps the kings will realize your predicament and come to your rescue."

''If the greedy women don't keep them perpetually freaked out until they forget they're already married. That Voracia has the potential, and that Demoness Claire's no slouch either. And if Nefra Naga's in on it too, they could be lost.''

"I do fear the possibility. It may be that they will need your aid more than you need theirs."

''Oh, damn, Justin, this is awful! This island was supposed to be the answer, not the problem.''

"Agreed. This is more of an adventure than I anticipated."

Then she heard something at the door. It was a faint bumping or scratching. It was the zombie, trying to get in.

She went to the door. ''Go away! Go away! I'm not going to marry you!''

The reply came faintly: ''Listen. We must talk.''

''We've already talked! I won't marry you! Go away!''

There was a pause. ''I'm not the king.''

''So you're one of his minions. I'm not going with you. Go away!''

Another pause. ''I am Zyzzyva.''

"That's the one Voracia mentioned. The zombie female who lives on the Isle."

''I don't care who you are!'' she yelled at the door. ''Go away!''

"You are becoming hysterical."

''I have a right to be hysterical!'' Breanna screamed. ''The zombies are going to get me!''

"There may be another interpretation."

''I don't want an interpretation! I want no zombies!''

"Breanna, think for a moment. All the women on this island want to marry princes. Who would Zyzzyva want to marry?"

"A zombie prince, of course. She—" Breanna froze. "Oh, my, Justin! Is it possible?"

"I think you should talk to Zyzzyva and find out. She might be your salvation."

"But I don't want to get near any zombie! They freak me out."

"I appreciate your concern. I was not overly fond of them myself, when I was human. But I think this could be what the Good Magician had in mind. Not your physical escape from Xeth, but your emotional escape. If he found another love."

"I think you're making sense. But I just can't bring myself to—oh, God, I'm a bigot, aren't I! I hate this." She discovered that her face was wet with tears. "What am I going to do, Justin? I just can't face her."

"Perhaps I can face her. Will you let me use your mouth?"

"My mouth? You mean like my eyes? You could talk?"

"I think so. If you allow it."

"Try it," she said, and released her mouth.

"Hello," her mouth said. It sounded like someone else.

She grabbed it back. "You did it! You can talk!" Then she let go again.

"I can talk," he agreed. "So I can talk to Zyzzyva. If you allow it."

"If you can take care of this, you can have any part of my body you want."

"But you will have to let her in," he said.

Breanna nerved herself. Then she walked to the door and unbarred it. She pulled it open.

"Please come in, Zyzzyva," Justin said. "We shall talk."

"Thank you." The zombie woman stepped inside. She was in much better health than Breanna expected; her decay hardly showed. That meant she had been caught soon after dying. Zombies seemed always to be decaying, but actually remained as they were when zombied. That should mean, in turn, that her brain was pretty healthy too. Her clear speech suggested that.

"Offer her a chair by the table. You can sit with the table between you."

Breanna was surprised for half an instant, then realized that of course he could still talk in her mind too. And she would much rather have the table between herself and the zombie, than nothing between them.

She walked to the table, pulled out a chair, and let her mouth go. "Please sit down," Justin said. "There are things we must explain."

"Thank you," the zombie repeated. Now Breanna noticed that the woman wore a metallic skirt and armored halter, and there was a small helmet on her head. A short sword hung by her right side. She was a warrior lady! She must have been killed in battle. No wound showed, but maybe that was closed up when she got zombied.

They sat at the table. "I am Justin Tree," her mouth said. "I am with Breanna of the Black Wave. She was kissed awake by King Xeth Zombie, but that was a confusion. She does not wish to marry him. The Good Magician Humfrey sent her to the Isle of Women, where she is supposed to find her reprieve. Do you understand?"

"Yes," Zyzzyva said. "That is why I came here. I was a warrior lass, but I died in action. The Zombie Master found me almost immediately, and revived me as a zombie. I decided I wanted to settle down and live as normal an existence as I could. My talent is consistency, and I wanted to settle down in life, so it remains my ambition in half-life. But no ordinary man would consider me. So I came here, hoping for my chance. But I am low on the list."

"So you would like to marry King Xeth?"

"Yes, that would be ideal. But I fear some other woman will get him first. I know that he wants to marry a living woman, and all the others here are fully alive. But I am the best preserved of zombie women, so I think I could accomplish what he wishes. So when I learned that he might be coming here—"

"I doubt many other women would care to marry a zombie," Justin said. "Even a zombie king."

"Some might. But if I could somehow intercept him, and persuade him, then he would never come here." Zyzzyva hesitated. "Unfortunately, as a warrior maiden I was never very good at romance. So it might not work."

"I could teach you!" Breanna burst out, grabbing possession of her mouth.

Zyzzyva glanced askance at her. "Your voice seems to have changed. Perhaps my perception has deteriorated."

"No it hasn't," Breanna said. Now that she had actually done it, she found it wasn't that hard to talk to the zombie. After all, she had talked to Xeth. "Justin was speaking for me, because I—well, never mind. I see you are a person, different from me, but still a person. Some folk don't like to associate with me because of my color, and I don't like that, but I guess I have my own prejudices. But if you can win Xeth's love, and marry him, then I'll be gloriously free. I think I can tell you how to do that. After all, he is a man."

"I would be most grateful if you would."

"Come on," Breanna said, getting carried away. "Most of what you need to know is this: men like to see where they shouldn't. So if you can show him your—you do have panties?"

Zyzzyva stood and lifted her metal skirt. Under it she wore metal panties.

"Will they do?" Breanna asked Justin.

"Yes, I believe so. They are quite competent. Now please avert your eyes."

Oh. Breanna pulled her eyeballs away. Obviously the panties *were* competent. They should have that much more effect on a zombie male. "Okay, the other part of it is how you act. You have to sort of look him in the eye and smile, and tell him how handsome he is. And if he grabs for you, the way men do—let him."

"But I always slew any man who grabbed for me."

Which was surely part of her problem. "Control the impulse. This time you want to—to let him have his way with you. Then he'll be yours forever. That's how it's done."

Zyzzyva hesitated again. "I spoke somewhat blithely of intercepting and persuading him, but that was my militaristic nature talking of a campaign. Now that I contemplate actually doing it, I am afraid."

Breanna stared at her. "You're human!"

The woman smiled wanly. "I am a human zombie. My living capacities are only slightly diminished. Unfortunately my living liabilities also remain. I fear that I will—will—"

"Will mess up?"

Zyzzyva nodded. "So maybe this is not a good idea. I'm sorry I bothered you." She turned toward the door and took a step.

"No you don't!" Breanna cried, going after her and grabbing her hand.

Zyzzyva whirled. A short sword appeared in her other hand. It glinted as it swung toward Breanna's neck. Breanna froze, horrified, unable to react in time to save herself.

The blade stopped just short of her flesh. "Oh, I'm sorry," Zyzzyva said. "I reacted automatically. You must never grab a warrior."

"Uh, I'm sorry," Breanna said, shaken. "I—I just—I just didn't want you to go. Because I still think I can show you how to do it."

"Do you really? Despite seeing how I react when touched?"

"That's rough, I confess. But there must be some way. Justin, what do you think?"

"Perhaps if she could still think of it as a military maneuver. The correct reaction could win the day."

"What correct reaction?"

"Perhaps a passionate kiss."

"Now I gotcha." Breanna returned her attention to Zyzzyva. "He says you can still be military. You can still react when touched. But instead of cutting off his head, kiss him. Can you retain your reflexes to do that?"

The woman considered. "Different situations require different reactions. I should be able to do that. It's as if to vanquish him, my weapon is a kiss instead of a sword."

"Right! Think of him as a demon. If you cut off his head it will just turn smoky and reform. But if you kiss him, you score."

"I will try," Zyzzyva said bravely.

"Rehearsal may be in order."

"Lets rehearse it," Breanna said. "Fortunately we've got a man here. Justin can use my body and grab you, and you kiss him instead of killing him."

"But it remains your body. You don't want to be kissed by a zombie."

That set her back. But Breanna hardly hesitated. "I'd rather be kissed by one than marry one."

So they tried it. Breanna stepped outside the door, then came back in. "I am King Xeth," her mouth proclaimed. "I am looking for Breanna of the Black Wave."

The armored woman turned to face the intruder. "I am Zyzzyva. You are really handsome."

Justin looked past her. "Where is Breanna?"

"She is modeling for you at the moment."

"Oops."

"Let try it again," Breanna said. "This time don't forget to bat your eyes and show your panties."

"Hit my eyes?"

"Sort of blink them at him. Like this." Breanna demonstrated.

"I will try," Zyzzyva agreed, abashed. "Eyes, panties."

Justin entered again. "I am King—"

"Hello, handsome." Zyzzyva lifted her skirt.

Justin's eyes locked on. He strode across the room and grabbed her by the shoulder.

Zyzzyva drew her sword. Then she froze. "Darn!"

"Practice makes perfect," Justin said with Breanna's mouth. "That's why we have rehearsals: to ensure that the real case is perfect."

The zombie woman nodded. "Not this," she said, sheathing her sword. "This." She stepped into Breanna and kissed her firmly on the mouth.

Breanna froze. She had never been kissed like that by a woman before. Justin took over. He reached down and stroked the woman on the bottom. Breanna felt Zyzzyva stiffen, then relax, accepting it.

They separated. "I think we are making progress," Justin said. "That was very nice, Zyzzyva. Now let's see if we can do it without miscue."

Both women were silent, so Justin acted. He walked toward the door and opened it.

There stood Xeth Zombie. Oh no! Breanna, freaking out, lost volition. But Justin handled it. "Come in," he said, and stood aside.

"Thank you," the Zombie King said. He stepped through the doorway.

There before him was Zyzzyva. She looked startled, but quickly recovered her military discipline. "Hello, handsome," she said, smiling.

Xeth hesitated. "Who are you?"

"I am Zyzzyva Zombie." She batted her eyes fetchingly. Then, remembering, she lifted the hem of her skirt. "I would like to marry you."

"So far, so good."

"I am King Xeth Zombie," he replied, advancing with his eyes fixed on that hem. "You seem remarkably well preserved."

"I was zombied only minutes after I died. I am the healthiest zombie female."

"Your flesh does look firm." He reached for her, but hesitated. "Still, I don't think any zombie female can—"

She stepped into him and kissed him. Now his hand fell to her bottom, exactly as Justin had demonstrated. Zyzzyva melted against him.

"Perfect," Breanna said silently.

The two zombies ended their kiss. "You are strangely attractive," Xeth said. "But I need a living woman, to—"

"I can do it!" Zyzzyva said passionately.

"But I am promised to—"

"I release you!" Breanna cried.

Still he was doubtful. "I don't know—"

"The bedroom is this way," Zyzzyva said, urging him toward it. "I have so much more to show you." She touched her metal bodice.

"Let's leave the house to them," Justin said.

"For sure," Breanna agreed. She stepped outside the open door, and closed it behind her. She felt wonderfully free.

10
Gals Galore

Bink watched Breanna enter the house. He was sure she would find it satisfactory; it looked very nice from outside. So she would have a place to stay. But they still needed to prevent the Zombie King from coming to the island.

"We have something to show you," Voracia said.

Bink looked at her. She stood with Demoness Claire and Nefra Naga. They were all remarkably lovely young ladies.

Then, acting in concert, they acted. Nefra changed to her serpentine form and slithered out of her dress. Then she changed back to human form, stunningly naked. Claire's clothing turned smoky and drifted away in the breeze, leaving her voluptuously nude. And Voracia's outfit reverted to its natural state of pink bra and pink panties, both tightly filled to overflowing. All three of them had perfect figures. All three smiled and batted their eyes and made a synchronized high kick with one bare leg. Then all slowly turned around in place, displaying every facet of every curve.

Bink was freaked into immobility. He had been married a long time, and seen Xanth's most beautiful woman in all states of dishabille, but this sudden surprise frontal assault by three lovely creatures caught him unprepared. It was a case of instant overload and male circuit blowout. He knew that his son and grandson were in the same state. The women of the Isle had sprung their trap the moment the three kings had been deprived of the protection of the girl.

"Take them to the retention pool," Voracia said without moving from Bink's locked view.

Women appeared from all over. Bink couldn't look directly, because he could not turn his head, but his peripheral vision showed them, and he heard them behind. None crossed in front of him, for that would have interrupted the freaking view.

He was tilted onto a cart and pushed still standing along the path, following the three exposed women. It was clear that this procedure had been carefully choreographed; there were no mistakes. Probably they had used it on other reluctant men. It was a system designed to see that no living prince escaped the island without being firmly married to one of its women.

In due course they reached the retention pool, which seemed to be an empty cavity covered by a flickering layer of light. Bink felt a prickling across his body as that membrane passed across him. Then he felt quite peaceful, as if all were right with the universe. But he still couldn't take his eyes off the three exposed women walking in front. They were just as fascinating from behind as in front. That was the magical thing about women: they could capture the male attention from any angle. Only their normal use of clothing allowed any men to function with reasonable efficiency.

At the bottom of the pool the wagons stopped. Then at last the three women covered up. Voracia's bra and panties thickened into halter and shorts and lost much of their compulsion; D. Claire's form was shrouded in smoke that became an appealing but not overly exposive dress; and Nefra donned her normal clothing.

Bink relaxed and rubbed his smarting eyes. He saw after images of flexing buttocks. He had had an overdose, and it would take his orbs time to recover fully. He looked around.

He was in a half formed chamber whose walls rose only to waist height, demarking rather than enclosing it. In it were two chairs and a bed. Nothing else. He saw that Dor and Dolph were in similar chambers.

He walked to the half doorway, but stopped. It was open, but some invisible panel balked him from leaving. He walked around the chamber, and found that similar material enclosed it. He climbed on a chair and reached upward. Sure enough, there was an invisible ceiling. He was confined.

He was not unduly worried, because he knew that these magical constraints could not harm him. But Dor and Dolph did not have his kind of protection, so it was better to share their fate for now.

Voracia approached the chamber. She walked through the doorway with no trouble. She sat on one of the chairs, gesturing him to the other. "I have decided that you, being the youngest, are my most appealing prospect," she said.

"I'm not young."

She shrugged, making her halter ripple. "Have it your way. Marry me, and we will leave the Isle of Women forever."

"I'm already married. You know that."

"You will have to renounce her. I will be your wife from here on."

"Never."

Her halter fuzzed into the bra, which of course it was all the time; only its appearance changed, to make it less evocative when she wished. Her short trousers remained. Thus her body was not completely compelling, but was a good deal more than indifferent. "There are certain things you must understand, Bink. No man leaves the Isle without marrying one of us; the only uncertainty is which one. If I am unable to persuade you, the others must have their turns. You will remain here until you accede to one. Your best course is to make an early agreement, so as not to be confined for a tedious period."

"I married Chameleon fifty six years ago. She has been an excellent and loyal wife. I will not renounce her."

She eyed him coolly. "Fifty six years. That is a very long time for a man who is twenty one years old."

"I was youthened. I am actually eighty one years old."

Voracia shrugged. Her bra became translucent. He tried to keep his eyes clear of it, but they were magically drawn to that translucency. "Then you are old enough to be realistic about your prospects. I doubt that you will encounter a better prospect for a wife than me."

"I won't encounter *any* prospect. I am already married."

Her bra became fully transparent. His eyeballs creaked in their sockets as he tried vainly to wrench them away. "I have a certain amount of time to make my case with you. If I do not succeed, I will have to give way to the next woman, who is D. Claire, unless she has already married one of the others. I think you would prefer me, all things considered, to the demoness. For one thing, only my clothing changes, not my actual body. You might find that reassuring." She took a deep breath.

Fortunately Bink's mouth was not incapacitated the way his eyes were. ''It is not a question of preference. I am not marrying any of you.''

She sighed. That was a considerable effect, considering her bare-seeming front. ''I see I shall have to use stronger persuasion.'' She stood and stepped toward him.

Bink tried desperately to look away, but his eyes were glued to her front, and their surfaces would have peeled off if he hauled on them too hard. He tried to stand, but she got there first and sat on his lap. She put her hand under his chin and lifted his head. He tried to resist, but felt strangely weak. ''There is a peace spell on the retainer pool,'' she explained. ''You can move and speak, but you can't become violent or resistive.''

''But that will not make me marry you.''

She angled his head until she could kiss him. He tried to deny it, but the fact was that her lips were very nice. He was lucky that these women hadn't discovered lip bomb. After a moment she broke it off. ''Now if you care to, we can adjourn to the bed, where I will delight you excruciatingly. Then you will be obliged to marry me, having by your action renounced your prior wife. That is really the easiest way to do it.''

''I'm not going to do it.'' But it was very hard to be sure of that. Would his talent consider seduction to be harmful?

''If you resist me, and the other women, we will then commence the second round. You will be given food and a pitcher of water. You may eat freely, but when you drink, you will commit.''

''Why?''

''Because the pitcher will contain love elixir. Whatever woman is with you at the time you drink will become the object of your insatiable affection. But she may not be your best partner. So you will be better off to choose for yourself, before thirst chooses for you.''

They really seemed to have it figured out. But they did not know that his talent was to be invulnerable to harm by magic. His talent seldom showed itself directly, but it was always effective. It had made it plain in bygone times that the loss of Chameleon was considered harm. So there would be some unusual coincidence that freed him from this marriage trap. Assuming his magic wasn't satisfied to have him be seduced and be quiet about it. That notion continued to unsettle him.

And of course, he reminded himself again, his talent did not necessarily protect his two companions. They were both younger than he, so probably more vulnerable to the temptations of revealed flesh. Thus it was probably better not to wait for his talent, but to find some better avenue for all three of them soon. He had to keep reviewing that, lest the distractions of the flesh make him forget. Voracia's firmly heaving flesh was almost touching his face, and that was about as distracting as it could be.

''If you do not respond in a moment, I will change my lower garment,'' Voracia murmured. It was no empty threat.

But what better avenue was there? He was trying to think, but that invisible bra right under his nose was beguiling him something awful.

''You asked for it,'' she said, and her trousers shrank into a tight blue panty. His eyes couldn't move, but her plush bottom was on his lap, and he could feel the change of color as well as of material.

But her ploy failed, because now he was unable to move or speak. He just sat there, staring.

''Time's up,'' a voice from outside the chamber called.

''Curses!'' Voracia cursed. She reformed her outfit into something relatively demure and got off his lap. ''Remember: you can still ask for me, if you wish.''

Then she was gone, and Claire was there. She did not sit on his lap; she simply picked him up with demon strength and laid him on the bed. She began to unbutton his shirt.

''Objection!'' someone called. ''Woman is not allowed to undress prospect. She has to persuade him to do it himself.''

Claire looked furious, but desisted. She lay down beside him, and kissed his face. Her lips made his mouth seem to float up to the ceiling and burst into a spectacular array of flying colors. ''You surely know how much fun a demoness can be, when she wants to be,'' she said. ''And when you marry me, I will get half your soul, which will make me have some decency and conscience, so that I won't leave you or otherwise embarrass you when you annoy me. So I can give you continuous delight unmatched by any ordinary woman, who would of course in time grow old and wrinkled.'' She kissed him again, as her dress fogged into nothingness.

''Sorry,'' Bink said, when she allowed him to speak. The rest of him felt as if it were floating up to rejoin his lips. ''I'm not marrying you.''

"Not even if I let you do this?" she inquired, taking his hand and bringing it to her bare breast.

"Objection!" a voice cried. "She's not allowed to make him do that! He has to do it for himself."

Claire's eyes fired out tiny sparks, but she let go of his hand. "So do it for yourself," she suggested, inhaling.

Somehow he managed to resist her charms, though it was teasingly difficult. She left him quivering with frustrated longing, but did not break his resolve. It had been shaken and dented and battered and kissed, but not actually broken.

Then she was gone, and Nefra was with him. He took some solace in the realization that this meant that neither Claire nor Nefra had prevailed against Dor or Dolph either. But the two other kings were surely weakening. There had to be a better way out!

"I'm sorry I had to deceive you," Nefra murmured as she lay beside him without clothing. "But we had to get that Black Wave girl out of the way; she was interfering."

That reminded him of Breanna. "What happened to her?" he asked.

"Prince Xeth Zombie arrived. None of us high on the list wanted him, so we guided him immediately to the house so that he could win Breanna."

"But she was trying to escape him!" he exclaimed. "That's why she came here!"

"Well, she let him into the house, and they have not emerged, so perhaps she changed her mind."

"You betrayed her too!" he accused her.

"I love it when you show emotion," she said, and planted a fierce kiss on him.

"It's negative emotion."

"That's all right. I'll take that for now. Would you like to rape me? That counts the same as a seduction. I promise not to resist effectively."

"Just get out of here!" he gritted.

In time she did. She was replaced by a more ordinary girl, fully and decorously clothed. "I am Loni," she said. "What color do you think my hair is?"

Surprised by this approach, he sat up and studied her hair. "Brown.

No, red. No, green. No—'' he was confused. ''I can't decide what color it is.''

''That's my talent: folk can't agree what color my hair is. I admit it's not much of a talent, but by the same token I am no threat to you. If you marry me I will obey you in all things, and do my very best to please you always. I would just love to be a princess.''

''I'm sorry. I'm not free to marry anyone.''

Her face clouded up, and so did her hair. ''But—but this is my only chance! It may be months before another prince comes to the Isle!''

Bink realized that she was young. He put his arm around her heaving shoulders, trying to cheer her. She turned into him and gave him a wet kiss. And he realized that whatever her age, she was just as determined and artful as the others. So he steeled himself and resisted her blandishments of whatever nature.

The next woman was small and elfin. ''I'm one of the Brown Knees,'' she said. ''See?'' She spread her knees as she sat on the chair. Sure enough, they were nice and brown. But in the process, she showed him well up under her short skirt, and he knew that she, too, was doing her best to seduce him in a hurry. He managed to blink his eyes closed just before they reached the freakout region.

The next was Molly Coddle. ''I just love children!'' she said brightly. ''I hope to get a dozen delivered.''

There had to be some way out of this! But the women were addressing him continuously, using every kind of artifice, and he couldn't concentrate.

''I am Lasha Lamia. I can create cloudstones.'' She demonstrated, forming a stone so light that it floated, yet was hard enough to use for construction. ''I could help you build a nice, light castle, that you could pick up and move when you wanted a change of scenery.'' She leaned forward, showing the scenery inside her loose blouse.

It was neverending! He was holding out, but how long could Dor or Dolph survive? Especially Dolph, who really was as young as he looked.

''Woof! I'm a real bitch.''

He looked startled. It was a dog—a talking female dog. ''How did you get in here?'' he asked.

The dog became a cat. ''I told them you might like a pet feline. How do you like me? I am Catrana. I'll purr if you stroke me.''

He stroked her, and she purred.

Then she became a teakettle dragon. ''I can be any creature you like,'' she hissed. ''Marry me, and be perpetually entertained.''

Oh—another demoness. ''Sorry, I don't need to marry a talking pet.''

''Oh, phooey,'' she swore. ''It worked for my friend Vera Similitude, with her two dogs Disa Pointer and Up Setter.'' She started unlacing her bodice. ''I'll never disa point or up set you.''

The next was tall, thin, and ugly. ''I am Tipsy Troll. I know you won't like me, so I'll shut up for my time and give you a chance to rest.''

''Bless you!'' he exclaimed, and kissed her.

She was so surprised she fell backwards onto the bed. This wasn't artifice, because she lay absolutely still and silent, letting him rest.

Now that he had a chance to think, a good thought came: what these women wanted were princes or kings. But there weren't enough in all Xanth to accommodate them all. But there were enough in another realm: Ida's moons. Because every person who ever existed, or would exist, or might exist was there. There should be hundreds of perfectly good princes who would love to have experience with women of real Xanth. If there were just some way to make contact.

And there was! Dor had saved that jar of sleep potion. They could go to those dream worlds and find princes, and—and what? The princes would not be able to leave their dream realm, and the women would not be able to go permanently to Ida's moons. Unless the Zombie Master found a way for his zombies to go, and—no, because the zombies' bodies would remain buried in Xanth. Real folk couldn't be buried like that. They would have to sleep on beds, and wake every so often to eat and exercise.

Tipsy got up. ''My time is done,'' she said sadly. ''I hope you enjoyed your respite.''

She was a decent woman. Suddenly he wanted to do something for her. He couldn't marry her, but maybe he could help her. ''Don't go,'' he said.

''Oh, but I have to. My time is up, and the Vine cousins are next.''

''Vine cousins?''

"Clinging and Bo Vine. They—"

"Stay," he said firmly. "I can't marry you, but maybe I can find a prince for you. And the others. I want you to stay and help me work this out."

"But I can't. My turn—"

Bink faced the door, and saw the line of women waiting there. "Tipsy Troll is staying with me, for now. We're looking for a way to find princes for all of you. Now back off, or I won't do it."

Surprised, they backed off. Bink turned back to Tipsy. "Here's the thing: I know where there are hundreds of princes, and I know how you can meet them. But I don't know how you can marry them."

"Oh, we'll make them marry us, if we catch them. At least those of us with formidable figures will." She glanced disparagingly down at herself. "Where are they?"

"On Ida's moons."

She looked blank. "Where?"

"Princess Ida has—" He paused, realizing that this could get complicated, and they might not believe it. "I'll show you. Then you can tell the others. Go to King Dor and ask him for the jar of sleep potion."

She nodded. She left the chamber, and returned soon with Dor himself, and his woman of the moment: Davina. She looked, reasonably enough, like the neighbor woman. Then came Dolph, with his woman: Fiona. She looked like the girl next door. But surely she was old enough, or she wouldn't be here.

"I realized what you were up to the moment she asked for the sleep potion," Dor said. "And I knew we had to come with you, so as to be together and stay out of mischief. But the women won't let us go alone."

Bink nodded. "We can do it with six people. I don't think there's a limit on the size of dream parties. Then the women can report on what we find."

Dor looked at the bed. "We'll need more space to sleep."

"Exactly what is happening here?" Davina inquired suspiciously.

"He's got an idea," Tipsy said eagerly. "To find hundreds of princes. I believe him."

Fiona shrugged. "I can live with an idea like that."

With that reassurance, the others soon dragged three beds out into the main area of the pool and put them together. Then the three men lay down on them, and the three women insisted on lying beside each of them.

Dor handed the jar to Voracia. "Give each of us a good sniff of this, then close the jar. And leave us alone until we wake. This may take a few hours, but may be worth it."

Except for the problem of the impermanence of contact, Bink thought. He would have to discuss that with the others while they traveled. But right now they had to handle the practical aspects of the visit. "You three women—hold our hands when you see us in the dream. This will be a wild trip for you."

Voracia unscrewed the lid and gave them sniffs. Each in turn sank immediately to sleep. Bink was the last.

When he slept, he found himself floating above the pool. The others were waiting for him. They all linked hands, and floated rapidly toward Castle Roogna. On the way Bink started to explain. "We are going to visit some very small worlds. But each is as big as Xanth when we get there. They are very strange. Stay close to us, and don't get alarmed. Remember, we are all dreaming."

The three women nodded, already impressed. "It was never our intention to let you out of our sight," Fiona said.

The ghost at Castle Roogna spied them and summoned Princess Ida, as before. She smiled and went to sleep, and they homed in on Dream Ptero.

"Oooo!" Fiona exclaimed as they fell toward the rapidly swelling globe. "It's growing!"

"Magic is different on this planet," Dor warned them. "Don't accept any favors from the natives, or you'll be diminished."

"No, that's Planet Pyramid," Dolph reminded him. "On Ptero they exchange favors."

"Nobody wants to exchange favors with me anyway," Tipsy muttered. Bink was to the right of the others, and she was holding his right hand, so was at the end of the line.

"You don't seem *that* ugly," Bink said. "I'm sure that by troll standards you are beautiful."

"Not so. I'm only half troll, actually; my father was human. He caught my mother in a net and trussed her up and signaled the stork with her and then departed. She was furious, but by the time she got free of the net there was nothing to do but go hide under a bridge. The stork found her anyway, to her chagrin. I'm homely by both troll and human standards, and not welcome among the trolls because of my polluted ancestry. So I thought I would marry a human man, but discovered that they didn't want me either. So I figured no one would notice on the Isle of Women, because there are so few men seen there anyway.''

''So you were just going through the motions, pretending to want a prince,'' Bink said.

''We'll, I'd marry a prince if he wanted me. But let's be realistic. If a regular man doesn't want me, why should a prince?''

Bink saw her point. Still, she seemed like a nice girl, when allowances were made. ''You're half human? Do you have a magic talent?''

''Yes, but it doesn't do me any good. It's the cold shoulder.''

''You mean you can ignore people?''

''No, I mean I can make my shoulder cold. Feel it.''

Bink let go of her hand and touched her shoulder. It was cold. ''I suppose that wouldn't make you comfortable to sleep beside,'' he said.

''Well, it's not cold all the time, only when I turn it on.''

''Can you make it hot too?''

''No, only cold. I seldom bother.''

''Does it make you shiver?''

''No, that doesn't bother me. But I guess the heated exchange from my shoulder makes my heart hot, and I hate being hot-hearted while cold-shouldering folk.''

The ground of Ptero was now rushing up, and they had to concentrate on their landing. But Bink continued to think about what he had learned. Tipsy had a warm heart, which no one appreciated. She had already done him a favor by giving him time to think instead of constantly trying to seduce him. She wasn't pretty, but she would be good for any man who cared about character more than appearance. That was of course the problem: he knew of no men like that. Even he himself liked Chameleon much better when she was beautiful than when she was smart.

They landed. The girls were surprised: ''There's no bump!'' Davina cried.

"This is a dream, remember," Dor reminded her. "But it will become more solid as you get used to it."

"I think it's fascinating," Fiona said. "I love dreaming like this."

"Now where can we find some princes?" Dolph asked.

"We'll have to ask," Dor said with regret. "That means exchanging a favor."

"Maybe that tower will know," Tipsy suggested, pointing to a nearby tower that seemed to be made of eyeballs.

Dor considered. "I wonder whether eyeballs are animate or inanimate? I can talk to them if they are the latter."

They went to the tower, which turned out to be huge. Big solid eyeballs braced the four corners of the base, and smaller ones were piled up to a towering top, where a single monstrous eye stared around.

"You can talk to it and see whether it answers," Bink suggested.

"What are you?" Dor asked it.

"I am the Eye-full Tower," it replied. "I see everything."

"Can you see where a number of princes are?"

"Certainly. Do you want to know where they are?"

"Yes."

"What service will you exchange for that information?"

"Well, I can talk with the inanimate."

"I can see that, old man. Now what will you exchange?"

"What do you want?" Dor asked.

"I want to get rid of that club soda that lurks too close."

They looked, but saw only a sparkling pool. "Where?" Dor asked.

"Go drink some soda and see."

"I'm thirsty," Davina said. She knelt and dipped a little cup into the soda. She sipped it.

Suddenly she was flat on her back. Fiona rushed to help her sit up. "It clubbed me," Davina said dizzily. Tiny planets whirled around her head.

Now Bink appreciated why the Eye-full Tower might not appreciate having the pool so close. Any splashing would get an eyeball clubbed.

But how could they move a pool? It happened to be in a hollow, with the land rising in all directions.

"I could push it somewhere," Dolph said. "If it were solid."

"I can make it solid," Tipsy said.

Dolph looked at her. "How can you do that?"

"Like this." Tipsy rolled back her sleeve so that her shoulder showed. It looked faintly blue, oddly. She lay down so close to the edge that the bare shoulder overlapped the pool. She angled her body so that the shoulder touched the surface of the liquid.

A film appeared on the pool, spreading out from the point of contact. Soon it thickened. "Hey, I'm cold!" the pool protested.

"That's ice!" Bink exclaimed. "From the cold shoulder."

The ice reached across the pool and penetrated to its base. "I think it can be moved now," Tipsy gasped.

Dolph changed into a bull dozer, perhaps inspired by the one they had seen on the Isle of Bovines, put down his horns, and pushed. The ice slid out of the hollow in one thick disk. Dolph shoved it on across the landscape, until it went over a ridge and slid down the far side, away from the tower.

"Now, if you care to tell us where those princes are—" Dor said.

"Fair enough. Follow the direction of my gaze to the horizon. There you will find Prince Town, where all the unemployed princes are getting educated. But you will have to cross more than one comic strip on the way."

"Thank you," Dor said. He oriented on the direction the towering eye was looking.

But the others were not quite ready. Fiona had gotten Davina to her feet, and the tiny planets had faded. But Tipsy remained on the ground. Bink went to her. "May I help you up?"

"Don't touch my shoulder," she gasped. "You'll freeze."

So he reached down and put his arm around her waist. It was quite warm. He lifted her, and she fell against him. Her chest was burning hot. No wonder she was gasping. It had been a considerable heat exchange.

"How can I help you?" he asked, concerned.

"No, I'll be all right when I even out." But she seemed to be in real distress. That amount of heat exchange must have stressed her system to the breaking point, even in a dream.

"How can I help you?" he repeated.

She blushed, but that might be another effect of the heat. "If you could stand to—to kiss me—"

He kissed her. Heat flowed from her face to his, warming him throughout. It wasn't physical heat, but emotional warmth. Because her heart was hot. She needed release from the agony of unrequited warm-heartedness.

He held her while her body returned to normal. Her shoulder warmed up and her bosom cooled. "Thank you," she murmured at last.

"Thank *you,*" he replied. "You enabled us to get the information we need."

They set out for Prince Town. Dolph could have changed form and carried them, but might have confused the direction, so they stayed on the ground.

Soon they came to a comic strip. "I think we had better mark our direction carefully and fly over this," Dor said grimly.

"Why?" Davina asked. "It looks like an innocent border."

The three men sent a glance circling around. They shrugged. Some things were best learned the hard way.

They stepped onto the strip. There was a pretty flower in the shape of a stomach. "Oh, what a pretty posy!" Fiona said, learning forward to sniff it.

"Wait!" Dor said sharply. "What is that?"

"That's a cute gastritis," one of several nearby crosses replied. Each of them was garbed in a dress. "Sniff it and you'll have one heaven of a stomachache."

Fiona jerked her head back. "Thank you for the warning, cross dressers," she said.

Suddenly a swarm of bright red ants crossed in front of them. Wherever they stepped, fire broke out. "Those fire ants are ringing us with fire!" Dolph cried.

They retreated—and fell with several splashes into a foul pond of soapy water. "What is this?" Dor demanded as he struggled to get out of it.

"Lake Hogwash," the pond replied. "To wash pigs like you."

There were even toys floating in the dirty water. Bink grabbed one that was in the shape of a word: LET. It was attached to a string that disappeared into the murky depths. "What are you?" he asked.

"Isn't it obvious, sewer-breath? I'm a Toy Let."

It figured. But it could be useful. Bink jerked hard on the string.

There was a loud sucking sound, and the level of the hogwash descended.

"What did you do?" Tipsy asked as she fought to stay clear of the small whirlpool that was forming.

"I flushed the Toy Let."

Soon they were standing around the drain in the bottom. All the hogwash has been flushed.

They looked for a way to climb out of the empty pool. Dolph felt among several disks that were perched near the edge. "Quit that, you bleepity bleep!" a disk swore villainously. It was of course a disk cuss.

Fiona found a way that led through another pool, one that had not drained. But she hesitated to try it. A number of small bug-like creatures floated in it. "What are you?" she asked it.

"I'm a sep tic tank," it replied.

"Those are sep tics!" Bink said, recognizing them. "They live in sludgy bays. They'll suck out our minds in the filthiest way."

They finally found a shallow section and helped each other out. Here there were a number of elastic loops. Whenever someone picked one up, it played music. Since they were easy to pick up—they stuck to shoes and clothing—soon there was a discordant medley. "I hate rubber bands," Dor muttered.

Bink came up against a clump of big-leafed plants. They bore fruit that hung down and pointed up. "Eat me!" the fruit begged.

Tipsy reached for one. "I am suddenly hungry," she said.

Bink stopped her. "Wait till we get out of the comic strip. Those fruits will drive you crazy."

"Why? What are they?"

"Bananas."

Meanwhile Fiona had brushed a huge toad. "Oooo, I'm going to fight the whole world!" she cried, looking for a weapon.

Dolph grabbed her and looked at her hand. "I thought so: you've got warts."

"Let go of me!" she raged. "I have battles to fight."

But Dolph got a piece of cloth and scrubbed at her hand until the warts came off. Then she relaxed. "Those were WARts," he explained. "They make you go to war."

"Oh," she said, abashed.

Tipsy saw a nice-looking pillow. "Maybe I'll sit on that and rest," she said.

"First let me check," Dor said. "What are you?"

"Sit on me and find out!"

"Don't get fresh with me. What are you?"

"Awww. I'm a pun cushion."

"I don't think you want to sit on that," Dor told her.

Bink kept his mouth shut, though he was curious what would have happened. It might have made jokes about getting to the bottom of things. Or bad smelling puns might have erupted beneath her.

The far side of the comic strip was close. They lunged for it, but a nasty little canine creature growled and menaced them. "Pay no attention to it," Dolph said. "That's a pet peeve. My sister Ivy used to have them all the time."

They charged by the peeve and burst out of the strip. They were in sad shape, with their clothing stinking wet and torn. The three girls had their hair straggling in assorted tangles, and their faces were smudged.

"We need to get cleaned up," Fiona said. "I see a pool over there."

"Why clean up?" Dor asked. "This is only a dream."

The girls circled a glance that said "Men!" Then Fiona spoke again. "All the same, we want to be clean—in and out of the dream."

"That's a cess pool," Dolph said innocently.

Fiona looked as if she had gotten another wart. But Tipsy spied a better prospect. "There's a well."

They considered the well. "What kind of well are you?" Dor asked it.

"Midas well," it replied.

"Might as well," Dolph agreed, and started lowering its bucket so as to haul up some water.

But Dor was more cautious. "What does your water do?"

"If you touch it, it turns you to gold."

Suddenly the girls lost interest in the well. "But we still must clean up," Fiona said desperately.

Then Bink saw a big bow. It had huge pretty colorful loops of ribbon, and several big arrows. "I believe that's a rain bow," he said. "That should do it."

He picked up the bow, and fitted a white arrow to it. ''I forget which color does what,'' he said, ''But we can try them all.'' He looked at the girls. ''You'll need an enclosure.''

''Why?'' Davina asked.

''So you won't freak us out as you strip to wash.''

She nodded. ''Point made. If you freaked out, we might be stuck here with no escape. But what is there to make an enclosure?''

''What is there?'' Dor asked the surroundings.

''Ahem.'' It was an oval sign:

''Content ahead?''

''Go find out,'' the sign said.

So they walked in that direction, and found a huge tent made of corn. It had a number of sections, and it was possible to draw on the corn silk strands to open the top to the sky. ''This will do,'' Davina said. ''It's corny, but sufficient.''

''But there's no water,'' Fiona protested.

''The rain bow arrows will make rain,'' Bink explained. ''I'll fire them over the tent. Just say when.''

The three entered the tent. In a moment items of their clothing were strung up over the edge of the enclosure. ''When!'' Davina called.

Bink fired the white arrow. As it passed over the tent, a sprinkle of rain came from it.

''Is that the best you can do?'' Fiona called.

Bink fired the blue arrow. A mild shower descended.

''That's better,'' Davina said. ''But we could use more.''

So he fired the red arrow. A wild torrent poured from it. ''Eeeeek!'' the three cried. ''It's cold!'' Onc of them jumped so high that enough of her showed to put a temporary freak on Bink's left eye. Dor and Dolph were watching too, but neither complained. Bink wondered which one they had seen. It wasn't the kind of thing he felt free to inquire about.

Soon they were done. Their clothing remained wet, but it was clean.

"Now it's your turn," Fiona said. "We'll fire the arrows."

So the three kings had to go in and strip, and soon they were drenched by the rain arrows. But they got clean. They put the wet clothing back on and emerged.

Tipsy looked at them. "That's better. Now we can meet the princes."

Davina turned to Dor. "The next comic strip we come to—fly over it!" she said severely.

The men smiled. The point had been made.

They got their direction and resumed travel. When they came to the next comic strip boundary, they made sure of their direction and then Dolph changed form and carried them all over it.

Finally they came to Prince Town. This was protected by thickly tangled ivy vines, some of them leagues long. Dolph flew them over, and they landed in a nicely laid out pattern of streets, buildings, and parks.

"Girls ahoy!" someone shouted.

Immediately they were surrounded by princes. They ignored the kings and focused on the women. But soon that focus narrowed to Davina and Fiona; dull Tipsy had been tuned out.

She rejoined Bink. "Even in a dream, I can't get the attention of a prince," she said with resignation.

"But you're a fine person."

"I think we've already been over that."

"A problem has occurred to me," Dor said. "How can living Xanth women marry dream princes? The two realms don't overlap in reality."

"That bothers me too," Bink said. "I was hoping we would figure out a way."

"I can think of something that might work," Tipsy said.

They turned to her. "If you can do that, we'll be in your debt," Bink said.

She smiled sadly. "But you can't marry me, even if you wanted to. So forget it. Here is my notion: maybe we don't need to have the realms overlap. All we need is to have plenty of that dreaming potion, so the women of the Isles can visit Prince Town whenever they want. They can marry princes here, and do whatever they want with them, and when they want to rest, they can simply wake up and be where no man can bother them. Most of them would appreciate that, though they wouldn't say so in mixed company.''

Dor nodded. ''That sounds good, for the women. But wouldn't the princes object?''

''I think they would be glad to see the women any time the women appeared. Apparently they are a long way from Princess Town. And they probably need time for their studies. So they might like half time too, especially since the women would be coming with romance in mind. I understand that men do have other interests, like jousting and gambling and watching nymphs run, that they don't necessarily care to share with women.''

Bink nodded. ''Astute assessment. Let's put it to the princes. Would they like part-time marriages to lovely women?''

They discussed it with the princes, and it turned out that the princes were indeed interested, provided they got to pick the women themselves. Davina and Fiona already had commitments from suitable princes. In fact they were not yet ready to wake; they had hot dates in mind.

So Tipsy Troll returned with the three kings. They simply went outside of Prince Town, held hands, and concentrated on waking up.

They woke in the retention pool. Davina and Fiona remained asleep. But Tipsy was able to make the report. ''In short,'' she concluded, ''every woman can have a prince in a dream marriage, without leaving the Isle. The princes are eager to meet all of you. All you need is the sleep potion and a place to lie down.''

The others were not convinced. But they released the three kings to roam the Isle while the matter was being settled. When Davina and Fiona woke, they would compare notes.

But Bink hesitated as they departed the pool. ''What of you, Tipsy?'' he asked. ''There doesn't seem to be much for you in Prince Town.''

''There's not much for me anywhere,'' she said sadly.

An idea had been simmering in the background, and now it moved hesitantly forward. ''Would you consider marrying a non-prince?''

''I'd marry anyone who wanted me. But no one does.''

''How about a man who molds things into other things?''

''Sure.'' It was significant that she didn't qualify her agreement, or ask whether the man was handsome or nice.

''I know a man who wants a wife. In fact he agreed to tell us something we want to know, if we bring him a wife from the Isle of Women. His name is Phil Istine. He's not a prince."

"But he wasn't thinking of a troll."

"But I think he might settle for one, with a bit of management."

"All right."

"Then stay with us. We must find Breanna and make sure she's all right. Then, when the women are satisfied with the dream princes, we can leave the Isle, and take you along."

They set off on the path toward the house Breanna had entered. But before they had taken many steps, there was Breanna herself coming toward them.

"Are you all right?" Bink and Breanna called together. Then they laughed, together.

11
Isle of Wolves

"I came out of the house, and you were gone," Breanna told the three kings. "I was afraid something had happened to you."

"Something did," King Dor agreed. "But we worked it out. What of you?"

"Something happened to me too, but now it's all right. King Xeth has found a good zombie woman to marry, and they are addressing the stork now. So I don't have to stay here after all."

"We'll be glad to take you home when we leave," Prince Dolph said. "Which should be soon."

"Thanks! I'm glad things are okay." Then she noticed that there was another person with them. "Hello. I'm Breanna of the Black Wave."

"I'm Tipsy Troll. I'm going with them too."

Breanna was surprised. "Not—?"

Tipsy laughed. "Not married, no. But they think there's a man there who will marry me."

"Oh. Okay." And of course she had known that none of the kings would have married any woman of the Isle.

"Indeed they would not," Justin Tree said. *"But I suspect that they have quite a story to tell, if they care to tell it."*

Breanna made a mental note to be sure to ask for that story, when the occasion seemed propitious. Then she thought of something else. "Justin, I guess my adventure is just about over, now that I've escaped marriage to the Zombie King, thanks to your help. So I guess that means we'll be parting company soon.''

"I confess that is a sad occasion for me. You have been fascinating company."

''And you have been great. I really needed your guidance.''

"But of course you have your own life to live now, and do not need any further intrusions."

''I guess.'' But she was dissatisfied. ''Justin, I know you have had enough of teenage girls by now.''

"As if there could ever be enough of them."

''Do you think maybe—I mean, if you don't have something better to do—you could maybe, sort of, well, stay around a little longer? Of course you don't have to—''

"I do not wish to impose, Breanna. I fear my presence limits your lifestyle. You have given me a fine adventure, and I can't complain."

''I wish you'd stay.''

She felt his surprise.

"You are not merely being polite? The Good Magician did say a year, or until we mutually agreed to end it, but of course I would not hold you to such a term."

''I'm being more like desperate. I think I don't want to go back to nothingness just yet, and that's what it'll be. But maybe I could sort of hang around with the three kings a while longer, and that's bound to be interesting. But I don't really know them, and you do, so if you could tell me what to do—''

"I would be glad to, Breanna. I am gratified that you are not yet tired of my presence."

''I'm not tired of it! I couldn't've made it without you.''

"I thank you for that sentiment."

They walked to the dock. There was the duck-footed boat. ''Will you take us back to the mainland?'' Dor asked it.

''Sure, when the women say it's okay. When the Isle interfaces again.''

''But that won't be until tomorrow,'' Breanna protested.

''No, that's the automatic cycle. The women can change it when they want to, to let an impatient prince in, or to take a married one out with his bride. We can go when Voracia says it's okay. She should be along in due course.''

"That's great," Breanna said, though she was speaking more for the kings than for herself. This did not seem like a bad isle, now that she had settled with Xeth.

They sat down to wait for Voracia. And while they rested, they exchanged stories. Justin's surmise turned out to be correct: the women had pulled a dastardly stunt, and only some good breaks and good thinking had gotten them out of it. Exactly as it had been for Breanna herself.

Voracia came down the path. "We're setting up the interface," she told the boat. "Take them back to Xanth." She glanced at Tipsy. "You're going too?"

"Yes. They think there's a man for me."

"Good for you. We've got dream princes galore. Davina and Fiona confirmed it, and will show us the way there."

They got into the boat, and it paddled across the pond and ran up onto the path on the other side. They were on their way.

They reached the shore, and the boat splashed into the sea. There was Xanth, as she gathered it had not been until the women set up the interface.

"Now may be a propitious time to raise the matter . . ."

Oh. Yes. "Uh, you said you would take me home."

"Yes, of course," King Dor said.

"Could you maybe wait on that? I mean, I'm grateful, but I'd sort of like to stick around with you a while, if that's not too much trouble."

King Dor glanced at the others, who nodded. "Certainly, Breanna. You have been of real help to us, and we appreciate it. We suspect that our own adventure, such as it has been, is about done, but you will be welcome to remain with us until it ends."

"Gee, thanks." She stifled a tear; she really appreciated their generosity. They were all good men, as well as being kings, unlike that bad Ralph.

They reached the other dock and disembarked. There were a few zombies wandering desolately around. "Oops, there's something I should do," Breanna said.

"We can keep you from the zombies," Prince Dolph said. "We'll simply fly away from them."

"No, I'm tired of running from problems." Breanna walked boldly up to the nearest zombie. "Hello. I'm Breanna, the one you've been chasing. But you can go home now, because your King Xeth has found love with Zyzzyva Zombie instead, and will marry her. They'll be returning here in a day or two, I think. Do you understand?"

The zombie seemed surprised. "Underzdand," he repeated after a suitable pause for cogitation.

"Good enough. You stay here to welcome them when they come." Then she extended her hand.

After another pause, the zombie extended his hand. Breanna grasped it firmly and shook it, not hard. It felt somewhat slimy, but she gave no sign of disgust. She had conquered her fear of zombies.

"Good for you, Breanna!"

Then she returned to the kings. "Okay, that's done."

Dor was talking with the duck-footed boat. He looked up as Breanna returned. "We have made a deal. It will be days before Para needs to service the Isle of Women, because their interest is now on dreams. Voracia will call if the boat is needed sooner. So we will exchange conveyances."

"So the boat is Para, with the two docks," Justin remarked appreciatively. *"There can be more meanings in a name than one expects."*

"Yeah, every time you figure you know something, there's more you don't know."

"I don't understand," Tipsy said. "I thought that man was near here."

"No, he's some distance south," Bink said. "But we feel there is one thing you need before you meet him. So we shall fetch it now."

"I don't mean to be any trouble," Tipsy said.

"They don't consider it trouble," Breanna said.

"They're nice people." She had come to know the troll-woman somewhat while they waited to cross back to Xanth, and knew she was warm-hearted. "You helped them; they're helping you."

King Dor, Bink, Tipsy and Breanna got into the boat again. Prince Dolph changed into a roc bird. He caught up the boat in his huge talons, spread his wings, and took off. Breanna saw that it was definitely easier to be carried in the boat than it would have been to be clutched by bare claws.

"Wheee!" the boat exclaimed, wiggling its feet. "I've been on land and sea, but never in air before."

"Me too," Breanna agreed, peering down as the land fell below.

"And me," Tipsy said, looking down the other side. "It looks just like a map."

"We're going to Mt. Rushmost," Bink explained. "For some lip bomb."

"A bomb!"

"You put it on your lips, and when you kiss a man, it just about knocks him out, in a pleasant way. We think that with that, you will be able to make an impression on Phil Istine."

Tipsy looked at Breanna. Breanna shrugged. "I haven't encountered this."

"I have. Long ago. It is a good ploy."

"But Justin says it's good," Breanna said.

Soon they came to a towering mountain. Dolph-roc glided to a landing at the edge of its upper plateau. He set the boat down, changed to manform, and jumped in as the duck feet got moving.

"We are looking for Karla, Sharon, or Chea Centaur," Dor said. "Or Serena girl."

"Go that way," the ground said, its voice moving in a particular direction.

They went that way, and came to an early evening fire where three winged monsters congregated. All of them were centaurs, and female.

"What, are you men back again for more punishment?" one of the centaur fillies demanded.

"I'm not a man, and neither is Tipsy Troll," Breanna said before it occurred to her that silence might be better.

"You're not winged, either," the centaur said disapprovingly.

"Karla, we come to ask another favor," King Dor said quickly. "We'd like to get some lip bomb for Tipsy."

The centaurs considered. "What use would a troll have for that?"

"She did us a favor, and now we want to help her get married. She's a good person. We think the lip bomb will enable her to make a suitable impression."

"Very well: we will give it to you. But you must demonstrate it on your two girls, so that they understand its nature."

"You mean, we must don it, and kiss our companions?" Prince Dolph asked.

"Exactly."

King Dor looked at the girls. "I don't know—"

But Breanna was curious. "Sure one of you can kiss me," she said. "I'll know you don't mean it, so it's no violation of the Adult Conspiracy, if that matters."

The kings looked doubtful, but didn't argue.

"All right," Tipsy agreed uncertainly.

Karla brought out a jar of red stuff. "Come here, King Dor," she said with a typically centaurian obscure smile. She took paste on her fingers and carefully smeared it on his lips. Then she did the same with Bink. "Now kiss them."

The king and the prince turned. Bink approached Tipsy, and Dor approached Breanna. "I apologize for the necessity," he said.

"Oh, at least pretend some enthusiasm," Breanna said naughtily. "It isn't as if I haven't been kissed by a king before."

He took her in his arms and put his lips to hers. It was sort of pathetic, that this middle-aged man thought his kiss could have any real effect. Then her mouth detonated, and she would have fallen spinning to the ground, except for the fact that he was firmly supporting her. Stars and planets careened in circles around her head. The experience was devastatingly pleasant.

She found herself limp in his embrace. "Do what you want with me," she murmured blissfully.

"Have no fear of that," he replied. "It is only a demonstration, as we agreed." He set her on her feet and let go, and she was able to stand somewhat unsteadily.

"That lip bomb is remarkable stuff," Justin remarked. *"Now I appreciate more fully why they believe it will help Tipsy Troll."*

"For sure. If Xeth had used it on me, we'd be married by now."

She looked around. Tipsy Troll was sagging against Bink, with little hearts floating up from her head. Obviously his kiss had been just as potent. "That's some stuff," Breanna repeated, awed.

Karla handed Tipsy the jar. "Now you know what to do with this," she said. "Go get your man."

"Now I know," Tipsy agreed dizzily.

"We thank you very kindly," King Dor said. "Perhaps you fillies can come to the big royal wedding next week at Castle Roogna."

"Oh? Who is getting married?"

"We don't know. But it will surely be a momentous occasion."

"We like momentous occasions," Karla said. "But we don't have invitations."

"I will try to get some made up for you," King Dor said. "We'll give them to you when you arrive."

The centaur frowned. "That's not exactly the way it is done."

King Dor shrugged. "I'm a man. I don't know any better."

"True. We'll try to attend."

"Ask Serena, Erica, and Aurora to come too," Prince Dolph said.

"We shall."

They got into the boat, and it ran toward the brink. The centaurs waved farewell, evidently intrigued by their mode of transportation. The boat charged right over the edge and dropped toward the distant ground. Tipsy and Breanna screamed.

Then Prince Dolph changed form, his feet grabbing the sides of the boat while his great wings spread and took up the slack. The fall became a rise. They were on their way.

"That was fun," the boat said. Breanna stomped a floor panel.

King Dor and Bink brought out handkerchiefs and wiped the remaining lip bomb from their faces. Breanna touched her own lips, where a trace of bliss lingered. She had had no idea that something like that existed. It was a devastating weapon in the war of genders, usable by either side. As it was, she had half a crush on King Dor, despite his advanced age.

They flew down to the ground somewhat south of the Isle. They landed, and Prince Dolph resumed riding in the boat. Soon they came to a man contemplating a loaf of bread. As they halted by him, the bread became a statue of a winged dragon.

"Phil Istine," King Dor said, stepping out of the boat. "We have brought you a wife from the Isle of Women."

Phil's eye fell on Breanna. "A black beauty," he said. "But isn't she about three years young?"

"Not me, white trash," Breanna retorted. "Her." She indicated Tipsy, who was carefully applying lip bomb.

"A troll moll?" Phil demanded incredulously. "I meant a human-type woman."

"She is half human," Bink said. "And a nice person with a warm heart."

"I don't care about her heart! She's a troll!"

"At least give her a try," King Dor suggested. "Kiss her."

"Why should I kiss a troll? It's no deal."

"Then let her kiss you," Bink said evenly as Tipsy got out of the boat.

Phil did not look pleased, but couldn't refute the logic because there wasn't enough to refute. So he stood disdainfully while Tipsy approached him and planted a hot kiss on his lips.

It was something to watch. The man fell back, spun three times around, and fell on the ground, leaving a trail of heart-shaped cloudlets. It would have been comical, if Breanna hadn't experienced such a kiss herself.

Tipsy went to help him sit up. "I'm sorry. I didn't mean to—"

"Okay, you'll do," Phil said. Then he glared at King Dor. "But still, she's a troll. That's only half a loaf. So I'll give you half a loaf in exchange: I'll just tell you who else knows where you live. Go to the king of the werewolves, in the Isle of Wolves."

King Dor did not look pleased, but Breanna saw that there was a certain logic to Phil Istine's decision. Tipsy was a nice woman, but she *was* a troll. With the help of the lip bomb she would surely make Phil about as happy as he deserved to be. Meanwhile, this meant that the three kings would need to visit another interesting place, and that Breanna would be able to enjoy their adventure a while longer.

Breanna went to Tipsy. "Could you spare a little of that lip bomb? I'd like to have it for an emergency."

"Certainly." Tipsy found a packet and scraped some of the red stuff into it.

"Thank you." Breanna put the packet away.

King Dor returned to the boat. "Can you take us to the Isle of Wolves?" he asked with resignation.

"Sure. It's not far from the Isle of Women."

"Very well. Please take us there now."

They got in the boat, and it padded toward the water, ran in, then paddled swiftly north.

Breanna looked back. There was Tipsy troll, waving. Breanna waved back, feeling a lump in her throat. They had gotten Tipsy what she most desperately wanted, a husband, but had they done right by her? The wrong man would be worse than no man at all, as Breanna's experience with Ralph had shown.

"Suppose Phil mistreats her?" she asked Bink. "I mean, some men are brutes."

Bink nodded. "I have a similar concern, though her talent of the cold shoulder could set him back if that proved necessary. That's one reason I decided to fetch the lip bomb. Can you imagine ever mistreating a man who kisses you with that?"

She pondered that. "No, I guess not. When King Dor kissed me, I would have done anything for him." She glanced in the king's direction. "Still would," she murmured.

Bink smiled. "The effect slowly fades. I was first kissed by Sharon Centaur, when we delivered Aurora Winged Mermaid there. I always liked centaurs and have had good relations with them, but I never saw them as romantic objects. That is—" he paused, awkwardly.

"I understand," Breanna said. "No storks."

"Yes. But when Sharon kissed me, I just wanted to please her. It wasn't the same as love elixir; I wasn't in love with her. But she seemed infinitely desirable, and if she had wanted to summon the stork, I would have found it harder to resist than I did when the Isle of Women tempted me. When I saw her again, I felt a thrill, as if we had been lovers, though we had not. If one kiss had such effect, what would several have? So I think Phil Istine will never mistreat Tipsy."

Breanna nodded. "You're a lot older than you look, and married, and Sharon is of a different species, but that bomb got to you. I'm too young and King Dor's too old, as well as being married, but if it were just the two of us in this boat, I'd be growing up real fast. So you're right: Tipsy's safe with Phil. I'm glad of it, because she's a good woman."

"Yes. Actually all the women of the Isle are good, just desperate. They treated us fairly by their lights."

"Just as you treat others fairly," she agreed. "You know, it's just chance that I met up with you, but I'm glad I did, and not just because it's a nice adventure. I'm learning a lot."

"It may not be just chance," he said.

"What do you mean? I was trying to escape Xeth Zombie, and you were trying to find your way home. Neither of us knew or cared about the other. I was even asleep when you arrived. So our paths crossed randomly."

"Let me see if I can explain. My life is less random than it seems, because of my talent."

"What *is* your talent, if it's okay to ask? They call you a king, which means you must have a Magician-caliber magic talent, but I haven't seen anything, no offense."

"My talent normally conceals itself from others," Bink said. "If I am able to tell you about it, it will be because you have some need to know. It is—" he hesitated, as if afraid something was going to stop him. "That I cannot be harmed by magic." He looked surprised. "And you must indeed have a need to know."

"I don't *need* to know anything. I'm just foolishly curious. Do you mean that if someone hurls a bad spell at you, it won't land?"

"More than that. No magical creature will do me harm, no magic plant will hurt me, no magic of the inanimate will act against me. But because someone might find a way to circumvent or nullify my talent if its nature were generally known, my talent conceals itself. So it usually acts indirectly."

"Fascinating," Justin Tree remarked.

"Suppose a dragon chomps you? That's pretty direct, and you'd need direct protection."

"Yes. So the dragon will not try to chomp me, or if it does try, something seemingly coincidental will interfere so that it doesn't happen. Another dragon might appear on the scene, distracting it, or it might fall in a hole it didn't see because it was looking at me instead of the ground."

"But then how can you tell that it is your talent protecting you? That it isn't all just coincidence?"

He smiled. "It protects me *through* coincidence. And few folk ever suspect. You can test this. Try harming me nonmagically."

Breanna was abashed. "Oh, I would never—"

"Not seriously. Just enough to ascertain that you could do it if you wanted to."

"Okay. I'm going to push you out of the boat." He was beside her on the seat. She put her hands against his shoulder and pushed. He tilted. She pushed harder. He was in danger of falling over into the water.

She desisted. "I guess I could do it, if you didn't fight back."

"Now try to harm me magically."

"But I don't have any—" Then she remembered the protection

racket. Was it still working? She tried banging her hand against the wooden seat, lightly, then harder, then harder yet.

"Hey!" the boat protested. "You're going to damage me!"

"Sorry, Para." The racket was working, because she had suffered no pain. She looked at Bink and raised her fist. "I have this magic protection, so I can hit without being hurt. Are you sure—?"

"Yes. Try to hit me."

"Okay," she said dubiously. She aimed a blow at his nose, but pulled her punch without touching him. "Bink, there's nothing stopping me. I can't do this to you."

"Do it," he said firmly.

So she aimed for his cheek and tried a light blow. It landed. "Bink, I tell you, there's nothing stopping me. I don't dare try to really—"

"Let me try it," Justin said.

"Okay." She relinquished control of her arm to him.

Her arm lifted, formed a tight fist, and shot directly toward Bink's nose.

The boat suddenly swerved, causing the fist to miss, and she sprawled halfway across Bink's lap. "Sorry," the boat said. "There was a piece of sharp wreckage I didn't see until the last moment, and I had to swerve. Usually I'm more alert."

Breanna picked herself up, unconvinced. "That was sheer coincidence."

"I don't think so."

"Let me try again." She addressed Bink, putting her right hand behind his head and lifting her left fist. "I'm going to hate myself in a moment," she said grimly. "But I've got to know." She shot her fist forward at his nose.

A large soft ball flew between them. Her fist punched into it, and it pressed against Bink's face, cushioning the blow so that he wasn't hurt. Where had the ball come from?

A snout poked out of the water. "May we have our ball back, miss?" the sea creature inquired. "Sorry it got in your way."

"Who or what are you?" Breanna asked it.

"I am a manatee," it said. "I was just playing a ball game with my family."

Three more snouts appeared. "I am his wife, the womanatee," a large one said.

"I'm his son, the boyatee," a smaller one said.

"I'm his daughter, the girlatee," the smallest one said.

A fifth snout appeared, rising into an animal head. "And I'm the Seal of Approval," it said. "Family games are good. You wouldn't want to interfere, would you?"

"Oh, of course not," Breanna said, embarrassed. She tossed the ball down to them.

The seal caught it expertly on its nose and flipped it to the nearest tee. The family game resumed as they swam away from the boat.

"Don't forget what you were doing," Bink reminded her gently.

Breanna considered. "I don't see how coincidence could stretch that far. That ball had to be deliberate."

"Yes. Not by the tees or you. By my talent."

"Okay, so you can't be harmed by magic. But that doesn't change the coincidence of our meeting. I could have come here any other day."

"On the contrary," Justin said. *"You were traveling because the zombie kissed you. The three kings were traveling because the zombies were stirred up looking for you. The events are connected."*

"I believe that we were required to interact," Bink said. "There must be some devious magical threat to my well-being, so my talent is acting to turn it aside by seeming coincidence. So it put us together, and is keeping us together. This adventure is clearly not yet finished."

"So my whole adventure is just to help you avoid some magical threat?"

"Not necessarily. My talent may simply be borrowing from what is most convenient. You were in the vicinity, so it arranged to have you join us. You certainly were helpful in getting us to the Isle, and in shielding us from initial problems with the women of the Isle. There may be more coming."

"Well, if that's why I'm here, I like it," she decided. "But what could threaten three Magicians?"

"It may not be a physical threat," Bink said. "It could be something that I need to get done, lest I be truly pained by failure to do so. I don't know what that might be, but perhaps it will be apparent after it has been accomplished." He paused, thoughtfully. "For one thing, Chameleon and I were youthened by sixty years, and there was surely reason for that. There must be something I can accomplish as a young man that I could not as an old one. I admit it's nice to be young again, physically, but so far I have seen no real justification for it.''

"It is a good question. Youth is not granted to folk just because they may want it. If it were, every living person would be perpetually young."

''I don't know. Being young doesn't seem all that great to me.''

"It is the nature of life to have unrealistic dreams. You should enjoy your youth while you have it."

''Maybe so.'' But she was unconvinced.

''Land ahoy!'' Prince Dolph called from up front.

''That's the Isle of Wolves,'' the boat said. It moved to shore, waddled onto the beach, and stopped. ''King Wolverton's den is down that path.''

''Thank you,'' King Dor said as they disembarked. ''I hope our trade of conveyances was worthwhile for you.''

''It certainly was,'' Para replied. ''I loved flying. And it was nice being able to talk aloud. And peering up under girl's skirts.''

''I kept my skirt close and tight!'' Breanna retorted hotly.

''But Tipsy Troll didn't, and her legs were pretty good, considering.''

''Well, good luck peeking under *other* skirts,'' Breanna said, mollified. She was discovering that this particular game could be fun to play, so her outrage was mostly for show.

They walked down the path, and the boat waddled to the sea and paddled smoothly away. On impulse Breanna turned and waved to it, and saw it rock from side to side, waving back.

"You are becoming more solicitous of others, including the inanimate," Justin commented.

''So?''

"I favor it."

Suddenly a wolf appeared. Its fur was metallic. It screeched to a stop when it saw them; the squeal came from its four paws scraping along the ground. Then it became a man. He was furry enough on the body to remain fairly decent. ''Who are you, and what do you want here?'' he demanded.

''We are three kings and a young woman, come to see King Wolverton.''

''How did you reach this isle? The interface is off.''

"We were conveyed by Para, the web-footed boat, from the Isle of Women."

"You couldn't have gotten away from there unmarried."

"We are married. The woman is beneath the age of marriage."

"Oh." The werewolf reconsidered. "I am Wolfram. Follow me." He resumed wolf form and loped back down the path.

Soon they came to a hill. A sign labeled it Wolverton Mountain. This was evidently the home of the king wolf.

Sure enough, a large wolf emerged from a den as they reached the top of the hill. He became a man. "Why, you are King Dor of Xanth," he said, surprised. "The one who makes things talk."

"You bet, bushytail!" the nearest stone called.

"Yes," King Dor agreed. "We accidentally drank some lethe water, and forgot where our home is. If you would be so kind as to tell us—"

"I'll be glad to—after you do a service for me."

"Listen, furface—" Breanna started.

But Justin cut her off. *"We are on their Isle. It is best to honor their conventions."*

"Of course," King Dor said smoothly. "What can we do for you?"

"You can talk my son Jeremy into doing his duty and starting training to assume the kingship when I pass on to that great other hunting ground."

"He doesn't want to be king after you?" King Dor asked, surprised.

"He is in a mottled funk, and doesn't want to do anything."

"Well, we'll talk to him," King Dor agreed.

King Wolverton led them to the mottled funk, which turned out to be a grove of mottled funk trees. "He is in there."

Breanna smelled a strong, unpleasant odor: the smell of the funk blooms. It made her feel sad. She knew that no funks smelled good, but mottled funks were the worst.

They entered the grove, and soon discovered Jeremy Wolf, in wolf form, asleep on a bed of funk berries. The smell was verging into stench. "Hello," King Dor said.

"Go away," the funk bed said.

Prince Dolph assumed the form of a wolf. "Woof!" he said.

Prince Jeremy opened one eye. It was obvious that he was a prince, because there was a small golden crown on his head. ''Woof!'' he retorted negatively.

So Bink tried. ''We'd like to talk to you.''

The face of the wolf became halfway human. ''What you would like has no bearing.''

''Let me try,'' Breanna said impulsively. She got down and planted a hot kiss on the face.

The eyes widened. The humanity spread from the face through the rest of the body, making him into a large and somewhat clumsy person. He still wore the crown. ''Wow!'' Jeremy said as a vaguely heart-shaped cloudlet dissipated.

"I think some of the lip balm remained," Justin remarked.

''Serves him right.''

Jeremy gazed at Breanna. ''How old are you, Black Wave maiden?''

''Fifteen, of course. What's it to you?''

Jeremy sighed. ''Too young.''

''Too young for what?'' she demanded, though she had a pretty good idea.

''Too young to be my ideal mate.''

''I'm nobody's ideal mate, and least of all yours. I've already been through all that with one king. What kind of a girl do you think I am?''

Jeremy assumed wolf form and stared at her. Then he returned to human form. ''I think you are an assertive runaway from your home village, with the talent of seeing in blackness, and a tree in your mind.''

"He knows!" Justin exclaimed, amazed.

''How do you know that?'' Breanna demanded, shaken.

''In my natural form I can read minds,'' Jeremy said. ''Unfortunately, I can't do it in manform. I constantly seek a way to have that part of my talent expanded. Do you know a way?''

''No! And I don't want you poking around in my mind, so kindly remain in manform.''

''You have spirit, and you're cute. I wish you were the one.''

''Well, I'm *not*. So why don't you do what your father wants and go into training for kingship?''

''Because of the curse.''

"What curse?" Nobody else seemed to be talking, so Breanna figured it was up to her.

"It is complicated."

"Well, maybe we can help."

"I doubt it. But you might as well know. When I was young I roamed out from the isle, across the continent of Xanth, heedless of anything. I had no fear of monsters, because I could read their minds, and evade them before they could close on me. So I was somewhat reckless, and I fear in retrospect, at times obnoxious."

"Express sympathy, now that you have him talking. We need to know his problem."

"Well, we all get that way at times," Breanna said.

"But I was chronically that way. Finally it caught up with me. In my brash ignorance I trampled a private garden of boysenberries and girlsenberries, ruining the crop. An old Curse Fiend Woman came out, saw the damage, and cursed me."

"The curse fiends all have the same talent: they can blast a hole in the ground or kill trees or blow people into oblivion with their curses."

"That must have been painful," Breanna said.

"This wasn't a normal curse. She was one of their ranking people, and had perfected a worse curse."

Breanna had an idea. "Can you project your thoughts too? So you can show me exactly what happened?"

Jeremy assumed wolf form. Then, suddenly, Breanna found herself in the trampled berry patch, with little boysen and girlsenberries squished all around her, their juice on her fur.

The old Curse Fiend appeared. "You despicable creature!" she shouted. "You have ruined my crop! May you be cursed to suffer as you have made me suffer."

"How's that?" Breanna Werewolf asked.

"These berries would have brought delight to courting couples, enabling them to recognize their ideal partners. So you will suffer the same loss of delight. There will be only one perfect life's companion for you, a foreign woman, but you will not be able to find her. She will have to find you, and you will know her only when she declares her love for you. But she will not know that you are her ideal mate, so will not look for you. And when she passes the age of twenty one without finding you, the two of you will never get together, and you will be doomed to be with some lesser creature, knowing that you might have had perfect happiness, but forfeited it by being thoughtless and stupid. Now depart, you cretin; the curse is complete.''

Breanna departed, her tail between her legs. She knew that every word of the curse was true.

"That is one awful curse! No wonder he is dejected. Why should he want to be king, knowing that he will never have his perfect love?"

She came out of it, and was herself again. The three kings were looking at her. ''Jeremy has a real problem,'' she said.

The werewolf, back in human form, nodded agreement. ''I have looked everywhere, but found no perfect woman. Oh, there have been many who expressed interest in me, but when they did, I know they were not the one. They just wanted to be princesses or queens. I want the one who will love me for what I truly am, not caring about my status. I must find her before she passes twenty one, or lose her forever. And I can't find her.''

''But that's not the curse,'' Breanna said. ''*She* has to find *you.*''

''I have searched by ranging widely, telling women of the curse, so that if any should be the right one, she will be encouraged to come to me. That is how I have tried to nullify that aspect. But it has all been for naught. I fear my true love has already passed the critical age, and I am forever lost.''

"This is a negative assumption. He is clearly in this funk because he has given up hope of success."

''Okay, Jeremy,'' Breanna said in businesslike fashion. ''Either she's over twenty one and it's too late, or she isn't. There's no point in figuring she's over, because that's hopeless. So you have to figure she's under, and you can still find her, or rather, have her find you. Because that's the only way you can possibly win.''

The werewolf prince gazed at her somewhat hopelessly. ''What can I do, that I have not already done?''

''Let's get some basics established first. If you find your true love, will you agree to start training for the kingship?''

''Yes, of course. I have nothing against it. It's just that without my true love, I have no ambition for anything else.''

''Okay. So as I see it, maybe you just need to make yourself more attractive to that ideal girl. Which is funny, in a way.''

''Funny? I'm depressed.''

''Not funny you; funny thought. I just came from the Isle of Women, where I was helping a lady zombie learn to be more appealing to a king. Now I have to show a prince how to be more appealing to a lady. I'm no expert, either way, but at least the lady zombie did get the king.''

''If you can enable me to get my true love, I will be forever in your debt.''

''Actually, I'm just trying to help the three kings. They've had a whole lot more experience with woman than I have.''

Bink laughed. ''But we lack one prime prerequisite: we are not female.''

"Which may be why you are here. The distaff perspective is required."

''The what perspective?''

"Female."

''Oh. Well, I'll do my best.'' She addressed Jeremy again. ''Now this perfect woman is foreign. That means she's not a werewolf?''

''At least is not a werewolf of the Isle of Wolves, though I have checked the local bitches too.''

''The local whats?''

"A female canine is a bitch. It is not a term of disrespect in this context."

''I knew that,'' she said, remembering. ''So she could be a different type of crossbreed, or even dull human.''

''She could be anything,'' Jeremy said. ''That's what makes the search so difficult.''

''For sure. But can we assume that she will have a human form, or can take that form when she wants to?''

''I don't know.''

''Well, let's assume it, because that makes it a whole lot easier. Because what little I know about women is all human. I can't help you learn to impress a bi— a nonhuman female.''

''That makes sense,'' King Dor said. ''And perhaps the conventions for different species are similar enough in essence to make it relevant.''

''Let's hope,'' Breanna said. ''Okay, so lets see if we can make you so appealing to women that the right one is bound to take notice. It would be better if we had a real woman, but I guess we'll have to make do with what's available. Which is a simple girl. If you can impress me, you can probably impress her.''

''I have impressed many women,'' Jeremy said. ''But none would have noticed me if I weren't royal.''

''Precisely. So let's pretend you are a completely ordinary werewolf. Ditch the crown.''

Jeremy lifted the crown from his head. He buried it out of sight in the funk. ''Now I am just another werewolf.''

''Right.'' Breanna looked around. ''Help me, guys. What comes next?''

''Perhaps you should be a woman passing by, and he tries to impress you,'' King Dor suggested.

''Okay. Impress me, Jeremy.'' Breanna walked just outside the glade, turned, and walked innocently back in. The three kings faded circumspectly into the background.

Jeremy became a huge wolf and rose up with a horrendous growl.

''Eeeeeek!'' Breanna screamed. ''The big bad wolf is going to eat me up!''

The wolf became the man. ''No go?''

''No go,'' Breanna agreed. ''I mean, impress me as a man. Like for a date.'' She walked out of the glade, and back in.

''Hello, luscious maiden,'' Jeremy said. ''Have a date.'' He proffered a thyme berry.

Breanna almost fell over laughing.

''I made an error?'' Jeremy asked, annoyed.

''My fault, I guess, for using a Mundane term. I meant a date, as in boy and girl go somewhere together and do something fun together.''

''But you are too young for that.''

''I don't mean storks!'' she exploded. ''Isn't there anything else on a man's mind?''

''Should there be?''

"At ease, Breanna. It was a natural misunderstanding on his part, and he reacted appropriately. He's a decent sort."

So she stifled her natural reaction, and used the occasion for some necessary education. ''Some subtlety may be in order here. Men may think that storks are in constant need of summoning, but women have other things on their minds.''

"They do?" The werewolf seemed amazed.

"Definitely. So get the stork out of your mind. Anyway, we're play-acting here, so my age is irrelevant. So don't think of storks, not because I'm too young, but because no woman thinks of them until late in the game. Make her love you, then maybe she'll think of the stork. Eventually."

"Actually, the women of the Isle of Women seemed to think of nothing but storks, according to the report of the kings."

"They were trying to nab a king. That's different."

"I suppose it is. I seems to be true that men have storks, or at least the act of summoning them, on their minds more than women do."

Jeremy shook his head. "This is more difficult than I ever imagined. How can women exist without constantly thinking of storks?"

"We have disciplined minds. So just try to figure out something that you and I might like to do together that has nothing to do with storks."

The man pondered, and cogitated, and thought, and considered, and reflected. Sweat formed on his brow.

"You stumped him."

Breanna almost laughed. "I guess I'd better give you a hint. How about taking a nice walk together?"

"Where?"

"Anywhere. It doesn't matter. The point is just to be doing it."

"This is strange indeed."

"Aren't there any interesting sights on the Isle of Wolves?"

"Well, there's the quandary."

"So let's take a walk and go see that."

"If you insist. It's really not much, especially with the masses."

"You aren't making this very interesting," Breanna said. "What masses?"

"The mass confusion and mass hysteria. People go near them, and—"

"I get the picture. Are there any other local sights?"

"There's the ink well. We draw buckets of ink up, and ship them to all other parts of Xanth."

Breanna made a gesture as of tearing her hair. "None of this will do. We'd better stick to boy–girl. Suppose we just walk around in a circle and make interesting conversation?"

"But you said that girls don't think of anything interesting."

Breanna opened her mouth, but Justin intercepted her expostulation before it got out. *"He means your refusal to think of stork summoning. Change the subject."*

Good advice, again. "I think I'm just going to have to tell you some things to talk about. But that means I won't be able to judge how impressive it is. We need another girl."

"One who doesn't know I am a prince," Jeremy agreed.

"For sure. Okay, first off, you'll have to notice how pretty I am."

"But—"

"I don't mean me personally! I mean any woman. You have to compliment her. You have to scratch for nice things to say about her. If she's got distinctive features, you notice them. Whatever they are. Even if they're really not much. Now try noticing me."

He studied her head. "You have lustrous long black hair."

She clapped her hands. "That's it! You're making me be flattered, and that makes me like you better. Try again."

He looked at her face. "You have glowing green eyes."

"Right on!"

He looked at her mid section. "You have a nice little—"

"Nuh-uh! Off limits. There's nothing in that region you're supposed to notice."

He looked at her chest. "You—"

"No!"

"But there's not much else to notice."

"Then get creative. And after that, with luck, she'll ask about you, and you must tell her something moody and feelingful, evoking her sympathy, and then follow up with whatever seems apt. Just keep the dialogue going nicely, and she'll get interested in you. Then if she's the one, you're home free."

"I never did any of this before."

"Which is maybe why you never got anywhere. Let's see what else we can arm you with." She looked around. "Any of you have suggestions?"

"The weather?" King Dor asked.

"Okay, Jeremy, if there's awkward silence, and you can't think of anything else, talk about the weather. Not bad weather; interesting weather."

"This all seems horribly far-fetched,"

"Women have far-fetched minds. Now let's review this, to be sure you have it straight. Then we'll have to go out and test it on a real woman."

They worked on it, and bit by bit he seemed to be getting it. But Breanna was really worried about whether it would every play in real life. This promised to be a long, grueling, and probably fruitless exercise. Meanwhile, she was tired; she normally slept in the daytime, and she hadn't had much of a chance yet today.

12
Impromptu Ingenue

They seemed to be making progress, but Dolph was bored. Teaching Jeremy Werewolf to impress women favorably might be a positive step, but the chances of him being able to impress the right one in time seemed remote. How long would it take? Days? Weeks? Months? They couldn't afford the time. They had a big wedding to get back to, back home—wherever that was.

He stepped back out of sight, then became a small bird and flew up to take a look around. The isle was quiet; it was late afternoon and the wolves were mostly snoozing.

He flew toward the mainland—and there was Para, the duck-footed boat, paddling toward the isle. Riding in it were Jenny Elf and Sammy Cat. He knew what that meant: Sammy could find anything except home, so the two had been sent out to find the three kings. To remind them to get on back home instead of dawdling. The three were more than ready to go home, the moment they could!

He was going to fly down and introduce himself, as Jenny was his friend. Then he thought of something: Jenny could be their ingenue! She was female, and of age, and didn't know what they were doing. So he had better not tell her anything; he would warn the others, and thus give Jeremy some real practice.

He looped down, and soon returned to the funk grove. He resumed his natural form. The awful smell of the grove hit him anew; he had become acclimatized, until he got a breath of fresh air. ''Jenny Elf's coming,'' he announced.

"Sent to find us," Dor said. "She will know where our home is."

"Yes," Bink agreed. "But we can't ethically leave until we solve Jeremy's problem."

"I was thinking that Jenny could help in that. She can be the ingenue."

"The ingenue!" Dor exclaimed.

Breanna glanced across at them. "What's this?"

"Our friend Jenny Elf is coming," Dolph explained. "She must have been sent to find us, because her cat Sammy can find almost anything. She can be the ingenue, because she won't know that Jeremy is a prince. He can try to impress her."

"Is that fair?" Breanna asked. "To put one of your friends in that position?"

"You think I'm going to chomp off her arm?" Jeremy demanded.

"No. It's just that—well, I suppose it's all right." She turned to the werewolf. "But make sure you remember that you're just practicing. You don't actually want to summon any storks. You want to see what works, so that you can go out and maybe win your perfect love."

"I understand," the werewolf prince said. "If I can impress her, maybe I can yet manage to break the curse."

"Meanwhile, what about the rest of us?" Dolph asked. "Won't we be in the way?"

"We can go eat, take a nap, or whatever else we fancy," Dor said. "But someone should stay, just in case."

"I'm dead on my feet," Breanna said. "I just want to sleep."

"You can have my bed, here," Jeremy said. "I'll go meet her outside the grove."

"She'll be looking for us, so we three kings had better meet her," Dor said. "But then we can move on. So why don't you go with us, Dolph, then change form and keep an eye on Jenny." He glanced at Jeremy. "It's not that we don't trust you, but if there is awkwardness, this ensures immediate contact with us. Probably there will be errors, and we'll have to explain things to Jenny. I'm sure she'll cooperate; she's a very nice girl."

"That's good. I'm suddenly very nervous. I have come to know Breanna, but this is a stranger. A thousand things could go wrong."

They organized and started out of the grove, while Breanna

plumped herself down, put her head on her crossed arms, and went to sleep.

Jeremy glanced back. ''Breanna is nice too. I'm sorry she's not the one.''

''She's a good girl,'' Bink agreed. ''Made better, perhaps, by Justin Tree's presence.''

''It must be nice to find such companionship.''

''Maybe it will happen for you.''

''Especially if you learn how to impress women,'' Dolph said.

They emerged from the grove. Their timing was right: Jenny Elf and Sammy Cat were just arriving. The elf girl was wrinkling her nose as if she smelled something horrible—the mottled funk, of course.

''Oh, there you are!'' Jenny cried. She ran up to hug Dolph. She was so small she seemed like a child, though he knew she was twenty; usually he didn't notice. ''You have to come back now. They are setting up wedding rehearsals, and you have parts to play.''

''We will, soon,'' Dolph said. ''But right now we have something else to do. Would you mind waiting with Jeremy?'' he gestured to the werewolf, who looked tongue-tied.

''Oh, sure,'' she agreed. ''Just don't be too long. I promised to bring you back to Castle Roogna within a day.''

''Castle Roogna?''

Jenny lifted a brow. ''You know. Home.''

''Home!'' Dor exclaimed, remembering.

Jenny laughed. ''You couldn't have forgotten, could you?''

''I'm afraid we could have,'' Bink said. ''We drank some lethe water by accident.''

''Oh, that explains it! We didn't know what was keeping you.''

''We will return shortly,'' Dolph said.

The three of them walked on, leaving Jenny with Jeremy. As soon as they went around a bend in the path, Dolph became an invisible winged man and looped back. He had always been able to change forms, but as he had grown older and gained experience, his talent had broadened and deepened, until now he could do much more. For example, he had learned to assume other human forms, so that he could make himself more handsome or muscular, or smarter. He seldom did it, because Electra liked him just the way he was naturally, but he could do it when he had reason. Now he had reason: he wanted to retain his full human intelligence, which could get cramped in small-headed bird form, yet be able to move silently without leaving footprints. So this form was good for that, and he would change it when he needed to.

He flitted back to eavesdrop on Jeremy and Jenny. He felt a bit guilty for not telling Jenny what was going on, but if he had done so, that would have spoiled Jeremy's test. He would tell her everything as soon as it was feasible.

The two were standing in the very kind of awkward silence that was supposed to be avoided. Dolph came up behind the werewolf. "Compliment," he whispered.

"You have nice spectacles," Jeremy said.

"Oh, they're just from a spectacle bush," Jenny said. "I can't see very well without them."

There was more silence. "Try again," Dolph whispered.

"You have nice hands."

Jenny held them up. "You like four fingers?"

"Four fingers!" he said, amazed.

Worse and worse. This wasn't working.

"You didn't know?" Jenny asked. "Then why did you comment?"

Jeremy stared at his feet. "I'm sorry. I was trying to say something nice, but I'm not good at it."

"Something nice? Why?"

"Do you really want to know?" he asked, dejected.

"Yes, of course."

"It's sort of complicated."

"Life often is. Tell me."

"I'm trying to learn how to impress women, because I am cursed not to recognize my true love until she comes to me, only she won't know it so won't come, so I need to be interesting enough so she'll want to."

Jenny digested that. "I guess it's a start. But I should think you would fare better just by being yourself."

"But I'm just sort of dull and clumsy, in this form."

"This form? What other form do you have?"

"I'm a werewolf."

"A werewolf!" Jenny exclaimed, delighted. "That's wonderful!"

"It is?"

"I always liked wolves. I'm a wolf-rider."

"You ride wolves?"

"Well, I did back home. But I never met any wolves here in Xanth, so I couldn't ride. Anyway, it isn't as if I could ride just any wolf."

"It isn't?"

"No, it has to be a wolf friend. That's—well, it gets complicated to explain."

"In my wolf form, I can read minds. May I read yours?"

"A telepathic wolf? Certainly; why not? I have nothing to hide, and you can get the concept much more quickly and completely."

Jeremy changed to wolf form. Jenny smiled and stroked his fur. She was a small girl, and he was a big wolf, so his head was as high as hers. She showed no fear at all; instead she was plainly delighted to be in the company of a wolf.

Dolph shook his invisible head. Suddenly this was working out, but not in the way expected. Jeremy hadn't impressed her by his attempted compliments, but by his basic nature, which Jenny happened to like. Did that count?"

Jeremy resumed manform so he could talk. "Your World of Two Moons—how wonderfully strange," he said. "I had no idea you were such a remarkable person, with such an exotic origin."

"Oh, I'm not remarkable or exotic," she protested. "I just came to Xanth by accident, chasing Sammy Cat. I'm strictly nothing much."

"Not as I see it." Jeremy hesitated. "I am strong enough to carry you. Would you like to ride me? In my wolf form, I mean?"

She clapped her hands. "Oh, *yes*!"

"I'll go very slowly, so you won't fall off."

"Don't worry about that. I won't fall off. An elf never forgets wolf-riding."

Jeremy resumed his wolf shape. He started to lie down, so Jenny could climb on him, but she didn't wait. She leaped, and was on his back, holding on to the long fur of his collar. He started to walk, slowly, but she showed no sign of unsteadiness. So he moved faster, and she had no trouble. He was evidently reading her mind, and knowing that she was all right.

Then he broke into a run. Dolph changed to invisible wolf form and followed. They charged along the path and on to the beach, where the wolf did his utmost, running swiftly along between the water and the jungle. Jenny never wavered; Dolph could see her smiling.

After a while Jeremy slowed, then stopped, and Jenny slid off. "Oh, thank you so much!" she cried. "That was the most wonderful experience I've had in years!"

Jeremy resumed man form. "It's nice being appreciated like that. You really do know how to ride a wolf."

"Yes, we are made for it. That's why we are small, so as not to be too much of a burden."

"You were no burden."

Jenny turned and hugged him around the neck and shoulders. Then she drew back, abashed. "Oh! I forget you had changed form. Hugging wolves is natural, but—"

"I know what you mean." He changed back, and she hugged him again.

Then she drew back. "What's this about the curse? I mean, how do you know there's only one woman for you?"

Jeremy resumed man form. "It's all part of the curse. If I don't find her before she passes twenty one, I'll never find her at all. So the three kings and Breanna are helping me learn how to— well, never mind."

"No, it's all right. You were supposed to practice on me?"

"Yes," he said, abashed.

"Well, then you should do it. Your woman must be growing older all the time. You need to get it straight as soon as possible."

"You don't mind?"

"Jeremy, for a wolf-ride I would do anything. Practice on me all you want; I want to help you."

"Oh, thank you, Jenny. This will help a lot." He paused, looking down at his feet again. "I'm sorry I was so clumsy. I mean, complimenting your hands when I hadn't even really seen them. But I do think they are nice hands."

"Four fingers and all?"

"I felt those hands grip my fur as you rode with perfect balance. I don't care how many fingers you have; they're great." He took one of her hands and kissed it.

"Oh." Jenny blushed.

"Sorry. I got carried away. I do clumsy things when—"

"Oh, stop it. I'm not embarrassed, I'm touched. Nobody ever did that to me before."

Jeremy looked around. "I suppose we should get back to the glade before the kings return and miss us."

"I suppose."

But he didn't change form, and she didn't make any motion. They walked along, looking out over the sea. Dolph wondered whether he should join them, but decided to remain hidden.

"You said a name I didn't recognize," Jenny said after a bit. "A girl?"

"Breanna. She came with the three kings. She was trying to teach me to be charming. It wasn't working very well."

"How did they get together with her? She's not of Castle Roogna."

"I didn't mean to snoop, but I did pick up some things from her mind. She was chased by a zombie, and I think the kings helped her escape. She helped them too. They were on the Isle of Women, and those women don't like to let royal men get away unmarried."

"But they are married already."

"Those women don't like to take no for an answer. They would have tried to make them renounce their existing wives and marry Isle Women. Anyway, the three of them and Breanna got away and came here. My father made them try to help me, before he would tell them where their home is."

"Well, I'm glad I got to meet you. I didn't know where they were, but Sammy found them." Jenny froze. "Oh! I lost Sammy!"

"He must be with Breanna. We'd better return now."

"Yes."

He changed, she jumped on, and they raced like the wind back the way they had come, with Dolph following.

They reached the grove as Bink and Dor were returning. "Look at that!" Dor exclaimed. "He's carrying her!"

Jeremy halted, and Jenny slid off. They were similarly abashed. "I know we should have been practicing manners," Jenny said. "We just got carried away."

"We didn't know you could ride," Bink said.

"I can't. Except for wolves. I'm a wolf-rider. When I met Jeremy— I'm sorry. I just got carried away. Literally. We'll practice now.''

Jeremy assumed manform. ''It was my fault. When I learned her nature—'' He skuffled his feet.

''I've got to find Sammy,'' Jenny said, walking on into the grove. Jeremy followed, and so did Dolph.

Sure enough, there was Breanna, asleep, with the cat snuggled up against her. The girl's eyes opened as they approached. ''Hello, Jenny,'' she said.

Jenny was surprised. ''Have we met?''

Breanna sat up. ''Not exactly. Justin knows you.''

''Justin?''

''Justin Tree, of the North Village. You have visited him. His mind is with me now, and he identifies folk for me.''

''Oh. I didn't mean to disturb you. I had lost track of Sammy Cat, so I thought he might be here.''

Breanna looked at Sammy, who was now stretching. ''Yes, he joined me in a cat nap. He's good company.''

Dolph realized that Sammy had been looking for a nap, so had found the cat nap.

''We'll get out of your way,'' Jenny said.

''No, I'm okay. That nap will hold me for a while. I can sleep at night if I have to. We need to get Jeremy trained.''

''Yes,'' Jenny agreed. ''But now that I know his nature, I relate to him as a wolf. That distorts my awareness.''

Breanna smiled. ''Something always messes up. I know how it is.''

''Maybe it's part of my curse,'' Jeremy said.

Both girls laughed. ''We'll just have to beat your curse,'' Breanna said. ''Now let's see how you impress Jenny, as a man. What do you do?''

Jeremy turned to Jenny. ''You have nice ears.'' Then he did a doubletake. ''Oops.''

''They're pointed,'' Jenny said. ''You hadn't noticed?''

He nodded. ''As I said, I'm just sort of clumsy in manform.''

''You're going to have to learn to notice things,'' Breanna said. ''So you can make accurate compliments.''

They continued to practice. Dolph, bored, wandered away. He was in invisible wolf form, so he changed to visible wolf form, so that he could relate to the wolves of the isle.

He spied a wolf racing in from the beach. The wolf looked worried and disgusted. ''What's the matter?'' Dolph growled in wolf-talk as the other passed.

''There's a zombie werewolf coming to the isle! I must tell the king, so we can repel it,'' the other growled, and raced on.

The werewolves didn't want a zombie werewolf? It occurred to Dolph that Breanna might be interested in that, after her experience with zombies. He trotted back to the funk grove.

''I think you're getting it,'' Breanna was telling Jeremy. ''But Jenny's right: she's *not* right, because she sees you as a wolf prince.''

''Prince?'' Jenny asked, startled.

''Oops, I messed up,'' Breanna said. ''Again.''

''Yes, I am a werewolf prince,'' Jeremy said. ''We didn't tell you, because I was supposed to impress you as a man, not as a prince. Instead I impressed you as a wolf.''

Jenny looked crestfallen. ''I guess that means you won't be free to— I mean a prince has better things to do than carry around stray elves.''

He put his arm around her. ''Jenny, I love carrying you! I'll be glad to do it any time. I never before encountered anyone who could ride like that. Or anyone who valued my wolfishness rather than my princeness. I want to be your wolf-friend.''

She shook her head. ''Princes have duties. They have to learn to be kings. They can't just run around with friends and explore Xanth.'' She looked at Dor. ''Isn't that so?''

''That is so,'' Dor agreed. ''And this is why we are trying to help Jeremy. He must abate his curse so he can be ready to be a king, in due course.''

''But I don't care about being king,'' Jeremy said. ''Not if I have to marry the wrong woman. I'd rather be a wolf-friend, and range all Xanth.''

''That would be second best,'' Jenny said, a tear in her eye. ''We can't let it happen. You must find your true love.''

Then Breanna noticed Dolph. ''There's a strange wolf here.''

Dolph changed form. ''No, it's just me. I just learned that there's a zombie werewolf coming to the isle, and the other werewolves don't like that.''

''The zombies have a right to exist too,'' Breanna said hotly. ''So they're a bit different from others; so's everybody. I'm black, Jenny's an elf, you're a shape changer—we're all different in our special ways. They should let it come here.''

''I thought you might feel that way,'' Dolph said.

''Let's go talk to King Wolverton,'' Breanna said. ''I think I've done more than enough mischief here. You folk can practice better without me.''

''That's not true,'' Dor said.

But Breanna was already in motion. ''I don't know how to ride, but is there some other form you could take to carry me in a hurry to the king?''

Dolph became a winged man. Actually he was himself with wings, another refinement he had learned. He picked her up and flew into the nearest patch of sky.

She looked around. ''Oh, this is as much fun as flying in that duck boat! Just don't drop me.''

''I wouldn't do that,'' Dolph said.

''I was teasing.'' She kissed him on the cheek.

He wavered, and had to correct his course. He knew he was blushing.

''Sorry,'' Breanna said. ''I get into more trouble by being impulsive.''

He spied Wolverton Mountain and glided down. The wolves had already gathered, and were in animated dialogue.

The werewolves paused as Dor landed and set Breanna on her feet. One approached them. ''This is a private matter,'' he murmured.

''No it isn't!'' Breanna retorted. ''You're discriminating against a zombie werewolf, and I won't have it. He's a person too.''

They stared at her. ''You are defending a zombie?'' King Wolverton demanded.

''Yes! Somebody's got to. All they want to do is get along, and they're not bad folk. They can be useful too. Suppose a gruesome monster invaded the isle, and it killed any of you who tried to stop it? A zombie can't be killed. A zombie could fight that monster, or maybe disgust it so it went away. That's why they have zombies to defend Castle Roogna. You should welcome that zombie werewolf!''

The werewolves passed a glance around. ''Sire, she is making sense,'' one said.

The king looked at Breanna cannily. "Some folk are great for recommending things for other folk that they wouldn't do themselves."

"Oh, yeah? Like what?"

"Like associating with zombies."

Dolph knew what was coming. The werewolves didn't know about Breanna's recent history. He kept his mouth shut.

"So you think I'm a hypocrite?" Breanna demanded. "That I wouldn't touch a zombie myself?"

"That is what I suspect," the king agreed.

"So if I touch that zombie, you'll let him stay here without trying to freeze him out?"

There was another glance. "That depends on the magnitude of the touch," the king said. "We will match your level of contact, in a general way."

"Okay, just watch me." She turned to Dolph. He picked her up again and flew toward the beach, while the others assumed wolf form and ran swiftly in the same direction.

"They think you're bluffing," Dolph told her.

"I know they do. But I'm not doing this just to embarrass them. I'm doing it because it's right."

"Is Justin Tree guiding you in that?"

"No, he's agreeing with me. It took me a while to get straight about zombies, but now I know what to do."

They reached the beach. The duck boat was just arriving. Dolph landed, set the girl down, and stayed back as the wolves caught up to him.

Breanna hurried out to intercept the zombie. It seemed to be male, in wolf form, and rather farther gone than Dolph personally liked. Would the girl be able to make herself touch him?

"Hello," Breanna said as the wolf got out of the boat. "Welcome to the Isle of Wolves. Will you defend it against all enemies, including gruesome monsters?"

The wolf nodded, and a bit of furry skin dropped to the ground. Dolph winced.

"Change form, please," Breanna said.

The wolf became a similarly decaying man. His eyes were sunken, and his lips had rotted away, so that his teeth were bare.

"I am Breanna of the Black Wave. I'm not a werewolf; I'm just part of the welcoming committee. Who are you?"

"Ztigma Zhombie."

Breanna paused, and Dolph knew she was consulting with Justin Tree. "Stigma? As in a mark of disgrace or disease?"

"Yez."

"Fair enough," she said. "Stigma, I'm going to give you a welcoming kiss. Hold out your arms."

The zombie did. Breanna stepped into that clumsy embrace, wrapped her arms around the decaying torso, and planted a solid kiss on the lipless mouth. She held that pose for a more than sufficient moment, then disengaged. "You will like it here," she said. "Now you can meet King Wolverton." She turned to face the werewolves.

"She did it," a werewolf said, shuddering. "We're stuck for it."

"So we are," the king said. "Well, a deal's a deal." He strode forward and shook the hand of the zombie. "Welcome," he said gruffly, and walked away, his hand stiff, as if needing to be plunged into a vat of boiling soap.

Dolph knew that after that, no other werewolf would criticize the zombie. He would get along.

Breanna walked back to join him. There was smear of ick on her mouth, and a chunk of rot on her shoulder. Her green eyes were staring, as if encrusted with sickly slime. "Help me," she whispered.

Dolph picked her up and flew her to another section of the beach, out of sight of the werewolves. He led her to the water, and then into it, setting her slippers on the dry sand. He scooped up a handful of sea and washed off her face and hands. Then he touched up aspects of her clothing, though this made them damp.

"I had to do it," she said. "But it was awful."

"You showed real courage," he said. "That zombie was far gone."

She became more animated. "But I survived it. And I got the job done. The zombies can't help the way they are. They don't deserve to be shunned."

"True. The Zombie Master, who makes them, is a nice man, and his wife, Millie the Ghost, is nice too. They are both human, but getting old."

"Who will represent the zombies when those two move on? I

mean, apart from King Xeth? Doesn't there have to be some living interaction?''

''Yes, I think so. I never thought about it.''

''I feel another impulse coming on. Is there time to visit there?''

''Time before dark? I doubt it.''

''Let's go anyway. Now. I want to meet the Zombie Master.''

''He may not be awake.''

''Well, then Millie. I want to know how they relate to the zombies.''

So she donned her slippers, and Dolph picked her up again, slightly dripping, and flew across the sea to the mainland, and then on over land to Castle Zombie. By the time they arrived, it was dusk. The castle was brooding in the shadows, but it could manage that almost as readily in full sunshine.

They landed at the drawbridge. ''Halsh!'' the zombie guard cried, losing a tooth.

Breanna stooped to pick up the tooth. ''Here,'' she said, returning it to the guard.

Zombies were seldom startled, but this one managed it. ''Thanksh.'' He put the tooth back in his mouth.

''We have come to see the Zombie Master,'' Dolph said. ''I am Prince Dolph, and this is Breanna of the Black Wave.''

''Thish whay.'' The guard led them across the mold-encrusted bridge to the mildewy front gate.

Breanna looked around. ''It's beautiful, inside.''

''Millie is a good housekeeper.''

''You sure can't tell by the outside.'' She tilted her head thoughtfully. ''Which I guess is true of people—and zombies.''

Soon they reached the interior office. This time the Zombie Master was there along with Millie. ''Why hello, Dolph! I did not expect to see you back so soon.'' He glanced at Breanna. ''But Aurora has changed significantly.''

''This isn't Aurora,'' Dolph said quickly. ''This is Breanna of the Black Wave. Aurora is with Erica, another winged mermaid. Breanna is the one King Xeth wanted to marry.''

''But she looks to be only fifteen,'' Millie protested.

''Yes. So she was not suitable. But Xeth didn't understand. Now he has decided on another woman—''

"Yes, Zyzzyva," the Zombie Master said. "We have word that they are coming here soon."

"But after her experience with zombies, Breanna wanted to learn more about them, so we came here."

"Well, I finally managed to locate Planet Zombie," the Zombie Master said. "It is well along in the chain, but most of its creatures and plants are zombies, and its rocks are well eroded. Now Millie and I will be able to retire there, together with any zombies who wish to come. I believe that the majority will. But there remains one problem."

"Who is going to run Castle Zombie," Breanna said.

"Yes. We are the only living folk here, and there needs to be someone living, because other living folk may have a certain problem relating to zombies. So we will wait a few more years, until we train in someone else for this. Then at last we'll be able to go and relax."

Dolph found this interesting. "Who will come here?"

"We don't know," Millie said. "Jonathan asked the Good Magician Humfrey, and he said he would work on it, but so far no prospects have appeared. We're looking for a man of experience and judgment, or perhaps a couple." She glanced at her husband. "We found that works well enough."

"The Good Magician will surely come up with someone," Dolph said.

"Yes, it is not an easy search," the Zombie Master said. "The man must have maturity, yet be young enough to remain for some time. The woman must be sensible enough to accept the presence of zombies. Age and youth combined."

A light flashed over Dolph's head. "Grandfather Bink" he exclaimed. "Bink and Chameleon! That must be why they got youthened!"

The Zombie Master's jaw dropped. "I never thought of that. Yes, they would be perfect. But they would have to want to do it. Do they?"

"I don't know. The subject never came up. I don't think Magician Humfrey ever spoke to them."

"Curious," the Zombie Master said. "Maybe he is waiting for them to think of it themselves. It's not the kind of position that anyone should be urged into; the desire should come from within."

''Maybe,'' Dolph agreed dubiously. ''Yet Bink was right here, and didn't think of it.''

''Some things take time,'' Millie said. ''I did not understand zombies at first. Maybe Chameleon does not.''

''Could be,'' Dolph agreed. He turned to Breanna. ''Do you want to see the rest of the castle?''

''I am curious,'' Breanna said. ''If it's not too much trouble.''

''I will be happy to give you a tour,'' Millie said. ''I don't see many living women here.''

''I guess you don't,'' Breanna agreed half ruefully. She glanced at Dolph. ''You won't mind waiting?''

''Go ahead,'' he said. ''I'll tell Jonathan about your experience with the werewolf.''

''Thanks.'' Breanna looked as if she were suppressing a grimace.

The old woman and the young woman went off. Dolph turned to the Zombie Master, who was looking at him with a question mark. ''We encountered a zombie werewolf coming to the Isle of Wolves. Breanna used to be scared of zombies, but once she worked it out with King Xeth she defends them. She got the werewolves to accept a zombie.''

''Oh, that would be Stigma. He had hoped to be with his own kind. But often there can be prejudice. How did she do it?''

''She kissed him on the mouth.''

''But he doesn't have any lips.''

''She kissed his teeth, I guess. It was a nervy thing to do. After that they couldn't deny him. They were shamed into it.''

''She must be more of a person than she looks.''

''I think so. She can be feisty and blunt, but she means well, and she learns from experience. After that, she was curious about Castle Zombie, so I brought her here for a visit.'' Dolph paused, then remembered something else. ''She *is* more than she looks. Justin Tree is with her.''

''Justin Tree! But isn't he firmly planted in the North Village?''

''Yes. But he craved some human adventure, so made a deal with Breanna. He shares her adventure, in exchange for his good advice. So she has the advantage of a truly mature perspective.''

''Interesting things are happening. I would never have thought of that.'' The Zombie Master changed the subject. ''Have you learned who is to be married at Castle Roogna? We received an invitation, and will attend, but we wonder.''

''No word yet,'' Dolph said. ''We're trying to help the Werewolf Prince Jeremy find his true love, so that we can get back in time for that ceremony. But it's not going well. He is cursed not to know his true love until she comes to him, but she doesn't know it either, so won't come.''

''That is a bad curse,'' the Zombie Master agreed.

''I understand that the Curse Fiend Woman who made it was really angry. She wanted him to truly suffer, and she succeeded.''

The women returned. ''It's such a lovely castle,'' Breanna said. ''Millie showed me everything.''

''It was nice to have an appreciative audience,'' Millie said. ''You must stay for tee and crumples.''

It was now full night. ''I think we had better get back to the Isle of Wolves before we are missed,'' Dolph said with regret.

''We can wait a little longer,'' Breanna said.

So they stayed for the refreshment, and it was good. Breanna asked for the recipe, and Millie gave it to her. Then at last they departed. ''They're really nice,'' Breanna said. ''I'm glad we visited.''

''To fly at night, I must assume another form,'' Dolph said. ''It may not be as comfortable for you.''

''That's okay. I needed to unwind, after—after Stigma. This worked just fine.''

Dolph became a large night hawk. She made herself halfway comfortable in his talons, and he launched into the night sky. His vision in this form was excellent.

''Oh, look—there's Xeth and Zyzzyva walking south,'' Breanna said.

He looked down, and sure enough, there they were. He had forgotten that her talent was to see in darkness. Obviously it was a good one.

They reached the Isle of Wolves, which did not seem to fade out the way the other isles did. Maybe they could relate to it because other members of their party were there. It would have been real mischief, otherwise! Dolph glided in for a landing near the grove, set Breanna down, and changed back to manform.

''Thanks, Prince Dolph,'' she said. ''I needed that break.''

They walked into the grove, and found the others sleeping. Prince Jeremy was in wolf form, and Jenny Elf was snuggled against his side, and Sammy Cat was snuggled against her side. Bink and Dor were nearby, with their own beds of funk. Funk had turned out to be good material for doing nothing on.

Rather than disturb the others, they shaped their own beds and lay down. The night was warm, so they needed no covers. In a moment Dolph was asleep.

13
Love's Labors

Jenny woke to find the others sprawled across the glade, on beds of funk. The funk didn't smell bad anymore; her nose had gotten used to it.

Today they had to find Jeremy's perfect woman, so he could be happy and focus on training for the werewolf kingship, and so the three kings could return to Castle Roogna and rehearse for their roles in the big wedding. The womenfolk, who paid much more attention to such things than menfolk did, were getting frantic.

Her eye fell on Breanna of the Black Wave. The girl was impetuous and assertive; Jenny liked that. She and Dolph had disappeared in the evening, so as not to interfere with the practice; Jenny wondered where they had gone. She would ask, when they woke.

Meanwhile, Jenny and Jeremy would go to the Isle of Women, because there were many women there who were looking for princes, and he hadn't been there before. So that was the most likely place he would find his true love. She and the others would try to coach him through the interviews. With luck, they would have success. Otherwise—

She didn't finish the thought. They *had* to get him settled. Not just because they had business elsewhere. Because he was a nice wolf under an awful curse. Jenny was especially sensitive to the problems of wolves.

''Say, maybe Sammy could find her,'' Jenny said aloud, seeing her cat. ''Sammy, where is Jeremy's True Love?''

But Sammy simply rolled over, asking to be stroked. Jenny did so, sighing. Sometimes he was like that. He could find anything except home, but he had to want to. Evidently he didn't care about this case. He was no longer a young cat, and had less energy than in times past.

Then she thought of something else, so obvious she marveled that it hadn't come up before. The Good Magician! Jeremy could go to him to ask about his true love. It would cost him a year of service, but it would be worth it, because it would get him the rest of his life happy.

The wolf opened his near eye. ''Oh, did I wake you?'' Jenny asked, feeling guilty.

He changed part way: just his head. ''Your thoughts did. The Good Magician? Do you really think he could do it, despite the curse?''

''Yes, he can find the answer to anything. I don't think any curse could stop him. So I think that if you don't find your true love today, you should go to him.''

Jeremy nodded. ''I shall do so. You folk have given me hope, and now you have given me the way too. I thank you for both.''

''You're welcome. But maybe you'll be able to save that year, by finding her today. I understand there are many beautiful women on the Isle of Women.'' Then she thought of something. ''But if they have all found dream princes now, maybe they won't be interested. Including your True Love, if she's there.''

''I think a woman should prefer a real prince to a dream prince, if she has a choice,'' Jeremy said. ''If she doesn't, then she's not the one for me.''

Jenny smiled. ''Maybe she would prefer to take both. One for her waking hours, the other for her sleeping hours. Would that bother you?''

Jeremy pondered. ''I don't like to seem jealous, but yes, it would. I think that my dream woman should love me completely, as I would love her, and not be interested in anyone else, awake or asleep.''

Jenny nodded. ''That makes sense to me. You don't want the wrong woman; the right woman wouldn't want the wrong man, either. So if she's there, she'll welcome you. I hope she is, and does.''

The werewolf prince smiled. ''Thank you. But there is also one big problem. They don't let any prince off their isle unless he marries one of them. That's why I never went there before. I knew that if my ideal woman were not there, they would force me to marry a non-ideal woman."

"But they can't *make* you marry one you don't want to!"

"Oh, they can, they can. They have ways."

"I don't see how. I mean—"

Breanna sat up. "They do have ways, Jen. The three kings would never have escaped, before, if Bink hadn't figured out a better alternative for them. He sent them to look for princes on Ida's moons."

"Oh, those! There would certainly be princes there!"

"There are. But to visit them, you have to be asleep. So if one of the Isle of Women women is right for Jeremy, she'll probably be satisfied to be with him instead of with one of the other princes."

"I should hope so!"

Breanna looked suddenly stricken. "I just thought—suppose his ideal woman is on those dream worlds?"

For an instant Jenny felt panic. Then it passed. "It doesn't matter."

"Doesn't matter!"

"Because every person who ever lived in Xanth, or ever will live, or ever might live there, is in those worlds. That includes the ones who are in Xanth now. So of course his ideal woman is there. But she must also be here in Xanth. Because why would the Curse Fiend Woman bother to curse him if it were meaningless? She knew that there *is* a perfect love for him, here in Xanth, so she cursed him to stop him from getting her."

Breanna pondered, then nodded. "That works for me. So she is accessible, if we can only find her in time. And I agree: the Good Magician should know. He solved my problem—not in the way I expected, but just as good, really—and he can solve Jeremy's problem. So let's give it one whale of a try today, and if that doesn't work, take him to the Good Magician. That will take care of him, and the rest of you will still be able to get back home in time for your big event."

Jeremy changed all the way, and stood up. His clothing came automatically with his human form, fortunately. Such things varied; some shape changers, like the naga folk, had to don their clothing each time they changed. "It sounds good. But what way do you have to get me off that isle unmarried, if we don't find her there?"

Breanna glanced at Bink, who was just waking up. "I'm sure there will be some way."

Jenny wasn't satisfied. ''It's risky. We need to be sure, before going there. Otherwise he might be forced to marry the wrong woman, and right after that the right one could turn up. That would really crown the curse.''

''She's right,'' Jeremy said. ''I think I would be better off not to risk it. I can go directly to the Good Magician. It is better to pay a year, than to risk a lifetime.''

Breanna shrugged. ''Sometimes things you never thought of turn up to change things. Like the lip bomb.''

''Like the what?'' Jenny asked.

''Oh, you don't know about that? I'll show you.'' Breanna delved into her clothing and found a packet. She opened it and dipped her finger into its red paste. She spread that on her lips. ''I wonder if this works on same-gender kisses?'' she said musingly.

''On what?''

''Let's find out.'' Breanna approached Jenny, and without further warning, kissed her on the mouth.

Jenny was so astonished that she almost fainted. Her mouth erupted into a shower of candy kisses. She seemed to be floating on a warm sea of rose petals.

''What was that?'' she asked as she wafted to the pleasant shore.

''I detonated some lip bomb on you,'' Breanna explained. ''It has quite an effect, doesn't it?''

Jenny wiped off her mouth as her heartbeat settled back toward normal. ''Yes. Don't kiss me again.''

The girl laughed. ''For sure not! I'm saving this for a boy. When. Eventually.''

''I wonder whether that would help me find my woman,'' Jeremy said.

''No,'' Breanna replied. ''Because it's artificial. You don't want to trick a woman, or force her; you want her to come to you, naturally. Lip bomb is more like effect without substance.''

Jenny had to agree.

Suddenly the duck-footed boat waddled into the glade. ''All aboard,'' it said. ''Now's the time.''

''But—'' Jenny started to protest.

''It will be all right,'' Bink said, climbing in. ''They let us go before.''

''But you made a deal! Jeremy isn't part of that.''

"Sure he is," Dolph said. "He's with us now."

"But the risk—" Jenny looked at Breanna. "You're a woman. You must have some sense. If that island is a man trap—"

"It's okay," Breanna said, helping Jenny into the boat.

"But—"

Jeremy shrugged. "They want to do it," he said, climbing in. "So let's do it."

Frustrated, Jenny gave up and got into the boat. She hoped that the others knew something she didn't. But she didn't trust their weird confidence. There was more than a whiff of a hint of disaster in the air.

The boat moved out of the glade, through the trees, and onto the beach. It plunged into the water and moved swiftly for the neighboring island.

"Who arranged this?" Jenny asked.

"I did," Dor said. "Last night, after we decided to try the Isle of Women."

"But we hadn't considered the risk then."

"I think it will be all right."

Jenny shut up. Sometimes the logic of men escaped her. But why did Breanna also agree to this risk? She at least should have more sense.

Soon they came to the Isle. The boat ran up on the land, making its way to the duck pond in the center.

There was a crowd of beautiful women. Chief among them was one in indecent bra and panties. Naturally all four men went immobile as their eyeballs locked into place. They would be no help.

"So you return," the woman said.

"Hello, Voracia," Breanna said. "You know the three kings and me. The others are Jenny Elf and Prince Jeremy Werewolf. We need to discover whether his ideal woman is here. Presuming that you women remain interested."

"Yes, we all have dream prince boyfriends now, but we want something for our waking hours too. We don't want to dream our lives away."

"We figured as much. But first you'll have to turn off your clothing."

"Oh." The woman's apparel became a halter and shorts. These

remained somewhat too suggestive for Jenny's taste, but at least the men were able to draw their eyeballs away with only slight sucking sounds.

"Let's just stay in the boat," Breanna said. "While you parade your women by. We hope that one of them will be the one."

The boat, agreeing, relaxed. It sank slightly in the water, its feet moving just enough to keep it stable. Jenny knew, because she peeked over the edge.

"But that's not the way we operate," Voracia said. "We each must get our turn to fascinate him."

"You can do that right here."

Voracia shrugged. "Very well. I am first. How do you like me, Jeremy?"

The werewolf eyed her thoroughly. Jenny could appreciate why. Voracia had the kind of face and figure Jenny knew better than even to dream of. "You look very interesting. But my concern is not how you look, but whether you are my true love. I will know only if you approach me, speaking love."

"I can do that," she said. She walked toward him, her hair flowing, her halter jiggling, her shorts tightening and moving most suggestively. Jenny was privately jealous, being forcibly reminded that her own body would never fill out clothing like that, or move like that. So she would never be able to fascinate a man in that manner.

"I love you, Prince Jeremy Werewolf, and want to marry you," Voracia said dulcetly as her clothing turned translucent. Jenny was jealous again: she could never lie like that, either. Oh, the woman surely wanted to marry him, but how could she love him, in just these few minutes? She just wanted to be a princess or queen.

Jeremy shook his head. "You are not the one."

Jenny was privately gratified, though she knew she shouldn't be. It was just that she thought that things like bulging halters and semi–see-through shorts should not decide a lifetime relationship. What about character? Compatibility? Harmony of lifestyle? Would Voracia even want to associate with him when he was in his wolf form? Yet the other women of the Isle might be no better.

"But how can you be sure?" Voracia said, her halter shrinking so that her bosom had to struggle to stay partly inside. "Come out of that canoe and join me, and I will show you such a good time."

"I don't want a good time. I want my one true love."

Her expression became less pretty. Her upper garment assumed the likeness of brands and brass knuckles, which Jenny realized made sense for a bra. "Then go soak your stupid head!" she flared, turning away. Her shorts condensed into a G-string so that her flexing bottom looked bare.

Jeremy's eyeballs began to steam. Breanna reached out to put her hand before his eyes. That broke his connection before the orbs were cooked. "Thank you," he gasped.

"Others will try something similar," Breanna murmured to Jenny. "Be alert, and rescue him quickly. I'm going to take a nap; it's my sleeping time."

The other women tried to impress Jeremy, flashing their charms and speaking lines of love, but one by one he turned them down. Some were gracious, some not. Some cried. Jenny saw how guilty that made the werewolf feel, but he would not accept any wrong woman. It was clear that he was both decent and a person of conscience, and this was not the delight it might have been for another man.

Jenny saw that the three kings, bored, were joining Breanna's snooze. Apparently the sheer amount of curvature being exposed had worn down their freakout circuits, and of course they had seen it before, when they were the ones being tempted.

"I am Polly Tician," the current woman was saying. "I love you, Prince Werewolf, and will make you happy for the rest of your years, with two carts in your garage."

"I believe you," Jeremy said, surprised.

"Wait," Jenny said, alarmed. "Find out her talent."

"What's your talent?" he asked Polly.

"I make others believe what I promise, but then I don't do it."

"You're not the one," he said. Then, privately to Jenny: "Thank you. She was persuading me, but you were right. Her promises are meaningless, however persuasive."

The next was a creature so ethereally lovely that it had to be artificial. Perhaps she was a demoness. Jenny was becoming increasingly cynical and disgusted by this process of mate-hunting.

"I am Miss Succubus," she said. "I lost my body in the Void, but managed to save my spirit. Now I can suck up whatever is near. If you would like a soft girl, I can suck up feathers and cloud-stuff. If you prefer a hard woman, I can suck up rocks. If you have a dirty mind—'' She glanced at the ground, and the dirt around her sucked up into her form, turning her brown. ''Unfortunately, I can retain substance for less time, each time, so I will eventually blink out of existence, unless I find true love. Are you the one to give it to me?''

Jenny was surprised, and she saw that Jeremy was too. This was a different girl, and a different approach. ''I don't know,'' the werewolf said. ''Will you speak the words?''

''No.''

Jenny and Jeremy were startled. ''No?'' he asked.

''Not unless it's true. As yet I hardly know you, so I can't love you.''

''She could be the one,'' Jenny murmured. ''She's honest.''

''But my curse requires the woman to come to me,'' Jeremy said. ''I can recognize her only if she approaches me with love.''

A muddy tear formed at Miss Succubus's eye. ''I can say that I wish it to be so, and that I hope to be the one. But I can't say—''

Jeremy stood and stepped out of the boat. He took the woman in his arms. ''Can you say that you feel it at least a little?'' he kissed her.

''Oh, yes!'' she replied after a moment. ''A little feeling, and a lot of longing.''

Jeremy looked sad. ''But now I know you are not the one. I'm sorry.''

''I'm sorry too,'' she said, her whole face turning muddy. She turned and walked away.

''I hate this!'' the prince swore. ''I hate what I did to her. But it was the only way to know.''

Jenny wiped away a tear of her own. ''The only way,'' she agreed.

He returned to the boat and resumed his seat.

The next woman was distinctly unimpressive. Her features were plain, her hair was straggly, and her dress was nothing much. ''I am the Iron Maiden,'' she said. She lifted her right hand, which carried an iron. ''I can iron anything. I'm a good, dull, housewife.''

''It's a useful skill,'' Jeremy said courteously.

''My other form is different,'' she said. Suddenly she was made of iron, with metallic features and a short sword where the iron had been before. ''If you need some fighting to be done—''

This was a surprise. But Jenny saw that this was in some respects an ideal woman, with both domestic and combat skills.

''Say the words,'' Jeremy said.

''I love you and want to—''

''You are not the one. I'm sorry.''

''I suspected that,'' the Iron Maiden said sadly. ''I hope you find the right one.'' She departed.

''Some of these are nice girls,'' he muttered. ''I would have been satisfied with either of the last two.''

''They are people, as well as women,'' Jenny agreed. She was increasingly impressed with the werewolf prince's humanity. He was truly searching, and did not like hurting others. But if none of the women here was the one, how would he escape the Isle?

A woman came running from left field. ''Danger! Danger!'' she cried.

Voracia stepped up to intercept her. ''Are you trying to break into the line, Krissica? Wait your turn.''

''No! There's something horrible happening,'' Krissica exclaimed, her feet moving as if she couldn't stop running. ''Things are trying to—to—it's awful!''

''Wait your turn!'' Voracia repeated, her bra and panties forming into metallic armor.

''But this is serious,'' Krissica said.

Voracia put her hands on Krissica's shoulders, making her stand still. ''What is happening?''

''They're—they're fighting,'' the woman gasped. ''And summoning storks!''

''You mean men are invading the Isle?'' Voracia demanded.

''No! Women are fighting women. And—''

''Girl, you're not making any sense. We don't fight among ourselves. And we certainly don't summon storks by ourselves.''

''This sounds like real trouble,'' Jenny murmured to Jeremy. ''And Voracia's being balky instead of checking into it. Maybe we should check.''

''But we have no authority here.''

''Somebody needs to do something, just in case it really is serious. Fighting and stork summoning? That can't be ignored.''

Jeremy nodded. Then he stood and stepped out of the boat, striding forward. ''This bears investigation,'' he said. ''Krissica, show the way.''

The woman turned and ran back the way she had come. Jeremy and Jenny followed. The three kings and Breanna remained asleep in the boat.

''Who gave you authority to decide anything?'' Voracia demanded, running after them.

He spared her a cursory glance. ''Do you have any other active princes on the Isle?''

''No, but—''

''Do you have any princesses?''

''No, but—''

''Then I rank you. I am trained to act when action is necessary, and it may be necessary now. If it is a false alarm, we will return to the boat and resume interviewing.''

Voracia opened her mouth, but nothing came out. Jenny was too busy running to look smug. The prince had shut her up. Because he was indeed a prince, a leader of people.

He glanced at Jenny. ''We had better hurry. Get on.'' He changed to wolf form and veered close to her.

Jenny leaped, grabbing fur. She drew herself up onto his back as he charged forward, passing Krissica. ''We'll check on it!'' Jenny called back to her.

They ran to the beach, and stopped. Jeremy changed back to man-form as Jenny dismounted. There was something peculiar happening. Plants were writhing, two by two. At the edge of the water, seaweeds were wrestling. Crabs were entangled with each other, trying to pinch off each other's heads while at the same time putting their bodies together. Insects were trying to sting each other while trying to do something else. Two women were fighting while stripping off their own clothes. Two birds flew in from nearby trees. Suddenly they tried to join together, while savagely pecking each other.

''What can this be?'' Jeremy asked.

''It looks like hate—and love,'' Jenny said. ''As if they drank from a hate spring and love spring. As if they are trying to kill each other while signaling the stork. But of course that's nonsense.''

Jeremy turned to Krissica, who was just catching up. ''Are there any love or hate springs on the Isle?''

"No!" she gasped. "But it sure looks as if—"

"Are there any on nearby isles?"

"Yes, on Selfish Steam Isle. It has springs of every kind. Folk go there to feel better or worse about themselves."

Jeremy gazed across the sea. There was a neighboring island with a cone in its center, belching smoke and vapor. "I think those springs have been heated to vapor. We are suffering an invisible cloud of love and hate elixir. So anything caught in it has a love/hate relationship with its closest neighbor."

"Yes!" Krissica agreed. "That must be it."

"We must take immediate action, because we don't know which way that cloud is moving. It could settle on the center of the Isle and ruin it. Krissica, go fetch as many women as you can, with bags. They must scoop up colored dust and bring it here."

"Yes," she agreed, and ran off.

Voracia arrived. Jeremy hardly glanced at her. "Voracia—go gather all winged creatures on the Isle. Bring them here as fast as possible."

"Winged creatures?"

"Time is of the essence! Do it!"

She turned and ran off.

"And we must enlist the help of the kings," he said. He glanced at Jenny. "Get on."

He changed, and Jenny leaped on. He ran swiftly back toward the center of the Isle. This was a side of him she hadn't seen before, but she realized that it had always been there. He was a prince, and surely had had some princely training, before getting cursed. He was a natural commander, who knew how to take charge in an emergency. This was certainly that.

They reached the boat, where the others were waking. Jeremy changed to manform as Jenny slid off his back. "Cloud of love and hate elixir," he said. "I've got one crew gathering colored dust, and another assembling winged creatures. Will you help?"

"I'll join the winged monsters," Prince Dolph said.

"I'll get the inanimate cloud to identify itself," King Dor said.

"I had better go with you," Bink said.

"For sure!" Breanna agreed, for some reason.

Dolph became a roc bird, and the two other kings grabbed onto his feet as he spread his wings and took off. The werewolf bounded back toward the shore. Jenny and Breanna were left behind.

"What can we do?" Breanna asked.

"Maybe direct traffic," Jenny said. "We can use the boat."

They got in the boat. "Do you know where the colored sands are?" Jenny asked. The boat was silent, and she realized that it couldn't talk when Dor wasn't present. But she hoped it could hear. "Take us there."

The boat splashed out of the pond and ran through the forest. It did seem to know where it was going. They passed a woman on her way somewhere. "Hey, Molly Coddle!" Breanna called. "We're on a mission to save the children from something dreadful. We can use your help."

The woman quickly joined them in the boat, and they hastily explained about the deadly invisible cloud.

They reached the colored sands section. A number of women were filling bags of it, but they were heavy. "Pile them in here!" Jenny called. "And come along; we have to hurry before that cloud moves."

The women did so, filling the boat. It ran on, slewing somewhat as it navigated curves, and came to the beach.

"Ho, ho!" a voice said, seeming from the air. "I'm going to put you into a killing mating frenzy!"

"Screech to a halt!" Jenny yelled at the boat. "That's the edge of the cloud talking, thanks to King Dor's presence. Don't cross into it."

A figure bounded through the woods toward them. It was Jeremy in wolf form. He changed in mid stride to manform. "Give the bags to Prince Dolph," he said. "Better yet, stay in the boat; he'll pick you up."

Then the roc appeared. The huge feet reached down, took hold of the boat, and lifted it into the air as the wings kept the bird hovering. The downdraft was fierce, blowing the women's hair across their faces, but they seemed too distracted to notice.

"It's all right," Jenny said reassuringly. "Prince Dolph won't let us drop."

They rose up high over the Isle. Then the roc squawked. "Same to you, birdbrain!" the invisible cloud responded.

Guided by that sound, the roc flew directly over it, then circled in place. ''Dump the dust!'' Jenny cried, realizing what it was for.

They opened their bags and emptied them over the sides. The dust wafted down onto the cloud below, and the vapor became visible. It had a certain cohesion, so that the dust tended to stick to its edges, outlining it as a huge blob.

''Now we can see it,'' Jenny said. ''Now we can blow it away.''

The roc flew down beyond the edge of the cloud and set down the boat. Then it flew to join the winged monsters of the Isle. All of them were rather pretty women; the term ''monster'' referred to a type rather than being derogatory. They watched as the creatures anchored themselves to the ground and began flapping their wings strongly. They made a draft that pushed against the cloud.

''Hey, watch what you're doing!'' the cloud protested.

''We are,'' Jenny called back with satisfaction. ''We're blowing you away.''

And slowly, with continued effort, they did just that. They blew the cloud away from the beach and the Isle, until it drifted offshore. Finally it got caught in a natural wind, and was swept away. The dire threat was over.

The women went limp with relief. Some went to the aid of the ones who had been caught in the awful vapors, and who were no longer trying to do anything deadly or obscene to each other.

Jenny, Breanna, Jeremy, and the three kings returned to the boat, and the boat waddled back toward the center pond. ''That was good thinking on your part,'' King Dor told the werewolf.

''Jenny nudged me,'' Jeremy said. ''She made me realize that the situation could be serious, and that I was the best person to take immediate action.''

They looked at Jenny. Suddenly she was blushing. ''I just—Krissica was so upset—Jeremy knew what to do.''

''Once nudged,'' Dolph agreed.

''Actually it was all such a coincidence,'' Jeremy said. ''That such an unlikely threat should occur right when there were folk visiting the Isle who could handle it.''

''Say, that's right,'' Dolph said. ''A real stroke of luck. Things could have been much worse.''

Dor glanced at Bink. Bink looked elsewhere.

Breanna perked up. "Justin says no, it was bound to happen sometime, with that Selfish Steam Isle next door. If the women hadn't been distracted by trying to impress Jeremy, they probably would have handled it well enough themselves."

"I guess so," Dolph agreed, not seeming much concerned.

They reached the pond, and the boat settled down again. The parade of hopeful women resumed. Jenny prompted Jeremy to say nice things about each one, and he was getting better at such social graces. That made the process go more smoothly, though none of the women were right for him. In fact he also complimented Jenny on her help.

But Jenny was increasingly uneasy. Finally she could handle it no more. "Breanna, can you take over here?" she whispered. "I have to go."

"But you're doing a great job," Breanna protested. "He's much better since you took over."

"Please."

"Okay. But come back soon."

Jenny got out of the boat and walked away. She blinked, trying to conceal her tears. She didn't want to make a scene.

She walked into the forest, sick at heart. What was she going to do?

Then someone followed her. It was Bink, so old yet looking so young. "Jenny, what is the matter?"

"Nothing, really," she said bravely. "It doesn't matter."

"You have been so helpful, and done so well. You have really helped Jeremy learn to impress women."

"That's the problem."

"The problem?"

She tried to stifle it, but it burst out anyway. "He's impressing me too."

"Well, of course. He's a werewolf prince. The two of you get along wonderfully."

"As a man." There: it was out.

Bink was silent for a moment, piecing it together. "So you are coming to like him yourself, and it's hard for you to help him impress other women."

"Yes. I know I have no right to be jealous, and I do want to help him. But I know I'll start messing it up, because my heart isn't in it anymore. So it's better if I just stay away, so as to give him the best chance. Breanna is pretty sharp; she can do it well enough.''

''Jenny, she isn't as good at this as you are. She's too young. How old are you?''

''Twenty one in a few days. What has that got to do with it?''

''The day of the big wedding?''

''Yes, not that it matters. It's a coincidence.''

''A coincidence,'' he repeated thoughtfully. Then he returned to the subject. ''Jenny, you have to go back. You relate to him better, because you're a wolf-rider. He was pretty much hopeless, until you came, and then he started improving. There is a continuing frisson between you. You can't desert him now.''

''But I can't *do* it anymore!''

''Then you must tell him why.''

''I can't do that. It would just make him feel guilty, and that would mess him up too. My best course is to quietly get out of his way.''

''No. He needs you. You must help him, or tell him plainly why not.''

''*You* tell him. Then he'll know, and I won't make an embarrassing scene.''

He shook his head. There was a strange glow in his eyes. ''I think this is something you have to do yourself.''

Jenny started to protest again, wiping the tears from her face. Then another person came along the path. Bink looked over her shoulder. ''Oh, hello, Jeremy,'' he said, as if this were only to be expected.

Jenny tried to run, but Bink caught her, gently but firmly, and turned her around to face the werewolf prince. ''Tell him.''

Others were approaching. This was becoming public. She burst into worse tears.

''Jenny,'' Jeremy said solicitously. ''What's the matter?''

''I can't do it,'' she blubbered.

''Jenny, I need your help. When you left, I started getting clumsy, as I usually am in manform. You understand me, and keep me looking good. Breanna says you have the touch, and you do. I need you.''

''I can't!''

''Why not?''

There was no way out. ''Because I love you myself!'' She was horrified when she heard herself speak; she hadn't meant to blurt it out like that.

He stared at her. Oh, she had done it; she had made the worst possible scene. How would this stupid little elf girl ever live this down?

"You're the one," he breathed.

Everyone was staring.

"I'm so sorry to have messed you up," she said through her tears. "I never wanted to do that. But you are just so nice, and so competent, and you're a *wolf.* I just got swept away. I'm sorry, I'm sorry." She turned and stumbled blindly out of the circle of people. Where could she hide?

"You're the one!" he repeated. "Jenny, wait! Don't you understand?"

Something wasn't making sense. She paused. "What?"

"You're my ideal love. I know you, now that you have declared. You are the one I will marry."

Now it registered. But she realized what he was doing. "That can't be. I'm not even of this world. You deserve so much better. Don't do this just because you feel sorry for me. Don't ruin your life." She stumbled on.

He strode after her and caught her. He turned her around. "You didn't know! You didn't suspect. You don't believe it. You are a foreign woman. You would never have come to me. That's part of the curse. But it's broken now. Jenny, I love you."

Her tears renewed. "Don't ruin your life," she repeated brokenly. "It's not worth it. For anyone."

"I didn't recognize you, though in retrospect it's obvious. A wolf-rider! One who loves both my forms. That curse blinded me. But no more."

She just sagged in his grasp and wept, not assimilating his explanation. "Let me go."

He didn't answer in words. He drew her in close and brought his face to hers. He kissed her.

The music of a thousand choruses sounded in her head. The explosion of a thousand lip bombs spread out from her mouth. The love of a thousand worlds suffused her body. All doubt was obliterated. She sank into blissful oblivion.

When she revived, she was lying in the boat. People were talking. "I think we know now for whom that big wedding is," Bink was saying. "Everybody loves Jenny."

"And why Jenny had to write all those invitations," Dolph agreed. "That's the bride's job."

"The Good Magician knew," Dor said. "She had to come to the Isle of Wolves, but the curse prevented her from knowing why."

"What a coincidence that it all worked out," Voracia said. "Prince Jeremy did find his true love here, so our requirement has after all been fulfilled."

"I don't think it was coincidence," Breanna said. "It was fated."

"I agree," Jeremy said. "She and I got along so well together, from the start. I think I was falling in love with her before I knew. But she had to come to me, because of the curse."

"Curses are difficult to navigate," Bink agreed. "They protect themselves, so they can't be nullified."

Jenny opened her eyes. Immediately Jeremy was there, leaning over her. "Now do you believe?" he asked.

"Now I believe," she agreed faintly.

"We will be married at Castle Roogna, on your birthday. Then I will proceed with my training to be king. But you will always be with me. I hope you won't mind being a princess or a queen, between rides."

"Just so long as it is with you."

He kissed her again. That put her out for the duration of their return trip.

14
Notable Nuptials

Justin found it interesting. He had never before been to Castle Roogna, because at the time he had been transformed to a tree it had been lost in the jungle for several hundred years. Not until Magician Trent returned to Xanth and revivified it had the castle become the center of Xanth society. Now it was impressive, with a well-kept moat complete with moat monster—Soufflé Serpent, of course—and two classy gargoyles spouting water at the front gate. He saw everything, because Breanna was looking all around, her eyes wide. She had never been here before either.

Princess Electra come to the gate to meet them, and to hug Prince Dolph. Justin had seen her only occasionally, as she was usually busy taking care of the twins, Dawn and Eve, who were seven years old. She didn't travel much unless they did, but they did sometimes visit his tree. She was in blue jeans, and didn't look much like a princess, but there was no doubt Dolph loved her. Queen Irene welcomed King Dor back, and an appealing if not lovely young Chameleon embraced Bink.

Princess Ida appeared. Justin recognized her because of her similarity to Princess Ivy, and the little moon that circled her head, and advised Breanna. "There is much to do, and we are short of time," Ida said. "So I will supervise the rehearsal. I think we shall need your help, Breanna."

"You know me?" Breanna asked, startled.

"We had news of your coming, and of your help to the three kings."

''Oh.'' And of course it did not need to be said that Breanna was the only Black Wave female in the group.

''I will show you to your room,'' Ida continued.

''But I can't stay here,'' Breanna protested.

Ida angled her head. ''Why not?''

''I'm not royal. I'm not even invited to the wedding. I'm nobody.''

''Oh, I think you are somebody. Jenny will make out an invitation for you. This way.'' Ida led the way into the castle.

The hall was huge, and the stairs were ornate. Breanna stared around in awe, and Justin was impressed. They had really fixed up the old castle.

''Here it is,'' Princess Ida said. ''Go on in.'' Then she looked right through Breanna's eyes to Justin. ''You too, Justin. We are glad to have you with us.''

She saw him! For a moment he was disoriented, and by the time he recovered, Ida was gone. He had been impolite by default.

They found themselves in a comfortable upstairs chamber. There was Jenny. ''Here is your invitation,'' she said, handing an envelope to Breanna.

Breanna looked around. Justin saw Sammy Cat sleeping on the bed. ''This is Jenny's room,'' he said.

''This is your room!'' Breanna said. ''I can't stay here.''

Jenny looked at her. ''We slept in a funk grove on the Isle of Wolves. Is this so much worse?''

''No! It's that you're the bride. I can't—''

''Please,'' Jenny said. ''Everything has changed so much for me that I feel dizzy. I can't properly concentrate. You were such a great help with all those women. Won't you help me through one more crisis?''

''Crisis?''

''This is to be the biggest, hugest wedding in years. I never thought I'd be in it. I never knew I had so many friends. I'm afraid I'll faint.''

''Do it,'' Justin said. ''Everyone else is busy, and she needs a female friend.''

Breanna caught on. ''Of course I'll help.''

''Thank you.'' Jenny sat on the bed, looking suddenly tired.

''You need a rest,'' Breanna said. ''You get it, while I find out what's going on.''

"Thank you," Jenny repeated. She lay down beside Sammy and closed her eyes. That reminded Breanna how Jenny had asked Sammy to find Jeremy's True Love, but the cat had simply asked Jenny to stroke him. None of them had caught on that Sammy had indicated Jenny herself. The curse had not allowed itself to be bypassed by the cat's magic.

Breanna stepped out the door, shutting it carefully behind her. "This way," Princess Ida said.

Breanna jumped, and Justin agreed with her. This was eerie.

"There is a banquet coming up, but I think Jenny is too tired to attend, and perhaps you are too, so it is better to have a meal in the room, and to rest."

"Uh, for sure," Breanna agreed. "But I promised to find out what's going on."

"Here is an itinerary," Princess Ida said, handing her a paper.

Breanna held it up, and Justin glanced at it. It listed all the upcoming events, with their times and the people expected to attend. The first event for Jenny was Wedding Rehearsal on the following day. "That will do," Justin said.

"Jenny said she didn't know she had so many friends," Breanna told Princess Ida.

"She's a nice person, and deserves them. But there is more to it. Her first friend in Xanth was Che Centaur, whom all the winged monsters have sworn to protect. Her second was Gwendolyn Goblin, now the Chiefess of Goblin Mountain and a powerful ally. Another friend is Sim, the Simurgh's chick, who will some century inherit the universe, whom Che is tutoring. So Jenny is extremely well connected."

Breanna whistled. "She never said!"

"She wouldn't. She doesn't see it that way. But she can't escape the royal wedding."

"I guess I can help her get through it."

Ida smiled. "I'm sure you can."

The castle kitchen had a hot meal packed and waiting. They also had a pitcher of rinsed cream, that the girls could use to untangle their messy hair; a cream rinse would be good for tangles. And a sweet-smelling deoder ant. Breanna carried it all back up to the room and set it down beside the bed where Jenny snoozed. A curl of scented steam wafted out and tickled the girl's nose, waking her. "Oh, food," she said. "I'm famished." She sat up.

There turned out to be enough for two, so they shared. They discussed the schedule. Then they took turns cleaning up and settling back down. Jenny went to take a bath, but retreated from the tub, blushing. Breanna looked, and discovered the problem: there was a shameless plug in the bottom. A mischievous princess must have put it there, some dawn or eve. She covered it over, and then they were able to bathe without shame.

There was another bed for Breanna, and suddenly she discovered how tired she was too. But Justin remained awake for a while, thinking about the interesting turn events had taken. Jenny had come to find the lost kings, and turned out to be the one to solve the werewolf prince's problem. But with that wedding, Breanna's adventure would be over, and it would be time for him to return to his tree. The prospect appealed less each time he considered it. Yet obviously he couldn't continue to impinge on the girl's life indefinitely.

Why was he so loath to end what he had always known would be a temporary association? He explored that, and realized that something surprising and rather embarrassing was happening: he was coming to like Breanna too well. She was young, and impulsive, while he was old and staid, and they had little in common. But she had increasingly good instincts, and was fun to be with. His life would be dull without her company. He would no longer be satisfied to be just another part of a forest, watching the sun cruise by each day, and the moon many nights.

Yet even that was not the whole of it. She would not stay young much longer, while he would just get older. He wished—

What did he wish? Nothing that was remotely possible. Even if he had his human body back, what point could there ever be? His peer group was about four generations removed from hers. If he were close to her age, then perhaps there might be a point in speculation. But he wasn't. So it was best not to bother her with his sad idle fancies. He would enjoy her company until the time came to separate, and then return gracefully to his tree and his fond memories. She would surely have a good life on her own.

With that settled in his mind, he relaxed, and slept, though without the innocent ease of Breanna's slumber.

Next morning there was a knock on the door, and Breanna opened it. There was Chameleon, looking barely older than Breanna, and another day prettier. "I brought breakfast," she said. "And there is something we must discuss."

"Come in," Breanna said.

This time there was food enough for three, so they all ate. Jenny looked improved, though still a bit vague.

"The zombies wish to attend the wedding," Chameleon said.

Jenny rolled her eyes. "Oh, no."

"Now wait a minute," Breanna said, speaking before Justin could stop her. Justin found that quality increasingly endearing. "What's wrong with zombies attending?"

"They would drive the other guests away," Jenny said. "Nobody likes zombies."

"I like zombies," Breanna retorted. "They're people too. They guard Castle Roogna. Why shouldn't they join its celebrations?"

Jenny looked surprised, while Chameleon looked speculative. "Perhaps they should," Chameleon said. "I can't stand them myself, but I remember how hard they fought to save the castle when the Nextwave came. And the Zombie Master and Millie are certainly good folk. Millie used to baby-sit our son Dor."

"And King Xeth and Zyzzyva will be getting married too," Breanna said. "Maybe they want to see how it's done."

"Maybe they could have a separate section," Jenny said.

The word "segregation" came to Breanna's mind, subvocalized so that he could hear it, but this time Justin managed to get there first. "It takes time to get over prejudices," he reminded her. "Jenny is offering a reasonable compromise. Remember, it is her wedding."

Breanna stifled her ire. She knew he was right: others could not impose their preferences over those of the bride. She forced a smile. "Maybe that will do. I could go talk to King Xeth and explain."

"That would be nice," Jenny said.

"Now we must do the rehearsal," Chameleon said. "The key people will be there, but informally garbed."

"You mean we can wear blue jeans, like Electra?" Jenny asked.

Chameleon smiled, in a way that made her show her age briefly. "Yes."

They went to the rehearsal. It was in the ballroom, which seemed far too large. The three kings were there, with their queens. And Jeremy Werewolf. Jenny ran to hug him, while the others took seats.

"Now the Groom will enter from the side," Princes Ida said, gesturing. Jeremy and Jenny separated, and he stepped to the side entrance. "While the Bride will be escorted down the aisle by the Father. Go to your places now."

King Dor got up and walked to the back. Jenny joined him. A puff of smoke appeared up front, and formed into a horrendous demon. "That's Demon Grossclout," Justin said. "He officiates at only the most prominent occasions."

"There will be music," Ida said. "But not at the rehearsal. Pretend you hear it."

But then Jenny bent over and ran out the back.

"What happened?" Dor asked, dismayed.

Breanna rushed out to find Jenny. She found her in the lady's room, looking ill. "Do you need healing elixir?" she asked, concerned.

"It's nerves," Jenny confessed, abashed. "I never expected to be married like this, and suddenly it seems overwhelming. I can't do it."

"Of course you can do it," Breanna said. "If I can kiss a zombie, you can marry a werewolf."

Jenny looked at her, and suddenly it was Breanna who was abashed. "I didn't mean it the way that sounded."

"I understand, I guess. But I just can't go out there. I was never important enough to rate all this attention. When I saw that stage up front—"

"Stage fright," Justin said. "We'll have to get that stage removed."

"But how do we get Jenny through the rehearsal now?"

"You do it," Jenny said. "I think I can handle it if I just watch, this time."

"But I can't—"

"Do it," Justin told her sternly. "It is only the rehearsal. We will get rid of the stage before the wedding."

"Where do you get off, telling me to do something like that?" Breanna flared.

"I am just trying to facilitate—"

"Well, don't! This business is complicated enough without your interference."

He was hurt. ''Interference! That's unfair.''

''Oh, so now I'm being unfair! Well, if you think so, why don't you just go back to your tree?''

''Breanna, I realize that you are under stress. Perhaps I spoke intemperately. But you are being unreasonable.''

''Well, I haven't had a century to learn reason! So go, get out, leave me alone.''

She had never before attacked him like this. His spirit was smarting. ''If this is what you wish, I shall of course depart.''

''Yes. Go.''

Sick at heart, he gathered himself for the jump back to his tree. He had known it had to end, but hated to have it end this way, on such a sour note. He discovered that he couldn't just fade from her; his spirit had permeated most of her body, and had to be drawn together into a compact mass before departing. But he accomplished this, and in a moment was ready to go.

''Fare well, Breanna,'' he said, trying to shield her from his grief of the occasion. Probably it was for the best, because his growing feeling for her was not licit, and needed to be abated.

''Justin—wait.''

He paused. ''Yes?''

''I—I'm sorry. Don't go.''

''But I understood that—''

''Justin, I'm a child. I threw a tantrum. But when I felt you withdrawing—I realized—please, I didn't mean it. I apologize. I jumped at nothing. I don't want you to go. Unless you really can't stand me anymore. I need you. I'm sorry. I—''

He felt enormous relief. ''Of course I will remain, if that is your wish.''

''I was bitchy. I—I've been tired of my parents always telling me what to do, and I guess you sounded like that. I struck out at you. But you are right, as always.''

''Not always. I—''

''Please. Can you forgive me?''

''Breanna, there is no need!''

''Yes there is!''

He was wary of another outburst, so yielded. ''I forgive you.''

''Thanks.'' Her face was wet with tears.

"Are you all right?" Jenny asked. "I didn't mean to make an impossible demand. I'm sorry."

"She thinks you were reacting to her request," Justin said. "She needs reassurance, if you don't mind my recommendation."

"No, I want it. I always want it. So I won't be childish."

"There is no shame in being your age. Still, I think Jenny does need this support."

So Breanna changed her position. "I'll be glad to. I—I just had to think it through. You come and watch."

"Yes," Jenny said faintly, looking less anemic. They returned to the ballroom, where King Dor waited, perhaps having been advised of the likely nature of the problem.

"I will sub for Jenny in the rehearsal," Breanna told the king. "If it's okay with you."

Dor, surprised, glanced at Jenny, who nodded. "That is good," he agreed.

"No it isn't," the floor said. "She should be in a skirt."

"Too bad for you," Breanna said, stamping hard enough to shut it up. "This is a jeans session."

"I wonder why a floor even cares what is under a woman's skirt," Justin said.

"The boards get bored," she replied. "So they try to stir things up. If women didn't react, the floor wouldn't bother."

"That is a remarkably mature perspective," Justin said admiringly.

"I have learned a lot recently, and I hope matured some," she said. "Especially in the last few minutes, I hope."

Then Princess Ida signaled, and they started the march down the aisle. Dor held out his elbow, and Breanna took it, and they got in step and walked slowly forward.

"I feel as if I'm getting married myself," Breanna confided to Justin. "It's a thrill, even though I know I'm too young and will never have a royal wedding anyway."

"Any wedding is a royal occasion," he assured her. He was so glad to have her back to normal! "When you find your beloved, whoever he may be, you won't care much about anything except being together."

"How do you know? Have you been married?"

"Never. But I have known many others who married, such as Bink and Chameleon."

''Bink!'' she said aloud, remembering. ''He's the one to take over Castle Zombie.''

King Dor shook his head. ''Dolph mentioned that possibility to him, but Chameleon absolutely vetoed it.''

''But isn't that why they were youthened?''

''It can't be, because the position has to be voluntary. Someone who likes zombies, or at least respects them.'' He glanced ahead. ''Now pay attention to the rehearsal; you don't want to mess it up for Jenny.''

''For sure,'' she agreed, and oriented on the wedding march.

Unfortunately that freed Justin for more thought. During his many decades as a tree, he hadn't thought much about this aspect of life. Now he couldn't help it. Breanna said that she felt as if she were getting married. Justin picked up that feeling, only for him the feeling was not general or nebulous, it was specific. He wished that he were standing by that stage, watching Breanna approach.

There was no fool like an old fool, he chided himself. He had allowed his interest in the girl's activities to shade into interest in her. He had let himself be carried away by the sudden surprise of Jenny Elf's revelation as Jeremy Werewolf's perfect love, and now fancied himself in a similar role. His fancy didn't care that he had nothing in common with Breanna—that he was too old, she too young, he a tree, she a girl with her future awaiting her. His common sense recognized the vision for nonsense, yet his fancy still longed for it. Even if she had any such interest, which of course she wouldn't, the dread Adult Conspiracy forbade any such relationship.

The answer was clear: he should keep silent about this ridiculous image, and return to his tree when the wedding ceremony was done. He would spare her any knowledge of his insanity. That would save both of them considerable embarrassment. And, of course, in time, the notion would fade, with no harm done. It might have been better if he had departed when they had their difference, but he couldn't make himself go as long as she wished him to remain.

But he knew that in due course he would have to go, and that he would grieve for that sweet foolishness. He had indeed been too long away from human life and activity. He had not allowed for the resurgent emotions of the human state.

Breanna reached the front of the hall. Jeremy looked at her, with a vulpine smile of mischief. ''Why Jenny, how you have changed.''

"I got really sick, and degenerated to this blackface," she agreed.

"Shall I kiss you and make you well?"

"Don't risk it; it might make you ill instead, and someone in the back row would faint."

He laughed. "Really?"

"No. More likely I would just turn into a frog."

"I think that if I had not found The One, you would have been a worthy substitute, Breanna."

"Not at my age, you handsome wolf."

He laughed again. "In three years, when you burst on the adult scene, all eligible men had better take cover. You are one cute creature in nature as well as appearance."

Breanna tried to blush, unsuccessfully. He had finally gotten to her. "Then I guess I had better line up a prospect before then, so as not to scare the whole Land of Xanth out of its magic."

Justin shook his nonexistent head. What a girl!

They got through the rehearsal, and Breanna returned to brief Jenny on the details. "Beware of Jeremy's sense of humor," she warned. "He threatened to kiss me."

"He doesn't even need lip bomb," Jenny said dreamily.

"If you get woozy during the real ceremony, hang on tight to King Dor's elbow; he's very steady."

"He's the Father of the Bride," Jenny agreed. "He's been through it before."

They retired to Jenny's room. "I'm sorry I got sick and put you on the spot," Jenny said.

"Oh, it was fun," Breanna reassured her. "It made me want to get married myself."

"Oh, do you have a man in mind?"

"There's one I would like, I think, but I don't think he's interested."

Justin felt another shock. Breanna had a man in mind? "You didn't take Jeremy seriously!" he said to her, appalled.

"No, of course not," she replied silently. "It's someone else, who's not married."

Justin was only partly relieved. He had had no idea that Breanna had noticed a man in the course of her travels. Was it someone who might return her interest? If so, she was too young. If not, then she would be disappointed. So either way, the matter was unsettling. ''May I inquire who?''

Breanna hesitated. ''If you haven't picked up on it, then I think you wouldn't understand.''

''Of course.'' He was gracious, but her implied reproof stung. Always before, she had shared her concerns with him. Now she wasn't doing so. He remained intensely curious what man she was thinking of, but refused to pry. She was an attractive girl—how well he knew!—and surely could make an impression on the man she chose. It was certainly her right to do so, within limits. So he wished her well, though the thought of her finding love and fulfillment elsewhere gave him an unreasonable pang. He would almost have preferred to return to his tree at the time of their argument, because then at least he might have retained some fond foolish illusions.

Next day the important guests began arriving, and Breanna was busy showing them to their rooms. Almost everyone else was busy with something, and Justin knew most of the guests, so this made sense. Castle Roogna was big, and seemed to get bigger to fill the need; that was one of the advantages of an enchanted castle.

The first to come was Clio, the Muse of History. Both Breanna and Justin were amazed when she introduced herself. ''Is there something historical going on?'' Breanna blurted, as usual before she thought.

''History is always in the making,'' the Muse replied. ''Every where, every time. However, some occasions seem more significant than others, and this is indeed one of those occasions.''

''It's really great, Jenny getting married to a prince.''

Clio turned a disconcerting gaze on them. ''That too,'' she agreed.

''What does she mean?'' Breanna asked Justin internally.

''I have no idea, unless the convenience of this gathering facilitates another important activity or decisions.''

''Exactly, Justin,'' Clio agreed. Then she closed her door, leaving them both trying to blush.

Then Good Magician Humfrey arrived, with a woman Breanna didn't recognize. Before anyone could think of looking askance, she introduced herself: ''I am MareAnn, Humfrey's fifth and a half wife. I was his first true love, but wouldn't marry him for 142 years because I didn't want to lose my innocence and with it my ability to summon unicorns. But later, having resided in hell, I concluded that much of my innocence had already been sacrificed, so I married him. Thus he obtained a half-wife of 142 years. I am the Designated Wife for this occasion, as the Gorgon is busy elsewhere.''

''Oh,'' Breanna said, somewhat taken aback. ''Well, I hope you enjoy the wedding.''

''I doubt it,'' Humfrey grumped.

''Oh, come on, you know that deep down under all those layers of grumpiness you do like the chance to get out and meet old friends,'' MareAnn said, tweaking his ear. ''As for me, I love weddings. I cry buckets.''

''But aren't weddings supposed to be fun?''

''Tearful fun. You'll see.'' They moved on into their chamber.

The next guests were unfamiliar to Justin, but Breanna almost fainted. ''Mom! Dad!'' she screamed, charging up to hug her parents. ''What are you doing here?''

''We received an invitation to a wedding,'' her mother said. ''We hoped it wasn't yours.''

''For sure!''

''And we thought it was about time for the Black Village to start spreading out,'' her father said. ''We need to interact more positively with the rest of Xanth, especially now that there are a number of black children with magic talents.''

''You bet!'' Justin saw that though Breanna had never mentioned her family, and might even have felt somewhat alienated from them, she did love them and was glad to see them. She was bubbling over with things to tell them. But soon they retired to their room; they had made a long trip here, and were tired, they said. Justin suspected that they did not want to get in Breanna's way. They were after all Mundanes, perhaps feeling out of place here.

A decrepit coach drawn by two half-dead horses drew up to the moat. ''The Zombie Master and Millie the Ghost!'' Breanna cried, dashing out to meet them. Sure enough, the two were just stepping down to the ground. But they weren't alone: King Xeth and Zyzzyva Zombie were there too, looking quite regal in formal clothing. Breanna greeted them all like the old friends they had become, and showed them to the castle's special cell in the cellar, where the local zombies congregated. This wasn't isolation; they had requested it.

The biggest surprise was a couple Justin didn't recognize, but Breanna did. ''Tristan Troll and Mouse Terian!'' she exclaimed joyfully.

''Yes, we are a couple now,'' the lovely woman said, hugging her. ''Thanks to you.''

''But how can you be in human form, away from your mistress?''

''Com Passion is here with me,'' Terian said, touching her pocket. ''In remote unit form.'' There was a little screen tucked there. As Justin looked, it formed a little female smiley-face.

''How clever,'' Breanna said enthusiastically. ''And is Com Pewter here too?''

Tristan touched his own pocket, where another little screen peeked out. Words appeared on it: GIRL LOSES INTEREST.

Breanna lost interest in the computers, but Justin didn't. As Breanna led the couple to their chamber, he questioned her, and learned that Mouse Terian was a real mouse, rendered, by Com Passion's power to change local reality, into human form for the occasion, and that Tristan served similarly as Com Pewter's mouse. It seemed that mice and machines were now dating, thanks to something Breanna had done before she met Justin. The girl just seemed to have effects.

The chamber for that party was small and plain, but in a moment it changed and became palatial. The computers had the power to change reality in their vicinity, and were using it.

A big tank was delivered, containing three lovely mermaids: Ash, Cedar, and Mahogany. They were respectively blonde, red-haired, and brunette, and attracted some attention as they diverted themselves in the moat. Certainly Soufflé Serpent enjoyed the company.

There was a rumble as of thunder, and a shadow passed across the castle. It was a monstrous bird, in fact a roc, coming in for a landing. The mermaids looked up. ''Here comes Roxanne!'' Ash called, waving. The roc wig-wagged, responding.

Jenny's friend Che Centaur arrived, with his friend Cynthia, both being winged centaurs. Che was to be an Usher, a position of honor. With them was Gwendolyn Goblin, queen of Goblin Mountain, another close friend. She would be the Maid of Honor. There had been no trouble from those particular goblins since Gwenny's ascension. There was one more member of that party: a huge glittering baby bird. ''That must be Sim, the Simurgh's chick!'' Justin exclaimed. ''Princess Ida said he was another friend of Jenny's.'' Now he realized why Roxanne Roc was here; she was Sim's nanny and guardian. She took her job most seriously, but knew that there was no threat to the chick in Castle Roogna. So she was visiting with the moat party, being too big to squeeze inside.

''I am so glad to meet you, Sim,'' Breanna said smoothly.

''Peep,'' the chick said, bobbing his head.

''That means thank you,'' Che said. ''He could read your mind, and project his response to you, but he feels that would be impolite, so he sticks to bird talk.''

Breanna smiled. ''I really appreciate that, Sim. I have all kinds of black secrets I'd rather not share.''

Sim nodded. There seemed to be a smile on his beak.

''I love weddings,'' Cynthia said. ''I can hardly wait until we have one, and start our family of winged centaurs.''

''But we're only thirteen,'' Che protested.

''I was older once, so I'm entitled to romantic notions. Do you think our foal will have a separate magic talent?''

''But our talent is making things, including ourselves, light, so we can fly.''

''That's a species talent, like walking on four feet. Do you see human beings limited to the talent of walking on two feet?''

Che glanced at Gwenny Goblin. ''I agree with her,'' Gwenny said. ''It's high time goblins had individual magic talents too. Why should my friend Gloha Goblin-Harpy be limited to flying?''

So he glanced at Sim, who this time projected a thought to the group: ''Flying is plenty of magic for anyone.''

Gwenny made a cute moue. ''That's right—side with your own gender, bird-brain. What does Breanna say?''

''Don't get into it,'' Justin warned.

So Breanna avoided the issue. ''I'm still waiting for Mundanes to find magic.''

They laughed, and moved on.

Two winged mermaids flew in, and joined the three at the moat. These were Aurora and Erica, whom the three kings knew. Soon after, another party of winged centaurs descended: the ones they had met on Mount Rushmost and gotten the lip bomb from.

Then Voracia arrived, representing the Isle of Women. And Tipsy Troll with Phil Istine, who had evidently worked things out well. And a handsome princely young man with a breathtakingly lovely young woman, who introduced themselves as Nimby and Chlorine. Justin had never heard of them, but they seemed to know everybody. He had been too long away from human society; he must have missed much. There was something odd about this couple, but he couldn't place it. They seemed somehow too knowing.

On it went, as it seemed that just about everyone who was anyone in Xanth came to attend the wedding. All for Jenny Elf, who had arrived mostly by accident nine years before, from the World of Two Moons, with her cat Sammy, and become very popular in Xanth. Justin was glad for her, as she was certainly a nice girl. But it made him much aware of what he had missed when he became a tree. Romance, marriage, enduring human interactions. Of course he could ask Magician Trent to transform him back to man form, but to what point? He would be cripplingly old.

Everything came together on the appointed day. Justin watched the proceedings through Breanna's eyes, and his sadness of joy increased. They had removed the stage, so that the girl did not get frightened. Jenny looked beautiful in her elfin way, and Jeremy Werewolf was darkly handsome. King Dor gave Jenny away in a royal manner, and for this occasion even the floor and furniture managed to keep their smart remarks to a minimum.

When it was done, King Dor announced that there would be a banquet for all after the reception. A reception line formed, with Jenny and Jeremy meeting the guests personally.

The worst was over. Breanna stepped back, wiping her face. ''MareAnn said that women are supposed to cry at weddings,'' she said. ''I thought it was applesauce, but I can't stop my eyes.''

''It is natural,'' Justin said. ''There is no shame in it.''

''But I don't believe in such idiocy.''

''Under that rebellion, you are a woman.'' She couldn't know how sincerely he meant that.

''I guess I am.''

''Anyway, I must confess that some of those tears may have been mine. There is just something about a wedding.''

''For sure.''

The odd couple approached. "May we speak with you, Breanna and Justin?" the lovely woman asked. "I am Chlorine, and this is my friend Nimby."

"Pleased to meet you," Justin prompted Breanna, though they had already met, passingly.

"Pleased to meet you," Breanna echoed aloud. "Sure, tell me what's on your mind."

"You have done Nimby a significant favor, and he wishes to give you another gift."

"But we never met before today."

"We have met, but you don't remember. That's what this concerns."

Breanna's confusion was one with Justin's. "He wants to give me something?"

"The gift of memory," Chlorine said. "On condition that you share it only with Justin."

"Okay?" Breanna asked Justin, unsure what this could be about.

"I agree," he said. "I am curious about this too."

"We agree," Breanna said.

"Look Nimby in the eye."

Breanna and Justin looked the handsome young man in the eye. The eye seemed to expand, becoming like a portal, and through it was a scene of a lovely woman and a donkey-headed dragon and Mare Imbri. Suddenly a phenomenal memory flooded through Breanna, and through Justin too, though it had not been his experience. This was the Demon $X(A/N)^{TH}$ in mortal form, and he had given Breanna her talent of seeing in blackness, in exchange for the right to watch her dreams. Breanna had agreed to the deal, then had her memory of the experience deleted. This explained how a girl originating in Mundania had come to have a magic talent.

Breanna became unsteady, but Chlorine took her arm to keep her balanced. "I made the deal," she breathed. "But then Imbri had to take away the memory, so no one would know about Nimby."

"Yes. Thanks to you, he has at last learned to dream. He has learned that dreams are not confined to sleep; they also represent a person's most cherished ambitions. This is so immensely valuable to him that though he will no longer watch your dreams, you may keep the talent—and the memory."

"But I didn't really do anything," Breanna protested.

"You gave permission, and this was enough. That enabled him to learn what he wished to, without having to depart the Land of Xanth."

"But if he had left, the magic would have gone too!"

"True. Most of it, at any rate. Just as the law of gravity would be repealed if the Demon E(A/R)TH departed from Mundania. The natives probably wouldn't like that. So we prefer that the Demons not travel too much."

"Amen!" Justin agreed.

Chlorine nodded, smiling. "We feel it appropriate for you to know the truth about Nimby. There may come times when you need to protect this knowledge from discovery elsewhere, as was the case with Magician Bink's talent. Do not reveal Nimby's nature to anyone else, any more than you reveal Bink's secret."

"You know about that?"

"Nimby knows about everything he wishes to. He thanks you for your assistance, and your discretion."

"Gee—thanks," Breanna said, awed. "I never dreamed—"

"You dreamed; you did not remember. And if you should ever encounter something that you suspect warrants Nimby's attention, focus on his name, and we will soon make an appearance." Then Chlorine looked through Breanna's eye to Justin. "And your own dream is not necessarily foolish. It can be realized, if you find the way before this day ends."

"But it's impossible!" Justin protested.

"No. Merely improbable." Then Chlorine and Nimby turned away.

"What dream?" Breanna asked.

"It's nothing. Just a completely foolish passing fancy."

"What dream?" she repeated more firmly.

"Please, this is nothing you wish to know about."

"Justin, if there's anything I really want to know about, it's whatever some adult says I *don't* want to know about. Come on—we're about to separate, so I won't have another chance. What was she talking about?"

He felt the pain again. "As you say, we are about to separate, our adventure together completed. There is no point in complicating it by an irrelevancy."

Breanna paused, and he knew by her expression that she was working out a strategy. "Suppose we exchange secrets? I'll tell you mine, and you tell me yours."

"No, that would not be wise."

"Here's mine: I don't want you to go, Justin. I know you want to return to your tree, but I wish you would stay. I mean, beyond the adventure."

"I would like to stay, but should not."

"Why can't you? I really need your guidance. You have helped me grow up so much, and besides I like your company. I like it a lot."

"And I like yours. But you have your own life to lead, without the complication of my presence."

"What's your secret?"

"I did not make your deal."

"Tell me anyway."

"I fear you would find it dismaying."

"Tell me, Justin. Please."

She was bound to have it. "It's similar in a certain respect to the situation Jenny found herself in. She—"

"She liked Jeremy too well. Justin—are you saying—?"

"I'm afraid I am. I like you too well, Breanna. So rather than embarrass you further—"

"Like a friend, or like a romance?"

"Like both. But of course that's ludicrous, because in actuality I am neither. I am an adviser and vicarious adventurer."

"But I'm young and impulsive and militant, and sometimes I blow up for no good reason."

"And I am old and staid and a tree, and sometimes I become too dictatorial in my advice. So there is no point in further discussion."

Another guest was approaching. "This isn't finished," Breanna said, and turned to meet the other.

But it soon would be, he knew. Perhaps that was just as well.

It turned out to be a pair of guests: Xeth and Zyzzyva Zombie. They were well-dressed, and looked very good, considering. He was in a suit and was handsome in a pale way, while she was in a low-cut formal gown that was attracting many gazes. Justin suspected that many guests did not even realize that these were zombies.

"We want to thank you for your timely help," Xeth said. "You introduced us."

''Well I just—you know,'' Breanna said, embarrassed.

''Whatever your motive, we appreciate the result,'' Zyzzyva said. ''We thank Justin Tree too.''

''You are welcome,'' Justin said through Breanna's mouth.

The couple moved on, mingling with the guests without awkwardness, and Justin was glad that Breanna had made an issue and gotten them admitted. They were well-preserved zombies—the very best preserved—and their nature hardly showed, but the principle was a good one. Breanna's surprising liberalization about zombies was carrying him along; zombies were indeed worthy folk in their own right.

''Now about that discussion,'' Breanna said to him. ''I thought you were mostly putting up with me, for the sake of having your adventure. I thought we got along well because you are so good at smoothing over my outbursts. At hiding your own feelings of disgust, and coming up with reasonable ways to interpret what you know is crazy, so I won't feel bad. Even when I went nuts and told you to go, you forgave me, instead of taking the chance to bug out. I thought you thought I was pretty much of a snot.''

''I never thought that!''

''Well, even if I was a perfect teen, there'd be things you'd find ridiculous. And I know I'm not perfect. That's why I need your guidance. You helped me get over my prejudice and be a better person. You never even saw me as black.''

''As what?''

''That's my point. Maybe it's because you're a tree. You understand about being different.''

''But you're not different, except in your inimitable character, which always did appeal to me. Your charmingly direct manner—''

''I'm just better with you than without you. That's why I wanted to keep you.''

''I can appreciate that. But now that you know my failing, there is no need to—''

''Failing?''

''I have admitted that I failed to maintain a proper objectivity with respect to your person. To keep the necessary emotional distance. This places you in an unfairly awkward position. It is in fact a tacit violation of the Adult Conspiracy. So it seems best to disengage immediately.''

"Let's see if I have this straight: you like me, so you want to leave?"

"That is essentially it, though I would use the word 'need' rather than 'want.' I need to vacate before I corrupt you."

"Corrupt me! Justin, you never did anything of the kind! You helped me grow up where I needed to."

"And now, by my transgression of emotion, I threaten to force on you the kind of awareness you should not yet encounter. I fear I have already said too much."

She pondered a moment. "I have to tell, you, Justin, I wasn't, as you would put it, entirely candid with you either."

"You have been more than polite, considering the affront."

"I said I like you. Like you a lot. But that's an understatement, hiding the truth. I've got a Jenny problem too."

"You are a good friend. Unfortunately I spoiled it. I wish you well with the man whose interest you seek."

Her bosom heaved. "I was right: you don't understand about that. But now I'll tell you. There is no man. Not like that, I mean. Justin, I think I love you."

"That is the very corruption that must be avoided! You can't—"

"Damn it, Justin, give me credit for knowing what I'm talking about. It isn't just storks or sex, it's love, and I think I know it when I feel it. I think I'm feeling it."

He was almost dumbfounded. "That isn't possible, at your age and my circumstance. You mistake a passing fancy for—"

"The hell I do! I don't want to keep you because you give me good advice. I want to keep you because I can't stand to lose you. But I didn't want to be a brat about hanging on to you, when I know I'm just a child in your eyes. When I thought you were just being diplomatic, encouraging me so as not to hurt my feelings. I guess that's why I blew up at you: I was mad because of the futility of my interest. But now that I know you care—"

"Oh, I do, Breanna! But this is absolute foolishness. We are merely mind companions. We can never be more."

Her jaw set. "I want to make love with you."

Justin reeled, mentally, emotionally. "This—this—even if it were possible, it would be forbidden, because—"

"I'm the one who rejected the Adult Conspiracy, remember? I

think a girl is old enough if she thinks she is. If she knows what it's all about. I do know. And if she wants to. And I do want to. With you.''

''This is unacceptable. Your age—''

''Justin, if I were old enough, would you do it?''

It was as though he were sailing in a tiny boat on a treacherous sea in a storm. He wanted to be honest, but it was difficult. ''I must confess I would want to. But even so, I wouldn't be able to. My age—''

''If you were young again.''

''But I'm not young, and in any event any such speculation would be corruptive to your innocence.''

''$$$$!''

The obscene expletive almost blew him away. ''Breanna, please!''

''Then stop pretending I'm innocent. You can't corrupt me, because I already know the forbidden words and deeds. Do you want me to spell out exactly how folk summon the stork?''

He knew she wasn't bluffing. ''I spoke figuratively. I am aware that you brought the knowledge with you from Mundania. But in experience, in this respect, you are innocent, and it would be a violation for me to even suggest that you take any such action with anyone.''

''All I want is a straight answer to a straight question. I think you owe me that much.''

He capitulated. ''If I were young, and you of age, and you wished to, yes, I would do it. Not because of the personal pleasure there might be, but because the sweetest thing I can imagine is simply loving you and being loved by you. But since you are too young, and I too old, it is no fit subject for speculation.''

''Well, I'm brash and impulsive, and I have a notion.''

''I must confess that it is your very boldness and animation that draws me to you. Life with you could never be dull, regardless of the surrounding circumstances. What is your notion?''

''We must talk with the Zombie Master again.''

''With Jonathan? How could that relate?''

''Let's find out.'' She marched across the hall to where the Zombie Master and Millie the Ghost were standing.

''Why hello, Breanna,'' Millie said. ''It is so nice to see you again.

We enjoyed your visit to Castle Zombie so much. You must come again.''

''Maybe I will, thanks.'' She turned to the Zombie Master. ''You're going to retire, aren't you?''

''When the Good Magician procures a suitable replacement for me,'' he agreed.

''And for me,'' Millie said. ''We thought that Bink and Chameleon might be the ones, but it turns out that they aren't interested.''

Breanna nodded. ''How about Justin Tree?''

The Zombie Master shook his head. ''He is almost as old as I am, apart from his vegetable state.''

''For sure. But would he be good to do the job, apart from that? If he resumed human form?''

The Zombie Master considered her question seriously. ''Yes, I believe he would. If he were interested. But the age—it does need to be a much younger person.''

''Someone Bink's age?''

''Yes. His present physical age. He is of course much older mentally.'' Then he did a double-take. ''Are you suggesting that Justin take the elixir of youth, as Bink did?''

''Yeah.''

''I think the Good Magician would provide it, for that purpose,'' Millie said. ''But there would still need to be a woman. The castle—the situation—would be too lonely otherwise. The zombies mean well, but they aren't good company on cold evenings.''

''How about a woman of eighteen, three years from now?''

The Zombie Master looked blank, but Millie understood immediately. ''Oh, Breanna, yes! That would be beautiful. You have already done so much for the zombies.''

''Yeah, I guess I'm the zombie lover. But it's not just for them. It's because I want Justin. I want him human and young. As he could be, if someone with some clout spoke for him. I thought that maybe if you put in a word to the Good Magician—''

The Zombie Master shook his head. ''I doubt I need to. This is surely what he has in mind. Assuming that Justin is amenable.''

Breanna turned inward, but spoke aloud. ''Are you, Justin? Take my mouth.''

How neatly she had put it together! He was overwhelmed. ''Yes!''

he said with her mouth. "But still, in fairness, I must point out that you are not yet of age to make such a decision. You must wait three years. By that time you may have reconsidered."

"How about this: we stay together that three years, just as we are now. Then we decide whether we still feel the same way, and want to do it. Maybe I'll have changed my mind, or you'll have changed yours. So we can stay together, or separate, or decide to take the position. Then we go to the Good Magician and ask him for the youth elixir. Then we go to your tree, and Magician Trent changes you back to human, and you take the elixir and turn twenty one. Then we get married and move to Castle Zombie for a long time, and stand up for the zombies when they need it. Does this make sense to you?"

Justin, amazed again, couldn't answer immediately. Her impulsiveness was absolutely delightful, but this was almost too much to assimilate. But Millie kissed Breanna, and the Zombie Master reached out and shook her hand. "It makes sense to us."

Breanna caught Bink's eye, and he came over with Chameleon. "You won't need to worry about Castle Zombie," Breanna said. "Justin and I may go there, in three years, when we're young enough and old enough."

Bink smiled. "I am glad to hear it. It is a most convenient coincidence."

Breanna laughed. "For sure! I'm glad you didn't take that position." She stepped close and kissed him. "Thanks."

Chameleon raised a brow. "Just what is your relationship with this girl?"

"There's just something about teenage girls that is appealing," he said, kissing her. She, of course, was now sixteen.

"I remember," the Zombie Master said, glancing at Millie.

Then the four of them dissolved into a dialogue about old times. Breanna faded back. "Come on, Justin—let's go somewhere and pretend that I'm eighteen and you're twenty one, and we're kissing."

"Do I have a choice?"

"Of course not. But let's not tell, okay? Not for three years."

But they were intercepted by another couple: Mare Imbri in human form, and her partner Forrest Faun. "Would you like a dream?" Imbri inquired.

"For sure! You know which one. Make it extra real."

"My love is very good at making the unreal extra real," Forrest remarked, patting Imbri's bottom.

"Are you trying to be a satyr instead of a faun?" Imbri asked him archly.

"No, I was trying to be more of a satire. The kind curse fiends hate, when they put on a play."

"This play will be no satire. It's more of a romance."

"But it wouldn't be proper to—" Justin started to protest. However, his heart wasn't in it. He longed for just such a dream.

Imbri looked into Breanna's eyes, and through them into Justin's eyes. "Dreams don't have to be proper," she murmured. "That's part of what the Demon learned."

Then reality dissolved, and Justin was a virile young man, and Breanna was a lovely black eighteen. They were alone in the glade that once had been filled by his tree form. It was some dream, whose naughty details they would never tell.

Epilog

The Good Magician Humfrey made his way to one of the few secluded spots on the Castle Roogna premises: the rose garden. The roses were beautiful, fragrant, and restful. He sat down amidst them, closing his old eyes.

"How nice to see you again, Humfrey."

He didn't open his eyes. "Go away, Clio; I'm not ready for another challenging historical nexus."

She laughed. "Have no concern; I will be occupied for some time recording this one. What a delightful girl!"

"Jenny is no girl. She's a married woman, thanks to our meddling."

"And Breanna?"

He nodded. "There are appealing qualities about her, despite her youth. She is direct and forthright and determined, and quite ready to challenge the status quo—exactly the kind of representative the zombies need to combat the prejudice of the rest of Xanth. When Mare Imbri told me about her connection with Nimby—"

"Nimby," the Muse of History repeated thoughtfully. "He gave her back her memory of his true nature."

"Just as Bink told her of the nature of his talent. It is all information Justin Tree may need, when he becomes the new Zombie Master. It is a more important position than most folk realize."

It was her turn to nod. "Indubitably. Bink is fortunate. He and Chameleon have a second youth to spend—all so they could serve as an example to those who needed to think of youthening to similar ages. So that they could achieve their necessary if unlikely destinies.''

``And so Bink could handle the rigors of the rest of the mission, and ensure via his talent that it not come to grief.'' Humfrey finally cracked open half an eye. ``Now if you are quite done reminiscing about the obvious—''

Clio laughed. ``For now. But brace yourself; the next volume promises to be more complicated, with a special irrelevant significance.''

The Good Magician groaned.

Author's Note

The last novel, *Faun & Games,* introduced the worlds of Ida's moons; this one explored them farther. Readers have asked me why Xanth has a hell and no heaven; I think heaven is somewhere among those tiny moons. They are larger than they seem from a distance, and there is room for everyone there, even princes and zombies, as we have seen.

I continue to hear from my readers, at a rate of about 150 letters a month, and some have more than puns on their minds. Consider this paragraph by Monica Ramirez:

> You know, life is funny. Jenny Elf got hit by a car, sent to the hospital, and put in your books. Other people who get hit by cars aren't put in novels, but that doesn't lessen the pain of their families any more. Unfortunately, I had a Jenny Elf experience lately. Not me, a friend of mine. Patricia Foley has been my baby-sitter since my earliest childhood, mine and my sister's. When my sister would ignore me, I would talk to Miss Pat, as I called her. We'd play board games, and we became close friends. But on February 8, she was crossing the street on her way to a doctor's appointment and got hit by a car, like Jenny. But unlike Jenny, there was nothing the doctors could do for her, so [they] disconnected the machines that kept her alive. I attended the funeral of my thirty-nine-year-old friend on Monday night. But they never caught the driver who

hit her; he just drove on. Most likely he was drunk. Why do people drink and then try to drive? It only results in pain and sometimes death. It's not fair. She didn't need to die. Please, Mr. Anthony, why?

It's really the wrong question. Drunk or reckless drivers do it because they can get away with it, because our legal system doesn't take the matter seriously. The drunk who took out Jenny Elf never paid any penalty. They don't give half a darn for the welfare of anyone else. The right question, as I see it, is why does our society allow this pointless mayhem to continue? Freedom is great, but what about the freedom of innocent folk to live in peace without being targets for any idiot with a bottle and a car?

Meanwhile my own dull mundane life continued during the writing of this novel. Last year I bought a right-handed compound bow and learned to fire it reasonably accurately. This time a reader, Dee Lahr (I suspect she's related to the nice demonesses, such as D. Light or D. Lirium) sold me her composite left-handed bow, and now I am slowly learning to fire it, considerably less accurately. A compound bow is always strung, and has pulley-cams that perform the seemingly magic trick of allowing you to hold the string with only, say, twenty pounds of pull—but when you release it, it assumes the force of fifty five pounds of pull, and propels the arrow viciously forward. Once I developed the muscle to draw that fifty five pounds, so as to reach the twenty-pound let-off, it was great. In fact I have now cranked it up to sixty pounds, because I'm doing this for exercise rather than entertainment. But the composite bow is simpler; it must be strung each time, which is tricky if you don't know how, and there is no let-off. So I work harder to shoot the arrows with considerably less force. But it's all good experience.

Last year, also, I bought a recumbent bicycle, that resembles a deck chair with wheels. You lean back and peddle out front, and the handlebars are under your seat. It's weird at first, but a superior machine and a great ride, because there's no stress on your arms, and no crotch-binding saddle. That set me up for the cycle I bought during this novel, not long after the left-handed bow: the RowBike. It's actually an exercise machine, but it can be ridden around the neighborhood. You row it, the seat sliding back and forth while you draw the oars, which are the handlebars, and move forward. But it's awful to balance, at first. You need lots of room to maneuver, but I don't have room, just a long narrow drive. So I went constantly off the sides and had to slam to a stop. But I'm making progress, and now can make the whole three-quarter-mile trip to the gate in one haul, though I do make constant involuntary S-curves.

So my adventure of life has not ended in my '60s. But it's not all good. Also in this period I developed a pain in my left upper jaw, together with pressure and cold sensitivity. When it got so bad that I had to take heavy-duty pain pills so as to get to sleep, I went to my dentist. By the day's end, I had had a root canal job done on a lower left tooth. They call it transferred pain; where I felt it wasn't where it really was. The discomfort faded, but I had to chew on my right side—which had some similar symptoms in the upper jaw, now that I couldn't avoid it. I returned in two weeks for a routine followup check—and got another root canal in my lower right jaw, to take care of the referred pain there. My mouth felt better, but in another two weeks I had a third root canal, in the upper right jaw, to clear up the smaller remaining sensitivity. The endodontist seemed to be getting quite cheerful with all that business I brought him. Each one means a reworked crown to follow, too. O joy! That will make my regular dentist happy too. No, I take care of my teeth. It seems that the weak point in the sixteen onlays (partial crowns) I had two decades ago—the experience translated into my dental science fiction novel, Prostho Plus—is the cement. Saliva breaks it down and the germs wedge in, and take out the nerve. So about half of those onlays have been replaced following root canals. Teeth are expensive to maintain. My advice, based on solid experience, is to choose parents with naturally perfect teeth, so that your tooth genes are better than mine.

As I set up to edit this novel, I was letting our ninety-one-pound dog Obsidian out into our fenced yard—we live on a tree farm, but the dog does not roam that, because there are alligators and rattlesnakes and other creatures we don't want hurt—when I spied an owl in our pool enclosure. Our pool has long since gone natural, somewhat in the manner of my teeth; frogs live in it, dragonflies hatch from it, and a tree poked a branch through its wire-net ceiling. We had a flap, catching dog before dog caught owl. Then the problem: how to get owl out of enclosure? I call her Jean Owl; she's a barred owl, a foot and a half long, a huge bird. No, not quite as big as Roxanne Roc. She's been around for years, and uses the trees in our yard for snoozing in daytime. Evidently she got in through the ceiling hole, and couldn't find her way out. So we propped open the doors, but though she would fly up and sit on the door-sill, she didn't catch on that it was a way out. Then her offspring, Junior, arrived. Instead of Jean flying out to join him, he flew in to join her. So now we had two owls perched on the pool railing by the door, not knowing the way out. Finally I took tools and ripped out the netting above the door. Then I circled around, sort of herding them toward it, and this time when the owls perched there, they hopped to the top of the open door, and thence back into the wilderness. So I was an hour late starting work, but Jean and Junior were free. All part of the fun of living in the forest, and we wouldn't be here if we didn't like nature. We have gopher tortoises living in their burrows against the north and south sides of the house; "Tortle" comes out to watch me practice my archery. Wrens try to nest in my bicycle bags; that's awkward, because I don't think they want their eggs to travel up to our gate and back each day. So I covered the back of the bicycle with plastic wrapping material—and they started building their nest in that. So I moved the bike and hung the plastic on an iron ring used for storing wood, and that worked; Carrol and Lina Wren are using it. As I edit this novel, there are perhaps five eggs in the nest. I suspect that in due course they will hatch into Wrenny and Gwenny and their siblings. We like wrens; they are brave little birds, and go after bad bugs. We just have to compromise a bit to make them feel at home.

Some readers may not be aware of the story of Jenny Elf, so I'll give a brief reprise. She started as Jenny Gildwarg in Mundania, age twelve, crossing the street on a school route, when a drunk driver cruised by the stopped cars and carried her away on his bumper. Fast help got her smashed body to the hospital, but she was given only a fifteen percent chance to survive. But she hung on, and was upgraded to fifty percent after emergency surgery. But she remained in a coma for months, until her mother, in desperation, wrote to her favorite author, in the hope that a letter from him might rouse her. So I wrote to Jenny early in 1989, and they read my letter to her, and the ploy was successful; she did come out of the coma. That was when it became apparent that she was almost totally paralyzed, being able only to wiggle one toe, move her right hand some, and her head some. She couldn't talk. Her mind was there, but not most of the connections to her body. So began a major one-way correspondence; I still write to her every week, eight years later, and the first year's letters were published as *Letters to Jenny.* Now she is twenty, and by the time this novel is published she will be twenty one. The character based on her, Jenny Elf, appeared in Isle of View, has made incidental appearances since, and now is married. I thought it was time. But Jenny in Mundania remains mostly paralyzed, though her computer is a big help. She can speak a few words, and with the aid of leg braces and a wraparound walker and nervous nurses ready to catch her if she falls, can walk a few steps. She has continued her schooling, and hopes to attend college, if the system can handle a person this physically limited.

And what of Breanna? Is there a real life analog? I thought not, but again, as I edited, I saw a page ad in the Sunday supplement *Parade* for an ''In The Limelight Barbie'' doll, patterned after the famous white Barbie, but black. She wears a snugly fitting chocolate brown gown, and a metallic cape with a lime-green inner lining, and is described as ''boldly stylish.'' I have my doubts about coincidence; I think that's Breanna manifesting in Mundania. Sort of having her fling before settling down to her life's work.

Suggestions have continued to pile in from readers at a rate faster than I can use them, so some notions I received in 1992 are still waiting for their spot. I try to use the oldest ones first, but they have to fit into the story, and some require special stories. So some old ideas wait, while some new ones get used. So the span of notions used this time date from 1992 to 1997, with most from 1995–96. The most recent is Happy Bed Monster, found orphaned by Sharon Ellis, so she sent Happy to me, and she arrived in FeBlueberry 1997. Happy's so young she still wears mittens on her six little hands, and hides under my keyboard. She didn't quite make it into Xanth proper, because nobody much was using beds this time, but she is with me as I type. Maybe she'll be in the next, *Xone of Contention,* the novel that will, as the Muse of History remarked, have a special irrelevant significance.

Some readers have commented on my relation to Xanth. Eugene Laubert spoke of Peer Xanth on Knee. Robert White says I am like the Demon $X(A/N)^{TH}$. Sure: a mule-headed dragon. But it is true that despite the humorous mythology, I do write these novels, and pretty much control what goes into them. Though I identify to a degree with all my characters, I am mainly the ogre. Ogres are justifiably proud of their stupidity.

Some notions were used indirectly. Pedro Léon de la Barra suggested that Xavier and Zora be given an adventure. That didn't happen, but their son Xeth does have an adventure in this novel. Each character seems to have his/her/its following, and readers are constantly suggesting that old characters be brought back to prominence. For example, Wayne Murphy asked for Dolph, and Dolph does have his chapters in this novel. But normally I don't list credits for such suggestions. I use both new and renovated characters as the story warrants.

Suggestions continue to pour in from readers. I counted 181 noted but not yet used, and some are ones I had expected to use here, but didn't. I have used around two hundred here, which is about the limit. Many readers like puns, but others don't. Some seem to be ambiguous; one told me I used too many, then finished his letter with a page of his own suggested puns. The fact is that I reject as many reader notions as I accept, because they duplicate ones already used or just don't work well for me. A number of readers want their names used as characters; I limit that, but do use some intriguing names on occasion. Each novel is a kind of balancing act, trying to make the best story compatible with reader satisfaction. Each novel will have some reader who believes it is the best yet, and some other who says it is the worst yet. The cri-tics, of course, think the series should be abolished. What I don't understand is why they think that no one else should be allowed to read novels that the critics personally dislike; why don't they just go read something else and leave Xanth alone? Assuming that the critics' agenda is not simply to make everyone else as miserable as they are.

Here, then, are the credits, listed approximately in order of use, except when several belong to one person: Breanna of the Black Wave—Rachel Browne; Ability to see only mundane things in Xanth—Gavin Lambert; Chewing gum, bananas drive folk crazy—Chris Swanson; barrister/bare aster flower—Rose Blaylock; Banana boat, catamaran for cats, doghouse/puptent—Katie Leonard; Fray D.

Cat—Brandy Stark; Perch—Chris Conary; Latchkey kids—Jennie Takata; Keyboard unlocks Writer's Block—Bryce Weinert/Kristina Courtnage; Xeth Zombie—Angella Castellano; Sleeping bag—Jennifer Walker; Zombie corps d'esprit—Bruce Morton; Penta-gone—Sarah Rushakoff; Hippo-crit—Katrina Brooks; Shortening, largening—Gordon Johnson; Mun Danish, Sapphire Fly; Midas Well—Robert Cobb; Glare of the sun—Megan Thorne; igNore folk—Jenny Wilson; Ayitym, who absorbs one property of what he touches—Nat J. Silva; Tyler, with a different talent each day—Tyler Hudon; William Henry Taylor—Addy Taylor; Ricky Golem—Katelyn Bundrick; Sea Attle—Shelley Robichard; Sea Mint—Michelle Detwiler; Cross Walk, VirginiTree—Andrew Crawford; Back Village should spread out—Dorcas Bethel; Sickly sycamore—Sarah Bennett; Night Foal for Night Mare, Flame Vine—Nicole Adkins; Ability to conjure any kind of seed—Catherine Coleman and Emily Waddy; Choose the breed of one's future children; fancy spot-on-wall picture talent—Eugene Laubert; Hearing from a distance—Ian Rhoad; Power to create a small void—Michael Tesfay; Conjure a geyser at any spot—Jeremy and Cameron Gray; C puns—George Kummerer; Transformation of the inanimate—Jeremy Schenefield; Alarmed Clock—Sasha Skinner; Time Fly, spasmo tic, irrelev ant, ench ant—Robin Tang; Fish Tank—Ben Chambers; Fish bowl with pin and needle fish, Miss Conception, Interpret, Givings, skeleton carrying boot rear, pair o' docks—Gwyneth Posno; Hair spray, cat scan—Heather Oglevie; Hare comb, Karla Winged Centaur—Karla Sussman; Mr. E—Stephen Stringer; Hackberry Tree, mud, suds, and hush puppies, sand witch, Che/Cynthia's foal should have a separate magic talent—Monica Ramirez; Cindy Centaur—John Newton; Root beer with roots—Stephen Vandiver; Jackpot—Brian Baurmash; Currant jelly—Michael J. Kaer; Mouse pad—Kelly Brown; Seymour Bones and Rick R. Mortis—Andrew van der Raadt; Smart Alec, winged goblins should have separate talents—Stephen Monteith; Magic Dust to Mundania—Avery Campbell; De Censor Ship—Meghan Jones; Liquidation—Brian Visel; Time line, chorus vine—Donovan Beeson; Clap hands for reports—Miguel Ettema; Seal of Approval—Nissa Cannon, Miguel Ettema; Reverse wood with lethe = memory enhancer, Toy Let, rain bow—Chris Efta; Forest of Forgetfulness, Chelle—Michelle Crim; Winged humans/birds—Billy Banks; Lady Bug—Abby Everdell; Mega bites—

Matthew Bohy; Gooey GUI—Steve Godun; Gnome Well—Rick Frazier; Metro Gnome, re-done-dance—Bonnie Sarkar; Across tics—Andrea Thomalla; Psycho tic, psycho path—Debbie King and Janice Rodriguez; Eye teeth—Juliana Boiarski; Bowling—Daniel Chambers; Lap dogs, hot dogs—Richard A. Medlin; Disperse, disso-lute—Morgan Stecher; Sidewinder—Pamela, John, Jeremy Rowe; Pain ting—Abby Everdell; Running commentary—Nicole Adkins; Running gag—Monique Craig; Wild roses for wild women, fire hydrant, rainbow trout—Justin P. Roth; Floor play—Frederick Douglas Bennet Sr.; Man who likes zombies—Michael A. Weatherford; Justin Tree to have adventure—Justin Henderson; Invisible castle, sticky situation—Arthur L. Bolen; Dream Catcher—description from one sent me by Karen Yoesting; Native American's dream catchers for night mares—Debbie King and Janice Rodriguez; Forget-me-not extract—Stacy Spitz; Sandy Sandman, goblin-harpy-dragon crossbreed—Laura Brown; Pop quizzes—Anne McAndrew; Govern mint—Chris Robinson; Ant onym—Arthur L. Bolen; Brilli ant, reli ant—Nicole Taylor; Thumb tax—Ryan Manzer; Midget roc bird, role for prior winged mermaid—Suzanne Schack; Aurora—winged mermaid—Ariel Aurora Dawn; Demons become dust devils in Time of No Magic—Andrew Crawford; Sea lion—Austin Hull; The Oliver Twist for poor boys—Allison Meshell; Uncle lions—Jessica Kross and Eileen Wang; Love spring make parental love for child—Meghan L. Card; The flew, lip bomb, Eye-full Tower, club soda, manatees, womanatees, boyatees, girlatees—Aaron Batista and Mike Burkholder; Couch potato—David Hoover; Firebreathing puppy, catfish—Douglas Laidlow and Andrew Gobeil; Story of the misplaced talent—Joy Boem; Serena Winged Girl—Serena Loder; Chea Winged Centaur—Laura Slocum; Sharon Centaur—Sharon Ellis; Erica Winged Mermaid—Erica Hendrix; Bad breath—Kristin Gardner; Living room—Jessica Mansfield; Sun glasses—Scott Josephson; Maxi and mini mums—Margaret Fitzgerald; Two-three-four-five lips—Garrett Perryman; Lip-o-suction, banana cream pie tree—Kurt Parakenings; Envelope/antelope—Tom Morgan; Talent of bringing characters and items from books—Jeffrey Sosnoski; Talent of molding things into other things—Derrick Walters; Bovine puns—David M. Gansz; Everblue, yellow, and green trees—Bethany Corvo; Dee Composed, Dee Ceased—Brenda Toth; Voracia, Zyzzyva, D. Claire, Nefra Naga—Susan Hatfield; Loni, with undecided hair color—Loni Mori; Brown Knees—Reneé Kuljis; Molly Coddle—Tiffany Stull; Lasha Lamia—Sarah Jo Wagner; Catrana Demoness—Cat Busch; Vera Similitude, with Disa pointer and Up Setter—Samantha Parsons; Tipsy Troll—Sarah Curran; Talent of the cold shoulder, heated exchange—Anonymous; Clinging and Bo Vine—Robert Gallup; Davina—Davina Viniana; Fiona—Fiona Rairigh; A cute gastritis—Miranda Futrel; Cross dressers, Brass ears—Ron Leming; Fire ants—Rick Raddue, Jennifer Henry, Jake Watters; Lake Hogwash—Travis McElroy; Disk cuss—Vasudev Mandyam; Sep tic—Allen Lupfer; Rubber bands—Andrew Graff; Pet peeve—Jerod Browne; Warts make war—Kelly English; CORN Tent Ahead—sign seen by Glenn Puro; Pun cushion—Sheila Cody; Jenny Elf gets a werewolf friend—Kim Livesay; Jeremy Werewolf—John Henry Wilson; Quandary, mass confusion and hysteria—Greg Clem; Ink well, shameless plug in tub—Dana Bates; Aspects of Dolph's talent—Rachel Choy; Polly Tician—Alan Little; Miss Succubus—Stuart E. Greenberg; Voracia's variations of bra-nds and bra-ss knuckles, the Iron Maiden's two forms (and lovely pictures)—Randy Dale Owens; Krissica—Krissica Montano; Selfish Steam—Rich Lynch; cloud of love/hate vapor—Carol Miatke; Cream rinse—Duane Hachten; deoder ant—Alexandra Roedder; Demon E(A/R)TH's departure repeals the law of gravity—Alina Vogelhut; Satire/satyr—Joe Barder.